# A Bad Boy is Good to Find

## Jennifer Lewis

Published 2013 by Mangrove
2637 E Atlantic Blvd #24692
Pompano Beach, FL 33062
USA


ISBN: 978-1-939941-01-5

For Jordan and Mia

Many thanks to the generous people who read this book at some point during its creation, including Kathy Altman, Melissa Beck, Phyllis Campbell, Anne-Marie Carroll, Elle Kennedy, Margaret Lukoff, Anne MacFarlane, Lynn Messina and Andrea Somberg.

# 1

"What is that?" Her brown eyes widened as her finger lifted off his skin.

She'd discovered his tattoo. He had a tendency to forget about it since it wasn't where he could see it.

"It's...a family crest." He stroked her cheek.

"Oh." She smiled. "I see. It does look like a fleur-de-lis." She touched it, then pulled her hand back under the sheets.

*Good save.* You learned to be resourceful when you had a flaming dagger tattooed on your ass. Somehow she'd gotten hold of the idea he, Conroy Beale, was descended from French aristocracy, and he didn't want to deprive her of that happy delusion. Who knows? Maybe he was.

Anything seemed possible lately.

"You smell nice," he whispered as he snuggled up closer. Lizzie Hathaway smelled like a plump overripe rose. Felt like one too. Silky skin on silky sheets in her comfy apartment. Heaven.

"It's a personalized scent. I had it mixed for me by an olfactory specialist at a scent boutique in the East Village."

"Cool." *Yeah, smooth, Con.* Rich girls did leave him speechless though. He pushed her long curls aside and kissed her hot cheek. "Roses and vanilla? Smells like sweetness and innocence."

"Smells can be deceptive."

"I don't doubt it." In this case, he thought the smell was pretty damn close. Despite her old-money New York upbringing, Lizzie was quiet and shy, more comfortable in a bookstore than a cocktail bar, and he liked her just fine for it. The world could use more sweetness and innocence. He sure hadn't run across too much until now.

"I wonder what your custom-blended scent would be." She brushed his chin with a fingertip.

Hmm. Axle grease and champagne?

Bottle it and call it Contradiction.

"What do you think would reflect me?" He looked her dead in the eye.

"Hmm…" Her plump pomegranate lips curved into a smile. Pretty. "Horses, sweat, and wild alpine flowers."

"I don't know about horses, but sweat, I can give you." They'd worked up quite a sweat already.

"Maybe the flower should be a fleur-de-lis?" She squeezed his butt and his cock leapt to attention.

"Sounds good to me." He leaned forward and kissed her gently on the lips. "You make me happy, Lizzie. You know that?" He buried his face between her breasts worshipfully and didn't try to hide the shudder of lust that followed. "You're a unique woman."

"And you're a very unique man."

*If you only knew.*

He looked at her steadily, not wanting to complicate things with more words. The less lies between them, the better, as they'd all come out in the wash sooner or later.

Her whole face shone with the unspoken connection between them that took his breath away. She tugged at his shirt buttons with a hungry look in her eyes. Lizzie Hathaway wanted him as badly as he wanted her and wasn't afraid to show it.

Which made him hard as a gun barrel.

Oh, Lizzie.

He trailed kisses down her pulsing neck, over her breasts and belly. Shucked off that blue satin and dove into the hot warmth waiting below, licking and cajoling her into a place where it didn't matter who they were or where they came from.

Her breathing quickened and he instinctively filled his mouth with a rosy nipple. As he suckled, burying his face in rose-scented warmth, she lost it—gushing low groans that unraveled him too. Lizzie genuinely drove him crazy with her lush, mobile body and her inhibitions all undone.

When the blood returned to his brain he slid off her. Slowly, reluctant to give up the delicious closeness that was the best part of sex. He cuddled up to her, settling his head on one soft arm, his cheek against her breast. Bliss.

She stroked his cheek affectionately and a sensation of perfect contentment softened his limbs. He'd take his moments of perfection where he could get 'em. So he'd let her get the impression that he was a big shot—was that a crime? Once they were married...

Yes. Married.

A hot, tight feeling in his chest told him his plan was right, even though some people might say it was wrong. His life had been a long strange trip, and he craved a permanent berth in Lizzie Hathaway's calm harbor.

He wasn't marrying her for the money, but the money would make it work. Keep her living in the style she was used to. It was her money, so her parents couldn't cut her off.

And once they were married he'd make her the happiest woman on earth for the rest of her life.

Ronkonkoma. Yaphank. Hampton Bays. Lizzie's blood pressure ratcheted with each green highway sign she passed. She'd left early to avoid the Friday night Hamptons-bound traffic, but now she wished she'd stretched the journey out as long as she could. She knew tonight wasn't going to be easy. Nothing in her life was ever easy.

For a start, it was no picnic being an "heiress." Everyone expected you to live up to some image of ultimate glamour they had in their head from reading too many princess stories as a kid. You were supposed to be a willowy blonde with roses in your porcelain cheeks and elegant hands that itched to play symphonies. You were supposed to be outgoing, confident and easy to talk to. Demanding and slightly arrogant, yet sweet and lovable.

*If you're not all that stuff, then that's your problem.*

She hit the exit for Southampton too fast and had to turn hard.

Sometimes you weren't a willowy blonde, you were a "big boned" brunette. Sometimes that "arrogance" was really insecurity, and your best talents were for things that no one appreciated.

And sometimes you fell in love with a person who wasn't exactly the handsome prince your parents had in mind.

*At that point you just have to take charge of your own goddam life.*

She slammed on the brakes and screeched to a halt, her bumper inches from a doe's chest. The stunned deer stared at her for a moment, then scrambled—hooves scraping on the tarmac—back the way it came, over the high privet hedge of an expensively manicured yard.

They all looked the same, these "cottages," because a gazillion dollars only bought you so much around here. A few thousand square feet of paneled oak and granite countertop and chemical-soaked lawn, the smell of the sea hovering off somewhere beyond the privet.

It was good that she'd come early, and not because of the traffic. Hopefully she'd catch her mother before she dove into a second bottle of wine.

She pulled into the driveway, gravel crunching under her tires and anxiety twisting in her belly.

*I don't care what they say.*

*I love him.*

*I'm going to marry him.*

"You are not." Her father's harsh tone made her jump, since he rarely issued more than a disinterested rumble in her direction. He hadn't moved, or even looked at her. Just stood there, in his "summer weight" suit, an unlit cigar in one hand.

She wobbled slightly in her high heels. "I don't understand why you don't like him. We all had a perfectly nice time last weekend, you said so yourself."

"That was in front of him, dear," said her mother from the far side of the room, where she refilled her glass with unsteady hands. "You'd hardly expect us to insult him to his face."

"I don't know why not. You think it's more polite to wait until he leaves, then stab him in the back?"

She'd seen that they didn't like him. The too-polite smiles. The too-witty conversations. Con saw it too, but he asked her to marry him anyway. He loved her in spite of her parents.

"No one enjoys a confrontation, Elizabeth." Her father surveyed her over the half-moons of his reading glasses. "There's no need to stir up drama."

"But why have a confrontation at all? What's wrong with him?"

"We don't know anything about him. Where he comes from, his family."

"He's from Louisiana," she protested. "What does his family matter? I'm not marrying them."

Her father gave a dismissive snort.

"Why are you sneering? Because his family is from the South?" Heat rushed her chest at the thought of them discriminating against someone so good and kind.

Her father removed his reading glasses and started to polish them. Anger bubbled up inside her as she saw that—once again—he planned to simply ignore her.

She groped for something to impress her father. "They're descended from French aristocracy!"

*He even has the family crest tattooed on his...*

Never mind.

"It's not so simple, dear." Her mother shot a glance at her father. "There are things to consider. Your legacy, for example..." She paused and sipped her wine. Looked almost nervous.

"My legacy? Who are we kidding here? We're garbage bag tycoons. The only reason we're sitting on pots of money right now is because grandpa perfected the disposable bin-liner. People take our product and shove it in the trash can, literally, so excuse me if I can't take it too freakin' seriously."

"You will not use language like that in my presence." Her father lit his cigar, and her lungs recoiled as acrid smoke rolled toward her. "And as you know only too well, Hathaway Industries is one of the foremost manufacturers of household products in the world today."

Anger stole her breath. "Why are we talking about Hathaway Industries? Why does everything always come back to 'the firm' and the embarrassment of money that's a millstone around all our necks?"

She paused and took a deep breath, heart thudding. "Conroy Beale is the man I love. He loves me. Since I've met him I've changed and grown in ways I'd never dreamed possible."

She smoothed the clingy black fabric of the elegant dress he'd helped her choose. The marcasite bracelet he'd picked out caught the golden light from the lowering sun. Strength seeped through her veins at the thought of him.

"Since I met him I feel like a new person. Look at me!" She gestured to her glamorous attire, the loose dark curls cascading over her bosom. "When did you last see me wear my hair down? When did you see me in a dress? I feel beautiful. I know I'm beautiful, and Conroy Beale has given me that gift."

"Well, dear, I'm not sure that dress is entirely flattering, given your ...endowments." Her mother sipped her wine and peered at her with soulless pale eyes.

Lizzie shrank a little, the way she always did under that withering stare, then tossed her hair and stuck out her "endowments." "I'm not ashamed of my body any more. I'm tired of creeping around, hiding myself under baggy clothes, trying out every crazy diet that comes along. I'm not meant to be a twig like you. I don't have that kind of body. Conroy loves me just the way I am, and so do I!"

Her voice gave her a shivering thrill as it rang out over the polished parquet and reverberated off the wall of windows. She wanted to yell at them for every hurt she'd ever suffered at their hands.

"I'm intelligent and creative. I don't need to sit in a dreary office designing promotional brochures so you can keep me tucked away in 'gainful employment' that won't embarrass you. I was going to be an artist—" her voice cracked, "an artist who created beauty and made people see things in a new way—"

"Now, dear, let's not get carried away." Her mother's low voice stuck her like a blunt knife. "You sprayed graffiti on canvas and called it art. I don't recall anyone clamoring to put you in the Whitney Biennial."

Lizzie's breathing got shallow. Once again she felt herself shrinking, withering, losing stature and confidence while gaining in bloated girth under that critical glare.

*Con. Think of him.* In her mind she squeezed his hand. *Remember all that strength and power and warm affection.* The adoring way his gaze roamed over her, heated her skin and swelled her heart until it was ready to burst. The most handsome man she'd ever met, the sweetest, the most skilled and inventive lover...

"I'm going to marry him."

"You are not." Her father didn't even look at her. He stared down at his cigar for a moment.

"Oh, for Christ sake. Tell her, Harold," snapped her mother. She slammed her glass down on the antique sideboard.

"Tell me what?" Lizzie frowned. The sun had sunk in the sky and now blasted through the huge wall of paned windows, a fiery orange ball that made her squint.

"You're drunk, dear. Don't make a fool of yourself,"

Her mother didn't even flinch, but Lizzie froze. Where was the thin-lipped pretense she'd grown up with?

"I'm going to bed." Her mom turned and looked at her. An odd look in her pale eyes chilled Lizzie and made her glance at her father. She noticed for the first time that her mother's hair wasn't carefully styled and her clothes were wrinkled. Her whole façade seemed to be slipping. Even her face looked older, its lines deeper.

Instead of turning to the curved oak staircase she walked toward the French doors, opened them, and slipped out into the garden. The dark backyard screeched with tree frogs for a moment before the door closed behind her with a thunk.

"Where's she going?"

Her father stubbed out his cigar on a priceless piece of Chinese porcelain, making Lizzie stare. "She's staying in the pool house."

"What?" Her voice was barely audible.

"Sleeping with the pool boy, too, for all I know." His voice had taken on a newly malevolent tone.

She started to shake. "I don't understand…" Pain shot up her calves from the uncomfortable high heels she shouldn't have worn.

"No, I don't suppose you do. You've led a sheltered life." He stared at her from beneath lowered brows. "A very sheltered life. But that's all about to come to an end."

She shivered involuntarily at the coldness of his tone. Her parents had obviously gone stark raving mad. She lifted her chin and screwed up her courage. "I have to go. I'm marrying Con tomorrow, and there's nothing you can do to stop it. I'm sorry you couldn't be supportive, but I…I…I…" Tears rose in her throat and she fumbled in her pocket for a tissue.

Her father cleared his throat. "Tomorrow I'll be indicted for securities fraud. Most likely I shall be convicted. The company is bankrupt. I am bankrupt, and I'm afraid you are too."

Lizzie blinked. The fiery ball in the sky outside the window stung her eyes. His words made so little sense that it was a full minute before she could muster a reply.

"But didn't you just say that Hathaway is one of the leading…"

"Stuck in automatic pilot. I should have inserted the word *was*."

Silhouetted against the fierce blaze of sun her father suddenly looked like a pathetic shadow.

"Indicted?"

"And imprisoned, most likely."

"Daddy…" She took a step toward him.

"Don't touch me. Don't come near me. I've destroyed your mother's life and now I've destroyed yours. I didn't like that fellow you brought here, but I doubt he'll want you now you're poor."

"Con loves me, though I don't suppose you can understand that. Besides, my money is in my own name. Grandpa left it to me."

"You granted me power of attorney. I'm afraid I betrayed your trust."

She blinked rapidly. The sky darkened as the sun slid behind the tall privet hedge. "It can't be gone. My advisor would have…"

"Rollins is implicated too. It was meant to be a short-term strategy, just until the market turned around. But the market didn't turn around." The growl of his voice trailed off. She couldn't even see his face in the eerie half-light but his words sank in like poison.

"Oh." Her own voice sounded strangely disembodied, like it came not from her but from all the expensive antiques, the Aubusson rug, the rare paintings. Or those that were left. She looked up through the gloom to her favorite Degas sketch and found bare wall where the little dancer had always bent over her barre.

*Everything's changed.*

She realized she'd slumped and tried to straighten her back. "Is there anything I can do to help?"

Her father looked at her. Or at least she thought he did, the room was almost totally dark. Then he laughed, an unearthly cackle that made her jump. She snagged a heel in the carpet then caught her balance on the back of the sofa.

"Do you really think that you could help me? A fat little nobody. The last of the great line of Hathaways." A vicious laugh hurt her ears as she stood speechless, her gut in turmoil. "You've got none of my fire. Probably your mother had an affair with the mailman before you were born."

*He's gone completely mad.* Panic set in and she found herself stepping back, edging toward the threshold of the room. She fled, heels clacking on the marble foyer floor.

As she crunched across the gravel to her car, every second felt stretched, oddly distorted, like her life was suddenly transformed by an evil spell.

She rolled down the windows as she pulled out of the driveway, gasping for air. She heard a dog bark and a car door slam. People in nearby driveways exhaled city fumes and dragged bags from trunks, ready for another ordinary weekend in the Hamptons.

Nothing in her life had ever been ordinary. The curse of the Hathaway fortune had seen to that. She'd been envied and sneered at and sucked up to and snubbed, all because of money she didn't earn and didn't want.

And now she didn't have it any more.

It should feel like a weight off her shoulders. The millstone of millions was finally gone.

So why, as she drove along Main Street, braking in the bumper to bumper Friday-night-in-August traffic, did she feel utterly naked?

Con would understand. He'd hold her and make her feel whole again.

And tomorrow they'd be married and start a new life.

Wouldn't they?

2

Lizzie was shaking by the time she got back uptown. She parked her car in the garage under her apartment building and dropped her keys getting out. She fumbled around in the dark looking for them on the ground and scraped her knuckles on the cement.

How would he react? He loved her and wanted to marry her, yes, but would he be disappointed that she didn't come with the brass ring?

*Who wouldn't be?*

She found the keys and shoved them into her pocketbook. She wouldn't need them to open the door since she'd left Con in her bed watching movies. It was nearly midnight after her long drive back from the Island, and she'd bet money—if she had any—that he'd still be there, warm and welcoming, crumpled sheets the only cover on his muscled body.

Con was always there for her. Never too busy to see her, to hold her, to massage her tight shoulders and cook a gourmet dinner with her. When she told her cousin Maisie about him she'd laughed and said he sounded too good to be true, and for once Lizzie had been the smug one. After two years of hearing about Maisie's engagement to Dwight the Perfect Fiancé and all the boring details of their years-in-the-planning wedding, it was a delicious coup to announce "I'm getting married on Friday." She didn't need napkins hand-embroidered with their entwined initials to declare her love for Con.

The elevator jerked to a stop on the eleventh floor and prickles of anxiety crept over her. How would she tell him?

Thick carpet absorbed the sound of her high heels in the eerily silent hallway. The apartment was in her father's name. She'd have to move.

She and Con would find a new home together. In a nice friendly neighborhood. Not this snooty Upper East Side co-op where you had to have old money to get past the board. Maybe they'd even get a house? Not a big fancy one, but somewhere pretty and comfortable, just for them. She and Con shared the same taste in everything.

Except olives. She liked them, he didn't.

She rapped on the door with her knuckles, trying to ignore the cantaloupe-sized knot forming in her stomach. She could make out the sound of the TV through the door, and her breathing quickened as she heard it flick off, followed by the tap of bare feet on the parquet.

Maybe she imagined that. How could you hear bare feet through a solid door?

*I'm not an heiress any more. Sorry.*

She heard the lock slide back and the door opened. Con smiled at her with that lopsided grin that sent her heart skittering every time.

"I missed you." His voice and those dark sleepy eyes were just what she needed. She stepped over the threshold and threw her arms around him. He responded instantly, wrapping himself around her, holding her tight—so tight—absorbing all the stress and hurt that dogged her.

With her head on his chest and his strong arms around her back, she felt safe. Everything was going to be okay.

"That bad, huh?"

It had been her idea to go tell her parents about their planned wedding. He'd wanted to get married and deal with the fallout later. He knew he hadn't made a top-notch impression on them last week, though neither of them could figure out why.

They'd decided to get married right away, with a minimum of pomp and ceremony. To make it just about them and their commitment to each other. They didn't have anything to prove.

"Poor baby." He kicked the door closed and kissed her neck, stroked her back. His warm soft lips on her skin, the tickle of teeth, his tongue on her earlobe sent her fears running and stirred up a swarm of excitement.

"Con, wait…"

He didn't. He kissed her cheekbone and her eyelid, swaying her as she closed her eyes. Already lifting her away to a place where only they existed and where thoughts of—

"Sweetheart, stop…"

He still didn't. His kissing became more insistent as his mouth roamed over her neck. His hands ran up and down her clingy dress, stirring warmth in her skin and making her breasts tingle.

Before she knew it she was on the bed with her legs in the air and Con moving over her in that magic way that always made her fall to pieces and rise up stronger, no matter how many times they made love.

When they crashed to the sheets together, panting and sweating, she clung to him. Wanted to hold tight to the bliss pouring through her body and soothing her hurt mind.

"Feeling better now, babe?

She nodded, still not wanting to speak and break the spell. She opened her eyes just enough to see his face. His strong features and harsh, masculine beauty always shocked her a little. Usually a neat "short back and sides," his straight brown-black hair hung in his eyes, which shone in the glow of the light from the hall. Soft with love.

She smiled as he kissed the corner of her mouth. "Why do I always smile when you do that?"

"Because you love me." He said it simply.

"I do love you. I love you more than I ever thought possible." She pushed his messy hair out of his eyes, and he smiled too. He lay next to her on the tangled sheets, head propped on his elbow, gorgeous muscles defined even in the scant light.

"Con?" She paused. Was it her imagination or did a tiny crease appear between his eyebrows. Maybe he'd picked up on her odd tone of voice.

"Yes, babe?"

*I'm not rich any more.*

She hesitated. Not sure what words to use. None seemed to sum up the magnitude of what had happened or to put it in terms that made sense.

"My father said I couldn't marry you."

"And what did you say?" There was definitely a furrow between his brows.

"I said I love you, and we're getting married tomorrow."

The crease eased a bit. "You had me worried there. I thought you might be about to break my heart."

"I'd never do that." Lizzie swallowed. "But about the money…"

"What about it?" He looked relaxed again, a smile spreading across his mouth.

He wouldn't care about the money—would he?

"It's gone." She looked right at him as she said it, wanting him to understand.

Con pushed up higher on his elbow, stared at her like he was trying to make sense of it. "What do you mean?" His smile faded a little.

"My dad gambled in the stock market and lost it all."

"But your grandfather left the money to you. In your name."

He did look worried. A saw blade ratchet in her stomach reminded her she'd eaten no dinner. Maybe that's why she felt lightheaded.

"He did, but I gave my father power of attorney. He's always managed it for me." She inhaled a shaky breath. "He's being indicted.'

"Indicted for what?" Con's voice had lost its velvet softness.

"Securities fraud. He says he'll be convicted."

Con stared at her. Her breathing became shallow, and she struggled to keep it inaudible. Suddenly chilly, she fumbled with the sheet and pulled it over herself. Con had to move to free it from under his body, and she could see tension in the taut six-pack of his stomach.

Panic snuck through her as the frown deepened on his handsome face.

"I'm sure it's a misunderstanding." He touched her chin. "We'll get it sorted out tomorrow."

"I don't think so." Her voice was a breathy whisper. "He said my financial advisor was in on it."

"So how much is left?"

"I don't know. Let me check the balance online. Gosh, what's my password, I don't even remember it. I must have it written down somewhere."

The glowing laptop screen illuminated their faces as grim reality sunk in. Not only was there no actual money in her brokerage account, but someone had authorized margin loans worth more than thirty million dollars. The margin had been called and all existing stocks dumped at market price two days ago. With two million still owed.

"Holy shit." Con chewed his finger in a way she'd never seen him do before.

"My job will be gone too, I suppose. We'll have to make it on your salary until I find something new."

Con looked at her like she was speaking a foreign language.

"I know it won't be easy." She took his hand and squeezed it. "But we'll be fine. I'll have to move out of the apartment since it belongs to my father, but we can find a place of our own. We can live frugally, start saving…"

A new sense of resolve filled the odd hollowness she'd felt since leaving her parents' house. Maybe in a weird way this would actually be for the best. "I don't have expensive tastes, I never have. I actually like the idea of living like a normal person. Of having car payments and mortgage payments and having to save for vacations."Con still stared at the laptop screen, his lips slightly parted. "Car payments?" he rasped at last.

"You know, buying stuff like regular people do, rather than plunking down forty thousand in cash. I know it sounds rude to ask, but how much do you earn?"

"What?" Con's dark eyes stared at her, uncomprehending.

"Your salary, what is it?"

"I don't have a salary." His voice had a strange sound to it.

"You get paid on a project-by-project basis?"

"Kind of...um, yeah." He raked a hand through his hair and stood up. The bedside light glazed his firm muscles as he crossed the room, cursed aloud, then strode back. He seemed oblivious to the fact that he was completely naked.

An icy trickle of fear crept along Lizzie's spine.

"You're a mechanical engineer, right?" She didn't like the ugly suspicion in her voice.

Con licked his lips awkwardly and ran his hand through his hair again. He picked up his black pants off the floor and put them on. No underwear.

"Why are you getting dressed? It's two a.m."

He walked back to her, took her hand and lifted her from the desk chair opposite the bed. Guided her to the middle of the room and pushed a stray curl out of her eyes.

"Lizzie. My lovely Lizzie." He squeezed her hands and reassuring warmth rose through her. Then he shook his head, and a pained smile flashed across his face. "I'm not a mechanical engineer. I never said I was."

"I don't understand... I thought..." She searched his face.

"I said my expertise is mechanical, and you guessed what you wanted to believe."

She racked her mind to remember the conversation. "So what *did* you mean?"

"I'm a mechanic." He looked at her, soft apology in his brown eyes. "I work on cars."

She blinked rapidly and felt her forehead crease. "But that time we tried to meet for lunch—Wheelock Engineering LLC, the sign said. Isn't that where you work?" She still remembered waiting for him outside the glass-fronted high-rise just off Lexington. Waiting and waiting, until she'd finally given up. Caught in a meeting, he'd said later. They'd never actually made the rain date for that lunch.

He rubbed his upper arm. The desk light highlighted a taut bicep. "I don't work at Wheelock Engineering. I do some work in the garage across the street. That's where I'd meant to meet you."

*What?* "There's a garage on that street?" She racked her brain and couldn't even picture it. As far as she could remember, all the other buildings were brownstones. That's why she'd assumed...

"Yes. Maybe you never noticed it. It's a small place." He shrugged, his expression guarded.

*None of this makes sense.* Lizzie shook her head. She'd never doubted for a second that he was successful, well-off, educated...

"But aren't your family Louisiana landowners, descended from French aristocracy?"

He hung his head for a second, hair falling into his eyes. He lifted his chin and met her gaze again. "I'm from Louisiana alright. And my family's been sitting on the same patch of swamp for as long as anyone can remember, but I'm about as aristocratic as that cockroach there." He nodded his head at the wall behind her.

She wheeled around and saw a small roach scaling the striped wallpaper. On sudden instinct she picked up a slipper and threw it, left a brown smear on the wall.

Her breath came in heaving gulps. "I don't understand... You said..."

"I didn't say all that much." He wiped a hand over his face and looked at her, his eyes so sad. "I let you do most of the talking. I love listening to you talk. When I'm with you I really do feel like some old-money Creole aristo with an avenue of live oaks back home." He lifted his hand and stroked her cheek.

*His soft touch felt as good as ever.*

She recoiled from it. "Who are you?"

"I'm Conroy Beale."

"That's your real name?"

"Yes."

She stared at him. "But you're not wealthy."

He paused, then shook his head. "No."

"What about that Range Rover you were driving when we met? Those don't come cheap."

"It belonged to a friend." He hung his head a little. "I never said it was mine. I helped you get your car going that first time we met, remember? I never said I was anyone but who I am."

The hero who'd saved the day by putting Evian in her empty radiator. She'd broken down on Third Avenue on her way back from the Island. Her rescuer had been dressed in Armani and driving a Range Rover—what was she supposed to think?

"I just made all this stuff up in my head?" Her head spun in all directions, trying to make sense of the cataclysm of information it couldn't quite process. One minute she was a wealthy woman with a charming, successful, fiancé, the next she was—

She didn't know what the hell she was.

A dupe.

He looked apologetic. "I guess you did make it up, a little bit. Believed what you wanted to believe."

Her heart contracted at the sight of his kind brown eyes. *He looked like Con.* The wonderful man who'd brought her out of her protective shell and turned her into a self-confident, sensual, loving woman. Who'd taken her dreary existence and blown it open like a window thrown up in a dusty attic.

Her chest heaved under her satin dressing gown. "So when you said I was... I was beautiful..." her voice cracked. "It was all a lie?"

"No. You're the loveliest woman I've ever met." He looked right at her.

"No, I'm not." She squirmed, suddenly conscious of her big breasts, her big thighs. "I should have known."

"You are beautiful. You're also a loving, passionate woman with a big heart."

*Am I?*

She stared at him. So breathtakingly handsome with his dark hair tousled and his chiseled features shaded by two days' beard. She couldn't help the stirring of warmth—more—at the sight of him.

"You're a special woman, Lizzie." His hands hung by his sides and in spite of everything she found herself wishing he'd reach up and touch her. That look in his eyes—he did love her, didn't he?

So he wasn't a mechanical engineer or a French aristocrat. Was that the end of the world? He was smart, no doubt about that. "Your college degree, what's it in?"

"I didn't go to college." Contrition in his eyes.

"What? But you said you went to… St. Swithin's. I thought that was where you studied mechanical… mechanic—" She racked her brain, trying to remember exactly what he had told her.

"St. Swithin's is a reform school in Natchez, Mississippi."

Her mouth dropped and an undignified "oh" escaped.

She gasped for breath. "So you took auto shop there and I somehow translated that into a summa cum laude degree in engineering?" Her voice shook. "Why did you let me believe all those lies?"

She stared at him, unable to reconcile the seductive image before her with the ugly reality unfolding behind it's shimmering surface.

"Oh, Lizzie. We were going to be so happy. I had it all figured out."

"But now I don't come with a lot of zeros in the bank, the deal is off, huh?" The room pulsed in hideous Technicolor clarity.

The sad look in Con's eyes almost affected her.

"I don't have anything to offer you," he said quietly.

"Is that so? What exactly were you planning to offer me prior to this latest wrinkle in your plan?"

"Happiness. I did make you happy, didn't I?" *Yes.*

She swallowed. "An illusion. I thought I was happy because I thought you were someone else. You lied to me, maybe not in so many words, but in the things you didn't say. And maybe you lied to me another way with all those gentle touches and long, heartfelt kisses I'm apparently such a sucker for. I *loved* you."

Her words hung in the air, ringing with raw pain and already in past tense. Everything had changed irrevocably. Totally. The happiness of the last few weeks—the life-transforming joy—lay in ruins.

Conroy Beale—whoever he really was—didn't say a word.

"What a freaking joke. I've been skipping around in my own world of delusion, happy little Lizzie, while everyone who supposedly loved me was coming up with some way to milk me like a cash cow. What was I thinking? Why would anyone actually love *me*? As my father so kindly said, I'm just a *fat little nobody*."

"You are not fat." He looked her in the eye. "Don't let anyone ever tell you that. You're perfect."

His voice dropped as he spoke. Like he meant it. For a second she felt a prick of warmth, a surge of the loving support that transformed her from a shuffling caterpillar into the beautiful butterfly she'd become.

Or thought she'd become before her wings were rudely snapped off again. Right now she'd like to climb back into her chrysalis and hide forever.

All those warnings from her parents about being "careful" and avoiding "the wrong sort of people." She'd scoffed at their small-minded cynicism—

*And fallen headlong into the trap of a scheming con artist.*

"You never did say you loved me, did you?" She stared at him through narrowed eyes. Trying to ignore the perfect features of his noble-looking face. "I said it over and over, like a freaking parrot, but you never did say it back to me." A panicked laugh rattled her chest. "Tell me, Con, with no bullshit or beating about the bush. Did you ever, just for one moment, love me too?"

He blinked and a muscle twitched in his arm.

"Come on. The truth for once." She held her breath. Horrible hope bloomed in her chest. Did his hesitation mean…

He hung his head and his silence deflated the last of her ego like a rapier.

Tears sprang to her eyes. She dove for the living room and slammed the bedroom door behind her. Scrabbled to find the clothes she'd torn off in her embarrassing frenzy of lust. She struggled to tug up her tangled pantyhose as the door opened and Con emerged from the bedroom, shirt half-buttoned. Him catching her there, undignified in her underwear, her unlovely body exposed in the harsh fluorescent light, made her cringe with shame.

"Lizzie."

Her heart leapt at the sound of her name on his lips. Her fingers fumbled with the nylon waistband. "Go away!"

He didn't love her.

He just wanted her money.

She picked her rumpled dress off the floor and pulled it on over her head. When she emerged from the fabric their eyes met and a pang of emotion rocked her.

*We're getting married today.*

No, we're not.

The whirlwind four-week courtship that felt like a fairytale come true...was over.

Fake.

A scam.

She jerked her eyes from his gaze and they fell to a half empty champagne bottle in the ice bucket on the coffee table. She seized it by the neck, spilling cold champagne down her arm.

"What the—" He slumped to the floor as the bottle thunked against his head.

Lizzie snatched up her wallet and shoved her feet into her uncomfortable high heels. Why not more pain?

Without a backward glance at the body on the floor, she slammed her apartment door and took off down the fire stairs, banging her heels on the concrete as hard as she could.

*Look out, world. The wheels have come off and I'm coming full speed ahead!*

# 3

Con parked his car outside the adobe walls of the Zen Mind Spa in Las Gordas, Arizona, and entered the front yard through a decorative wrought-iron gate. The forbidding desert stretched for countless miles outside, but lush grasses and babbling fountains marked his arrival in an oasis of luxury.

"I'm here to see Lizzie Hathaway." He addressed the aerobicized receptionist. Her blonde ponytail bobbed as she picked up the phone. Plinking samisen music fell around him like drops of water and confident people in workout clothes cruised through the lobby as he waited.

"I'm afraid she's not picking up." She turned and glanced at the wall of keys. "Would you like me to page her? What's your name?"

He cocked his head. "I'm here for her birthday. It's a surprise."

He held her gaze ruthlessly.

"Oh." She blinked several times.

"Would it be okay if I just went up there and knocked on the door? I have a present." He lifted the gift bag he carried and the tissue paper inside it rustled.

"Of course." She smiled and pushed her chest out. "It's room sixteen. At the end of the corridor."

He smiled. "Thanks."

Polished wood doors with brass numbers lined the Saltillo-tiled hallway. Would she try to knock him unconscious again? Probably, and he couldn't blame her.

He still woke up at night, sweating at the memory of her question.

*Did you ever, just for one moment, love me too?*

And his chilling silence.

He still wondered what would have happened if he'd said *yes*. He'd fought that urge with every cell in his body and in his heart he knew he'd done the right thing. He'd let her off the hook.

What did he know about love? Everyone he'd ever loved was gone. He was all loved out for one lifetime.

He took a deep breath. He hadn't seen her since that fateful night over a month ago and excitement mixed with apprehension as he raised his fist to knock.

Muffled music—Katy Perry?—crept out around the door frame. He knocked louder.

"No, thanks! My inner yogi is on vacation today," came a rude shout from the other side of the door. *Lizzie*. His pulse picked up.

He knocked again. The music jerked off, and he heard feet clomp over tiles. The door flung open.

Then slammed shut.

"Lizzie." He grabbed the handle. Was that really her?

"Get lost."

"Please, let me in for one minute." He needed to see her and reassure himself she was okay. He ached to hold her again, but he knew better than to get his hopes up.

"Go to hell."

"I drove all the way from New York to see you."

"You shouldn't have bothered." He heard something clatter to the floor.

"Can I at least get a look at you?" From what he'd glimpsed through the crack, an appeal to her pride might work.

He was right. The lock clicked and the door opened a crack.

"Look but don't touch, buster."

She pulled it open. Joy roared through him at the sight of her—alive, whole, healthy. But the hardness in her eyes made his throat tighten. "You look different."

She let out a hollow laugh, peered at him through mascaraed lashes. "I've been pursuing a little self-improvement. What do you think?"

*A damn shame*! That's what he thought. Knew better than to say it, though. "You look... amazing."

"I think so. Who knew I had it in me?" She did a twirl, then teetered on her high-heeled sandals. His heart seized and he resisted the urge to grab and steady her. "Champagne?"

She seemed completely unaffected by the sight of him. Had he thought that one look into his brown eyes would make her fall at his feet?

His gut recoiled at the prospect of drinking this early. It was 10:30 in the morning and she'd apparently had a glass or two already. "Uh, sure. Champagne sounds good."

She sashayed across the Saltillo-tiled floor and he followed her into the room. A smallish Southwest-style bedroom with stuccoed walls and rustic pine furniture. The big bed unmade, clothes and cosmetics strewn about. French doors opened onto a terrace—they'd come in handy.

"You lost weight." He couldn't help saying it. Feeling it with a pang of sorrow. A white tank top molded to her sports-bra squashed breasts and whittled waist.

"Yes." She turned to him with a triumphant grin.

Even her face was thinner, cheekbones standing out.

"And you straightened your hair." His heart sank at the sight of all those glorious curls pressed out of existence.

"Yes, thank God! Who knew it was so easy?" She tossed the sleek mahogany mane over her shoulder as she turned from him. Con swallowed hard. What had he expected?

She filled a champagne glass she'd retrieved from a carved armoire and handed it to him. The lovely soft arms he used to rest his head on were hard with muscle, tanned.

The big brown eyes he used to lose himself in were cold. "So, what the hell are you doing here? Despite appearances to the contrary, I'm still flat broke." She slurred a bit, but didn't seem to notice.

"How much are you drinking?"

"As much as I can." She raised her glass and plastered on a smile before taking a gulp of champagne.

He drew in a breath. "I came because I'm worried about you."

"You're worried about me? Don't tell me you believe what you read in the gossip rags. I'm used to being the fat wallflower, so I'm enjoying my newfound celebrity. Look at this." She snatched a newspaper off the bed. "'Lizzie Hathaway dances the blues away. The glamorous former heiress laughed when asked about her father's recent indictment for stock fraud. Cutting up the dance floor at L.A.'s newest club, Breakdown, she and cousin Maisie Dixon turned heads until five in the morning. Speculation about her father's...' blah blah blah. Who cares about Hathaway freaking industries?" She flung the paper down.

"Is your cousin Maisie here too?"

"She was. Left for some kind of job. In *television*." She raised her eyebrows at the last word and shook her head. "I'm glad she's gone. I'm tired." She sipped her champagne. She had shadows under her eyes.

She slipped her hand into a bag of Cheetos on the counter. "Like a Cheeto? I've discovered they're the perfect food. Dairy, grain, salt and sugar. A bag of Cheetos and a case of champagne and you're good to go." She crunched the orange Styrofoam peanut between perfectly straight white teeth. "I'm going to write a diet book. "The Champagne and Cheetos diet," using myself as a testimonial." She indicated her slim body with orange-powdered fingers. "I think it will be a mega-bestseller, don't you?"

"I bet it will. How much have you lost?"

"Twenty pounds! In little more than a month."

"Jesus." He ran a hand through his hair. How was that even possible? Certainly wasn't healthy.

It was all his fault, though.

"Now let's look at you." She peered at him, scrutinized him from head to toe, teetered in her heels. "Disgustingly good-looking as usual. And you must be the only man on earth who could drive nearly three thousand miles and arrive in Arizona in one hundred degree heat without a single wrinkle in his white dress shirt. Your nose looks a little different though, if I'm not mistaken."

He touched his nose. She wasn't the first person to comment on it, though it looked the same to him. "You broke it."

"Did I?" Her high pitched laugh hurt his ears.

"Blacked both my eyes too." He managed not to smile. "I deserved it."

"You damn well did. Let's drink to that!" She raised her glass, then swigged more champagne. "I left you for dead and I haven't looked back."

He steeled himself against her hatred. What had he expected? "I don't think you've looked forward either, have you?"

"What do you mean?" She frowned, weaved and grabbed another Cheeto from the open bag.

"What are you doing with your life?"

"Living it to the fullest!" She hiccupped and sprayed some orange powder at him. "Sorry." She frowned. "No, actually, I'm not at all sorry. I'd like to dump this whole bag on you and your crisp white shirt, but that would be a waste of the perfect food and it's not easy to get around here."

"You can do what you like to me. I don't mind, I had it coming. But I can't watch you do this to yourself."

"No one invited you to watch anything. I don't know what you're doing here. You said you needed to come in for one minute, and your minute is up. Get out." No emotion showed on her flawless face.

She looked at him so coldly that the air squeezed out of his lungs. *Oh, Lizzie. What have I done to you?*

He'd made mistakes before. He hadn't been able to save the people he loved, and he lived with that guilt every day. Since then he'd done a lot of things he wasn't proud of in the name of survival. He couldn't change the past, but he could take responsibility for hurting Lizzie and try to make things right. "How are you paying for all this? Don't you owe your brokerage two million dollars?"

"That's their problem, not mine. I've discovered the joy of credit cards."

"You're running up credit?"

"I sold some old jewelry too." She peered down her nose at him. "But don't get excited, there's none left now."

"What are you going to do?"

"Drink, not eat and be merry for tomorrow we may—" Another hiccup made her rock on her heels.

His heart clutched and he grabbed her arm. "Lizzie. Come on, you're killing yourself. Come with me and we'll get you sorted out."

"I said the jewelry's all gone. There's nothing in it for you!" She spat the icy words as she wrenched her arm from his grasp.

"I don't care about your money, but I can't let you drink like this. You didn't drink at all until you met me."

"Had no idea what I was missing!" Her lipsticked mouth twisted into a fake grin. "I have to thank you for showing me the light—which looks especially golden through the bottom of a bottle of champagne. Cheers!" She drained her glass, then slammed it down on the table. "Now get out."

Time for plan B. Actually it was plan A, since he'd pretty much assumed she wouldn't go willingly.

"I brought you a present." He lifted the flower-patterned bag filled with pink tissue paper.

"Oh, how touching. Now take it with you when you piss off." She picked up the champagne bottle and refilled her glass, spilling some on the table.

"How much have you drunk today?" He didn't manage to sound casual.

"Don't worry, dear, it's my first bottle. Whoops, it seems to be empty. Lucky thing I have a case in the fridge." Her empty eyes stared at him in mute challenge. Devoid of all the love and laughter he'd once put there.

"Won't you at least see what I brought you?" He shook the bag and a metallic clank sounded under the rustling tissue paper.

"Gold ingots? Those would come in handy."

He stepped toward her, crowded her. She didn't smell like roses anymore. She wore a heavy, harsh scent probably designed in ε Paris lab.

"You'll need both hands to lift it out." He raised the bag. She looked at him, suspicious but curious, then dipped both hands into the bag. Lifted out a pair of chrome handcuffs.

"What the—?"

He pushed her onto the bed and pinned her with his weight while he grabbed the handcuffs and clamped them on her wrists. She struggled and shrieked but was no match for him.

"I'm sorry," he murmured as he pulled the wad of cotton primed with knock-out drops out of a Ziploc bag buried in the tissue paper and covered her mouth and nose. She stared at him, plainly terrified, as her body went limp.

"It's for your own good," he whispered. She couldn't hear him, and he hoped no one else had either. Lucky her room was at the end of the hall.

The next part of the plan promised to be tricky. The French doors to the garden were a blessing, but he still had to get her out there and over the low stucco wall that surrounded the property. And he needed to bring her stuff. Since money was tight now, everything counted.

He rooted around under the bed and in the closet looking for a suitcase. Nothing. She'd come here empty-handed after braining him with the champagne bottle. He found an expensive looking shopping bag from some store in Beverly Hills and shoved all her clothes into it. Mostly skimpy workout stuff. Piled a load of cosmetics on top, keeping one eye on the door. The strappy sandals took up less space than sneakers, so he took them instead.

He left the Cheetos behind. And the case of champagne. He scribbled a note about settling the bill later and forged her girlish signature on it.

With the bulging shopping bag slung over his shoulder, he flipped the lock on the French doors and propped one open with her sneaker. No one outside. Good.

Her limp body felt like a sack of lead. Her newly toned muscles flopped, arms hanging, as he tried to get a good grip on her.

*I'm so sorry, Lizzie.* Her straightened hair hung in a shiny curtain as he carried her over the threshold, out onto a tiled patio. The heat smacked him in the face, and he adjusted his arms around her chest.

He kicked the sneaker out of the door frame and eased the door closed with his foot. He wanted it to look like she'd slipped out the front door when no one was looking, skipped out on the bill.

The wall was a problem. For a moment he contemplated sneaking around the inside of it and strolling out the front gates. Nah. Too much chance of being seen through a window. The smooth stucco rose only chest high, but he couldn't step over it. Regretfully, he leaned over and lowered Lizzie's limp body as far as he could...

Then dropped her.

He grimaced as she fell to the sun-baked dirt and rolled, hair sprawling in the red dust.

*I, Conroy Beale, will never again do anything dishonest, low-down, underhanded—*

He hugged her limp body to his chest and shuffled along on his knees through the sandy dirt, making sure to keep his head beneath the level of the wall. One of her feet dragged, no matter how he tried to hoist her higher. The sight of his car gleaming in the sun around the corner made him limp with relief.

An invisible cloud of heat exploded in his face as he opened the passenger door and shoved her in. He jimmied her into position and propped her with his arm so she wouldn't flop forward and bang her head on the dash while he buckled her seatbelt.

He tossed her bag in the back seat and climbed into the driver's side, relieved the vintage engine started on the first try. Hoped she couldn't feel any pain as her short shorts and skimpy top left plenty of flesh exposed against the scorching leather seats.

*I'm so sorry Lizzie.*

*I wanted to make us both happy. I never meant to hurt you.*

Her sleeping body exhaled fumes from the liquor percolating through her system. A distinctive smell he'd known since the cradle, that never failed to turn his stomach.

Soon he'd have her tucked up in bed, with a good meal and plenty of water to drink. He'd get her dried out and straightened up. Then they'd figure out what to do next.

# 4

"What on earth?" Freezing daggers pricked Lizzie's skin and roused her from a distorted dream.

"Thank God." A man loomed over her, face in shadow. Behind him a showerhead pelted her with tiny drops of icy water.

The scream she let out practically pierced her eardrums. Before she knew what was happening he'd wrapped his arms around her and lifted her out of the tub.

"You had me worried there. I don't know what's in that stuff I gave you. Guess I should have asked."

*Con.* Of course. Her heart both sank and rose at the same time. Funny how it could still do that when it was *broken.*

She kicked and struggled as he carried her out of the bathroom into a tiny hotel bedroom.

"Where am I?" she shrieked, as he lowered her onto the bed.

"Shhh. A motel in the desert."

She scanned the room as he disappeared back into the bathroom. Garish geometric curtains and a wood-grain TV suggested a time warp to the 1970s.

He reappeared with a towel and started to rub. Conroy Beale, onetime man of her dreams, looked different with his shirt soaked and streaked with red dirt and his hair sticking in all directions. "You'll get a mean headache soon, but after a rest you'll feel good as new."

"I thought I killed you." She flopped back on the bed as an anvil fell on her head. At least that's what it felt like.

He disappeared back into the bathroom and emerged with a paper cup. "Drink it."

"I can't, my head hurts too much. What am I doing here?"

"I kidnapped you."

"You're an idiot. I'm broke, remember? Besides, my parents wouldn't waste money on a ransom for me." The cold emptiness threatened to close over her again. "Champagne, I need champagne!"

"That's the last thing you need. Drink this water and I'll get you some more. I'll bet you've been drunk an entire month."

"Best month of my life," she rasped. Her head was too heavy to lift.

"I'm not going to have your death on my conscience, so your boozing binge ends right now."

"What nonsense. Champagne isn't booze. It's made from squeezed grapes, you know. Healthy and delicious... Ow! Stop banging my head like that!"

"I'm not. I'm a good five feet away from you."

The furniture shifted and twisted as she tried to focus. She could barely keep her eyes open. "Take me back to Zen Mind. I have yoga class at two and I can't miss it."

"Yoga's over. You've been out five hours. I thought you'd never wake up."

A hollow laugh rattled her ribs. "I'm almost sorry I did. Would have been fun to leave you with a body to dispose of." Even in blurred half-vision he looked revoltingly handsome—all intense dark eyes and wild dark hair. Bastard. "Who am I kidding? You probably have experience disposing of dead bodies."

"Stop talking and get some sleep."

"I don't think so! I just woke up, in case you've forgotten. And I can hardly relax around you. In spite of the fact that I nearly married you, I don't have *any* idea who you are."

"Someone who cares about you." He said it softly.

Her heart tripped and she cursed herself for it. How many other things had he said to her with such breathtaking sincerity that had turned out to be—

"Utter bullshit!"

"It's okay. I don't expect you to believe a word I say. I'm just here to help you get dried out."

"Get another towel then. My hair's still wet."

He walked into the bathroom and she rocketed off the bed toward the door. She was fumbling with the lock when he emerged with a curse. Suddenly she was on the floor, crushed under him.

"Ow, my head hurts. Everything hurts. Where's my stuff?"

He picked her up and carried her back to the bed. Settled her down and tucked her in. His arms were strong and warm and she didn't have the energy to resist.

"I brought all your things in a bag. I'm not going to hurt you." His voice soothed her as he patted her hair with a white towel. "Get some sleep."

She couldn't find any more words, so she closed her eyes.


Lizzie crept back to consciousness, her mouth dry as a scoured pot. *Water. Must get water.* Thin light sneaking around the curtains suggested dawn.

The sound of breathing alerted her to the presence of her captor sleeping next to her on the bed. He lay on his stomach, one arm under his head, the other touching her pillow. Dressed only in a pair of blue boxer shorts.

She'd given him those shorts.

Humiliation flooded back on a wave of adrenaline.

She lifted her head and pushed aside the tangle of hair blocking her vision. His strong back rose and fell with the steady breathing of deep, dreamless sleep. A peaceful expression softened his masculine features.

*She'd like to disturb that peace.*

But first, she needed water.

She eased off the bed in incremental movements, anxious not to creak the mattress. Crept across the stiff carpet into the bathroom and eased the door shut. She stuck her head under the faucet and gulped back water in breathtaking icy swallows. Drank and drank and drank until it tasted like thick cream pouring down her throat.

At last she threw her head back and inhaled air. The sight of her face in the mirror made her gasp. Her hair, recently wet, had sprung back into a nightmare of tangled curls. Smudged mascara and eyeliner gave her eyes manic intensity. She scrubbed it off with the damp corner of a towel.

The skimpy T-shirt and shorts she'd had on yesterday hung over the shower rail, alerting her that she stood there in only her bra and panties.

*He'd undressed her.*

The thought of his fingers on her skin made her flesh creep with... With disgust, surely. How could she feel anything else for him? He'd handcuffed her, stolen her away and locked her up in this strange motel.

Her clothes were damp, like they'd been washed. She lifted the blinds and peered out the small, slatted bathroom window. Featureless desert stretched out toward a distant mountain range. Where the hell where they and why? What did he want with her?

And more importantly, what had he done with those handcuffs?

She found them in the back pocket of the pants he'd removed and left folded on a chair in the bedroom. She slid them out, along with the key, and held them behind her back. Held her breath.

She crept to the bed on bare feet, heart thudding in her ears. Opened one chromed bracelet very slowly, careful not to jingle the chain. Then the other. The first one would wake him and she'd have to get the other one on before he could gain control of the situation. He was strong and quick.

She decided to start with the arm stretched across her pillow, then she could sit on the other one until she got it fastened.

Deep breath. She lifted one leg—doable, thanks to all that yoga—and spanned him with it. Moved the cuff through the air.

Snap. It was on. She crashed down on him, backside on his, yanked his cuffed arm down and cuffed the other.

Hah!

He spun on to his back, knocking her to the mattress, and she scrambled to her knees. He grimaced as the cuffs dug into his back, then shuffled into a sitting position, hands behind him.

His eyes caught her off guard as surprise turned to humor. She realized she was panting audibly, and she tossed her hair out of her face and drew herself up.

Still in just her underwear, she sucked in her stomach. "Where are my dry clothes, you jerk?"

"I forget." A wicked smile hitched the corner of his mouth. The mouth that used to kiss her into oblivion.

"Never mind, I'm sure I can find them." She didn't like to turn her back on him so she eased off the bed and backed away. He shifted position, as if getting comfy. His smile broadened.

"Hey, you look good."

Against her will, her nipples tightened. She sucked her stomach in a little further as she backed toward the wardrobe.

"You do. Damn." He grinned at her. "I thought you got all skinny, but you didn't. You look *nice*."

"Stop looking at me!" Suddenly every overly curvaceous inch of her bulged in all directions and she fought the urge to look down. She felt more clear-headed than she had in a month. She'd been strutting around like Madonna in her drunken haze—maybe she was still fat after all?

She ripped open the dark brown closet.

Empty.

"Is the bag in the car?" She mustered a stern, schoolmarm expression.

He nodded, excited grin still spread across his face.

"Don't look now, but your shorts are bulging. Any minute something's going to come poking out and there won't be a damn thing you can do about it."

"No," he said wistfully. His eyes drifted over her breasts and belly.

She grabbed a discarded sandal off the floor and brandished it over her shoulder.

He winced.

"Oh, you don't like pain? Well, let me tell you, you don't know anything about pain. Someday you should try sitting right on top of the world, then falling all the way off it."

*I did.*

Did he say it or did she read it in his eyes?

"Oh, yes, of course, silly me. Poor little Conroy got cheated out of all those lovely millions. How could I forget?"

His lips twitched, but he didn't say anything. Just regarded her steadily with those dark eyes.

A harsh laugh slipped out. "You'd think the fact that your name is Con would have tipped me off, wouldn't you? I guess you know a good mark when you see one."

He shifted on the bed, uncomfortable. *Good.*

"Well, you marked me alright. I'm a completely different person now. Like I flipped inside out overnight. No one's going to catch me with my pants down again. Ever!" She slammed her sandal against the wall over his head. He ducked as the shoe fell to one side.

She realized she'd forgotten all about sucking in her stomach, and her breasts heaved with each angry breath. She pulled his shirt off the back of the chair and shoved her arms into the sleeves.

"Car keys?"

"No way."

"I just want to get my bag."

"Nope."

"I need some clothes."

"You've got some." He flicked a glance down at the shirt.

She made a show of wiping at a rusty smear of dirt on the front. "This shirt is filthy. You really should take more care with your appearance."

He met her challenging stare with a twinkle of humor. No one took more care with his appearance than Con. Of course now she knew why. Appearances were pretty much the full show. He'd combed his hair. Even after sleep it still lay neatly, one straight lock dipping to his eyebrows.

A hand crept up to her own fright wig of disordered curls. That infuriating grin crept back across his insolent mouth.

"You didn't get it permanently straightened."

"Of course not. That would fry it. I had it ironed."

"Do they use a real iron for that?" Innocent curiosity. She picked up the other sandal.

"Just asking." He shrugged. Shifted his bound arms, which bunched the well-exercised muscles of his chest and stomach.

She tore her gaze from his torso and settled it on his face with as much hostility as she could summon. Which was quite a lot.

"I hate you. Now why don't you tell me where the car keys are, and I'll drive away and you can forget you ever met me."

"How do I know you won't drive straight to the nearest bar and start slamming Fuzzy Navels?"

"I wouldn't be caught dead drinking a Fuzzy Navel."

"Well, whatever you ladies drink when there's no man around to laugh at you. Baileys." He smiled. "Didn't you drink chocolate milk the first time I took you out?"

Heat rushed her face and she was glad of hair to hide behind. "That was a lifetime ago." Her voice sounded thin.

His apologetic silence deepened her embarrassment.

"Why did you ask me out that day?" she asked after a long pause.

"Because I wanted to get to know you."

"Because I was driving a Mercedes and you thought I might be rich? Well, I'll be honest too. I thought you were rich. Nice suit, Range Rover. You didn't earn those on a mechanic's salary, did you?"

"No." Con shifted. A pained expression flitted across his face.

"Did the Range Rover belong to her?"

"Who?" His brow furrowed.

"Your sugar mama, of course. The one you traded in for me." She kept her voice steady. Steeled herself against the answer. "Don't lie to me. It's all over now, and I'd just as soon know the truth. The real truth."

Con looked away. "Yes, the Range Rover belonged to a female friend."

*I knew it.* "What's her name?"

He hesitated, then shifted his shoulders. "Frankie... Frances Allen." He blinked twice as he said the name. "She knows you."

"She does?" She racked her brain. "Wait a second, is she the one who just married the Greek shipping tycoon?" A thin, pretty woman she'd met a few times at parties with her parents. Not as old as them but not young either. Maybe mid-forties.

"That's her." He didn't meet her eye.

"So what did Frankie Allen think of you pulling moves on me when you were out driving her car?"

"We were just friends by then. I was doing her a favor by taking her car into the shop that day. When I told her I'd met a girl called Lizzie Hathaway, she was happy. She figured you and I might be a good match."

Lizzie stared at him. "How considerate of her to approve your new lover. She must care deeply about you." Acid in her voice.

She saw his Adam's apple move as he swallowed. "Do you have any idea how sick that is?" Her head shook as she spat the words at him.

He looked sad. *Aw, poor baby.*

"How did you get mixed up with Frankie Allen in the first place? I'd hardly imagine you run in her circle."

"Do you really want to know?" He dipped his head slightly.

"Sure, why the hell not?" She crossed her arms over her chest in a protective gesture.

"You know my car?"

"The gold Mercedes? Is that actually yours?"

"It's mine now. It belonged to Frankie back then, and it had a problem with the distributor..." He paused, looked at her cautiously. "I was working at a garage uptown, and she arranged to have me drive it to her house in Greenwich when it was fixed. Once I got there she

offered a big tip if I'd come take a look at the broken
motor on her Jacuzzi." He hesitated.

"And soon you were coming over to service a totally
different kind of body."

He nodded.

"She gave you her car?"

"It's from the late sixties. Takes a lot of TLC to keep
it running smooth. She knew I was the only person who
could keep it purring like a kitten." His look of
satisfaction irritated her.

"So when exactly did you stop sleeping with her?"
She braced herself.

"More than a year ago. She was getting over an ugly
divorce when I met her. Once she was ready to start
seriously dating again, I didn't fit the bill." He shrugged,
but his expression didn't quite match the casual gesture.

"So she gave you your walking papers. How romantic.
Did she give you money?"

He met her gaze. "She helped me out. Taught me how
to act, how to dress, bought me some clothes." His face
was grim.

"How sweet. So you were a charity project for her?
Her little Pygmalion. And the final triumph would be
seeing you married off to a plump heiress?"

"I never wanted to hurt you."

"You wanted to marry me for my money, then dump
me and keep half and you didn't want to hurt me?" Her
voice rose to a screech.

"I didn't plan to divorce you." He spoke quietly.

"Oh, so let me get this straight, you wanted to marry
me, live high on the hog with me and keep me fat and
happy for the rest of my days?"

He licked his lips again. Shifted his shoulders.

The idea sank in and gave her a strange queasy
feeling. "You really planned to stay married to me?"

"Yes. I think we'd have been a good team." The
wistful look in his brown eyes worsened the sensation in
the pit of her stomach. She ignored it.

"And, er, how did you plan to conceal from me that
you spend your days under a car rather than in an office?
That kind of illusion must take a lot of work to sustain.

You wanted to keep it a secret until we were legally married, and then you'd spring it on me?"

"Pretty much."

His quiet acknowledgement sent a flash of raw pain shooting high.

She stood there, panting, staring at him. She could picture him discussing her over cocktails with Frankie Allen. They must have schemed to string her along and keep quiet about his true identity until it was too late.

*All the while, she'd thought she'd found a man who truly loved her.*

How could something so beautiful, so perfect, that brought her such shining happiness, have turned out to be a big joke at her expense?

She shook her head, tangled curls blurring her vision. Hard breaths came like sobs, but she managed to get her breathing under control. Lifted her chin.

He grimaced as he rearranged his arms again. "You've had your fun." His voice was gruff. "Can you please take the cuffs off?"

That nasty hollow laugh shook her again. "Had my fun? That's where you're wrong. I'm just getting started."

# 5

"Okay, okay, you sweet-talked me. Again." She unlocked the cuffs and oddly it was a relief to see Con stretch and flex his wrists.

She tried to ignore the ripple effect in the muscles of his back as he rolled off the bed and stretched.

"We made a fair deal. You get the car keys. I get the handcuff key."

"How did you know I wouldn't take the car keys and hightail it out of town, leave you here for the maid?"

"Because you're not like that."

"More fool me." She jingled the car keys between her fingers. "You must really trust me—to let me go outside and get my clothes before I unlocked you."

"I'm a good judge of character." Con still wore nothing but the pair of blue boxers she'd given him. All tan skin and toned muscles, dusted with black hair. She averted her eyes.

"You can spot a sucker from fifty paces?"

"Something like that." A wry look. "We need to get you some food. We passed a diner on the way here. Let's go there and get a good breakfast. How's your head feeling?"

"What head? I lost it over a man, remember?"

"When did you turn into such a wiseass?" He picked up his pants.

"I guess around the same time that someone made a total ass of me. Those pants are dirty. I brought you some clean ones from the car." She picked up a pair of black pants she'd found in his luggage and threw them at him.

He caught them with one hand. "Now that's just what I mean, about your character." Shook them out and put his foot in. "Thoughtful. I appreciate it." His polite smile made her want to slap him.

"Did you bring my Cheetos?"

"I did not."

"I'm on a strict diet. Do you want me to blow up like a balloon again?"

"I want you to be strong and healthy. 'Cheese food' is not a balanced diet." He zipped his pants. She tossed him the clean white shirt she'd brought, without paying any attention to his flat stomach.

She glanced down at her exercise ensemble, dark gray yoga pants with a stripe to match the short lime-green tank top. Now that she wasn't high as a popped cork she felt more than a little self-conscious. At least neither of them was skintight. She'd cringed when she snatched down the skimpy two-piece she'd had on yesterday from the shower rail.

"Let's go." Con tucked his shirt into his pants, which as usual looked like they'd been custom cut to hug his... Never mind. He whipped out a comb and slicked his hair back, revealing the proud line of his cheekbones. He stroked his chin. "Mind if I shave?"

"Yes." That's all she needed. Chiseled perfection with smooth skin. "I'm hungry, let's go."

Con gathered up his stuff, loaded up the car and went to pay the motel bill. Lizzie deliberately climbed into the driver's seat. It went against all her instincts, but she felt this display of bravado was necessary to establishing a certain balance of power.

Of course if she had any moxie at all she'd put the key in the ignition and drive away. But—as Con had pointed out—she wasn't that kind of girl. Shame.

She rolled down the windows. No A/C from the looks of it.

When he returned, his brow darkened at the sight of her in his seat. She blinked innocently.

"I'll drive," he growled.

"No, actually I will. I'm sure I'm just as good at it as Frankie." She shot him a menacing look.

Con silently walked around to the passenger seat and climbed in. Fastened his seat belt.

A stick shift? Uh, oh. She hadn't noticed that when she got in. She turned the ignition and tried to remember which pedal was which. Left foot on the clutch, let it up slowly…

A horrible grinding sound rose from the engine as the car inched forward and then stalled.

"I'll drive." He spoke through gritted teeth.

"No, it's okay, I'm just a little rusty. I'll get it this time."

She let out the clutch, applied gas and with only minor scraping sounds the car lurched forward. Thank goodness she didn't have to reverse out. She drove to the lot entrance and stalled hard.

"Please…"

She ignored him. Started it up again, pulled out onto the highway and made sure to stay in first as long as possible to really drive up his blood pressure. Only when the engine sounded like it was about to catch fire did she shift into second with a smile. "Nothing to it."

When she finally shifted into third after whizzing along in second at about fifty miles per hour, she could swear she heard him exhale. They drove for miles through featureless brown desert, her hair whipping about her face. The sky was painfully blue.

"There's the diner," he said, audibly relieved, as a glint of metal appeared on the horizon.

She downshifted and pulled into the dusty lot of the 1960s-era diner with maximum grinding of gears. Stalled to a halt diagonally poised across two parking spaces. This was fun.

Con wiped a bead of sweat from his upper lip.

Inside, Lizzie settled into an aqua booth, enjoying the air-conditioning.

"I'll have a small fruit salad and a glass of water, please," she said with a smile. Her stomach protested loudly, and she slammed the greasy menu shut to silence it.

Con glared at her for a moment. "I'll have the blue-plate breakfast, with the eggs scrambled and a short stack. Whole-wheat toast." He smiled at the waitress. "Two of those, please."

"You have quite an appetite." Lizzie arranged her napkin on her lap as the waitress moved away.

"How are you feeling?" He shook out his napkin.

"I'm not sure. How do you suppose a gong feels after it's just been banged?"

"Need some aspirin?"

"No thanks. Pain can accelerate spiritual growth."

"Is that the kind of thinking they feed you at Zen Mind?" He took a sip of his water.

"No. No pain at Zen Mind. Mostly manicures, shiatsu massage, hair ironing, that kind of thing. I'm not sure if there's a connection between hair ironing and Zen Buddhism, but it's very chic."

"I don't doubt it. Very expensive too, I bet."

"It's only money. When you owe two million dollars, really, what's a few thousand more?"

A crease appeared between his eyebrows. "You'll regret getting into debt."

"Have some personal experience in that area, do you?"

"I learned everything the hard way. I just want to help you out so you don't have to do the same." His frank gaze threatened her defenses.

She steeled herself against it. "What makes you think I need help?"

"The stories I read about you on the Internet and in the papers."

"You searched for me on the Internet?" She ignored the funny fluttery sensation that gave her. "I told you, they make up lies."

"Do they? When I found you, you were drunk in the morning and living on Cheetos. That's actually worse than what I read."

"If we're going to be blunt, let's be blunt. No one gives a crap about me. I was just an easy pocket to pick, for my parents as well as you. It's empty. So who cares what I do with my life?"

She expected him to protest, to say he cared. He didn't. He just looked at her. A look so filled with pity it knocked her right off balance. She grabbed her glass and drank water and looked anywhere but at Con while the waitress put her fruit salad in front of her.

Canned, with slippery radioactive peaches and a Dayglo cherry on top.

The waitress returned with two steaming plates loaded high with eggs, bacon, sausage and pancakes. She moved the fruit salad to the side and set one of the plates right in front of Lizzie with no prompting from Con. She returned with two plates of toast, butter and jam.

"God I'm starving." Her confession was a relief.

Con smiled. "Good. Eat up." He buttered some toast and took a bite.

She loaded a fork with eggs and sausage and almost had an oral orgasm as she chewed it. "I'd forgotten what actual food tastes like," she murmured through her mouthful. Con beamed and took another bite of toast. "At Zen Mind it was either tofu teriyaki with wheatgrass juice, or contraband Cheetos and champagne. Hey, why are you eating toast when there's all this other good stuff?"

"I like toast." He took another neat bite. Chewed it with his lips closed. Dark lashes a girl would kill for hid his eyes.

"You know, it's a damn shame you aren't a moneyed aristocrat. As far as I'm concerned, you've got everything it takes: You drive with the roof down at eighty miles an hour and don't have a hair out of place; you hang around in custom-made Italian suits like you're wearing sweats; and, last and most important, you're an arrogant SOB who's out to get his and screw everyone else. Maybe you were switched at birth or something? Where were you born, anyway?"

"Nowhere you'd know." He popped the last of the toast triangle in his mouth and dusted his fingers over the plate.

"No, really, I want to know. You don't have a Southern accent, now that I think about it."

"We don't all talk the same, you know."

"Your accent almost does sound a little French. Maybe that's why I cottoned onto the French aristocracy thing so easily. What's the name of the town?"

"Like I said, you wouldn't know it." He picked up a jug of syrup and poured some on his pancakes.

"So what's the harm in telling me?"

"You'll laugh."

"Good, I could use a laugh," she muttered through a mouthful of eggs.

He hesitated. "Mudbug Flats, Louisiana."

A snorting laugh did escape. "You're kidding, right?"

"Nope." He kept a pleasant poker face. "Heart of Cajun country."

"It sounds...lovely." She snorted again. "I'm guessing it's known mostly for mud and mosquitoes."

"Ah, but that's where you're wrong." He picked up another toast triangle and buttered it with deliberate elegance. "*Mudbug* is another word for *crawdad*."

"Crayfish."

"That's right. Best eatin' in the state of Louisiana. Millions of the little critters right there at your feet." He winked, a gesture to match the phony backwoods accent. Took a bite of toast.

"This gets better all the time. Let me guess, you grew up in a trailer?"

Con held her gaze. "We couldn't afford that kind of modern luxury, I'm afraid. Just the old shack, the flat-bottomed boat and the one hog."

She couldn't help smiling. Didn't believe a word he said, but she was getting curious all the same. "Do you still have family back there?"

"Hell if I know." He finally picked up his fork, speared some pancake and put it in his mouth.

"How long have you been gone?"

"A long, long, long, long, long time. Now stop dredging up the distant past and let me enjoy my meal."

Lizzie watched the man across the table from her eat with careful precision. The more she learned about him, the less she knew.

She'd learned a lot about herself, though. She'd never trust her instincts again. He'd stolen something precious from her: trust, faith.

Hope.

He took a sip of his freshly topped-up coffee. Met her eyes for a minute with a cautious glance that made her catch her breath and look away.

What kind of heart really beat behind that carefully polished exterior?

*And how could she drive a stake through it?*

Tempted as she was to destroy Con's most cherished possession, she let him drive the car after breakfast. She figured she'd play along with whatever he had planned, let him get relaxed, then as soon as they got to a decent-sized town she'd give him the slip and head... Where would she head?

*Her head hurt.*

"Scenic overlook. Let's go do some sightseeing." Con beamed with goodwill. Probably thought he was a knight in shining armor rescuing her from the dragon of strong drink.

Shame he was the one who'd thrown her to the dragon in the first place. She'd gotten pretty cozy with it too. Maybe those maidens in the old days didn't want to be rescued either.

"I've never been to the Southwest before," he said cheerily, downshifting as they approached what appeared to be the rim of a vast canyon. They were in the middle of nowhere, not a single person or car in sight.

"I have. It all looks the same. Lots of flat, treeless land and a mountain in the distance. There's always a mountain in the distance."

"A very metaphorical landscape."

They climbed out of the car and approached the edge of the Canyon. Lizzie got a shiver of vertigo peering down at the dry river bed a hundred feet or more below.

"If you didn't go to college, and spent your teen years in a reform school, then how come you sound so educated?"

"Books." Con peered over the rim too. A breeze flicked his hair. "Always been a big reader. You can learn pretty much anything from books."

"You're smart too. I guess that's how you managed to trick me."

He didn't try to defend himself.

"So if you're so smart and you love books, then why didn't you just go to college and get a high-paying job?"

He looked at her as if the question was some kind of joke, then stared up at the inevitable mountain range on the horizon, toothed peaks cutting into an indigo sky. "The world doesn't work the way you think it does."

"I'm from New York City. I've hardly grown up in a bubble."

"You were cushioned in a nice soft bubble on the Upper East Side. I'd give anything to have had the kind of upbringing you had."

"Yeah? Look how well it's worked out for me. Twenty-five years old, no money, no job, no family, no *real* friends and no freaking idea what to do with my life."

"That's why I'm here." He extended a hand, and she flinched as if it might burn her. "I wasn't going to run off and leave you that night."

He took his untouched hand back.

"Yes, you were. You just wanted to marry me for my money. Without it you had no use for me. You didn't love me." She swallowed hard as the memories clouded her painfully clear mind.

He stared up at the mountains again. "I'm not capable of love. Maybe I was once, but that part of me is dead. I'm not really capable of anything other than survival."

"My, how dramatic. If you're such an emotional robot you hide it well. You did a bang-up job pretending to care about me."

He looked at her. "I do care about you."

She squinted at him. The sun hurt her eyes, and his words hurt her heart. She didn't believe them.

Didn't believe anything anymore.

He held out his hand again and she fought a mad urge to take it, just to steady herself.

"I'm here to teach you how to survive too."

"Oh, great. Maybe you can show me how to change the oil in your car and I can get a job at Jiffy Lube. I have a college degree and three years of experience. I think I can take care of myself, thank you."

"That's the attitude I was hoping for." He moved and sunlight hit his face, lighting up a smile. "When you took off, I didn't plan to chase you down. I figured you wouldn't want me to. But I kept close tabs on you and after a while I could see you needed a friend. How does your head feel?"

"Don't keep asking about my head. I'm trying to forget it's there." It didn't hurt any more, but the clarity was agonizing. Everything clear, crisp and sharp, the landscape, the cloudless sky, her sense of loss.

All that blue emptiness made her reckless. "So if you weren't planning to leave, would you have..." She stopped herself. Took a deep breath. The chasm gaped, dark in front of her. She turned to stare at him. "Would you have married me that Friday, just like we planned?"

"Yes. I made a promise to you."

The sun flashed and the sand seemed to shift under her feet. Did she hear him right? He grabbed her arm as she stumbled back, trying to figure out the meaning of what he said.

"You really would have married me?" The words drifted out of her mouth, toneless.

"Yes. I'll marry you today, if that's what you want."

His strong hand held her arm fast. Reassuring. Kept her up while the world tilted under her. He held her gaze with resolute dark eyes and a hard-set jaw.

"That's not what I want." She managed to spit out the words. "Not at all."

Something painful rose in her throat, and the next thing she knew Con's arms were around her, her head on his chest as her tears wet his shirt.

He was willing to give up his freedom and marry her.

Not because he loved her.

*Because he pitied her.*

She couldn't stop the choking sobs that hurt her throat or the tears that dripped from her chin. His hand rubbed

her back, caressed her shoulders. "Shhh," he whispered.
But she couldn't.

She looked at him through her tears and saw the face
that was the embodiment of all her dreams of Happily
Ever After. She'd had no doubts. No fears. He was perfect
and they'd live an enchanted life.

*The world doesn't work the way you think it does.*

Her chest hurt.

"Come on, you'll feel much better if you..."

She never knew what he was about to suggest because
her mouth closed over his and silenced his tongue with
hers. Their lips met with a breathtaking explosion of
chemistry. Her hands roamed over his face, into his hair,
along his powerful neck and into the collar of his shirt.
The hot sun and the feral scent of his hot skin made
thoughts evaporate before they could form. She untucked
the back of his shirt and slid her fingers under it, traced
the straight line of his spine and dug her fingertips into
hard muscle.

He shifted his hips, pushed his body against hers so
she could feel his arousal. Instant, like her own. She
pressed her breasts to his chest, nipples straining her bra.
His cupped hand on her buttock lifted her, deepened their
kiss. He ground his hips against her, and she pushed back,
harder.

She sat on top so he was the one lying in the dirt. She
kept her eyes open, watched his face as she increased the
rhythm and intensity and took them both to the quivering
edge.

His hands explored her body with that familiar touch
that felt like a celebration of every inch of skin, every
curve. Soft groans tickled her ears as she leaned to lick his
closed eyelids, graze his neck with her teeth. She had to
struggle to keep her head, not go adrift in arms that felt so
loving.

He never opened his eyes. Trust? Or because he didn't
want to see her? Wanted to imagine she was someone else
the way he pretended he was?

She sensed his climax coming with a thrill of power.
She'd never stayed so detached during sex. She
discovered she could enjoy the pleasure but not lose

herself in it. Keep emotion tightly buttoned down as sensation surged to her toes.

As Con came, hard, with a low animal sound and his eyes squeezed tight, she faked her own orgasm. Loud breathing, a high pitched moan. Her eyes open the whole time.

She'd never done that before. Could he tell? If so he didn't say. This was the new Lizzie, the one she planned to forge herself into. The one who knew how the world worked and played it her way.

The one who could rip arrows out of her chest and throw them on the ground without feeling anything like the agony ripping through her right now.

She climbed off him, her hands trembling.

"Hey, where are you going?"

She put her pants back on. Con was one of those supposedly rare men who actually like to cuddle and caress after sex. He loved nothing more than being entangled under warm sheets, snoozing, whispering and hugging. If anything she'd say he was more blissed out by that than by the act itself.

But she'd show him what he could do with his pity.

She inhaled a shaky breath. She wouldn't have guessed she was capable of enduring this much pain, but here she was, still alive.

What else was she capable of? She intended to find out, and Con would learn too—the hard way.

# 6

Lizzie squinted in the sun, keeping her distance from the edge of the canyon. "So, what is that thing on your butt?" She stared at the tattoo as it disappeared into a pair of neatly pressed pants. He seemed to have an inexhaustible supply. Probably had a deal with the Devil that banished wrinkles from his wardrobe.

"A flaming dagger." He pulled a gleaming white shirt from his bag and shook it out.

"A gang tattoo?"

"Kind of. Protective coloration."

"On your butt?"

"It's a long story. Better there than on my face, right?"

"Was that before or after you went to reform school?" She dragged out the last two words. Con didn't look at all ruffled. He whipped out a comb and slicked back his hair.

"During."

"Must have been a nice place."

"Very educational, let's put it that way."

"Is that where you learned how to lie, cheat and steal?"

Now he looked hurt. He tucked the comb back in his bag. "I didn't do any of those things."

"You told me that tattoo was a family crest. That's not a lie?"

"A gang is a kind of family." The half-smile that crept across his face let her know he didn't think he was fooling anyone.

"Don't snow me with semantics, please. I may be naïve, but I'm not stupid. How did you end up in reform school anyway?"

"It's a long story."

"Everything's a long story with you. I'd like to actually hear one of them."

"Maybe another time."

He zipped up his bag. Slipped his bare feet into dusty dress shoes. Apparently today the illusion only extended to his ankles. "You hungry?"

"No. Do you have any plans beyond feeding me back to my fighting weight?" Her hostile tone began to grate even on her nerves. "Damn, being a bitch is exhausting. If I lighten up a little, don't take it personally."

Con's eyes twinkled. "I'll try not to. Come sit down, get out of the sun for a while."

He'd put the top up on the car and the passenger seat beckoned. Her fake tan didn't give much protection from the blistering Arizona sun. Underneath it she was already freckling. "Alright."

Con climbed into the driver side and they sat there, side by side, inches from each other. She could smell his sweat and the scent of sex. A crisp white shirt couldn't hide everything. Strong, brown hands rested on his knees.

She shifted her attention to the big brown desert out there. "So, tell me, Con. Have you ever been really happy?"

"Sure. I can honestly say I've never been happier than when I was with you."

She rolled her eyes and tried to ignore an odd flutter in her chest. "I mean when you weren't living a charade." She turned to stare at him. "Or have you been acting some kind of role since the day you were born?"

His chin kicked up, like she'd clocked him on it. Not such a bad idea. Then again, if anything, the little bump she'd added to his nose made his profile more distinguished.

"I guess you could say I have been pretending things were different for most of my life. Not because I wanted to…" His voice trailed off and he turned those soulful brown eyes on her.

"Maybe I should give that philosophy a try. Mmm, who do I wish to be? Let me see..." She drummed a finger on the dashboard. Turned her eyes on him with an intense stare. "I'd like to be me. The way I was before I met you, before my nearest and dearest bled me dry and left my bones out to bleach in the sun." Her throat seized up as she spit out the words.

"Were you really happy?"

"Of course not! But no one is really happy. We figure out a treadmill to run on, and we keep running. I had a pretty good situation back then. It sure beat being a penniless dupe who's lost all faith in herself and others!"

She stared at him, her face heating.

"You were happy with me." He said it so quietly that she thought she might have imagined it. "Maybe living in a world of illusion isn't such a bad thing?"

His soft voice and steady brown-eyed gaze threatened her barricades. She shored them up by wondering what else he might be hiding from her. "Apparently you're still living there. I already know you're a garage mechanic with a juvenile record and maybe an eighth-grade education, but you're dressed like a stockbroker. Who are you trying to fool? Yourself?"

His dark eyes narrowed slightly, and a glint of humor covered the pain she saw there. "Maybe." A slight smile played across his lips and an odd sensation crept up her spine.

"Well, I guess if you've got even yourself fooled, you must really be good."

Silence shimmered between them like the desert heat.

She fidgeted in her seat, uncomfortable, battling a sudden urge to take his hand and hold it. To be nice to him. "Can we drive somewhere? All this sitting still is reminding me how my life is going nowhere fast."

Con started the engine. "You're a cool chick, Lizzie. You know, I think I like you even more now you're showing your dark side."

"That makes two of us. Where's my lipstick?"

"I think you put it in the glove compartment."

She fished it out and applied a thick smear of frosted plum. Checked the results in the side mirror and finger-fixed her smudged eyeliner. She even looked like a bitch with all this makeup on. Maybe there was something to be said for dressing the part.

"Where are we going?"

"Anywhere you like." He looked downright cheerful.

"I like a town. With people in it. All this emptiness is creeping me out."

"Your wish is my command."

Con carried their bags as they walked into the glittering marble lobby of the Desert Palm Hotel in Phoenix. He'd muttered about it looking expensive. She'd laughed. What did he expect? He was escorting Lizzie Hathaway, accustomed to only the best. She wouldn't need to give him the slip. He'd be begging her to get lost by the time she was done.

"My fiancé and I would like a room," she said in a syrupy voice. "Do you have a bridal suite?" She turned and gave him a loving look. He shot her back an equally fake smile.

"We certainly do." The receptionist beamed. "And you're in luck, it's vacant. It has a lovely view of the Phoenix skyline. Would you like to hear the rates?"

"I'm sure whatever you're charging will be fine. Won't it, sweetie?"

"Sure," said Con tonelessly.

"Your name?" The receptionist's smile stretched across her face in a crimson arc. Lizzie widened her own to match.

"Lizzie Hathaway."

"Lizzie Hathaway…" She wrote it in a log. "I recognize you! Your picture was in the paper after that party at the Coco Club a couple of weeks ago."

*It was?* Apparently she'd lost a day or two somewhere along the way. Lizzie kept her smile fixed in place. "I've been sowing some wild oats, but I'm ready to settle down now. Aren't I, darling?"

"Um, yeah." Con seemed to be having trouble keeping up.

"I'm so glad to hear that. When I read about what happened..." She leaned forward conspiratorially until Lizzie could count the individual pores on her heavily powdered face. "With your inheritance." The last word was a ponderous whisper. She shook her head with a tragic look on her face. Lizzie's smile wobbled. "It's a terrible shame. I said to Zelda, that poor girl is all alone in the world, without a penny. She's probably never worked a day in her life..."

"Actually I'm a graphic design specialist." She stepped back from the desk to get away from all those pores oozing prurient interest. How did this totally strange woman know enough about her to gossip with her friend over coffeecake? The thought gave her chills that competed with the air-conditioning.

"Zelda will be so tickled that you're getting married. I can't wait to tell her! And such a handsome fellow too." She shot a simpering glance at Con, then gave Lizzie a big, warm smile that made her want to sink right down into the marble floor and disappear. Her little joke on Con had backfired, and now she'd sparked yet another embarrassing rumor about herself.

Her heels clacked on the marble as they followed the bellhop to the room. She cringed at the sight of herself in the mirrored walls of the elevator, her hair the size of a category-three hurricane.

The bridal suite was embarrassingly luxe. Marble glittered on every surface, silver love-birds flew across the walls, and the heart-shaped bed was a cheerful affront to good taste. The city sprawled below the huge picture window, with more of those damn mountains in the distance.

"How do they know about me?" she hissed at Con when they were alone. He'd already started unpacking.

"Same way I do. You've been in the papers."

"People actually pay enough attention to remember my name and talk about me?" She shuddered.

"It's the kind of story people eat like candy. Riches to rags." He hung a shirt in the closet. "And Hathaway Industries is nationwide. They've been closing factories and shutting down offices everywhere. They defaulted on their pension plan. It's been big news in every state in the country, though you've probably been too drunk to notice."

"Jesus." She sank onto the bed. "Zen Mind didn't allow media. It clutters the mind. The only article I've seen was the one I showed you. Maisie gave it to me. What else has been going on out there while I've been in a Cheeto-and-champagne-induced haze?"

"You do know your father's being held without bail pending trial?"

"Yes. House arrest. I'm sure he got the ankle bracelet specially made by Brooks Brothers." She stood up swiftly. Her head hurt. "I wonder what they have in the minibar?"

"No, you don't." Con slid across the room and blocked her with his body. Caught hold of her by the hips as she pretended to tackle him. She completely ignored the stirring male scent of him.

"Unhand me, sir!"

He obeyed. His crooked smile made her heart hurt. "Just a half a glass of beer? It has B complex vitamins."

"Nope."

"I need it to rinse my hair. It brings out my brown highlights." She fluffed the hurricane.

"I'm sure you'll manage without."

"You're cruel." She threw herself on the bed. "I can't believe newspapers are making money with my sob story. That doesn't seem right. If anyone gets the money, it should be me."

"I won't argue with you."

She heard him hook another hanger over the rail. Apparently nothing interfered with his attention to his immaculate wardrobe.

"Maybe I could sell my story to *Vanity Fair*?"

"I don't think *Vanity Fair* would pay enough for it to be worthwhile."

"*People*?"

"That's more like it. But your story's pretty much out there already, so I'm not sure what you could add."

"Are you trying to say people on the street know more about me than I know about myself?" She flipped into a sitting position.

He shrugged and hung another shirt in the closet.

"Maybe I can sell them on something they don't know about me." She bit her lip. Tried hard to get her brain to work. "Something I haven't done yet."

"Like marrying me?" He winked at her as he fished a pair of black slacks out of his bag.

She watched him slide them neatly over a trouser hanger. A fiendish plot germinated in her brain.

"Like marrying you..." She said the words slowly, testing them on her tongue. Con's joking suggestion was ripe with possibilities. In fact, it presented an intriguing way to get revenge on Con, embarrass her parents, turn the tables on the media—and make some money into the bargain.

*I'll marry you today, if that's what you want.*

Afterward they could get divorced. She'd be a gay divorcée. It sounded sophisticated, bitchy and mean, all the things she'd decided would constitute her new persona.

"You're crazy," was Con's response when she shared her plan.

"Why? I'd think a show like *Entertainment Tonight* would love to cover our wedding."

"But you don't want to marry me." Infuriatingly, he hadn't even paused in his unpacking. He lined up neatly rolled socks in a drawer.

"Sure I do. What are you unpacking everything for? We'll be leaving tomorrow."

"I know. I just like to get settled in wherever I am."

"So you can pretend you're the kind of person who'd actually stay in a hotel like this?"

"I'm here, aren't I?"

"Yes, but only because I insisted."

"Makes no difference. I'm here and I'm going to enjoy it. Would you like me to unpack for you too?"

"Sure. Why not?" She lay back on the bed. "And I'm serious about the marriage thing. You're a good enough faker to pretend to be madly in love with me for a few weeks. I'll even give you half the money."

"I don't like it. It's deceitful."

"That's downright hilarious, coming from you."

"Look, I never set out to hurt anyone..." He rolled a belt and put it in the drawer with the socks. She could practically see the hair on the back of his neck standing up.

"No, you just set out to put one over me so you could live the good life. That's all I'm doing. They're making money off my misfortune. All I want is my fair share. You said you'd marry me, I'm just asking you to fulfill your promise."

Con ran his fingers through his hair, messing it up. She ignored the way that made him look more handsome. "I said I'd marry you, and I will..."

"And we let the media in on it." She leapt to her feet, hands on hips. "Is that so much to ask?"

"Yes, if you plan to get a divorce right after it. That's not a marriage, it's scam."

"Okay, maybe we won't get divorced after it. Maybe we'll fall madly in love and live happily ever after. Oh, wait, I forgot... You're not capable of love. Bummer." *Christ, she could use a drink from that minibar.*

Con ran a hand over his face. "I care about you, Lizzie."

"So you keep saying. If you care about me so much, then help me out with my little plan. Heck, maybe no media will be interested. In that case, you're off the hook. Okay?"

Con looked mildly relieved. "Okay. If no one's interested, you'll forget all about it?"

"Deal."

Some research time on a hotel computer and several phone calls later, Lizzie had been politely turned down by *People* magazine, the *National Enquirer* and *Entertainment Tonight*. She was waiting for a callback from *Access Hollywood* and the *CBS Early Show*, but the production staff she'd spoken to did not sound optimistic. Con whistled cheerfully as he shaved in the shiny marble bathroom.

"Don't be so chipper. They all took my call. I'm going down to the computer to do some more research."

"You're not going anywhere without me." He switched off the razor and ran a hand over his smooth chin. Her traitorous stomach jumped.

"Your lack of faith in me is so inspiring."

"Just protecting you from yourself. Maybe we can go out and grab some dinner."

"The Desert Palm has a rather lovely little restaurant, I hear." She was in the midst of attempting to wind her hair into some kind of bun and it fought back with vigor. She stuck pins in to stab it into submission.

"I was thinking more along the lines of a Big Mac."

"Such a romantic. I'm Lizzie Hathaway, you know. I don't eat Big Macs. Especially not now I'm slim." *Well, okay, not actually slim.* The full-length mirror in the bathroom had made that clear, even with a flattering sheen of steam on it. Slimmer. And planning to stay that way.

"Alright, Lizzie Hathaway, how about a veggie sandwich from Subway?"

"Oh, be still my heart." She placed her hand over it. "It's the kind of date I always dreamed about." Her hair exploded from its knot and fell over her shoulders.

Con's face cracked a smile. "You look beautiful with your hair down."

"Still with the charm. You don't give up, do you?"

The mirror had also made it clear she was still no beauty without her makeup. Right now she wasn't wearing any, just to spite him.

"I'm not trying to charm anyone. You just make me smile." Humor gleamed in those infuriatingly seductive eyes. Lucky they had no effect on her any more.

"Are we going down to use the computer or what?"


Lizzie teetered on the edge of the heart-shaped mattress, sleep still a distant fantasy. The pan-seared salmon she'd insisted on churned in her gut. At the time it had seemed like a point of honor, now it just felt like an indigestible extravagance.

All her life she'd hated snobbery and expensive status symbols. Now suddenly she was insisting on "the best of everything" just to get back at Con? It only made her feel worse when he went along with it, emptying his wallet to give her things she didn't really want.

Did he have to breathe so loud? How offensive of him to sleep deeply when she couldn't catch a single wink. And sprawled arrogantly over his side of the bed as if he hadn't a care in the world.

Every time she thought she might be close to drifting off, a stray thought bloomed out of nowhere and scattered her fluffy sheep. A renegade memory of how safe she'd felt with Con's warm arms around her. *Never again.* The thought of her proud father with an ankle bracelet under his crisp pant cuff and bored law enforcement employees monitoring his activities. *He deserved it.*

She remembered how her mother used to always tuck her in at night with a kiss. Even if they'd barely spoken all day, or if she'd been berating Lizzie over her weight or her hair or some other chronic failing. The day always ended with a kiss. *That wouldn't ever happen again.* She buried her face in the pillow so any stray tears would disappear into the hotel-issue pillowcase without pricking her skin. Willed her breathing to stay even.

They'd all betrayed her. Schemed and planned and defrauded her. Left her with *nothing*.

Maybe if she just pressed her face into the pillowcase hard enough she'd stop breathing and all the pain would go away.

*Or not.* She flipped onto her back, eyes staring into the darkness. Con grunted softly, and before she could roll out of the way, he'd turned onto his side and slid an arm over her.

*Excuse me?*

Still asleep—apparently—he shuffled closer and wrapped his arm around her torso. The sleepy, spicy scent of him acted on her like lavender bath salts. Soothing.

The warm weight of his arm drew tension from her chest.

Oh hell. She turned her head and buried her face in his clean, soft hair.

And the next thing she knew, it was morning.

# 7

The phone calls didn't go any better the next day. Lizzie and Con sat opposite each other at the table in their hotel suite, her pages of scribbled notes covering its lacquered surface. He looked smug as he browsed the want ads in the local paper and announced he'd need to use his phone soon.

"You're looking for a job in Phoenix?"

"Sure, why not? Nice weather."

"I'm not staying here!"

"Why not? We'll get an apartment to share. I've looked at the prices. We can rent a nice place quite reasonably. Maybe even one with a pool."

"You are out of your cotton-picking mind."

"Got any better ideas? Your brilliant scheme doesn't seem to be going over so well."

"They're all interested in the idea, but they don't think it's big enough."

"Maybe you need to approach a smaller media outlet?"

"Are you actually making a helpful suggestion?"

"I want you to give it up so I can start using my phone to get us a real life going here. We've got bills to pay."

"We do? As I recall, *I'm* the one with the crushing debts. You can waltz off any time you like. I won't come running after you." Why did that thought make her ribcage tighten?

Con just indicated the phone. "Whenever you're ready."

*Not yet, Buster.* She had one more phone call to make. One she'd been dreading.

She sucked in a breath as she dialed the number.

"Celebrity Access," drawled a bored-sounding receptionist.

"Maisie Dixon, please."

Con shot her a look and went back to his paper.

She'd come up with her "televised wedding" idea partly because Maisie had gone to work for a cable channel that did that kind of thing. A hitherto unexpressed competitive streak made her want to get her story on a better network than Maisie's. No such luck.

"Hello?"

"Hi, Maisie, it's Lizzie."

"Lizzie, Darling! How are you? Still whooping it up?"

"Pretty much. Listen, Con and I have decided to get married—"

"I thought he turned out to be a scoundrel."

"True love can overcome all obstacles." She ignored Con's raised eyebrows. "I don't care that he's a penniless, uneducated garage mechanic—" She paused while Maisie made choking noises into the phone. "Yes, I know, I didn't tell you that before. I was too proud, but it's true." She winked at Con. "Anyway, since I'm now flat broke, and of course he still is too, we're looking for a media outlet to televise our wedding, kind of a Cinderella story in reverse. Are you okay?"

Maisie's squeaky reply suggested she was nearly speechless with delight. Typical. Whenever Maisie "helped" Lizzie it was with the intent of somehow belittling her, ridiculing her, getting the upper hand. Anything to pay Lizzie back for having been born to the richer branch of the family.

"I'm the associate producer," Maisie was practically hyperventilating with excitement. "I'll have to talk to the boss, but this is just the kind of thing he loves."

*I know. Small-time pseudo-celebrities making an ass of themselves.* Apparently her self-destructive binge had washed up a sense of humor because now she found it funny rather than humiliating. Con pretended to read the newspaper.

Maisie came back on the line. "He'll be out of a meeting any minute. I'll call you back when I have an answer."

"Great! Chat later." She hung up and shot a smug smile at Con.

"She went for it?" He looked up from his newspaper oh-so-casually.

"She loved it. Has to talk to the boss, though. She'll call back."

Con ran a hand through his hair. "I know she's your cousin, but she may not have your best interests at heart."

"Are you kidding? She's been out to get me since Christmas of 1990 when I got a life-sized Barbie specially manufactured by Mattel to look just like me, and she got only three of the regular ones and a Barbie mansion and car."

"I could see how a disappointment like that could break a girl's spirit." His eyes gleamed wickedly. "You'd better watch out."

"Don't worry, I can handle her." She crossed her arms over her chest. "Your sugar mama will take care of everything. I'll get them to fly us to an exotic locale, pamper us with luxuries and pay us into the bargain."

"You're very optimistic."

"Maisie will make it happen. She won't be able to resist."


Sure enough, by the next morning they had a deal. Con did some touch-up ironing on one of his already wrinkle-free shirts, while Lizzie sprawled on the heart-shaped bed discussing dates and contractual details with a production assistant.

"You realize you're going to have to pretend you love me?" he said when she hung up.

She watched the muscles of his back move as he swept the iron back and forth.

"I can fake it. And I know you can too. You've had lots of practice."

Con unplugged the iron. "You've been unable to disguise your utter hatred of me since I came to get you."

"Aw. Have I hurt your feelings?"

"Don't you worry about my feelings. But I don't believe you'll be able to pretend you can stand me, let alone that you love me."

"Oh yeah? Watch this." She leapt off the bed and sauntered across the room while he wrapped the cord and put the iron on a table. Came up behind him and slipped her arms around his waist. Stood on tiptoes and put her lips to his ear. "I love you."

Ouch. *Sticks and stones can break my bones but words can never hurt me. Especially not if I'm saying them myself.* His warm, tan skin burned her hands.

"Do you?" His words shivered into her ear as he turned slowly and slid his arms about her waist.

"Of course not, you jerk!" She jumped away, heart pounding.

"See what I mean?"

"Okay." She shoved hair off her face. "This may take some practice. Let's try it again."

She walked up to him, staring him right in the eye.

"You look like you want to bite me, not kiss me." His mouth fought a smile.

"Let's take it step by step, shall we, sweetheart? Put your arms around my waist again." She braced as he circled her with them.

"You need to relax a bit."

"I'll worry about myself. You just do your part of the act." Why did he have to smell so damn good? He never wore cologne, but he had this infuriating spicy scent anyway. Probably his shampoo. She'd have to pour it out.

She stood on tiptoe again and puckered up. Scrunched her eyes closed. Her nipples accidentally bumped his chest, and she suppressed a curse as they instantly tightened.

Just a reflex. Nothing personal.

She pressed her lips together as the soft heat of his breath met her skin. A memory of yesterday's kiss in the desert flooded her brain. She pecked at him like a hen and pulled back.

"There. See?"

Con chuckled. "I don't think anyone would find that too convincing. They'll want smooches. Soul kisses."

"Ugh. How unhygienic."

"That's not what you used to say." He tilted his head, appealed to her with narrowed, soulful eyes.

*Faker.*

"I didn't know where you'd been. Now I know, I'll be more cautious, thank you."

"Why'd you kiss me yesterday?"

"Just wanted to see how easy you were." She tossed her hair. "Got my answer."

His eyes narrowed further. He didn't believe her. "You made love to me."

"Hah. I wouldn't call it that. I scratched an itch." She held his gaze with every ounce of self-possession.

*What the heck had she been thinking yesterday?* She really had no idea. Revenge. That's it. Using him like he'd used her.

How convenient that he'd had a full pack of condoms in his luggage for just such an occasion. Who'd used who?

"Are you afraid to French-kiss me?" His eyes met hers with a challenge.

"Of course not." She swallowed hard.

"Prove it. It'll be good practice for the dog-and-pony show you've signed us up for."

"I'd rather kiss a friendly pony, but here goes."

She took a deep breath as if preparing to dive under water. She stepped toward him, and he to her. She flung her arms stiffly around his neck, and his circled her back.

She could smooch him full on the mouth and not bat an eye. And she'd prove it to him.

She parted her lips slightly, licked them to provoke him, still holding his gaze. He winked at her. Damn! Why'd he do that?

He lowered his head, and his mouth closed over hers. His hands settled on her waist, and the pressure of his fingertips increased as he slid them up the vertebrae of her spine. His tongue played over her lips, sparking an irritating shimmer of sensation. He kissed just hard enough that she had to push back. Then his tongue parted her lips and touched hers with a tiny frisson like an electric shock..

She wasn't sure exactly when her eyes slid closed, or when her fingers moved up into his hair, or exactly when her nipples started to demand the touch of his fingers—and get it.

Or when she leaned in to rub against him, deepening their kiss with her tongue. Or when she began to run her fingertips up and down his back, feeling the ridges of hard muscle under his starched shirt.

But it was a low moan from some undiscovered range in her vocal cords that snapped her back to her senses.

She jerked away, panting. Con stood looking at her. Narrowed eyes shining. Lips soft, still moist.

Her hand flew to her mouth and she stepped backward, trying to gather her thoughts.

She tugged her hands behind her back, the traitors! Wound her fingers together to hold them there. Who knew what they'd do next? How the hell had that just happened?

She tossed her hair and took a deep breath.

"See?" Her voice sounded odd. "I told you I could do it." Her breasts tingled.

The merest hint of a smile tugged at the corner of Con's mouth. He looked cool as an iced martini. Not in the slightest bit bothered or flustered or... Bastard.

"Very nice. I think you'll be able to fool them." He hadn't moved an inch. "And I admit, I'm rather looking forward to it now."

"Don't get excited Nothing's going to happen except for the cameras." She unknotted her hands and tugged at the hem of her skimpy top. Wished her peaked nipples didn't show through it.

"You'll have to fool the crew too. And cousin Maisie."

"Piece of cake. With a professional con man at my side, how can I fail?"

Con's jaw stiffened. "Don't you think we should try to be nice to each other?"

"Why? We're doing this for the money. Once we have it we'll both be back on our feet and we can go our separate ways." She turned away and went into the bathroom for a glass of water. His annoying spicy taste lingered on her tongue.

She gargled noisily and spat hard. "Can't be too careful about germs. You'd better start packing. I asked them to book me a flight to New York for tonight so we can meet and discuss details tomorrow.

"A flight? What about my car?" Con stopped tucking his shirt in and stared at her.

"Don't worry, I didn't forget about your precious car. You can drive back while I handle the meetings. The location needs to be settled before the shooting can start, so that gives you until next week."

"How do I know you won't start drinking once you leave?" He frowned at her.

"I swear on the pieces of my broken heart." She pressed a hand to her chest. "I want this to work so I can get myself together again."

"Okay." He kept his eyes on her for a moment, as if trying to decide whether he believed her, then he smoothed the front of his shirt and examined his cuffs. "So where are they thinking of sending us?"

"Let me see, they sent me a preliminary list." She marched to the table and rifled though all the papers she'd printed out from the hotel's guest computer. "Here we are. Hmm. There's three in the Caribbean: some new place in Anguilla, a Sandals Resort in Negril, Jamaica, and the Atlantis hotel in the Bahamas."

"Cool!" Con grinned.

"Cool? Are you kidding? It's probably over a hundred degrees in any of those places in September. And I wouldn't be caught dead at Atlantis."

"I saw an ad for it. You can swim with sharks."

"Been doing that all my life, thanks. At least the human kind can't rip into your flesh with their teeth. Luckily there were some other options. A cruise to Alaska…"

"Sweet!"

"Stop interrupting. A golf resort in Virginia horse country, an inn on the coast of Maine, and a trendy bed-and-breakfast in the Napa Valley. I think the last one gets my vote. At least it won't be too sweaty there at this time of year."

"Come on, you can go to California any time. Can't we go abroad? I've never left the country and I'd love to go to the Caribbean. Alaska sounds fun too, and it wouldn't be too hot there." Glowing puppy-dog excitement was certainly a new look for him.

"Thanks for your input. I'm sure the staff of *Celebrity Access* and I will be able to select a location that will work for all of us."

"Yeah. Who am I kidding? They all sound good. A five-star hotel with comfy beds, gourmet food, people waiting on us hand and foot…"

"Just your cup of tea, isn't it? Well, enjoy it while it lasts because this time it won't be forever."

Con whistled while he packed. His boyish enthusiasm for a lousy week at a decent hotel almost affected her. But not quite.

Her fiendish plot involved a little twist she had neglected to mention to him. And after that kiss—which demonstrated that she might be crazy enough to lose her head over him again if she didn't keep it screwed down tight—she was more determined than ever to put it in motion.

# 8

Maisie poked her head out into the reception area and watched her childhood rival teeter across the terrazzo floor. That phone call had been a delicious surprise and frankly things were looking way up here at *Celebrity Access*. "Lizzie darling! Come in."

Cousin Lizzie had decked herself out today in a garish red suit that showed off her thick calves. She may have lost a few pounds, but she still wasn't skinny, poor thing. From the looks of it she'd straightened her hair herself—really, she should know better. "You look spectacular, sweetie." She kissed both cheeks. At least she'd stopped wearing that awful rose concoction that made her smell like an old woman.

"Come in to my parlor," she said, annoyed to find herself feeling a little nervous. She ushered Lizzie into her cramped, windowless office. Don had promised her a better one but she was beginning to learn a bit about his promises. She stepped over a pile of paper on the floor.

"Excuse the mess. I inherited it. We're so madly busy I don't have time to go through it. Do sit down."

Lizzie eased herself gingerly into the chair opposite the desk.

"We're just waiting for Don to get out of a meeting—story of my life! But really, it's a dream job." She plastered on a smile. "I was so happy to get your phone call. How exciting to produce my own cousin's love story! Do tell me more about this man of mystery. I can't believe you were so secretive with me. Honestly, I'm a bit put out about it."

Downright peevish, in fact. With all the champagne she'd poured into Lizzie, she'd never dished the dirt. Just said her swain had broken up with her when he found out she wasn't rich anymore. She never let on he wasn't the Southern blueblood she'd mooned over.

Lizzie tossed her hair behind her shoulder, tugged at the hem of her suit jacket and looked Maisie right in the eye. "I'm sorry I didn't tell you, but I confess I was a little embarrassed about it. I mean, he didn't even graduate from high school, and he has a gang tattoo on his butt. But I'm madly in love with him." Her lips settled into a cool smile.

Maisie realized she was dribbling cappuccino onto her blouse, and she snapped her mouth closed. She snatched up a tissue and dabbed at the stained silk.

Lizzie tipped her head slightly. "Obviously Mummy and Daddy wouldn't let me marry Con if they knew the truth, so I made up a story about him coming from Louisiana gentry."

She had the audacity to smile warmly and toss her crudely straightened hair over her shoulder again. "Horribly devious of me, I know, but the stakes were high, at the time. Who knew I was as poor as a church mouse myself?" She shrugged, still smiling that chilling smile.

Maisie found herself blinking and staring. As much at Lizzie's newfound self-possession as at her bizarre revelations. "I wondered why you never introduced me to him."

"I know what a keen judge of character you are. I'm sure you'd have sniffed him out in a minute."

"And there I was thinking you were worried about me stealing him away from you." Maisie forced a cheerful smile.

"Oh, I wasn't worried about that. You only did that once." Lizzie returned her icy smirk. "And really, I'm sure you were doing me a favor stealing my first and only boyfriend. What if I'd married him? I'd never have met Con. I can't imagine my life without him."

They blinked at each other in a smiling standoff. Maisie didn't know how to play this new Lizzie. Usually barbed remarks were enough to get her lip quivering, but now they seemed to bounce right back and poke her in the eye.

*Onward and upward.* "I remember something about you cursing the ground he walked on and never wanting to see his face again as long as you live. Why is he suddenly back in your good graces?"

"Oh." Lizzie giggled and waved a hand in the air. "It was all a terrible misunderstanding! When he came all the way to Arizona to find me and beg me to take him back…" She paused, closed her eyes, put her hand dramatically to her forehead. "I knew we're meant to be together, money or no money. It's a true love match." Her eyes shone with tears.

*Scary. But funny as hell!*

"That suit is quite something. Were they auctioning off the wardrobe from *Dynasty*?"

Aha! The lip quivered. She wasn't entirely impervious. Must have thought she looked good in it, poor thing.

"Is Conroy joining us today?"

"No, unfortunately he had to drive his car back from Arizona."

"You couldn't hire a driver for that?" *Sorry, couldn't resist.*

But Lizzie didn't even cringe. "We're penniless, Maisie, penniless! That's why we need your show to make our wedding dreams come true."

"Of course." Wedding dreams! This got better every minute. She hoped they'd pick Atlantis. She'd put on a "dream wedding" there to make Hathaway eyeballs pop right out.

She looked right at Lizzie and nodded. "Lizzie darling, *Celebrity Access* will make *all* your wedding dreams come true."

Gia the perky little production assistant stuck her head in the door. "Don's ready!"

"Marvelous. We'll be right in."

Don, executive producer for the "documentary production" arm of the Celebrity Cable Network, including Maisie's show *Celebrity Access*, was a middle-aged man with a thick head of gray hair and a deep salon tan. "Come in, Lizzie."

"Thanks." Lizzie felt horribly self-conscious in her ketchup colored suit now that Maisie'd compared it to something from *Dynasty*. She probably should have worn one of the outfits Con chose. He had far better taste, but none of them fit any more. She'd bought this one from a resale shop on Madison Avenue in trade for a pair of Jimmy Choo sandals she'd never wear in her newly sober state.

Maisie handed some papers to each of them. Without the soft filter of inebriation, her cousin intimidated her. When she'd been drunk it almost felt like they really were friends, but now the habitual cat-and-mouse relationship Maisie had always enjoyed with her threatened to send her scurrying again. She took a deep breath.

"So, Lizzie, Maisie tells me you've met the man of your dreams and you'd like our show to put on your wedding." Don rested enormous tanned hands, fingers interlaced, on the oak conference table.

"Yes. As you've heard, my family has fallen on hard times." She tossed her head like a down-but-not-out Scarlett O'Hara. "I've always been wealthy, but with my father under indictment and my bank accounts empty, I hardly know what to do."

Don leaned forward. "I've seen a tremendous amount of press coverage about your family in the last few weeks, and you've attracted some attention of your own lately, mostly with party-girl Maisie here." He shot an arch smile at Maisie. "So what can you bring us that's *new*?"

"My love story." She clasped her hands together. "Conroy Beale and I are meant to be together. He's from a poor background, and my parents fiercely opposed our marriage, but—as you know, I'm sure—nothing can stand in the path of true love."

His brow furrowed.

Had she overdone it? As a journalist of sorts he probably had a more sensitive bullshit detector than other people.

"He's very handsome," she quickly added. "Really, women swoon for him. He'd have been quite out of my league if I wasn't wealthy. But even now that I'm not wealthy, he still wants to marry me." Fake smile.

Guilt at her deception began to creep through her at the thought of taking their money, but nothing she'd said was an outright lie. Maybe he didn't actually want to marry her anymore, but he'd offered.

*Damn, she was starting to think like Con.*

"I like it." Don's leathery face creased into a toothy grin. "I think if we can do it quickly enough we'll grab some midseason switch viewers. Can you begin shooting next week?"

"Absolutely." The sooner she could get this whole charade over with, the better.

"Perhaps Maisie's told you, but in this company we don't waste time hemming and hawing. We get the show on the road. Location?"

"Well," Lizzie drew in a breath. "I know you sent us a list of locales, and they are all lovely. But Con and I have our hearts set on a very special place."

She paused, looked down at her hands, then up at him with intense faux-sincerity. "Con is from a tiny town in Louisiana, a sweet little place in the mangrove swamps, and we'd love to return to his birthplace to exchange our vows."

"Mangrove swamps? I thought those were in Florida?" Don's eyes narrowed.

"Cypress swamps?" Lizzie flushed. "I'm afraid I haven't been there, but Con's told me so much about it. It sounds charmingly rustic."

"Humph. It could work. What's this place called?"

Lizzie licked her lips. "It's called, um, Mudbug Flats." She kind of murmured it.

"What?" One of Don's impressive gray eyebrows shot up.

"Mudbug Flats." The name rang though the air. Suddenly this all seemed like a terrible idea.

"That sounds like hell."

"Don," Maisie leaned forward and cleared her throat. "You have a glamorous New York City heiress, traveling to a Louisiana bayou town called Mudbug Flats. It has a charming fish-out-of-water quality."

"Humph. You know, she just might be right." He looked at Lizzie. "I hired your cousin because she knows the right people. Goes to the right places. She's got class, so I'll defer to her on this one if that's what she wants. If Lizzie Hathaway wants to get married in Mudbug Flats, Louisiana, then *Celebrity Access* will make it happen."

He reached a hand across the table. Lizzie suppressed a nervous giggle and shook it. *It was going to happen.* Exhilaration and terror surged in her veins.

"Gia, can you track down the nearest big, fancy hotel. Maybe an old plantation or something? I want to move on this fast. The guest list is your job, Maisie. I'd like a truckload of New York high society, all the Hathaways' old cronies and those people you hobnob with."

Maisie blanched. "Um, I'm not sure that..."

Lizzie cut in, terror streaking along her nerves. "Con and I would prefer an intimate wedding. Just the two of us and a witness or two."

"Humph." Don's face wrinkled up. "I do think a Rockefeller or two would add class. Maybe Donald Trump?"

"Maybe Donald Trump," said Maisie with a poker face.

Lizzie struggled to keep a beatific smile in place. Somehow an anonymous television audience didn't seem nearly as frightening as the possibility of a crowd of former "friends," who were quite capable of flocking down to enjoy the spectacle. Maisie didn't seem to like the idea either. She was probably describing her "journalism" career rather creatively at cocktail parties.

"That's settled then. I'll leave all the details to Maisie. *Sitcom Stars of the Nineties* is tanking on Tuesdays, and Ty's looking for something to fill the slot. Let's move on this while the story's hot." He stood and extended his hand to Lizzie. "I'm glad you came to us. We'll put on a wedding you'll never forget."

As Lizzie tried not to wince at his hearty grip, his words echoed in her mind with grim foreboding.

Don left the room and Gia scurried after him.

"Good save," said Maisie with a swift exhale. "I suspect you don't want your Spence classmates there any more than I do."

Her penetrating gaze made Lizzie wonder if her cousin suspected she wasn't entirely on the up and up. Maisie might be a heartless bitch, but she wasn't stupid.

"I prefer to keep things simple. If we had to invite several hundred people it might postpone our wedding for weeks, even months, and Con and I just can't wait that long." Another fake smile. Maybe she could paint one on with lipstick and save her facial muscles the trouble?

"Well," Maisie rubbed her hands together. "I must say, I'm looking forward to it. I hope Gia can find a nice place to put us all up. I'd better talk to her and make sure she's not calling the local Holiday Inns. Let me tell you, they *need* me around here."

"I'll bet they do."

"And since I've been planning my own wedding to Dwight for two years, I have contacts at all the finest bridal suppliers. We'll give you a wedding fit for a queen." Smug smile. "I do hope Conroy won't feel too out of place."

"I'm sure he'll feel quite comfortable in the familiar surroundings of his hometown." She sipped her cappuccino. Hoped her forked tongue didn't show.

"I admit I'm rather curious to see picturesque Mudbug Flats. Gia will be doing all the advance scouting, though. I've got this *Princess Anastasia Rediscovered* mess to clean up. It airs next week, and the voiceover isn't even recorded yet. Don did it himself, and now I've finally convinced him it's not working, I have to find someone else to record right over the edited film. Can you imagine?"

"I can imagine almost anything. My imagination has quite taken flight lately. I do have to ask, though…" Lizzie leaned forward and narrowed her eyes. "What on earth convinced you to take a job here?"

Maisie leapt from her chair and gathered her papers. "Even Christiane Amanpour had to start somewhere, darling."

"Where are you?" Relief warred with anger at the sound of his murmured hello. She'd begun to think she'd seen the last of him.

"South Jersey. Coming up the 'pike. How're you doing?" Con's voice cut in and out like they were about to lose the cell connection.

"Why didn't you answer my calls?"

"I've been driving Had the phone turned off to save the battery."

"What's taking you so long?" She paced back and forth in the cavernous empty living room of her parents Southampton house.

"It's a long drive. I'll be up there in a couple of hours. I'm going to stay with a friend."

"No, you're not!" she shrieked. *Get a grip, Lizzie.* She'd been panicked for the last day and a half that he'd done a runner. Now she had him on the phone there was no way she'd let him get into the clutches of a "friend." "You'll come stay here. I'm at my parents' house. You know where it is."

He'd been there once. On the ill-fated meet-the-parents visit.

"Yeah, I can find it. You sure?"

"Why not. There's no one here but me. The place is up for sale." She glanced at the bare walls, the curtainless windows. "Plenty of rooms, we'll barely see each other."

"Alright. I'll see you soon."

The hollow sensation in her gut crept back when she hung up. Her footsteps rang out on the bare wood, the rugs long gone. No furniture. The door had been unlocked, left forgotten by a real estate agent. The house looked strangely smaller with no furniture, more generic, not a real place at all but a kind of stage set for a play that had folded.

It was nearly four hours before she heard the scrunch of tires on the gravel. She'd spent the last one pacing back and forth, mind revving with doubts. *He won't show up.*

*He'll leave you high and dry and lying to Maisie about why your wedding is canceled. You've been a fool to trust him or anyone else.*

She stormed out the front door and stood with her hands on her hips as the familiar gold Mercedes convertible, top down, rolled to a stop on the rather weedy driveway. Glare on the windshield hid Con from view and an unwelcome surge of exhilaration made her hold her breath as the door opened.

He emerged, hair uncombed and pants wrinkled. No shoes, either.

"You look terrible. Isn't it illegal to drive barefoot?" She hoped her snippy words concealed her excitement.

"Nice to see you too." He shot her a smile, then leaned in to retrieve his bag from the back seat. "I'm exhausted."

"I can tell from looking at you."

"I'd kill for a shower."

"Good luck. The power's turned off so there's no water." *Why did she have a sudden irrational urge to hug him?* Relief he hadn't ditched her, that's all.

"The pool got water in it?" He walked toward her.

"I guess so. I haven't looked."

"That'll do. Can I come in?"

He tilted his head, and she realized she was still barricading the doorway, arms akimbo.

"Um, sure." She turned and walked into the house, a mass of odd sensations roiling in her stomach. Why had she thought this would be a good idea?

Oh, yes, to stop him from hooking back up with Frankie or whoever. She couldn't trust him.

"Jesus. What happened to the furniture?"

"I think it all got auctioned off. The only stuff left is junk no one wanted. Most of my junk is piled up down in the basement."

"Where's your mother staying?"

"She's gone to an ashram in India. To find herself." Her voice sounded flat.

Con stared at her in amazement. "Your mom, in India?"

"It's a popular vacation destination, you know." She shrugged. She didn't understand it any better than he did, but she didn't need to let him know that. "Put your bag down anywhere you like. It doesn't matter."

He dropped it on the floor right where he stood. That lopsided grin creased his tanned face.

"What are you smiling at?"

"You. It's good to see you."

"I can't imagine why." She fought the warm sensation his smile churned up in her stomach. "I only want you here because I don't trust you."

"Can't blame you. Mind if I take a dip right now? I haven't washed in three days."

"I can tell. I can smell you from here," she lied, trying not to smile. "Did you sleep in your car?"

"Yup. Not too comfy." He lifted up his arms and stretched. "I'm kinked up like a pretzel."

"The pool's out back," she said, unnecessarily. Where else would it be? She was trying to distract herself from the spectacle of his tanned chest and bulging biceps as he stripped off his shirt. ' I've got an extra towel."

"'S okay. I've got one." He bent over and fished a white towel out of his bag, and she followed him out the French doors. The hot sun of the Indian summer beat down on the browning, unwatered grass. Crabgrass had made inroads into the lawn in the month since the gardener was let go and maintenance reduced to a weekly mowing.

"It's all set, you know, the show. I've even chosen the dress. It's worth fifteen thousand dollars." Her voice still sounded flat, like a recording. Maybe she was trying too hard to keep emotion out of it. To keep emotion out of anything.

"Fifteen thousand? Is it woven out of solid gold?" Con dropped his towel on the slate terrace surrounding the pool. They'd even taken the cedar Lutyens-style benches. Uneven blades of grass crept over the edges of the patio.

"Pearls. Freshwater. They're sewn all over it in a kind of rippling pattern. It's pretty."

"Sounds nice. Do you get to keep it?" He unbuckled his belt.

"No. Sorry, you won't get a cut of that."

"Hey, I don't want anything from you. I'm just here to help you out."

She held her breath as he unbuckled his belt and slid his pants down over his strong legs. Cleared her throat. "I appreciate the help. The money from this show will give me some breathing room to get myself together and get a job." Her heart jolted as he slid his boxers down past his muscled thighs. "What are you doing? You can't take your underwear off! Someone might see."

"No one around. And all these tall hedges." He stepped out of his boxers, stark naked and dangling. She felt a flush creep up from her neck.

He took two powerful strides to the greenish pool, drew himself up, and did a graceful, shallow dive into the water. He swam a few strokes, pulling himself through the water with ease, then flipped over onto his back, droplets of water streaming off his face and hair.

"Damn this feels good. Why don't you come in too?"

"No thanks. The filter's been turned off for a while. There are probably all kinds of nasty bacteria growing in it."

"Smells okay to me. And the temperature is heaven." He dove deep under the water and swam almost the entire length of the pool, causing Lizzie's eyes to widen, before he burst up for air, hair dripping into his eyes. "I haven't swum in a long, long time. I've missed it."

"Where did you learn how to swim? I don't picture your shack having a pool out back."

Con laughed. "A pool, no, the bayou. Flowed right past the old homestead. Right into it sometimes. I was swimming before I could walk." He shook his head like a dog, scattering water droplets over a wide area. One stung her arm.

"This back in lovely Mudbug Flats?"

"Yes, and don't say it like that. It's beautiful there. You've never seen it."

*I will soon.* "Do you wish you could go back there?"

"Hell, no! I'd sooner walk to the North Pole on bare feet." He dove under the water again.

Lizzie felt a nasty curl of guilt unfold in her chest.

*Don't forget, he never loved you.*

*He only wanted your money.*

Deep breath.

Con surfaced again. "Oh, man, I was sticky and dirty. The hotel in Phoenix left me with barely enough money for gas." He scrubbed his face. "That place was expensive."

She tried to ignore a twinge of guilt. "Well, don't worry, the show will cover all our expenses. It's negotiated into the contract."

"You won't hear me complaining."

*That's what you think.*

She touched her belly, which was flatter than ever. Nerves and no money for food. No car to drive to the store either, lucky thing the house was close to the train. "The only problem is how we're going to eat until we get there. My credit cards are maxed out. That's why I had to come back to the ancestral homestead. Think you can catch a deer and skin it?"

Con chuckled, treading water in the deep end. "I'll think of something."

He went out to get dinner, wet hair slicked back, the top down on his gold convertible. He returned nearly three hours later with two large pizzas on the front seat of an elderly Corvette with a loud engine rattle.

"What on earth…?"

"Ham and Mushroom still your favorite?"

"Sure, but where's your car?"

"Right here." He gestured to the Corvette, dingy black with white scrape marks on the rear wing.

"Where's your Mercedes?"

"Sold it."

Her gut tightened. "Why?"

"Money, of course. Lemonade okay?"

"Sure. But you loved that car." Why was she feeling guilty? That car was a gift from his ex. Payment for services rendered. "It's your pride and joy."

"Times have changed."

He slammed the door and scrutinized the Corvette for a moment. Nodded thoughtfully. "Wanna eat outside? This breeze is nice. We could eat by the pool."

"Uh, sure." She still couldn't believe he'd sold his car. And for this scratched-up piece of junk? Why did that make her feel uncomfortable all over?

"How much did you get for your Mercedes?"

"A lot." He plunked down on the grass and offered her a slice of pizza. "More than it's worth."

"Who bought it?"

"A guy who admired it. There's a lot of money rolling around this town. I'd be a fool not to take advantage." He took a big bite of pizza.

"Well, you certainly know how to do that." she snapped, tense.

He shrugged and took another bite.

"So where did you buy this thing?"

"Saw it in a driveway with a *for sale* sign when I was on my way to the store. It called out to me."

"What was it calling you—Sucker?"

Why did she have to keep sniping? She took a sip of lemonade. Bitter, like her.

"It's a Corvette."

"Is that supposed to mean something to me?"

"Nah. You're a girl. Trust me, it's an investment." He took another bite of pizza. Chewed it. "It's really nice here."

The setting sun pierced the trees with long shards of harsh light that bounced off all the windows. An unpleasant reminder of her last visit. "Appearances can be deceptive."

"I wouldn't have minded growing up here." He stretched out on the grass.

She looked up at the house that was so familiar she barely noticed it. A vast shingle-style "cottage," weathered dark brown except for the white trim and the rusty new layer of cedar shingles on the arching rooftops. Too big for the puny one-acre backyard. She'd never understood why her parents didn't buy a house right on the dunes, but they liked being in town.

"I hate it here. We only came in the summer, but you try being the fat girl on the beach in a town like this." She sipped her lemonade again. She had no appetite for pizza.

Somehow the loss of Con's car made her feel empty. Another beautiful thing that was gone for good.

"Wouldn't bother me. Not if I had my own pool." He leaned over and dipped his fingers in the water. Circles flew out across the shimmering surface.

"You probably would have liked it. You're an upbeat kind of person. Guess I'm just spoiled rotten and don't know how to be happy." She lay back on the grass. Crabgrass prickled her neck. "Do you know why I'm looking forward to this TV show?"

"Why?"

"Because it's going to be perfect. The dress, the cake, the flowers, everything. And do you know why it's going to be perfect?"

"Why?"

She'd closed her eyes, shutting out the sunset.

"Because it's fake. An illusion."

"The cake is going to be fake?" She heard the grass next to her crinkle.

She laughed. "You know? It probably will be. A real cake would melt under the lights. The icing would slide right off. They'll have to spray it with all kinds of gunk to hold it together. Maybe they'll just make it out of cardboard and spackle. Oh Con, why is illusion so much better than reality?" She opened her eyes, and he was right there beside her on the grass.

"Maybe reality is better." His dark eyes looked serious and good humored at the same time.

"Nope. I've been up to my neck in reality lately and it stinks. Do you know I called three of my so-called friends to ask if I could come stay with them and not one called me back? My mom is AWOL. My father is under house arrest in their Manhattan brownstone. I couldn't go there." She shuddered. Not sure if it was the memory of her last encounter with her father or the image of him in an ankle bracelet. "My old apartment is gone too. Repossessed by the co-op for fees owed, or something. I found out from the doorman who wouldn't let me in. Like I said, reality stinks."

"Look on the bright side. It's a beautiful night, nice and warm, you've got this great pizza to eat and a friend to share it with." His eyes glittered with the last of the sunset he squinted against.

She picked a fleck of dried grass off his collar, trying to ignore the funny feeling in the pit of her stomach. "Yeah, a guy who drives a ratty old used car. What a catch. I liked you better when you were a French aristocrat with a gold Mercedes."

"Me too." He smiled ruefully. "But I guess it's time I grew up."

"Not so fast. I'm just warming up to this illusion thing. I need to pick up some tricks of the trade."

"Yeah? Well…" He looked at her, a half smile lifting his lips. "The first rule is to live in the moment. Don't fret about where you've been or where you're going, just love the summer breeze when it's on your skin."

"It does feel nice." She closed her eyes, blocking out his smile.

"The second rule is to appreciate the people you're with. Enjoy the good things about them and forget the bad."

Her eyes snapped open. "So instead of focusing on the fact that you are a deceitful con-artist, I should concentrate on how you're actually a pretty caring person and give a great massage, that kind of thing?"

"Exactly." His eyes sparkled. "And don't forget my well-toned physique."

"How could I? You put it on display with such casual ease. I bet there are women all around us with binoculars trained over the hedges hoping you'll skinny-dip again."

"Only if you'll come too."

"Oh, they'd love that. Maybe a journalist will get a picture of my fat white ass for the local paper."

"What did I say about focusing on the positive?"

"I guess it's going to take some practice."

"Kind of like kissing me?" A smile tugged at his lips and a shimmer of unwelcome heat stirred in her belly.

She scrambled to her feet. "I think I've had enough practice there, thanks. I'll wait until I'm getting paid before I do that again."

# 9

They shared the damp-smelling mattress in the pool house because it was the only one that hadn't been carted away. Lizzie spent the night with her face to the wall, hating that she slept so much better with Con snoring softly into her neck.

In the morning she gulped down some leftover pizza and took the train into the city to organize more details of her Dream Wedding.

Gia had found a pre-Civil War plantation house with beautifully landscaped grounds in Terrebonne Parish, not far from the apparently miniscule hamlet of Mudbug Flats. At least in the pictures the house was stunning, Greek revival columns supported deep verandas and gnarled live oaks dripped with Spanish moss. Con would love it. Why did that give her a tickle of pleasure? Wasn't this supposed to be about punishing him?

Luckily there wasn't too much time to think about Con. It was "accessory day" and by noon her mind boggled with taffeta trains and hand-netted demi-veils, freshwater-pearl-drop earrings, embroidered garters and hand-dyed satin sling-backs with intricate beading. The office bustled with assistants from designers all over the city bearing a train of extravagance.

She wouldn't have batted an eye at all this stuff back when she was wealthy. Couldn't have cared less. Now the pretty trinkets mocked her. More beautiful because they were unattainable, except on temporary loan.

She could say a lot of bad things about Maisie, but the girl worked like a galley slave. Lizzie was honestly impressed with how she juggled details and handled multiple phone calls without breaking a sweat. But one thing puzzled her.

"Maisie," she said, between bites of Cobb salad. "Why are you and Dwight having such a long engagement? Why don't you just tie the knot?"

"It takes time to plan the perfect wedding." Maisie sorted through a box of Calvin Klein dinnerware samples. "Dwight knows that a society wedding is an occasion to be taken seriously. It shouldn't be rushed. You only get married once in a lifetime."

Lizzie almost choked on a crouton as a stab of raw pain shot through her. She'd been so excited to marry Con and spend the rest of her life with him.

Or with the person he'd tricked her into thinking he was. How could she have been so blind? So naïve?

*Because she'd wanted so badly to be loved.* Loved for who she really was, not the thinner, hipper, more witty version of herself her parents always seemed to hope for.

To be able to give love to someone who loves you in return was the best feeling she'd ever known. She'd never imagined she could be so very, very happy.

A strange sound emerged from her throat and she covered it with a cough. She realized she was gripping her napkin in a clenched fist, and she made a show of fluffing it out and spreading it on her knee.

Conroy Beale hadn't loved her. He'd loved her money.

Raw agony flickered into quiet fury as Maisie held a dish up to the light. Lizzie sat up and cleared her throat. "Those ones with the fleur-de-lis pattern—they're perfect. Definitely use those." She forked some salad into her mouth, shoved her hurt feelings back down where they belonged and wrapped them in barbed wire.

"You like them? I was thinking they were a bit subtle. Almost too European. I want a Grand Old South feel."

"Trust me on this. They look just like the tattoo on Con's butt. We'll have to make sure he bares it on screen some time."

Maisie's shocked stare made her worry that she'd overplayed her hand.

But, as her cousin's mouth quirked into a sly smile, another thought dawned on her: an image of Maisie enjoying a one-on-one viewing of Con's well-formed backside.

Lizzie had kept Con away from the offices so he wouldn't get wind of her plan, so he and Maisie still hadn't met, but she strongly suspected Maisie would simply have to try screwing her fiancé. It wasn't in her nature to pass up a challenge like that.

She had that thought firmly in mind as she walked the short distance from the train station to the house that evening. The beat-up Corvette was still in the driveway. The hood was propped open and some tools lay on the gravel, but Con was nowhere in sight.

"Con," she called out as she approached the door. She was hungry. She'd forgotten to borrow money from him to buy lunch so she'd had to make do with salad.

*I need Con for his money.* The thought made her want to laugh or cry, she wasn't sure which.

"Con, where are you?" She stepped over a socket wrench. How did she know the name of it? The front door was ajar.

"Con?" She called up the winding staircase, her voice echoing off all the bare wood and uncovered walls.

"Hello." A woman emerged in the upstairs hallway and Lizzie jumped.

"Who…? What. .?" Words sputtered and died in her mouth. Blood whirred in her ears as the woman descended the stairs, hand on the railing. An elegant woman of forty or fifty with a smart yellow suit and glossy hair. "Lizzie?" She held out her hand to shake.

Lizzie stood there open mouthed as flames of white hot rage snapped through her. It wasn't Frankie. This woman was a brunette and she remembered Frances Allen as a pale blonde, so it must be another one of Con's "friends."

The woman drew back her hand and tucked her shiny hair behind an expensive earring. Offered a lipsticked smile. "Conroy is getting dressed."

"Get out of my house!" An undignified high-pitched shriek.

"I'm sorry?" The woman didn't seem all that flustered by her outburst. She looked at Lizzie rather curiously.

"Lizzie, hey, this is Amanda." Con appeared at the top of the stairs, immaculate as usual, wet hair combed back.

"I don't care who the hell she is! Get her out of my house right now. And throw your own sorry ass out after her." Her heart pounded. She was so angry she could barely see.

"She's the Realtor." Con bounded down the stairs. "She stopped by to see why my car was in the driveway."

Lizzie froze. She looked at the woman, who was now staring at Con with a secretive smile.

The brunette lifted her chin. "I'm sorry I complained. It's just that first impressions are so important to a buyer. It's called curb appeal."

"I told her I'll put my car in the garage, so it doesn't lower the tone of the neighborhood." He winked at Lizzie.

Lizzie stood very still as a crimson tide of humiliation washed over her.

"Mr. Beale explained that the car is a hobby project of his, and I quite understand. I'm so sorry for the inconvenience." The Realtor looked like she was trying hard not to laugh. Lizzie felt like slapping her.

"It is a shame that your family removed all the furniture already. Houses show so much better when they're occupied, but I know the family has been in a rather difficult situation. It would be advantageous to turn the electric back on and get the landscape service to do more than mow. I'm doing my best to sell it, but the market is rather slow now that we're into the off-season—"

"I need to use the bathroom, excuse me." Lizzie pushed past the woman and heading for the stairs.

"Isn't the electricity turned off?" the reedy voice called after her.

"It flushes just fine with a bucket of pool water," hissed Lizzie, her face still burning.

"Anyway, thanks for stopping by," said Con. "I'll make sure the place looks neat."

"So sorry to make a fuss, but obviously this property is rather a challenge anyway, what with the notoriety..."

Lizzie slammed the bathroom door, blocking out the noise. There was no bucket of pool water because they always used the downstairs bathroom. Just a window to stare out at the tree-fuzzed horizon. *Make it all go away.*

"Lizzie." She heard Con coming up the stairs. She rubbed her face in her hands, then remembered her makeup. She was wiping smudged eyeliner off with a fingertip when he flung the bathroom door open.

"Do you mind? I'm in the bathroom."

"I know you aren't really using it. What did you make all that fuss for? Did you think I was..." He stopped and let a smile creep across his mouth.

"What was I supposed to think? You're here alone, and a woman comes out of the bedroom?" Irritation pricked at her.

"I couldn't get rid of her. She kept saying she needed to check on stuff. I was just getting cleaned up when she showed up."

"You were in the pool?"

"No, I'd gotten out, thank God," he grinned. "I had a towel on, but I had to come up here to get my clothes. She followed me. Came in to check out the bedroom after I got dressed."

"Probably the most exciting thing that's happened to her all year." Lizzie couldn't help smiling. She didn't mind that snotty Realtor thinking she and Con were an item. He was impressively gorgeous. Let her go back to her cronies at the agency and blab about the hunk in the towel at the Hathaway place.

That line of thought stopped her in her tracks. She and Con were not an item. Not any more. He was only here at because she'd roped him into her TV-show scheme. Was she doing this whole phony wedding thing because she wanted the world to see her with Con? To admire and envy her because he was, well, hot?

She felt a blush creeping back.

"What?" Con lifted an eyebrow.

"Nothing. I'm starving, do you have money?"

*Gee, that sounded great.*

Con smiled. "Yup. Car's not running though, I'm in *media res* with the transmission."

"You are the only person in the known world who would speak Latin while referring to engine repair."

"I'm a one-off."

"Thank God for that. We can walk to Main Street and get something to eat there."

"Sure, I just need to get the car in neutral and push it into the garage. Don't want the place looking scruffy."

"Screw her. Leave it right where it is."

"Okay."


An extended massage by Con had her feeling almost relaxed the next morning. Her shoulders kinked right up again when Maisie charged at her as she entered the *Celebrity Access* offices.

"Cajun or Creole?" Maise fired the question at her then looked down at her clipboard, pencil poised as if ready to grade the answer.

"What?"

"Con's heritage, I know it's French, but is he Cajun, or Creole? It matters, you know. The food. We're choosing the menu today."

"What's the difference?"

Maisie glanced down at her clipboard. "One is based on French cuisine, and the other is…based on French cuisine." She raised an eyebrow. "But they're different."

"Hmm. How about a bit of both?"

"Why don't I call Conroy and ask?" Maisie raised an eyebrow.

Lizzie's pulse jumped. "Cajun. Mudbug Flats is the heart of Cajun country." Wasn't that what he said?

"Good. We're going to bring the chef with us from New York, and I had three lined up to choose from—all native Louisianans—until I found out about this Cajun and Creole thing. This narrows it down to one."

"Does *Celebrity Access* really care about making sure all the details are fully authentic?" Lizzie was ready to laugh.

Maisie blinked. "I'm here now, so we care," she said stiffly. "My reputation is on the line."

Lizzie kept a straight face. "I'm sure Con will be touched by all the trouble you've gone to. But why bring a chef from New York? Don't they have plenty of them down there?"

"Quality control, darling. Once you leave Manhattan you just never know what you're going to get."

By the time she returned home she was bloated with delicious samples from the West Village restaurant where the Cajun chef worked. She'd tried to think about her waistline, especially in front of Maisie, who didn't seem to eat at all, ever, but the food was just too good. At least she wouldn't have to beg Con for dinner.

Con was nowhere to be seen as she walked up the driveway, but she could see light coming through the garage window.

She went in through the side door. Con, dressed in only a pair of athletic shorts, was applying newspaper and masking tape to the windshield.

"Why did you put it in here? I told you to leave it outside. And how come the lights are working?"

"Hey, nice to see you too." He winked. She made sure not to look at his bare chest.

He pulled another piece of tape from a huge roll with a loud rasp. "Brought the car in to keep dust off while it's painted. I called the electric company and got the lights turned on."

"How did you do that? You're not a Hathaway."

"I didn't tell them that." *Rasp.* "You're a spray gun artist, right?"

She narrowed her eyes. "I did some work with spray guns in college."

"Still got the equipment?"

"It's in the basement."

"Good. Let's go get it."

"Why? Are you going to use my spray gun to paint a *car*?"

"No. You are."

"I am not."

"Let's go look at your tools anyway, okay?"

She wasn't sure quite how it happened, but at 1:00 a.m. she was standing in the garage, wielding a spray-gun loaded with #522 Black Ice. Con had the nerve to go yawning off to bed after patting her butt in the most infuriating way and telling her he was sure she'd do a great job.

She'd do a great job alright.

Even the respirator couldn't dull the invigorating scent of enamel that always made her want to paint the town red. Or black or whatever else was in there. She couldn't think why she hadn't painted in so long.

Con had made a big deal about how with Corvettes you had to maintain the integrity of the original. Respray the exact original paint color, keep everything just the way it was.

Come on! This car was from the 1980s. Hardly a priceless antique.

And she wanted to see Con's jaw drop.

At first she thought she'd do something funny like paint cheesy flames all over it. But the base coat spraying had reinvigorated her muse and she figured she might as well get creative. She'd found quite a few cans of the automotive enamel she used to use, lids tightly sealed and the remaining paint fresh. Spent the last forty-five minutes cutting templates out of bits of leftover cardboard moving boxes. Then mixing colors with a drill mounted paint stirrer to create a palette of metallic off-blacks.

As her design took shape, her guilty glee at messing with the vintage-car integrity of Con's "investment" mutated into the sheer joy of creation. Her fingertips tingled with the thrill of making images, and her mind buzzed with ideas, urging her to try new things, push the envelope of possibilities.

It was almost dawn when she was finally satisfied. The car's panels shimmered with overlapping shapes in various shades of silvery black, almost seeming to ripple as her eyes scanned over them. The effect was subtle but powerful, transforming the car into a living thing rather than a hunk of metal. She lowered her respirator and pushed the button on the garage door opener, ready to let some air in now the paint was pretty much dry.

At that moment, Con appeared in the doorway leading from the house, light shining behind him. "How come you're up so... Holy shit."

He came down the stairs, eyes riveted to the car. A nasty sting of fear raced through her. Would he be mad? Really, really upset? He had sold his beloved Mercedes to buy this thing, after all. His money was tied up in it.

Hell, he asked her to do it. She didn't volunteer. Still, she stiffened, searching his face for signs.

He looked up at her, eyes wide. "You're a bad girl."

She raised an eyebrow, swallowed hard.

"But you're very, very, good." His eyes wandered back to the car, and he walked around it. He stopped and put his hands on his hips, surveying the pattern of interlocking shapes snaking around the rear. "I've never seen anything like it."

He stood there silent, still wearing nothing but shorts. Her pulse threatened to break speed records.

At last he looked up at her. "Did you spray the clearcoat yet?"

"No, so I guess I can re-spray it all black." She spoke between gritted teeth

"Are you kidding? I just think you should sign it first. Maybe right here, on the rear bumper."

Was he poking fun at her?

"A Lizzie Hathaway original? No, thanks. I'll be anonymous."

"If it was mine, I'd sign it." He walked around to the other side. Let out a low whistle.

He wasn't kidding. He was genuinely impressed. The realization gave her a warm thrill of pride.

"I can't believe you've been hiding all this talent under a bushel."

"Creative spray painting is not a highly valued skill in this society."

"Maybe not in your kind of society, but there are plenty of people out there who will appreciate this, believe me." He walked around the far side, peered at the lowest part of the car, checking out the details.

Did he think she'd skimped on the corners, done a sloppy job? She bristled. "I did all the edges, didn't leave anything out."

"I can see that. You've sprayed a car before, haven't you?"

"Never, only did it on canvas. The finish is a lot more beautiful on metal."

"I'll say. I want to see some of these canvases of yours. Do you still have any?"

"Sure. They're down in the basement under a tarp." She'd noticed them lurking in a corner. A little surprised her parents hadn't disposed of them.

"Can we go see them?"

"I guess so."

Con insisted on bringing them all upstairs out of the basement gloom. He hung the huge canvases—some of them six feet across—on the nails left vacant by the Degas sketch, the Corot landscape and all the other vanished beauties. The rising sun illuminated the overlapping, interlocking shapes and colors, sparkled off the metal-flecked highlights.

"I haven't seen these in years. Not since I graduated from college." They brought back memories. Happy memories of being alone in her college studio cubicle, painting into the night, with music blasting in her headphones. Back when she was going to be an artist.

That was before she came home to her parents' laughter and the offer of a boring but respectable job in the family firm.

Con wasn't saying anything. He just kept walking around, hanging the pictures. Annoyingly he was still wearing only his shorts, so it was hard to avoid the bulge and flex of gym-toned muscles as he hefted the big canvases into position.

There were eight of the large ones and about twelve smaller ones. The sun beamed across the wood floors by the time they were all hung. "The place looks like a gallery," she murmured. Embarrassed to see her hopes and dreams shimmering on the wall.

"Sure does. We should get some people in here. Would you mind selling them?"

"Selling them? Who'd want to buy them?"

"I don't know. I'm no art critic, but I think they're beautiful. I'd want one."

"You can have one. Shame you don't have a wall to hang it on." She snuck a sideways glance at him. Did he really like them? Why did that give her a funny feeling? "Besides, I suspect you're my only fan. My teachers didn't like them much. I didn't have enough conceptual bullshit to go along with them or something."

Con stood, hands on hips, surveying a gray-and-silver abstract with amorphous shapes melding into each other. "You're an amazing woman, Lizzie."

"Yeah, right. If I was so amazing I'd have stuck with my so-called passion instead of forgetting all about it as soon as I got out in the real world."

"You got sidetracked. It can happen to anyone. But you're an artist."

A shiver of sensation rippled through her as he said it. *Am I?*

She wanted to run and hug him, but she held herself in check. She was just sleep deprived and hopped up on paint fumes. If he did admire her work, it was only because he saw dollar signs popping out of it. Like he said, he was no art critic.

Still, that was the best night she'd had in ages. In fact, it almost rivaled all those nights of steamy passion she'd shared with Con before their One True Love went down the crapper.

"Well, thank you. I'm glad you like my work. Now I have to go get ready, I've got a train to catch."

"On no sleep? No way. Go to bed."

"Can't. I'm meeting with the florist at 9:30 and it's a very long train ride. I'm already running late. I'm glad the hot water's back on as I'll need it to get all this paint off my skin." A fine black mist covered the backs of her hands and arms, not to mention her ratty gray T-shirt and jeans. "I'm off to shower."

"I can help you scrub." He winked at her.

She narrowed her eyes and gave him a dirty look. Then she turned and fled before she started wanting to hug him again.

He'd given something back to her. She wasn't sure what, but it made her take the stairs two at a time.

# 10

The smell of roses made her feel sick. Reminded her too much of the "old days" only a few weeks earlier and that stupid scent she wore.

"No roses."

"But roses are the bloom of romance," protested Sven, floral artiste of the minute. "You cannot marry without roses."

Three pale pink roses, each almost the size of her head, mocked her from a handblown glass vase in the center of the conference table.

"Oh, come on, Lizzie, they're lovely." Maisie ripped off a pink petal. Sven winced. "Not a sprig of baby's breath in sight, thank God. I love what you've done, Sven, it's luxe, yet wonderfully modern. I think it's perfect."

"But the bride…"

"The bride will love it. Besides, she'll be too busy to think about flowers."

Maisie glowered at Lizzie as Sven gathered his blooms and departed. When the door closed behind him, she leaned across the table. "Are you nuts? No roses?"

"I'm sick of roses. They're so…Predictable."

"I'd think you'd like that about them. You used to be the rose queen. You even smelled like one." Maisie shuffled her papers into a stack.

"Those days are over." Lizzie stretched. "Since I met Con I'm a new woman."

"You certainly are different, I'll give you that. I can't wait to meet this mysterious Con. He must be quite a character."

"Oh," Lizzie looked her right in the eye. "He is."

"So really, no guest list? What about his friends and family in the area? His parents? Siblings?"

*Does he have any?* Her questions about his family had been met with swift evasion. For all Lizzie knew he'd emerged from the swamp on webbed feet, alone. While she was curious to find out where, and who, he did spring from, she was a little nervous about it too. She couldn't bring up the subject of a guest list without tipping him off to their destination, and she certainly didn't want to do that.

"Con and I want our wedding to be an intimate celebration of our love. Just the two of us. As if we were getting married on a deserted island."

"What about your parents?" Maisie's steely gaze made her stiffen.

"Maisie, you know my father is under house arrest." She wasn't going to be cowed.

"Your mother, then? What does she think about the wedding?"

*No idea.* She'd tried calling the ashram and been told her mother had left for an expedition into the mountains. With no contact information.

"Just the two of us."

"And Donald Trump. Ha ha. Luckily, it's far too short notice to get any real celebrities so I can pretend I tried and look all sad when I tell Don no one could come. He loves the tight timetable on this show so he won't complain too much. You came along at just the right time. All the new season shows are bombing so he was ready to grasp at straws. It was this or buy a new Brazilian soap opera, and frankly, you're cheaper."

"I'm honored to be the final straw for Celebrity Cable."


Even in the late-afternoon sun, Lizzie could see lights on inside the house as she walked up the driveway. It was one thing for Con to get the electricity turned on, but did he have to run up the bill like this in broad daylight? She'd begged off a styling meeting and taken the long train ride back early. Who cared how the stinking napkins were folded? Their flight was booked for the following day, and she wanted to get her stuff together. Get her head together.

She pushed the door open. "I'm back." Dropped her bag inside the door. Heard voices.

The voices were coming from outside. Con and a woman.

The Realtor. She wasn't going to make an ass of herself screaming like a shrew over Con again. Jeez, anyone might have thought she actually cared if he'd been between the sheets with some middle-aged harpy.

Still, she didn't stroll around the back and say hi, either. She crept across the wood floor of the living room, past all her brightly lit paintings, to the French doors. They were standing near the pool, backs to her.

And it wasn't the same Realtor.

Must be another one. *You're the de-facto homeowner, go out and introduce yourself.* She lifted her chin and headed for the French doors out to the pool area.

"Hellooo" she called, aiming for breezy confidence. Stepped onto the bluestone terrace. But her confidence withered and died as the woman turned and she saw that this time it actually was Frankie Allen. Aka Mrs. Stavros Gianopolous.

He'd brought her here. To her house.

"Lizzie, hi!" Con waved.

She froze. She didn't even feel anger, just deep hurt. Humiliation.

A woman he'd been in bed with—who'd paid him with expensive gifts for it—and he was standing there talking to her by her pool.

She struggled for breath as they walked toward her.

"Lizzie, you know Frankie… Gianopolous, right?"

"Yes," she managed.

"Hi, Lizzie."

"We were just talking about your paintings. Frankie's a collector. I thought she'd be a good person to ask for advice about how to sell them."

Lizzie stared at him, then at her. She was beautiful, in a fragile, birdlike way. Translucent skin stretched over fine bones. Thin as a rail.

"Lizzie, they're stunning. I've never seen anything like them. I'd like to buy one myself."

"No." The word flew out on instinct. "They're not for sale."

Con had the wisdom to hold his tongue, and there was a pleasantly uncomfortable pause.

"Congratulations on your wedding, Lizzie. You're marrying a very special man."

Lizzie glanced at Con, who ran his hand through his hair awkwardly. She noticed with a jolt that he wasn't dressed up. In fact he looked downright scruffy in navy sweatpants and one of her old T-shirts. Somehow that made the little scene disturbingly intimate.

"Why didn't you marry him, then?" she shot, unable to control herself.

Frankie didn't even flinch. "He's far too young and handsome for me. He deserves a lovely girl his own age, like you."

Had he told her the wedding was a sham?

"I was so sorry to hear about what happened to your father, Lizzie. He was so well liked. He told the most wonderful stories. I was at a dinner party with him once..."

Heart pounding, Lizzie cut in. "Thanks for the memories, but I'd like to get changed. These high heels are killing me. Con, darling, could you unzip me?"

Con's eyes widened. She turned her back to him and Frankie. The dress she wore had a long zipper from neck to waist.

Con unzipped it.

"Do excuse my lack of formality, but after all this is my home. At least until someone buys it."

"Frankie's looking for a place in the Hamptons."

Lizzie blinked rapidly. Did Con really mean to try selling her parents' house to his ex-lover?

Words rushed from her mouth. "I'd recommend a house on the beach. The town's frightfully built up. The traffic is terrible on weekends." Her voice shook as she realized this woman was probably rich enough to buy the house and not even notice the dip in her bank account. It was barely four million, after all. Chump change to the wife of a Greek shipping squillionaire.

She straightened her back. Put on a poker face. "Has Con given you a tour of the bedrooms?"

Frankie just looked at her. "He loves you very much."

Con flinched and stared at Frankie.

"I know," she said, wondering why Con had lost his cool just then. "We're both head over heels."

Con cleared his throat. "Frankie said you should wait until after the TV show to promote the paintings. She thinks you can use it as an opportunity to pitch yourself and your artwork and raise the price."

"But you'd like to buy one now—get in on the ground floor, so to speak?" Lizzie stared at Frankie. Held herself stiffly. "And if you buy the house too, you won't even have to move it."

Frankie smiled apologetically. "I think your paintings are beautiful, and you're a very talented artist. I also think I should not have come here today. Don't hold it against Conroy. He has a good heart, and I'm the one who should have known better."

"Thanks for your ringing endorsement of my fiancé, and of course cash donations are always welcome. But then you knew that already, as far as Con is concerned, didn't you?" Her voice was getting shrill.

"Lizzie—" Con took a step forward.

"It's alright, Con." Frankie held up her hand. "I'm leaving and I really do wish you—both of you—all the best."

Lizzie wondered for a tense moment if she'd kiss Con goodbye, but mercifully she just turned and left.

When she was out of earshot, Con grimaced. "Shit, I'm sorry Lizzie. I guess I didn't think it through."

"I suppose someone with your dubious background couldn't be expected to know that it's bad manners to bring your ex-lover to your fiancée's house. Trying to sell it to her was a nice touch. What's next?" Her hands were shaking.

"I'm sorry. I just know she likes art and buys a lot of it. And I figured if she bought the house, that's one less thing to worry about." He shrugged. Looked genuinely contrite.

"You always were one to focus on the practical details," she said icily.

"My survival instinct might be a bit too well honed. But on that note, I sold the car."

"Already? You mean it's gone?" Another stab of loss.

"Yup. Easiest sale I ever made."

"But I never even took a photo of it—" She cut off her whiny lament. Didn't want him to know how much she'd looked forward to seeing it again.

His brow crinkled. "I didn't know you wanted a photo."

"We artists do that before we sell work. For our portfolio. For posterity. Not that I've ever sold any before, of course, so this is a first."

"I'm sorry. I didn't realize. I called a friend and he hooked me up with a guy who came over and paid cash for it."

"How much?" She couldn't hide her curiosity.

"Fifteen thousand dollars, and I paid four for it."

Lizzie's mouth dropped open.

"It was your paint job. That Corvette was kind of a rare model, so with an authentic paint job it would have been worth quite a bit more too. The kid I bought it from didn't know what he had. But even though you ruined it for the collectors' market," he raised an eyebrow, "the Lizzie touch lifted it into a league of its own. You rock, babe."

He lifted his hand to high-five her. She just stared at it. And frowned. "Eleven thousand dollars profit for two days work? How come you don't do this all the time? Even my father wouldn't sneeze at profits like that."

"Like I said, it was your paint job that made the money. I just got it running well. Anyone could do that. You want the cash?" He looked infuriatingly pleased with himself.

"No, you can hold it for me—isn't that the expression? Oddly enough, I trust you with money. It's my heart I wouldn't let you near." She gave him a withering look. "I'm sure Frankie was touched to get your phone call. Probably thought you wanted to blackmail her."

Con chuckled. "Seriously, she's a nice person. You can trust her."

"How can you say that about someone who dumped you for a rich old Greek?"

"It was understandable. I don't have money." He shrugged.

"People don't always marry each other for money, you know, shocking as that may seem. That's probably why Frankie thinks you love me, because you're marrying me even though I don't have money now. Unless you lied and told her you love me." The idea gave her a quick thrill.

"I didn't say anything. I guess she just took the situation at face value."

"Using your usual strategy, I see. But speaking of taking things at face value, why aren't you dressed up? Didn't you want to make a good impression on your ex?"

"Nah. She knows me too well."

"Better than I do?"

He crossed his arms over her T-shirt, which fit him rather more snugly than it did her. "I decline to answer on the grounds that I may end up sleeping in the backyard."

"Well, I guess that's an honest answer, anyway. And you'll need a good night's sleep because the flight is booked and we're leaving tomorrow."

"Where are we going?"

"Surprise!"


Lizzie was already in bed, back to him, as Con climbed in. The cool night air still tickled his skin as he eased under the cozy covers and stretched himself along the delicious warmth of her body.

"You're cold," she muttered.

"There's a nip in the air." A nip in her voice too. She wasn't going to forgive him for bringing Frankie. "You're nice and toasty."

"That's me, a warm body."

And how. He'd left his underwear on so as not to piss her off, but he couldn't resist shifting into the curve of her lovely, round butt. All that soft skin in soft cotton underwear was a balm to his tired body.

"I tidied up the flower beds and edged the lawn. Looks neater now. Should help the place sell." The fumes from the weed wacker still hung in his nostrils. His way of apologizing.

"Good. Just do me a favor and don't sell it to anyone you've slept with, okay?"

"Deal." He slid his arm around her waist. She flinched slightly as his fingers touched the bare skin of her stomach, then she relaxed into his touch.

Damn it felt good to have her back, even under these strange circumstances. Yes, it hurt that she'd dumped him so fast when she found out he wasn't rich, but he could understand her being mad that he misled her.

He'd missed her so much it itched like a raw burn. Those few weeks they'd had together had been a little piece of heaven on earth. She'd brought out a part of him he'd never dared show anyone before—heck, he'd asked her to marry him! He really and truly wanted to spend the rest of his life with her.

He'd brought out something new in her too. She'd softened and warmed, come alive. Come out her protective shell.

Shame it was back now, and harder than ever.

She was tough now, with a fierce edge that...drove him crazier than ever.

God he loved her body. Still soft and curvy in all the right places.

He let his fingers play over her stomach.

"Stop that."

"Stop what?" He buried his face in her curls.

"Touching me." Her stomach quivered under his touch.

"Can't help it. The bed's too small."

"That doesn't mean you have to...fondle me."

"Just letting you know that I'm right here if you've got any itches need scratching." Sparring with the sassy new Lizzie got him going even more.

"No, thanks. I prefer cortisone cream."

"Yeah?" His thumb "accidentally" brushed her nipple, and he noticed with a jolt of pleasure that it was hard. "Sometimes creams don't work. When the itch is too deep."

"You'd know." Her voice was icy. "Scratch any itches for Frankie today? I bet a wrinkled Greek can get tiresome after a while."

Ouch. "You know I wouldn't do that."

"Do I? Why not? There's nothing between us but a business agreement so you don't owe me any debt of fidelity. I'd feel no guilt about sleeping with any handsome, available men who happen to be interested. Not that any are, of course, now I'm flat broke."

"I know one who is, " he whispered into her thick hair.

"Trust you to call yourself handsome."

"I'm not? A guy could get sensitive, especially if his nose got broken." He teased his tightening erection against her butt.

She stiffened. "I feel an uncomfortable bump. Kindly back off."

"Maybe there's a pea under the mattress?"

"I believe it's a thorn in my side."

"Aw, come on. Wouldn't you like to screw me again? Fuck me hard and toss me aside like you did back in the desert? I wouldn't mind." His cock throbbed at the memory.

"I hate to repeat myself. Now back off or you're out on the patio." She flipped over to face him and her breasts grazed his chest as she glared at him.

"Okay, okay, I'll be good." It caused him pain, but he backed off a few inches onto a chilly part of the sheet. "Go on and go to sleep, I'll do the same."

She turned over again, flicking her hair in his face, and settled down with her back to him.

You'd think since he was going along with her wacko plan she'd at least share a little affection with him. He didn't like this whole game she was playing and couldn't help a nasty feeling it was going to blow up in their faces. But, she felt he owed her and he couldn't argue with that.

And as long as they were still together, anything was possible.

# 11

Con's enthusiastic grin sent a stab of guilt straight to Lizzie's heart as he settled himself into the leather seat of the corporate jet taking them to their surprise destination. She'd convinced the show to fork out for the jet on the grounds that she was *the* Lizzie Hathaway. The real reason was more practical. If they'd taken a commercial flight to, say, New Orleans, Con might have figured out their destination at the airport and balked.

"Pretty slick." He fondled the leather armrest like it was a woman's thigh.

Lizzie crossed her legs and snapped her seatbelt closed. "It's just a plane. I can't believe you've never been on one before." An odd thought tweaked her. "How old are you, anyway?"

"Same age as you." He jumped up from his seat and walked around the plane, peering out the windows and studying the door into the cabin. Avoiding her glance.

She blinked at him as her guilt evaporated completely. "Why am I not surprised? For some reason I believed you were twenty-nine, but now I know better than to trust any information I acquired back when I was the target of your money-grubbing affections. Let me see, I think I asked you how old you were, and you said, 'How old do you think I am?' then laughed and looked delighted when I said twenty-nine. So naturally I assumed..." She paused and shook her head.

He shrugged, rueful expression undercut by twinkling eyes.

She stared at him. "You look at least thirty, by the way."

"A hard life will do that to you." He shot her a cheery grin and settled into his seat. "This is the life for me."

"I guess this is all excellent practice for your next attempted conquest. I'm sure you'll have her eating out of your hand as you describe all the details of a private jet that you will just delicately hint is all yours. I can see you making mental notes about everything here in preparation." Lizzie ignored the way her legs responded as if he was stroking them.

"Nice, though, isn't it?" He stroked his armrest again.

"Whatever. Planes all look the same to me. A way to get from A to B."

"Speaking of which, d'you think I should ask the pilot where we're going?"

"No!" She said it too fast and loud. "We're under contract. If they want to it be a surprise, lets keep it a surprise."

"Are they going to film us as we get off the plane or something?"

"I don't think they're going to film us at the airport— there's a car meeting us there—but they're definitely going to film us arriving at our destination."

"I don't get. What's the point of making it a surprise?"

Lizzie tried to look casual. "I guess they want those expressions of heartfelt joy on our faces. They said it was going to be somewhere special, that would mean a lot to us."

A crease appeared between Con's eyebrows. "What exactly did you tell them about us?"

"Nothing but the truth. Or at least what I've been told is the truth. One never really knows around you. Though naturally not the whole truth."

Con's frown deepened. With his sun-scorched skin and expression of hard-won wisdom, he didn't look even close to twenty-five. Was he bullshitting her again?

Now the gloves were off, she didn't think he'd lied to her. He'd been good to her in his own misguided way. She shook her head at the memory of Mrs. Frankie

Gianopolous on her lawn. Did he think you could just charm women into anything?

Con peered out the window during the flight. Lizzie closed her eyes, not wanting to see his gleeful enthusiasm over every new detail he spotted out the window.

Okay, so maybe he really was twenty-five.

But her plan wasn't cruel. She was taking him home. Yes, she wanted to put him on the spot and make him sweat. She wanted to see the real Con, not the slick, polished version that led her up the garden path. If he had an embarrassing past he'd tried to leave behind, it would be character building for him to face up to it. Maybe he'd form new loving relationships with all the relatives he'd left behind and he'd thank her for turning his life back in the right direction.

Right?

She glanced out her own window. He had to have realized by now that they were heading South.

"I think it's going to be Mexico." He settled back in his seat with his hands behind his head. "I can't wait to see you in a bikini."

"What a scary thought. Luckily, I don't have one."

"Why are you so down on yourself? You had a beautiful body before you starved yourself half to death, now you have a beautiful body by anyone's standards."

Why did he have to wear that expression that looked so much like genuine concern?

"Trust me, women are more critical about these things. Next to Maisie I look like a hippo. I could work out day and night for a year, and she'd still find something to chuckle over. I'm sure she was laughing her ass off at me wearing all that skimpy gear she helped me pick out at Las Gordas. Probably going around calling me La Gorda."

"I thought you two were such great friends while you were there."

"I thought so too. Of course I was drunk as a skunk the whole time, no small thanks to Maisie. With the hindsight of sobriety I can see she was having fun with me the way a cat has fun with its prey before it bites its head off."

"Aren't you stepping into her jaws, then, by going on her show?"

"I'm in control now. She's in my jaws."

"Hardly. She'll be the one doing the editing."

"But I'm writing the script. It's not as if any of this is real."

"A typical reality show, then."

"Exactly. And with your acting skills it should be better than most."

"I'll tell you straight up. I don't like it."

"I know. That's part of the appeal for me." She shot him a dry smile.

"I'm impressed that you trust me to go through with it." Con looked at her, expressionless.

Lizzie froze. Would he? Or would he screw her? Or more likely, would he screw Maisie and then they'd both screw her? Suddenly all that empty air under the jet threatened to suck her screaming into an abyss.

She struggled to look composed. "You have a bizarre sense of honor. I believe you when you said you'd have married me that day. I believe you'll marry me now."

"And divorce you." He spoke softly, eyes narrowed.

The breath squeezed out of her lungs. She held his gaze. "Yes. And divorce me. By age twenty-six I'll be a gay divorcée and you'll be off on your merry way to seduce some other hapless heiress."

"That'll be tricky if I'm famous as the man dumped by Lizzie Hathaway." Humor twinkled in his eyes.

"This show is going to blow your cover. What a tragedy, you'll never be able to pretend you have a private jet as everyone and their dog will know you're just a gold-digging grease monkey."

A muscle flickered in Con's cheek, and she suffered a stab of regret over her snobbish jibe, which was the kind of thing her parents would say. It felt dead wrong to insult his profession, which he obviously enjoyed and was good at.

But he'd preyed on her hopeful naiveté, exploited her trust. He deserved to feel pain.

She looked out her window. Blue sky for miles.

"You can see why I was afraid to tell you the truth," said Con after a pause. "You'd have tossed me out on my ass."

"As you so richly deserve."

"But think about it. You didn't love me because I was a big-shot engineer, or because my folks had some fancy estate on a bayou. You loved me because of the good times we had together. The dinners we cooked, the walks in the park holding hands, the long conversations about books, music, life. The kissing and hugging and…"

"The hot sex." She hissed it between tight lips. Tried to ignore the odd tug she felt as memories forced their way back.

Con looked at her with those deep brown eyes. "None of that was fake. I had the best time of my life with you."

Shit. He was getting to her again. How did he do that? She couldn't deny that it was the best time of her life too, by a long, long, long way.

Then she remembered. "I thought you were someone else. Someone who loved me."

She looked right at him. Steeled herself against his masculine profile, those dark, soulful eyes.

He held her gaze. "I wanted to be that person. Someone who could love you the way you deserve. But that part of me is…Broken."

"That makes two of us."

He looked at her, eyes so sad, as silence roared between them over the hum of the engines.


Con got a nasty feeling in his stomach as the pilot asked them to put their seat-belts on in preparation for landing.

They'd never left the continental United States.

All those snake-curving rivers, all that lush green beauty—he'd never seen it from the air before but he was pretty sure it was the Mississippi Delta he'd spent some seriously rotten times in. And that glimmering fat ribbon down there had to be Old Man River itself. They'd probably flown right over his "alma mater" down in

Natchez. And if he wasn't very much mistaken, right now they were coming in for a landing in…

Louisiana.

He glanced at Lizzie. Tight-lipped, she adjusted her seat-belt—she'd never unfastened it—and stared out the window.

*You have good food to eat, a roof over your head, you're helping Lizzie get back on her feet. You aimed too high and got your wings burned off. You called the tune, and now you have to pay the piper. Deal with it.*

He'd been honest when he told her he couldn't love her. When you loved people, you lost them and it ripped your heart open and bled out all the good stuff. Left nothing but the working parts.

Turned you into the kind of person who could deceive someone you cared about.

He took a deep breath and straightened his cuffs. Braced himself as the plane descended toward a sliver of tarmac shimmering in the afternoon heat. A couple of bumps and they were down.

He forced a smile. "We're here."

"Yes." She didn't glance at him. She looked nervous, stiff, her fingers fumbling with her seat-belt clasp, eyes darting about.

"We don't have to go through with this, you know," he said softly. "You don't have to be a liar. We can tell them it was a mistake, that we're not ready to get married or something."

He held his breath and cursed himself for wanting to marry her anyway. It made no sense, but—

She turned on him, eyes wide. "I'm not a liar. I'm marrying the man of my dreams, remember?" She yanked her bag down from the overhead compartment. "You were the man of my dreams not so very long ago. I'm just playing fast and loose with chronology."

He held out his hand to take her bag. She ignored it.

"Where are we?" he asked the middle-aged pilot who had emerged from the cabin.

"This is the Houma-Terrebonne airport in Houma, Louisiana."

*I knew it.* Con managed a polite nod and glanced at Lizzie.

She stood rigid as they waited for the door to open.

What the hell were they doing here?

He shouldn't have told her where he was from, but he'd vowed to himself he wouldn't lie to her anymore. Wouldn't even bend the truth. He'd turned over a new leaf, and he wasn't going back.

*Whatever you've got coming to you, you deserve it.*

A deep, ugly voice from the past echoed in his head. Made his fingers curl into fists.

"This way, watch your step!" The cheerful pilot gestured to the stairs  Con indicated that Lizzie should go first, and she did, tossing her hair stiffly behind her shoulders.

Heat and humidity wrapped around him. A black limo idled on the stained tarmac, shining in the sun. A driver got out. "Miss Hathaway?"

"Yes." Lizzie handed him her bag and climbed into the car with no further preliminaries. Con put his own bag in the trunk.

"Where are we going?" he asked the driver, fear snaking in his gut.

"Some place called the Dumas Plantation."

The name sounded vaguely familiar, but he wasn't sure why. Probably near home.

Home. What a funny word for your own personal hell.

He climbed into the car with Lizzie and closed the compartment between them and the driver.

He leaned close enough to feel the heat from her skin, to smell the traces of perfume that clung to it. "This is no surprise to you. You told them to choose Louisiana."

"I always said you were smart." She held her chin high, corkscrew curls of hair trailing over her shoulders.

"Why?" To punish him? What had she found out? His gut tightened, and he swallowed hard.

"So you can visit your 'ancestral home.' Go back to that fantasy plantation all your pretend ancestors came from." She turned to him, eyes flashing. "Be the lord of the manor for real."

He frowned. "You're kidding."

She pulled her hair up and twisted it into a knot. "Nope. It's real. Do you like the idea?"

"Can't say I do." He'd rather be any place on earth than here in Louisiana. This place held all the guilt and shame he'd tried so hard to run from. Things he couldn't even think about without—

He blew out a breath of air and shook his head. Looked at the smooth, slightly flushed skin of her cheek as she stared out the window.

"You said that when you were with me you felt like you really were an aristocrat with an avenue of live oaks, so now you'll have your live oaks if only for a few days."

She didn't turn to look at him, but her voice sounded soft, almost nostalgic. Had she really planned this as a kind of treat? Maybe he'd misjudged her. She'd been so hostile lately he thought she was out to draw blood from him any way she could. Maybe she still had a little bit of heart left that he hadn't broken.

"That's sweet of you. I mean it." Damn. He was touched. Wanted to give her a hug. Wanted to kiss those warm soft lips he couldn't get near anymore.

Almost forgot it was part of a scam they were pulling on a cable network and the viewing public.

She turned to him again. "I do hope there are no outstanding warrants for your arrest in the state of Louisiana."

"Nope. I think the statute of limitations has expired on all of them." He winked and actually started to relax a little. Who'd have thunk it? Here he was, back in Louisiana, a grown man and master of his own destiny.

Well, not really, but he would be once Lizzie had her fun with him.

He'd been afraid of the whole state for ten years, almost shivering when he heard the name, but now he could fly right in here in a private jet and go about his business.

He stretched and took off his jacket. Folded it up and placed it on the seat beside him. It wasn't until they drove out of the airport complex and pulled onto the highway that old haunted feeling crept over him again and threatened to suck the life out of him.

He'd left this place to save his own hide, and there was no running from the guilt that came with that choice.

The car drove along quiet back roads for an eternity. A feeling of foreboding crept up on Lizzie like the Spanish moss that engulfed the trees.

Since they'd left the highway the landscape was eerie and desolate and several of the houses they'd passed seemed to be abandoned ruins. Sometimes a new house was built right next to the crumbling wreck of an old one, the past hunkered in the backyard like a ghost. Bayous and deep swamps gleamed through the trees around them.

"So this is where you're from, huh?"

Con stared out the window, transfixed, silent for most of the ride. "Yeah."

"It's kind of creepy."

"Yeah."

"Kind of beautiful too."

"Yeah."

Con's slick charm had apparently been left behind in New York and he stared out the window, not talking unless she did first. She was relieved when the car finally pulled onto the promised avenue of live oaks and began its approach to the Dumas Plantation.

"Wow." Con craned forward to peer out the windshield. The bright white Greek Revival mansion loomed at the end of the driveway, windows shaded by deep verandas on both floors. "It's huge."

"It has to accommodate the entire crew, and the wedding will be in either the garden arbor, or the indoor ballroom, depending on the weather."

"Indoor ballroom." He smiled. "I like that."

"And look, there's the first camera." She tucked her hair behind her ears and tugged at the hem of her T-shirt, anxiety shooting up her spine. "At least I think that's a camera." The lone cameraman looked so unimpressive, no lights, no giant microphones, just a scruffy guy with a camcorder on his shoulder.

A girl with a clipboard came running to the car the moment it stopped. Gia. Breathless and sweaty, her fine hair sticking to her forehead.

Fierce heat and humidity rolled in as Con lowered the window.

"Hey, guys, have a decent flight? Great. That's Dino, the camera guy. He's going to take some handheld footage of you arriving as soon as I get out of here, okay, so just act natural, head up to the steps and whatever you do, don't look at the camera. I'll meet you inside." She slammed the door and scurried away without giving them time to get a word in.

"Act natural, but don't look at the camera." Lizzie licked her lips. "This should be interesting. It seems so rude not to say hi to the camera guy."

They climbed out of the car and a weird fake smile attached itself to her lips. She waited for Con to join her, but he'd gone round the back to get their bags. There was some fumbling and muttering with the driver about who'd carry the bags, and Con finally joined her, empty-handed, with his own weird fake smile fixed in place. He offered her his arm, and she took it gratefully.

The walk up the rather cracked driveway took about three hours. At least that's what it felt like. She could feel her hair bushing out in the sweltering damp air and sweat droplets moistened the skin between her breasts.

"Isn't it lovely," she murmured, sounding about as natural as a singing Barbie.

"It's magnificent," replied Talking Ken. Oh, lord, this was going to be a really long few days. Her entire body felt rigid, a walking robot, as they marched past the cameraman, eyes firmly fixed on the front door.

She stumbled on the gray-painted wooden steps and suppressed a curse, but Con's strong arm stopped her from falling. When they opened the door, Gia was right there with her clipboard.

"Let's do that again," called the cameraman, just as Lizzie was about to dive into the welcome shade of the interior.

She turned to greet the man she'd so pointedly ignored, but he didn't notice as he was busy doing something to his camera.

"He wants you to get back in the car and walk up again. It's often more natural the second time." Gia smiled. "More real."

# 12

Lizzie's sandals squeaked on the polished wood floors as she trailed behind Gia during their tour of the house. She could smell fresh paint on the walls and even the draperies looked brand-new—expensive reproductions in luxurious fabrics. Fine antiques occupied the rooms with stately confidence that implied they'd been there since the house was built.

The only serious snag seemed to be a lack of air conditioning. The system had died and apparently they were waiting to install new duct work before replacing it. The kitchen was a relic from the 1930's, with monstrous white enameled appliances and a sink large enough to gut a pig, but since the show had brought a genuine Louisiana chef with them from New York, that wasn't her problem.

Their tour ended in the master bedroom, which unfortunately Gia expected them to share. The four-poster bed loomed in the middle of the room like a prison with only four bars. Con already sprawled across it, the jailor.

"C'mon, babe, you know you sleep better wrapped up in my arms." He tipped his head and smiled softly at her, for the benefit of Gia and Dino, who stood in the doorway.

She stiffened. Unfortunately, it was true. She had such a terrible time sleeping lately she'd take a tranquilizer if it would help her rest. Con's arms were cheaper and more readily available, if no less addictive.

"To be honest, we don't really have a spare bed," said Gia. "Other people would have to double up if one of you takes another room."

Lizzie smiled stiffly. "I'm just worried about shocking the viewers." Thank God the camera was off for now.

"No sweat," said Dino with a dimpled grin. He was a young guy with messy black hair and an easy manner. "Our viewers are pretty open minded. The show's slated to air right after co-ed wrestling so whatever you do will look pretty tame."

Lizzie cringed. "Right then, we'll share this room. It's lovely, thank you." Her smile ached. "I'll take a quick nap if you don't mind." It was the best she could come up with short of saying, please leave.

Con winked and smoothed a spot on the bed with splayed fingers. Gia giggled. God, she was practically drooling over him. And he'd already established an easy rapport with Dino the cameraman and Raoul the makeup guy, who'd announced that Con didn't need makeup. His expression had suggested there wasn't quite enough makeup in the world for her.

Gia waved at Con and smiled at Lizzie. "Catch you later! Dinner's at seven and don't forget we'll be filming as you come down the stairs."

"Looking forward to it!" Her smile made one last gargantuan effort, then collapsed as the door closed behind them.

"Get off the bed " she growled, hurling herself onto it.

"I don't think so." He shifted onto his side, looking disgustingly comfortable.

"What the hell are you playing at? I swear, next time you call me babe, I'm going to slap you."

"I've always called you babe."

"Not in public."

"True." He stretched, flexing his muscles until they cracked. "But we've never had much of an audience before, have we? I never met your friends. You kept me pretty much under wraps."

"I'm a quiet, reclusive type." She stared up at the brocade hanging over the bed, relieved it looked freshly laundered. "I like to keep to myself. That way I don't have to worry about people trying to trick me and lie to me."

Her nerves were frayed from keeping a smile fixed in place all afternoon. A question she'd never thought to ask before had popped into her brain almost as soon as they were trapped under the stare of the camera. "When we arranged to meet for lunch that day, and you didn't show up, and you let me think you worked in the Wheelock Engineering office building, rather than in some garage across the street—was that something you planned?"

Con's expression darkened. He looked away to the window. "No." He ran a hand through his hair. "No. I didn't plan it."

"So what happened, exactly?" She crossed her arms over her chest.

He took a deep breath. "I knew you'd gotten a mistaken impression of what I did for a living. At first I liked that you made all the wrong assumptions about me. That you thought I was successful and educated. It felt good." He gave her a wary look.

"You were curious to see how well Frankie's polishing had worked?"

"Yeah, I guess that was part of it, in the beginning. But we were getting more serious, you know, past the flirting stage. I could see myself in a real relationship with you and I figured it was time to set you straight. That was why I asked you to meet me at work. They hired me pretty often and I was hoping to get a full time job there. It was a nice place, neat, well run—" He shrugged. "Anyway, I got held up by a customer, showing him what I'd done to his car, so I was rushed and late and looking out for you while I was still working. I went into the bathroom and cleaned up. When I came out, you were standing across the street outside that office tower."

He paused, and his eyes took on a shadowed look. "You looked so beautiful. So ladylike and elegant and…perfect. I could tell you thought I worked in that office building." He rubbed a hand over his face. "When I saw you there I had a weird feeling. I suddenly knew that if I told you the truth about me…I'd lose you." He shot a dark, piercing glance at her. "And now I know I was right."

Was he? Her parents would have had a fit if they knew she was seeing an uneducated mechanic. And Maisie. And her so-called friends...

But she could have made up her own mind. Followed her heart.

If she'd had the chance.

"You shouldn't have tricked me." Her voice trembled. "You should have let me make my own decision." She swallowed hard. "When were you going to finally tell me the truth? On our wedding night?" She bit her lip, willed back the tears.

Con swallowed. "I thought that maybe if we were already married..." He looked down.

"I still could have divorced you, you know." Her voice cracked as she spat the words at him.

He looked down. "I'm sorry Lizzie. You know I am. Don't cry."

She avoided looking at him. "I'm not going to cry." She cleared her throat to get rid of the scratch in her voice. "I wouldn't give you the satisfaction. And just because you let me wait there for forty-five minutes while you stood across the street watching me and waiting for me to leave—" She gulped a shaky breath. "You are sleeping on the floor tonight."

"It's bare wood." He tilted his head and looked at her with those big dark eyes that so easily turned her into a sucker.

"It'll be just like home, back in the shack." She fixed her eyes on him, steeled herself against all emotion. "Which we'll be visiting tomorrow with the camera crew."

Con sat up like a shot. "What?"

"You didn't think we'd come all the way down here and not visit scenic Mudbug Flats?"

Con stared at her, his mouth slightly open. Blinked. "Why?"

"So I can see where you come from. Meet your family." She rolled onto her side and tried to look relaxed. "It wouldn't be a real wedding without family. And unfortunately mine are temporarily indisposed." She extended into what she hoped looked like a casual stretch. "I tried to track Mom down at the ashram, but she'd left. Gone to climb a mountain or something. Probably scaling Mount Everest with Martha Stewart." Her voice sounded flat. "Anyway, we'd better get dressed for dinner. Formal, remember? Glittering candelabra, plates laden with local delicacies."

Why did Con still have that strange expression on his face? He was truly rattled.

Good. He deserved it.

Tension crackled through her as she eased herself up of the bed and padded across the polished wood floor to the closet.

She slid a blue spaghetti strap dress off the hanger, spread it on the bed and removed her clothes. She could still sense Con's eyes on her as she stripped

His silence was creeping her out. Was he really so afraid to go back where he came from? What was the big deal?

As she unhooked her bra, she felt his hard stare soften.

Men. They'll drool over anything. Don't take it personally.

She ignored the way her skin tingled under his appraisal. She fastened her new strapless bra and slid into the dark blue silk. Arranged the shoulder straps over her newly rediscovered collarbone.

"You look pretty."

He wasn't smiling. Still tense, on edge, no doubt dreading tomorrow's little homecoming. That should give her a thrill of victory, but somehow it didn't.

"I'm going to Raoul to get my face painted on. I'll see you later."


Raoul applied eyeliner to her lower lid, then surveyed her through narrowed almond-shaped eyes. He had razor edge bone structure like Miles Davis, black hair shaved almost to the dark skin of his skull. An aura of masculine menace offset by feminine grace that boldly announced his sexuality.

"Girl, your man is fine." He spoke with slow deliberation.

"Thanks, I guess." She blushed.

Raoul chuckled. A low, rather threatening sound. He set her nerves on edge. Too cool. She'd never met anyone like him and he knew it.

"So you're a Hathaway, huh?"

Lizzie flushed darker under the thick layer of foundation and powder he'd applied. "Yes."

"No need to blush. I'm honored to be in the presence of a member of high society." He penciled an arch into her brow. Surveyed his handiwork, then looked into her eyes. "But your lover isn't high society, is he?"

"Um, not really, no."

Ugh, why was she getting so flustered? Partly because it was so damn hot that sweat was slithering down her spine, but mostly because she had a feeling those sharp eyes could see right through her.

He caught her eye in the mirror again. Spoke slowly. "I think that's just beautiful."

She swallowed.

He fluffed more blush on her cheek with a huge brush. "Romantic, you know? Two people who love each other, not getting hung up on the rules of society." He brushed a knuckle against her now flaming cheek. "You are burning up. Let me get you some water."

She gasped with relief as he turned away to pour some out of a jug. Did he know she was a fraud?

He handed her a glass of iced water and she gulped some down. "Thanks."

"Most people spend their lives conforming to what everyone else wants of them, and they don't follow their heart, you know?" He drew a line around her lips, and she had to wait until he was done before she could croak a yes.

"Hold your lips still there, no pouting. Not until I'm done anyway. Then you can pout and kiss all you like. Mess it all up." He winked at her and her stomach tightened.

He'd know if she'd kissed Con or not. She'd have to smear it on the back of her hand or something.

Raoul brushed lipstick on with a tiny brush. She couldn't even glance at herself in the mirror, afraid her nose was growing longer by the second. The discomfort of his close scrutiny made her skin crawl.

And the thought of kissing Con for the cameras made her chest burn in the most uncomfortable way.

"Love," he said, as he dotted some shimmering stuff in the middle of her upper lip, "is a powerful force in the world. Don't fight it, don't ever fight it."

She nodded, trying to look like she believed this was sage advice. Something about Raoul told her not to get on his bad side.

"You're done, and if I may say so, you look ravishing."

She risked a look in the mirror. Gasped.

"Oh, my gosh, is that me?" He'd gone for a completely different look than the cheery young makeup artist at Las Gordas. Total va-va-voom, complete with heavily lined eyes, high arched brows and full pouty lips. Like she'd escaped from a fifties B-movie.

"Wow. Lizzie, is that you?" Gia rushed up behind her. "You look unbelievable. Raoul, you are truly a magician." Lizzie flushed darker than ever. Had she been such a toad before?

"The hairdresser hasn't made it yet. I can't get him on his cell."

"That boy is…" Raoul rolled his eyes.

"He's very talented."

"I'll give you that. But I'd make other plans if I were you."

"It looks kind of funky the way it is." Gia picked up a curly piece of Lizzie's giant frizzed-out bush of hair.

"No! Please, it must be straightened. I have a flatiron in my room. I can do it myself."

Raoul picked up a hair-dryer and blew the end of it, like a six-gun he'd just fired. "Have no fear. Raoul is here. Master of all trades and jack of none."

"Oh, Raoul, you're a savior," Gia breathed.

Lizzie shrank back into the chair, dreading more meditations on True Love.

"What have you done to my Lizzie?" Con's voice startled her.

"Made her a knockout." Raoul admired his handiwork.

"She was already a knockout. She doesn't need a lot of paint and stuff."

"Don't worry, sweetheart, she'll take it off in the bedroom. It's for the cameras. The lights can really flatten you out. Why don't you sit down here, homeboy, and I'll punch you up too."

"I'll sit down, but keep your hands off me." Con settled into a chair with an easy grin. There probably wasn't a person on earth who made him uncomfortable. "Raoul tell you him and me were gym buddies?"

*What?* She managed to keep a straight face.

Raoul made a sucking sound with his tongue. "I can't believe you're still going to that trashy place."

"Hey, the equipment works."

"The clientele is strictly low-rent. But then maybe that's why you fit right in." He winked at Lizzie.

"You're probably right," Con said cheerily. "But don't knock it. They got a StairMaster."

"That must be why your buns look so tight. Or are you still a weights-only man?"

"Weights and running."

"Ah, running. Now if I'd taken that up, maybe I could have caught you before Miss Hathaway here." He raised an eyebrow. "But I bet she appreciates you keeping yourself in such fine condition."

Lizzie wished she had more hair to hide behind. This must be the gym Con had always left for in the morning before heading to work. Anyone working out next to him probably knew more about him than she did back then. Probably still did.

"Don't get nervous now," said Raoul, holding up a hank of her hair. "Conroy is not one to kiss and tell. You won't catch him bragging about his conquests over the Nautilus machines. Not that that dump has any." He shot a glance at Con. "Keeps his thoughts to himself, this boy," he murmured. "More's the pity. I'd love to know what's going on under those still waters."

*You're not the only one.*

Con didn't bat an eye. "Nothing more to me than meets the eye, right, Lizzie?"

"Yes, sweetie," she said stiffly.

Con leaned in and kissed her on the lips. Gave her a shot of warm tongue that made her toes tingle, then pulled back leaving her glossy lipstick smudged and her dander sky-high.

"Sorry, Raoul, I couldn't help myself."

"Get your bad-boy ass out of here."

With her hair ironed into a gleaming mahogany sheet, Lizzie wilted under the glare of the cameras as they sat at the dinner table.

Huge lights on metal stands blasted the large dining room with an intense blue-white glare. Fat cables trailed over the floor, ready to trip the unwary and the fine antiques and ornate plaster moldings shrank into the shadows.

The table glittered with crystal, with the fleur-de-lis plates she'd chosen. A Lalique bowl bulged with lush tropical fruit, glasses sparkled with wine already poured and heating under the lights. Soup shimmered in the bowls, souring and congealing in the heat. The illusion of a delicious meal to be shared by lovers.

When the reality was anything but.

Dino adjusted something on a monitor. "Can you put another scrim on the backlight? I'm getting some glare."

Lizzie rested her aching cheek muscles while the camera was off. Con tugged at his too-tight collar. Winked at her. She glared at him.

Neither of them had managed to eat the congealed soup. Starving, she'd grabbed a red delicious apple from the Lalique bowl. Wax.

"Let's see if we can make it more real this time," chirped Gia. "More natural. Maybe you could hold hands over the table or something?"

Lizzie managed not to grimace. She picked up her hand and flung it down on the table like a rubber chicken she'd been hiding under the tablecloth.

Con took hold of her fingers. His hand looked rather brown and rough against the sheen of the white damask tablecloth. His fingers closed around hers and Lizzie took a deep breath. Sweat trickled down her back underneath her blue dress.

"You okay?" he mouthed.

"Or course," she mouthed back. Why did he have to look so freakin' sensitive and caring? Shame she couldn't snark at him here in front of everyone. She shot him a warm smile. "Your hand is sweaty."

"So's yours."

"I'm surprised my dress isn't soaked through," she murmured. "It must be a hundred and fifty degrees right here. I think my wine is about to boil."

"I know, I know. I'm terribly sorry." Gia picked her way to the table over the trailing cables. "I've told Maisie and she's ordered a slew of portable air-conditioning units to be delivered tomorrow. Honestly, we'd stop shooting, but we really need to get some establishing shots, just stuff to work into the story, or we won't have time. We're on such a tight schedule. Dino, darling, are you nearly ready? Our stars are wilting."

Dino mumbled something while pushing an array of buttons on a deck of whirring machines. "Alright, just make some natural conversation, it doesn't matter what you say as it'll probably just be used for cutaways and that kind of thing."

A tense silence followed. Lizzie could feel about ten pairs of eyes on her.

"The house is lovely, isn't it," she said with a pained smile.

"I think you said that when we arrived." Con's eyes gleamed with humor.

Irritation streaked up her spine. "Why don't you say something then?"

"It's surprisingly difficult to chitchat when there's a camera and a crowd staring at you."

"It's good practice for our wedding." She stared right at him, wishing she'd paid more attention in speech and drama class. "I'm so looking forward to it, aren't you?"

"Oh, yes, I can't wait until we're *man and wife*."

He spoke slowly, voice low and dark, and as he said it she felt something on her leg.

His bare foot.

What had he done with his shoe? She twitched her leg back and grabbed her soup spoon. Dipped it into the congealed mess in her bowl, prickling with annoyance.

Then she felt it again. This time on her crotch. She tried to snap her knees together, but his leg was already blocking the way and she bumped against the hard muscle of his calf. His toes rested gently against the thin layer of her satin panties.

It was too hot for pantyhose.

She gasped, trying to keep a straight face. Con just sat there staring at her. His toes wriggled.

*I will not be aroused.*

"Warm in here, isn't it?" He winked.

Bastard.

The gentle movement of his toes, and now the ball of his foot, stirred up sensations she didn't want to feel. Heat swelled in her groin as fury stirred in her heart. She shifted in her chair, trying to pull back without letting the crew know what was happening under the neatly pressed white tablecloth.

Con massaged her crotch gently with his foot. His face and upper body remained motionless, only the twinkle in his eyes was active. Her nipples sprung to attention, pushing into the satin of her bra, and her breath got shallow.

"It is terribly hot," she hissed. "And I can see you're uncomfortable in that rather formal suit. There's no need to get all dressed up for me, you know. We're going to be married, so you can just relax and be yourself."

Con's eyes narrowed.

She faked a "natural" looking sip of her hot wine.

"I'm quite comfortable." He wiggled his toes. Her clit throbbed.

"Really, darling, I know I'm burning up all over and I'm barely wearing anything at all." She indicated her expansive uncovered cleavage.

Con blinked, fought a smile. It was good to feel that she still had some power over him, even while his damn toes were revving her engines without permission.

She leaned forward, pushing into him. Challenging him. "Heatstroke can be dangerous."

"I'm used to the heat. I'm from these parts, remember?" He raised an eyebrow. She held his gaze. He picked up his warm wine and sipped it. A mistake, from the pained expression that flitted across his face.

She had the upper hand now.

"Sweetheart, give me your jacket." She pulled her hand from his grasp and extended it. "Now."

Her heart pumped loudly as she waited to see if he'd comply. His toes still rested against the moist satin of her crotch. He'd promised to do this her way. Was he a man of his word?

She enjoyed a flush of triumph as he pulled his foot back, regret in his eyes. He shrugged his shoulders out of the jacket. Held her gaze with a dark stare that made her stomach quiver. He handed her the jacket, lifting it high over the table.

"Your tie." Sweet smile. "Come on, sweetie, we can all see your collar is tight."

Without blinking or breaking eye contact, Con slid a sinewy finger into the knot of his silk tie and loosened it. Pulled it off and handed it to her.

She dropped it on the floor, right on top of his expensive jacket. She wasn't going to look away first.

She could feel the crew's excitement. Everyone was deathly quiet, totally still, the only sound in the room was the hum of the lights.

"Go on, unbutton your collar."

Con obeyed, still staring her down, his eyes black and fuming. The surge of power she felt scared her a little. What could she make him do?

He undid the button below his collar. Then the one below that, and the cuffs.

Still holding her gaze he untucked his shirt and pulled it over his head in one swift movement.

Lizzie held her breath, blood pounding, as he balled it up—still without blinking—and handed it to her.

She took it, looked away, gasping for air as she dropped it on the floor and accidentally tipped her plate, spilling soup on the table cloth.

Con settled back in his chair, shirtless. Then turned to the stone faced waiter standing out of view of the camera. "Could you bring me some ice, please?"

Lizzie gulped.

At the urging of someone off screen, a uniformed waitress silently approached and removed their bowls of uneaten soup. Lizzie nodded her thanks. Con didn't nod or move at all. Just sat there, totally relaxed, as if he ate a bare-chested banquet every day of his life.

The satin sheen on his tanned skin looked positively ornamental, unlike the sweat rolling down her back and soaking her dress. Her antiperspirant had failed miserably, and her whole face probably shone with thick droplets. Her skin hummed, still aroused, even without his touch still on it.

She'd called Con's bluff and he'd raised her.

His perfect six-pack mocked her, along with the full curve of those gym-pumped biceps.

"Your chest is so tanned. I guess that's from working out in the hot sun fixing all those cars." She wanted to remind everyone that he wasn't really the lord of the manor. Somehow removing his shirt had made him look more regal and imposing, not less.

Con tilted his head, gave her a long, sensual look with those narrowed black eyes. "I guess so, babe, but the last car I fixed up you did most of the work, remember?"

Lizzie's mouth fell open.

"You're a hard worker, and very talented."

"I... I..."

His toes were on her ankle now. Sliding up her calf very lightly. Her whole body tingled with a scary mixture of rage and arousal that left her speechless.

"We're a great team, you and me." He reached across the table, holding his hand out for hers.

Her face heated as she realized—cameras on— she had no choice but to take it. *He's my true love.*

He squeezed her hand in a way that made her belly quiver.

"I think that once the world finds out about what you can do with a spray gun, you'll be well on your way to getting rich again."

He squeezed her hand again. Like he was giving her a signal. Had kind of a serious expression on his face. Was this his crude way of trying to boost her artistic career on camera?

"Painting is just a hobby," she hissed.

"It shouldn't be. I've never seen anything like the work you did on that Corvette."

Pride shimmered through her for a split second before she realized Maisie was going to see this and laugh herself into a coma. She kicked Con under the table with the spiked toe of her shoe.

He flinched, surprised.

Just then the waitress put a glass of ice next to his wineglass.

Con picked up the glass, which looked ridiculously delicate in his big hands. In fact, all of him looked bigger now, without the civilizing veneer of clothing. He pulled a cube from the glass and rubbed it over his skin, on the back of his neck and down between his pecs. Then he held it out to her. "Here, babe."

She blinked. She could feel the crew's ears pricking up. She had to take it. He was her true love, right?

She cupped her palm, and Con pushed the melting ice cube in to it.

Dropped his eyes to her cleavage.

Her breasts seemed to rise under his gaze, nipples standing to attention. She stiffened her spine. Water from the ice dripped down her wrist as she drew her hand back and rubbed the cube over her collarbone, up her neck. An icy thrill. Con winked.

Jerk. She tried to ignore the uncomfortable heat still throbbing inside her, vying with the cool trickle of water between her breasts.

Con licked his lips slightly, almost imperceptible, and she shuddered. Damn him! She dropped the remaining fragment of ice on the floor, dragged her eyes from his muscled chest looking for any distraction. She reached for a glossy apple, then snatched her hand back when she remembered they were made of wax.

"Where's the food?" Con said casually. "My woman's getting hungry."

More punishing heat flooded her face, and she wondered if anyone had ever died of embarrassment on camera before.

Gia scurried forward. Gestured to Dino to stop rolling. "They're having trouble in the kitchen. Can't get the stove going." She grimaced. "It was working okay earlier, but there's something wrong with the gas range." She came closer. "The chef is having a hissy fit."

"Maybe Con should look at it. He's mechanically inclined." Lizzie said, gathering what was left of her wits.

"Sure, I don't mind." Con pushed his chair back, stood up and wandered off into the kitchen. On those bare feet he'd been tormenting her with.

Lizzie dotted her napkin over her heavily perspiring face.

# 13

Out in the backyard, Con rapped on the metal propane tank connected to the range in the kitchen, and it rang back a familiar reply. He tried not to laugh out loud. Clearly this was not going to be the week of all-expenses-paid luxury he'd envisioned.

"Empty," he called through the darkness. "You got another tank?"

"I don't think so. I'll have to order one from town tomorrow," Gia replied from the doorway. No one had followed him out into the pitch-black garden. It was a relief to get away from the cameras and lights for a moment.

The chef, a serious New York City prima donna, was fuming and stamping and smoking cigarettes in the kitchen, and Con was pretty damn hungry. Something about shrimp had been mentioned earlier and his stomach was growling for it "Got a barbeque?"

"Not sure. I didn't notice one," called Gia.

He walked back to the brightly lit door where the crew thronged, peering anxiously into the garden. "We can build a fire back here on the patio if you'll help me get some wood together."

"I bet there are all kinds of huge snakes and spiders and bats out there. I heard the insects down here are ten times the size they are back home," said Gia. "I think I'd rather starve."

"Nah, just friendly creatures out here. If any zombies start coming out of the swamp I'll let you know. Come on, I'll get started, and you guys figure out where to build the fire."

The garden was pretty well manicured so he had to walk almost all the way to the bottom, where the bayou gleamed in the moonlight. Fallen branches from the gnarled old trees were stacked in a couple of neat piles. Their limbs pricked and scratched his bare chest as he walked back across the cool grass.

Several crew members had ventured tentatively onto the patio by the time he came back. Dino videotaped as they helped him stack the wood in a circle and lit it with matches. Dry Spanish moss crackled and spat as kindling.

"Where's Lizzie?" he asked, as the fire started to take.

"I think she's in the kitchen, talking to André," said Gia. "He's the chef."

Con had a sudden nasty vision of Lizzie left unattended with all those bottles of wine. "I'll go find her."

"Sure."

He noticed the camera's mechanical gaze on him as he strode across the warm slate of the patio. He probably looked like some kind of backwoods bayou hick with no shoes or shirt and he felt a little clench of embarrassment.

Just what Lizzie wanted, no doubt, and he'd played right into her hands.

"Lizzie?" He pushed into the enormous kitchen, bright light making him blink.

The chef leaned against a vast table in the center, drinking red wine from a large tumbler. A stained apron covered his ample belly. A cigarette, burned nearly down to the filter, dangled from his lips.

"You seen Lizzie?"

"She was here a minute ago." Hints of a local accent like his gave him a start. "Went upstairs, I think." The chef lifted a black eyebrow. "Took a bottle of champagne from the fridge."

Shit. Con pushed out into the dining room, picked his way past all the cables from the now-dormant spotlights and took the stairs two at a time. "Lizzie!"

No answer.

"Hey, Lizzie, where are you?" He strode down the dim hallway. Ancient light fixtures gave off thin yellow light. The door to their bedroom was closed.

He knocked once, then pushed it open.

Lizzie sat on the bed, eyes on him, hands wrapped around an open bottle of champagne. His chest tightened. In two strides he crossed the room and snatched it from her.

"I didn't take a sip," she protested.

"You were just thinking about it?" The chilled bottle sweated cool droplets into his palm.

"I was contemplating my options." Her makeup had run in the heat, and he resisted the urge to neaten her smudged mascara with his thumb.

"Why? Everything's going your way. You've tricked me into coming back here to the swamp I crawled out of, and it's all being captured on camera. You should be ecstatic. What's the problem?"

"Where is the camera?" She glanced nervously toward the door.

"I don't know. I don't really care, but I do want to know what's making you want to drink again when I'm doing this all your way. For you."

"I don't know." She lay back on the bed. Her dress was soaked through at the waist. "I didn't know it would be so hot."

"So it's hot. Drink some water, take a bath. Big deal." He put the champagne bottle down on a walnut sideboard, taking care to slip a magazine under it so it didn't make a ring on the wood.

"And it just doesn't feel...right."

"What doesn't feel right? It doesn't feel right to tell people that beneath my expensive suit I'm just an uneducated mechanic? Why not? It's the truth, isn't it? And tomorrow you'll get to see the sorry place I grew up in, which, believe me, will live up to your every expectation and then some. You've got me right where you want me, so what gives?"

She looked like she was about to cry. He snatched a tissue from a box on the sideboard and handed it to her. "Here."

She blew her nose into the Kleenex. Tears shone in those big brown eyes. He had a sudden strong urge to put his arms around her, which he resisted. "It doesn't feel right to make me undress in front of the camera to show you have power over me?"

She leaped off the bed and walked to the other side of the room, wet dress sticking to her skin.

She couldn't look at him.

"Or it doesn't feel right to do that stuff and then pretend like you're all excited about marrying me? That's it, isn't it? It's the embarrassment to yourself you hadn't figured on. You were so hell-bent on showing me up as the loser you think I am that you didn't realize it would make you look like a loser too."

"I hate you!" She pulled off her shoe and threw it at him. It smacked loudly into a wooden bedpost.

"Yeah? So how come you can only sleep when you're in my arms?"

"You're nothing to me. You're nobody!" Her eyes flashed. Sticky tendrils of wet hair curled up around her face.

"So you keep trying to prove, but apparently I'm not dropping dead because of it." He shrugged. "I'm learning quite a bit about you, though." He paused. "I'm the naïve one. Do you know I really thought you'd be okay with me once I told you the truth about me. I figured, hey, I make her happy, she loves me, it'll all work out."

"I didn't love you!" she sobbed. She bent down to pull off her other shoe, but lost her balance and pitched forward, grabbing the bedpost to steady herself.

The bed creaked loudly and shifted. "Woah." He grabbed a thick wood post and tried to hold it steady as it tugged against him, shifted, and came loose from the bed base. It weighed a ton and he couldn't stop the motion. "Look out, it's coming down!"

He dived toward her, knocking her out of the way with his body and slamming them both into the floor in the corner of the room.

In slow motion, with a cacophony of creaks and a cloud of malodorous dust, the entire four-poster structure above the bed twisted, listed, then collapsed and crashed to the wood floor with a thunderous series of bangs and crunches.

His body covered hers completely during the bed's descent, so he was relieved when the noise stopped and he'd sustained no puncture wounds. "Must've been rotten."

Hot, angry and struggling to escape, Lizzie's lush body was having an unfortunate effect on him. He eased himself off with considerable regret.

She sat up, panting. "You practically killed me!"

"I didn't want you to get hurt. You're alright."

"You tore my dress. Look!" He glanced down. Her plump breasts heaved against the blue fabric, one breaking free where a strap had snapped. *Nice.*

"Stop staring, you beast! Help me up."

"Sure." He couldn't stop the grin ripping across his face. The sting of her hand on his cheek slowed its progress. Okay, so maybe he deserved whatever punishment she had in store for him. The delicious crush of her soft body under his had brought back way too many beautiful memories.

He offered her a hand, and she climbed heavily to her feet, one shoe still on.

"Let me help you with that." He lifted the flap of blue fabric that had fallen, exposing a see-through strapless bra. His thumb brushed against her nipple, and a jolt of raw lust shot through him.

Yes, he was a beast.

"Get away from me!" she shrieked. Dust clung to her hair and skin. His too, no doubt.

Footsteps clattered in the hallway. "Someone's coming." He snatched a tissue from the box. "Let me fix you up." She stood still while he dabbed at her smudged mascara and brushed dust out of her rapidly curling hair.

"What the hell's going on in here?" Roger, the sound guy, a big redhead no older than Gia, came crashing into the room. Dino followed, camera on his shoulder.

"Bed fell down." Con glanced down at the remains of the posts where they lay under brocade curtains crumpled into elegant whorls on the floor.

"Holy shit," said Roger, with a grin. "Cool."

"Get out of the shot, Rog," murmured Dino.

"Oh, yeah, sorry." Roger pushed out of the room. "Just wanted to make sure everyone was okay."

"We're fine." Con grabbed Lizzie around the waist. "It just collapsed. Must have termites or something."

He could feel Lizzie trembling in her damp dress. Her chest heaved indelicately as she struggled to control her breathing. She held up the torn section of her dress with clenched fingers and teetered in her one shoe. It was pretty damn funny. He gave her a squeeze around the shoulders and a kiss on the cheek. "It's alright, babe, no real damage done. Next time we have a lover's tiff we'll take it outside."

Her mouth fell open.

He planted another kiss on her cheek, enjoying this far too much. She'd dragged him here to get revenge on him and try to hurt him, so he didn't feel bad about having some fun at her expense.

"We did not break it," she rasped.

"Um, yeah, right." He winked at her. "Don't want to get sued. Who owns this place anyway?"

Another face appeared in the doorway, one he hadn't seen before. An icy looking blonde in a white suit.

Lizzie let out a tiny shriek.

"Darling, what happened?" The blonde pushed past Dino and into the room.

"Maisie." Lizzie's voice was barely a whisper.

One arm still around Lizzie, Con held out his hand. "Hi, Maisie, I'm Conroy. Glad to meet you."

So this was her, huh? The family resemblance was nonexistent. Maisie was tall, pale and thin, with poker straight hair and piercing light blue eyes.

She took a bold stride into the room and gripped his hand with force. "Conroy, it's a pleasure. I can't believe Lizzie's kept you under wraps for so long." Her eyes grazed his bare chest for a fraction of a second, then locked back on his. "I just got in and heard this terrible commotion. Lizzie, darling, are you alright?"

"I'm fine," said Lizzie, hoisting her dress higher over her breast. "Except for my dress, which got torn when Conroy gallantly threw himself between me and the falling bedposts. Without him I don't know what would have happened."

Maisie glanced down at the bed. "We're thoroughly insured, thank goodness. Dino, get some shots of the wreckage. Lizzie dear, is that a scratch on your cheek?" She reached out and Lizzie flinched.

Con felt a surge of protective instinct. "She'll be okay. She just needs to catch her breath. Maybe we should all go outside and get something to eat. Just give us some privacy so Lizzie can change."

"What a shame we didn't capture the collapse on camera," mused Maisie, a finger on her chin. "I'm here now so we'll make sure we don't miss any more key events, won't we, Dino?"

Con did not miss Dino's lowered brows. Gia had already scurried away. In fact, everyone had made themselves scarce since the appearance of the infamous Maisie.

Maisie touched his chest with a finger. Her nail scratched his skin, causing his right pec to flinch. What the hell was she up to?

"Dust. Powder post beetles, I expect. They can be such a scourge in an old place like this. We'll get someone up to clean this mess up before bedtime."

She leaned into Lizzie, who stiffened, and gave her a swift kiss on the cheek. "In with a bang! You're full of surprises lately. I can't wait to see what happens next."

Then she turned and left the room, white pants swishing and heels clicking on the wood floor.

They were left alone with Dino, who shrugged. "Sorry, boss's orders. Gotta shoot the mess, then I'll get out of your way."

Lizzie stepped back, pressing herself into the wall, and Con stood in front of her, shielding her from the camera. Now that Maisie was here, for some reason he didn't want Lizzie on camera not looking her best. They waited until Dino left with a gruff nod, then Con closed the door.

"The next time we have a lover's tiff we'll take it outside?" Lizzie's voice was shimmering steel.

"Hey, you were the one throwing shoes, not me."

"I never threw a shoe in my life until I met you."

"I can tell. You could use some practice."

"I'm serious. You bring out the absolute worst in me. I was a perfectly respectable person until you came into my life and turned it upside down. I was polite, calm, dignified." She put her hands on her hips, which caused her to drop the ripped neckline of her dress and reveal her lovely breast. "Now look at me!"

Con struggled to stop the grin sneaking across his face. "You look good to me."

"Shut up before I hit you."

"You already did, remember?"

"And you didn't even flinch. I guess it happens a lot."

He shrugged.

"Turn me back! Turn me back into that nice, normal person who didn't go around yelling or throwing shoes at anyone!"

"I'm not a wizard. And if I was I wouldn't want to change a thing. You're a woman of fire and passion, an artist, so it's no surprise if you need to throw a shoe from time to time."

"I am not! And don't you dare bring up my art again. Next thing you know they'll have me painting a car for the cameras."

"Hey, that's not a bad idea. Maybe I could pick up a nice—"

"Don't you even think about it!" Her eyes blazed. Any minute now her bra would burst too, he thought hopefully.

"You enjoyed painting that car."

"I did not." She lifted her chin.

*Don't push it, Con.* "Alright, why don't you get changed, then we can go down and get some dinner."

She shot him a glare, and he tried to shrug it off. It honestly hurt that she didn't respect him. That being smart and resourceful and well read didn't mean anything. Without a pedigree he really was a nobody to her.

*Yes, he'd been naïve.*

He still missed their days of warm intimacy. An intimacy underpinned by his deception and destroyed by it.

So she'd brought him here to humiliate him. Sure, it hurt. He wasn't easy to humiliate—been through far too much already—but hurt, that was another thing. And she didn't have any idea of the world of pain she'd jacked open by bringing him back down here.

The prospect of visiting his childhood home made him want to run and hide. Not—as Lizzie thought—because it was pokey and run-down, which it no doubt would be, at least by her standards.

*Terrible things had happened there.*

Was his father still alive? His veins stung with sheer terror at the thought. Here he was, twenty-five years old and still scared to death of the man. How old would he be now? Less than fifty. Even with the drinking there was every likelihood he'd still be there, bloodshot eyes staring and mouth quick with a curse that cut to the bone.

"Aren't you getting changed?" Lizzie's voice interrupted his dark memories.

"No, I'm okay." He brushed some dust off his pants.

"You're not going to put a shirt on?" She frowned at him, her voice rising.

Oh, so now she didn't want him walking around shirtless?

"Nope. It's hot, and I'm in the mood to keep it real." He shot her a glance and she looked away. "You look nice." She'd changed into a fresh pair of pale blue capris and a matching flowered shirt. Fresh as a spring flower. The lovely woman he'd hoped would help him forget the past and build a new life.

The woman who'd slapped him down when he told her who he really was. Or wasn't. And she didn't even know the half of it.

"Could you help me get this mess into a ponytail?" She held out a white scrunchie.

"Sure." He took it and smoothed her hair back, gathered it into a single cascading fall, and stretched the scrunchie around it. Doubled it and pulled the hair through again. Smoothed a flyaway strand and tucked it behind her ear.

The kind of intimate gesture he loved. And apparently didn't deserve to enjoy except under false pretenses.

"What's the matter with you? I've never seen you look so down." She stared at him, brown eyes penetrating. Did she actually care, or was she looking for another opportunity to grind him under her heel?

"I'm fine."

"So you keep saying, but I know better than to believe you." She brushed dust off his shoulder. The thoughtful gesture and the touch of her soft fingers made him swallow.

"Hey, what's this?" She crouched and picked something up off the floor.

He glanced down as she picked up a yellowed envelope from under a crumpled brocade bed curtain.

"A letter, and it's not opened. How odd. And look, here's another." She pushed back the heavy brocade to reveal a little stack of letters splayed on the wood floor. "I wonder what they were doing in the bed? Look, they have stamps and postmarks on them. They've been through the mail. I wonder why they were never opened?"

She knelt down on the floor and held up one of the letters to the light. A nasty sensation snuck up his back.

*Those letters gave him a bad feeling.*

"It's none of our business. Let's go eat."

"In a minute, wait." She gathered up the fallen envelopes. "They were hidden inside this bedpost. Look, it broke right where the hollow compartment was. It's exactly where I hit it with my shoe. I can see the mark made by the heel." She brushed dust off the splintered wood. "How odd. Doesn't this make you burn with curiosity to know who lived here?"

"Curiosity killed the cat. Come on, let's go." Some dead person's letters? Gave him the creeps, shivers right up his spine. "I'm going anyway. Are you still pretending to be my fiancée or have you gone off that idea?"

He held his breath a little while he waited for her reply. On the one hand this whole charade stank to high heaven, but on the other, if it worked out they'd end up legally married, and then there was always hope that...

*The old warm loving Lizzie would come back?*

Sweat prickled his neck.

*Get over it, Con. She didn't love you, she loved your Richie Rich alter ego.*

"I'm coming, I'm coming." She scrambled to her feet, clutching the letters. "Don't mention these to anyone, okay? I'm going to put them in my suitcase."

"I won't say a word." He held out his arm, and she took it.

"So now you've met Maisie, what did you think?" Her arm tightened as she asked.

"She's tall," he said diplomatically.

"Tall, blonde, beautiful and a complete bitch. Don't make me look like an ass in front of her."

"I'll do my best, but as you've pointed out, my manners can sometimes be lacking."

She stopped, grabbed his arm. "I'm serious. You owe me, remember?"

"I agreed to help you earn some money, not to have you try and break me down on national TV. If I'd known we were coming back here, I'd never have—"

"I know, I know that's why I didn't tell you. But now we're here, can we just make a go of it? There's fifty thousand dollars for maybe a week's work and half of it is yours."

He let out a low whistle. She'd never mentioned the exact dollar amount before and he was impressed. "I'll try to be on my best behavior."

"Darlings!" Maisie's voice rang out in the hallway. "I was just coming to see what happened to you. I know you lovebirds need your privacy, but we have a show to shoot here. Come on, come on." She gestured for them to hurry. "The reason I rushed down here is because Don and I agreed that I should appear in the show as on-camera talent, as your cousin, of course, but also as a sort of Barbara Walters-style interviewer."

"What?" Lizzie froze. "I thought you were an associate producer."

"I am, I am, but in a small company like ours, one person can take on many roles. That's why it's such a marvelous place to grow my career."

"Doesn't Barbara Walters make everyone cry?" Con asked dryly.

Maisie chuckled. "Conroy, you're a card. I can see we're going to have a lot of fun together. I love this shirtless thing you have going here."

"Lizzie made me take it off. She thought I looked hot."

Maisie raised a pale eyebrow. "I heartily concur. And no shoes either?"

"They were getting in the way." He squeezed Lizzie's arm and felt her stiffen. That under-the-table hanky-panky had been pure fun.

"I love it. Very natural. Our chef has risen to the occasion and come up with a marvelous barbequed shrimp recipe. Do hurry or it'll all be gone. They're like ravening wolves!"

Maisie strode off and Lizzie sagged with relief.

"Hey, this wasn't my idea," he muttered.

"Shut up," she snapped. Then she shoved her arm more tightly through his, and marched him down the stairs.

# 14

"What time is it?" Lizzie pulled the sheet over her as the door opened.

"One." The light from the doorway turned Con into a silhouette. Still shirtless, with his clothes under his arm. He unbuttoned his pants and slid them off, then headed for the bed.

"Floor."

"Come on, babe, you know you won't be able to sleep without me."

"Wheelock Engineering. That's all I have to say."

She turned her back to him. Not wanting her eyes to adjust to the silvery outline of his muscled body in the moonlight. She was going to wean herself off him, starting tonight.

"Alright, babe. But if you change your mind..." Without so much as rolling some clothes into a pillow, he eased himself down on to the bare wood.

"I won't." She flipped over, trying to get comfortable on the soft feather mattress. If anything, the heat and humidity were more oppressive in darkness. An almost-full moon blazed through a crack in the brocade curtains, picking out the plaster moldings around the high ceilings. A billion tree frogs screeched a high-pitched symphony.

She'd been lying here in the dark for two hours, hearing the voices of the crew—and Con—laughing and talking and having fun. She'd come up early, had all she could take of sitting outside under the stars with Con's arm around her. She couldn't laugh and talk and have fun with the cameras on her when it was all fake. The pretense was exhausting.

Con got along with everyone. Easygoing, quick witted and charming. He already had Maisie eating out of his palm. When Lizzie announced she was off to bed, he'd jumped to his feet to follow her upstairs to the Bridal Suite like the doting fiancé he so convincingly pretended to be.

But she needed to be away from him more than any of them. "Oh, no, sweetheart, please stay up. You're the only one who knows how to keep the fire going." He'd looked her in the eye, read her thoughts and stayed outside.

Sensitive bastard.

She'd spent some time studying the little stack of yellowed letters. No return address, just the address of the plantation house written in neat cursive. Ballpoint pen.

She hadn't had the guts to open one. Yet.

Con shifted on the floor. Hardwood with no carpet. He'd have a pretty rough night. Maybe she should offer him the comforter since she wasn't using it anyway?

*Stop being a wuss.* He deceived you and made a fool of you and turned you into the kind of person who throws shoes.

She tossed again. A very soft mattress could be surprisingly uncomfortable. A cramp seized her calf and she grabbed her foot, pulled the toe back hard and rubbed her knotted calf muscle, cursing under her breath until the ball of tension released.

Her dad probably wasn't sleeping too well either. The ankle bracelet stayed on even at night, and his activities were under constant surveillance, particularly since his coconspirator, her former "financial advisor," had disappeared without a trace. Probably sunning himself on a Caribbean island. She'd picked up several weeks' worth of mail being held at the post office in New York and discovered a long letter from her father. He'd apologized for squandering her inheritance and letting the family down. He regretted the cruel things he'd said to her that last day at the house. He'd been overwrought, almost psychotic.

Or so he said.

He'd promised to try to make it up to her and her
mother. He'd written so persuasively that she almost
forgave him.

Almost.

The promise of a large inheritance had warped her life
in many ways, cramped her existence. *Now, dear, don't
forget, people know who you are.* She'd accepted the
limitations, held up her end of the deal.

*Daddy's a busy man, darling.*

It had been a tradeoff— money instead of love—and
he'd reneged on his end of the bargain.

She heard Con shift. Maybe just a pillow? She really
didn't need all four of them...

*Sucker.*

She'd been a sucker for her father and a sucker for
Con, and she'd never be a sucker again.

That little game of footsie earlier had left her
irritatingly aroused. Simple body mechanics of course,
but frustrating.

She hadn't had sex since the showdown in the desert.
During their whirlwind courtship, four heavenly weeks,
they'd done it almost every day. Sometimes several times.
So easy, warm, inviting. A blissful connection and shared
release.

*Don't think about it.*

She tossed again, dragged the sheet over her. She
could still hear laughter from downstairs. The crew were
whooping it up and having a great time. They were all
young, free and single—like her—except that she wasn't
really like them. Money had stood like a wall between
herself and other people. She'd never had those easy,
comfortable friendships other people her age enjoyed.

*Except with Con.*

"You okay, babe?" His murmured question startled
her. Had he somehow heard her thoughts?

"Of course," she snapped. "Go to sleep."

And he did. Within minutes she heard his breathing
slow and deepen. When she leaned over the edge of the
bed, incredulous, she watched his broad chest rise and fall
in the bright moonlight. He lay on his back, sinewy arms
at his sides, totally relaxed. Expensive dark designer

briefs hugged a bulge that suggested he might already be enjoying a good dream. Long muscled legs extended carelessly over the floor as if he lay cushioned on a cloud.

How on earth did he do it?

She wondered what lay in store for them at his real ancestral homestead. His obvious apprehension made her nervous. Wasn't that just what she wanted? She'd come here to rub his nose in the humble roots he'd so artfully concealed. To blow his cover on national TV and punish him for his deception?

Now they were here he didn't even put up a fuss about going. He didn't look happy about it, but he didn't seem embarrassed like she'd expected.

She couldn't figure him out. Which was, of course, how she'd gotten into this mess in the first place.

She didn't sleep a single second all night long. In the morning her neck was killing her and her head ached. Con hadn't moved a muscle. Just lay there, lips slightly parted, relaxed expression on his revoltingly handsome features, big sexy body sprawled on the bare wood.

She'd just decided to accidentally step on his hand on her way to the closet, when a knock on the door jolted him from his unseemly repose.

He flew onto the bed and flung his arm over her. "Come in."

She resisted the urge to elbow him off, grateful for his quick reflexes. Honed, no doubt, while scrambling out women's bedroom windows.

"Maisie!" She pulled the sheet up higher and tried not to recoil from those all-seeing ice-blue eyes.

"Don't you two look cozy, sorry to interrupt."

Con had circled Lizzie with his arm and snuggled against her, spoon fashion. She could feel a sizeable morning erection against her butt.

"That's okay." Con spoke lazily. "We're practically in-laws, aren't we, Maisie?" She could feel his smile and it raised the hairs on the back of her neck.

"So true. What a sweet thought." Maisie snapped on a smile. "I'd love you to come down for breakfast, darlings, though I can see Lizzie needs some attention from Raoul first."

Lizzie cringed. Her flattened hair probably stuck out all over like a Vandergraf generator and she could pack her new wardrobe in the bags under her eyes.

"We did have rather a wild night," she managed.

Con buried his face in the back of her neck and kissed it. "Maisie doesn't want to know what we were doing all night."

*Oh, she'd eat it up like pie, believe me.*

"You're right sweetheart. Sometimes I forget myself when I'm with you." She settled her hand possessively on his big thigh. Steeled herself against the delicious spicy warmth of him at her back. He deserved full marks for playing along.

Maisie's smile remained firmly in place. "I'll send Raoul up. Oh, and Con, if you want to go shirtless again, that's just fine."

"You don't have to really go shirtless, you know." Lizzie sat in front of the dressing table mirror, trying to get the comb through her snarled hair.

"I'm a performer under contract. I wear what the director tells me to."

She glanced at his reflection in the mirror. Was he smiling? "Well, I'm the real director here and I'm telling you to wear a shirt."

"What if I don't want to?" He buckled his black leather belt.

"If you don't want to, then don't," she snapped. "I just think it's rather undignified." The waistband of his Italian slacks sat low enough to reveal the top of the fine line of black hair below his belly button. Low enough to be unpleasantly suggestive.

"Since when are you concerned about me being dignified? I figure this whole trip is designed to rob me of any false dignity I might have assumed. And you know what? I'm okay with that. I guess dignity isn't all that important to me in the grand scheme of things."

He moved up behind her, his low-slung waistband clearly visible in mirror. He put his hands on her shoulders and started to massage. "But I think it's sweet that you still care enough about me to defend my rights."

"I don't care about you one bit. If you want to prance around half naked it's fine by me. Go for it." She deliberately avoided looking at his broad fingers as they dug into the tender knots at the base of her neck.

"Jesus, you're wound up. Did you sleep at all last night?"

"Yes." *No.*

Not a frigging wink. She'd rather die than let him know that, though. She glanced at his face in the mirror.

"What are you laughing at?"

"I'm not laughing."

"Your eyes are laughing." She bristled, tightened up the shoulders he was trying to loosen.

"I'll tell them to stop. Relax, let your shoulders go."

She pushed her shoulders down, bent her neck forward and closed her eyes. Con had magic fingers and could zero in on a tension point from fifteen paces. "You've missed your calling, you know," she moaned, as he unkinked a hump beside her spine. "You could have been a masseur."

"Maybe I'll be one yet."

"I'm serious. I've had a lot of professional massages, especially out at Las Gordas, and you're better than any of them. It's amazing how you can be so gentle and so firm at the same time."

She instantly regretted the compliment. One with sexual implications, no less. "You could hang out a shingle, Come and Get Conned. I'm sure you won't have trouble attracting female customers."

Her barbed suggestion caused a slight hiccup in his massaging rhythm, then he continued with renewed vigor. "You wouldn't mind your husband putting his hands all over other women?"

"You're not my husband." Why did it hurt to say that?.

"I will be soon." He dug his thumbs into her neck with insistent pressure.

"Not for long."

A movement inside the door made her start. "Raoul!"

When had he come in and how much had he heard? Con's hands fell from her shoulders. He hadn't heard Raoul either.

"Hey," said Con.

"Hey yourself," replied Raoul, giving his bare chest a lingering once-over. "What're you trying to do, raise the temperature around here even higher?" He fanned himself, straight-faced.

"Maisie's orders. Do I look like an ass?"

"Best piece of ass I've seen in weeks. But we digress. I have work to do." He turned to Lizzie, still poker-faced. "Heard you need some primping. Can see it's true. You look like you've been in a boxing ring. Where's your icepack?"

"What icepack?"

"The one you are supposed to keep ready to reduce puffiness around your eyes in the morning."

"I didn't know I was supposed to have one."

"Ignorance of the law is no defense. They've probably got some iced-up shrimp downstairs we could use instead."

Con chuckled.

"Hey, I'm just kidding." He smiled, revealing unnaturally even white teeth between his thin lips. "There can be a lot of tension on a set and I like fooling around. Don't take me too seriously. Anyway, the hairdresser still hasn't shown up, so I'm doing double duty again. If things get ugly, we can go into my personal wig collection."

"Raoul does celebrity impersonations. In drag," said Con. "Goes onstage at the Copa."

Lizzie forced a laugh. She snuck a nervous glance at Con, who was slicking back his hair with a comb, biceps artfully displayed by the motion.

Raoul savored the view with her for a moment.

"I don't really see her in the Monroe or the Joan Crawford, do you?" He raised an eyebrow at Con. "Maybe the Veronica Lake?" He lifted up a semi fried hank of Lizzie's frizzy, flattened hair. "But you're definitely going to need one of my wigs if you keep trying to straighten. This humidity is a red-hot bitch."

"I like it curly." Con put his comb down on the dressing table in front of her. "I think Lizzie's hair is beautiful in its natural state. Wild and lovely, just like her."

He leaned in, all spicy scent and warm muscle, and planted a featherlight kiss on her cheek. Left her skin humming and her face heating. Bastard. "You always look beautiful to me, babe," he said. "See you downstairs.

She noted with deep satisfaction that he picked up a shirt on his way out.

"You're a lucky woman," said Raoul after Con had left the room.

"Yeah," said Lizzie, with no conviction whatsoever. How much had Raoul overheard? And what might he do with that information?

"So, shall we wash it and see what happens?"


"Lizzie, darling!" Maisie beckoned to her from the floodlit dining room.

She came down the stairs rigid with self-awareness since she'd noticed a camera trained right on her. Raoul had used some kind of greasy gel on her hair that made it hang in stringy tendrils about her shoulders. She looked like a wet wood nymph. He'd talked her into wearing cutoff jeans by some SoHo designer and a halter top with a built in bra, so she was a wet wood nymph who'd dipped into Daisy Duke's wardrobe. She'd been rather impressed with her swamp-sexpot look in the age-spotted bedroom mirror, with Raoul standing behind her claiming jealousy. In full view of the crew, with 3200 Kelvins of artificial daylight blasting her from every direction, she felt like a balloon in the Macy's Thanksgiving Day parade.

"Wow." A grin spread across Con's face. "I like this look."

She cringed at the blush creeping up her chest, which was pushed into view by a large quantity of industrial-strength underwire.

Maisie stood off to one side, grinning like the Cheshire cat. "Cut!" She strode forward. "Goodness,

Lizzie, Raoul does get creative doesn't he? Shame it took so long, but I imagine it was a lot of work." She picked up a clump of "wet look" hair. "I was just telling Con about our plans for the day. We're going to drive over to Mudbug Flats—" She lingered over the name a bit— "after breakfast. You two are taking a sweet little white Jeep we've rented. Of course, they'll be a cameraman in the car with you, but the rest of the crew will be in a van."

Maisie paused to look at her clipboard. Lizzie paused to regret ever coming up with this stupid idea.

She glanced at Con. He stared rather too intently at his cup of coffee.

"So, darling, the only snag is that when we tried to scope out the exact location, we couldn't find it, so Con will have to show us the way."

Con seized his cup and took a sip, without looking up. His shirt was on and buttoned.

"Your family will be expecting us, I imagine?" Maisie looked at Con.

Family? Lizzie felt a drip of sweat trickle down her back. It hadn't really sunk in that Con could have a family of real people. He certainly never mentioned them. What would they be like? What on earth would they think of her? She swallowed hard.

"No one's expecting me." Con's voice was throaty. "I've been gone a long time. Haven't stayed in touch."

Maisie stared at him, her smooth brow furrowed. "Reallllly?" she said slowly. "So this is sort of a prodigal-son-returns type of piece, then?"

Con licked his lips. No sign whatsoever of his usual polished charm. "I don't know what kind of piece it's going to be."

"But you will be able to find the place?"

"If it's still there, I can find it." He pressed his lips together. Lizzie tried to catch his eye but couldn't.

"Alright then, we'll go there and see what we see. Make a day of it." Maisie smiled brightly. "Breakfast!" She indicated a spread on the table. "Let me get out of the shot for a moment."

Con seemed to recover himself as Lizzie sat down with a plate of spiced sausages and scrambled eggs.

"Looking forward to seeing the old place?" she said brightly. Took a bite of her eggs. Squinted under the harsh spotlight.

"I haven't been back in so long, I don't know what to expect." His worried brown-eyed gaze threatened her defenses.

*Don't fall for it. Picture him chuckling about you with Raoul over the free weights.*

"I understand. Change can be so traumatic. I hardly recognize the block on East 66th Street where I grew up.." She smiled, bracing herself against any unwelcome emotion.

She noticed Maisie snap to attention and give some kind of signal to Dino. Maisie strode forward and sat down at the table next to Con, opposite Lizzie. Lizzie braced herself.

"Morning, Lizzie, Morning, Conroy," she said, brightly. A kind of 'on-air' glow made her smile shine whiter. She spoke to Con. "We're all very excited to be here with you for this little homecoming. As you know, Lizzie grew up in a luxury brownstone in one of New York City's finest neighborhoods. As cousins we spent many beautiful Christmases gathered around the fresh-cut tree in the magnificent living room of that house, surrounded by Van Dykes and Gainsboroughs."

"In a way it was the end of an era, a time of unsurpassed luxury and genteel living, when the Hathaway family was riding high on the success of the company founded by Lizzie's grandfather, Ezreel Hathaway."

Con, who had retained something of a poker face during this barrage of backstory, couldn't keep his lips from twitching with mirth at the mention of Grandpa Ezreel.

"Rising from the ashes of the depression, the Hathaway company brought new advances in sanitation into the homes of millions and created jobs in all fifty states. Now after decades as a beacon in American industry, the company is gone, the workers laid off, and the Chairman and CEO Ronald Hathaway—" She pressed a slim hand to her breast. "My uncle and Lizzie's father is facing a jail sentence for stock fraud. Unbowed by the disgrace to our family, Lizzie has boldly struck out on her own and claimed a new life with you, Conroy."

Lizzie squirmed as sweat tickled her back. She glanced at Con, who gave every appearance of having been a professional poker player at some point in his checkered past. Entirely possible, of course. Though his eyes were fixed on Maisie, somehow his entire posture and bearing seemed to project one thought.

*I told you so.*

Lizzie gritted her teeth.

"So, Conroy, how do you feel about marrying into such a famous—now almost infamous—family?"

Lizzie tensed.

"People are people," he said. "When I met Lizzie, I knew she was the woman for me." He cocked his head, exuded confident charm.

Yeah, right. *That's my kind of money* was your only thought.

"Now, Conroy, Lizzie was still a wealthy woman, with the expectation of a large inheritance when you met her."

Lizzie's last bite of sausage lodged in her throat.

"How did you react when you found out she was wiped out in the stock scandal?"

"It was a shock, of course, but Lizzie and I both feel it's for the best." He leaned into Maisie a little.

Lizzie's eyes widened.

"Lizzie and I want to live a simple life. As she'll tell you herself, she's never had expensive tastes. She's looking forward to living like a normal person for a change. To having car payments and mortgage payments and having to save for vacations. We're excited about building our own American dream."

Lizzie realized her jaw was hanging open. If she wasn't mistaken that was almost word for word the little speech she'd given on that terrible night. When she still believed in Con and thought they could make a life together. That moment of desperate hopefulness rang in her heart. Stung her with fresh pain at how totally she'd loved him.

"And *Celebrity Access* is delighted to be able to set that dream in motion with a wedding you'll never forget." Maisie beamed.

*Please don't talk to me.* Lizzie tried desperately to gather her thoughts, to catch her breath. She could feel Maisie getting ready to launch a missile in her direction, and she couldn't take the heat. She caught Con's eye and shot him a pleading glance.

Con cleared his throat. "It was Lizzie's idea to come back here to Louisiana. We're from very different backgrounds, and Lizzie wanted to see where I'm from."

"Where you're from," repeated Maisie, in a sonorous imitation of Barbara Walters. "Did you grow up in an antebellum mansion like this one?" She arched a slim brow.

"No." Con narrowed his eyes slightly. "No, I grew up in much…simpler surroundings."

"A stark contrast, I imagine, to the lap of luxury that nurtured your fiancé?"

"No doubt."

"You told me earlier, Conroy, that you haven't been home in a long time." Maisie lowered her voice, leaned forward. "Is this homecoming somewhat difficult for you?"

Con didn't flinch. "It was Lizzie's idea, like I said, but she's right. It's something I've put off far too long."

"And on that note, we have a journey to make. A journey to Conroy's hometown. A little place in bayou country, known to its inhabitants as Mudbug Flats." Maisie held her smile in place for a count of three. "Cut."

Con leaned back in his chair, obviously relieved the inquisition was over. Lizzie's head buzzed with his words—her words—that she'd said in another lifetime.

"A good start, I think. Thank you, Conroy." Maisie looked disgustingly pleased with herself. In a pale beige power suit that set off her rather subtle coloring, she was elegant and composed. A perfect on-air interviewer. Lizzie could already envision the fifty year retrospective of her illustrious career in journalism, beginning with her very first on-air story…

*This one.*

She closed her eyes and willed away an incipient headache. "Let's go." She wanted to get this Mudbug Flats ordeal over with and get back to the world of hand-trimmed seamed silk stockings and artfully arranged roses that was at least familiar.

*Twenty five thousand dollars. You can do it.*

# 15

**"If** it's still there, it's down the end of this road." The hair on the back of Con's neck stood on end as he steered the Jeep into the cool shadows of the familiar cypress swamp. He'd half expected the trees to have blown away or sunk or been cut down. They weren't all that far from the big house where they were staying, but it felt like another world. Neat trailers with cars in their driveways flanked the narrow road and reassured him that they were still in ordinary America, not on a trip into a murky underworld he might not come back from alive. He was glad most of the homes looked tidy and well kept. He didn't want Lizzie, or anyone else, to get the wrong impression.

Though why he should care, he had no idea.

"So is this Mudbug Flats?" Lizzie's voice sounded tight.

"Not yet. Mudbug Flats is kind of the end of the line. We'll get there soon."

The line of houses came to an end and trees crowded the road. They went a stretch of half a mile or more without any sign of human habitation. They had the windows up to keep the A/C in and the bugs out, but he itched to roll them down and inhale the sweet honey smell of the swamp, to fill his ears with the lively bustle of birds and insects. Right now he could feel the camera trained on his right ear as he drove. Could smell Dino's acrid sweat.

As they emerged from the darkest grove of trees his stomach tightened. His mind expected to see the pale blue walls of Tim LeJean's old place. Nothing.

"This is the town." His voice caught as the Jeep hung up on a pothole in the road and they lurched forward. Lizzie steadied herself with a hand on the dash.

"What town? I don't see anything."

*Me either.* A nasty cold sensation snuck up his back. Miss Dee's store used to be right there on the left, big oil drums of produce stacked in front of the porch, fishermen smoking in the plastic chairs outside. He didn't see anything there now except an overgrown clearing. Was the town totally destroyed? Gone?

No. A wall appeared through the thick cypress canopy and came into view as they drove further. "That's the Gaudry place." Relief loosened his chest. Joe Gaudry's cabin looked solid and immovable as ever on its high pilings, sun beating down on the gray wood. "Shall we go see if anyone's home?" He had a powerful urge to talk to someone. Even mean old Joe Gaudry. Get a heads-up on what to expect.

Procrastinate.

"No, let's keep going to your place. We can come back."

"Okay." No turning back now.

*Would Danny be there?*

A rocket flash of anticipation surged through him and stung his fingers. A painful swell of hope and fear made him grip the steering wheel tighter.

*You abandoned him.*

Shame crept over him, and a host of shadowy memories loomed like the ancient cypress. A smart new trailer on the right caught his eye, and he wondered who lived there. Two yellow lawn chairs flanked a colorful kid's wading pool. A neat ring of yellow flowers surrounded a statue of the blessed virgin.

*Holy Mary, mother of God, pray for us sinners, now and at the hour of our...*

The Jeep slammed into another pothole. The blacktop had deteriorated once they entered Mudbug Flats. Not surprising, since the population seemed to have largely vanished. He glanced at Lizzie.

"You alright?" The look of genuine concern in her eyes touched him someplace that hurt.

"I don't know," he replied honestly. The camera was trained on him, but somehow it didn't bother him. It felt almost natural, like the eye of God.

God? What the hell was he thinking about God for? Was God now haunting the swamp he'd abandoned all those years ago?

He realized his chest was heaving. The click of his mother's rosary beads flashed into his memory.

Holy Mary, *mother*...

He slammed on the brakes. "I can't do this."

"What?" Lizzie lurched forward then turned to him, tucking a tendril of hair behind her ears.

"I didn't tell you... I don't... I can't..." He couldn't formulate words or thoughts as painful memories rushed his brain. Thoughts he'd shoved down and locked up for years pushed to the forefront of his consciousness.

Lizzie's hand touched his arm, her fingers soft, squeezing the skin.

"It's okay." She sounded wary, like she didn't believe it.

"It isn't," he whispered. He could hear the camera whirring. "It isn't okay."

"Con," she said softly. "I don't know what's out there for you, but I do know that you need to face it." She squeezed his arm again.

Their eyes met. For once there wasn't a trace of anger, malice or cruelty in her face. Just compassion. "You know you do."

Something stirred in his heart, and he nodded and jerked the stick shift back into drive.

What was he afraid of? The old man and his fists? The camera was protection, not that he needed it anymore. He wasn't a skinny kid cowering under the house. He took a deep breath.

Danny wouldn't be there. He'd be twenty-one by now, gone off to lead his own life, if he'd lived long enough to

have one. The grim realization brought an emptiness that
almost passed for calm.

Lizzie's hand stayed on his arm as he drove. She
rubbed it, intending to be reassuring, but her touch stirred
up more anxiety. She'd regret this maybe more than he
would.

He wasn't going to be able to play it the way she
wanted.

His blood pressure ratcheted as he noticed Remy's
house was gone. Just the stilts were left, poking up out of
black dirt. The road itself was dirt now too, flecked with
an occasional hunk of tarmac, but looking like it washed
out regularly.

And there it was.

Nothing.

He threw the car into park, jerking them all forward
again.

One ragged wooden stilt stuck up out of the muddy
dirt.

Nothing and no one there.

"This is the place," he muttered. So low he could
barely hear his own voice. "Must have washed away."

Lizzie had a hand pressed to her mouth.

A terrible wave of relief swept over him, followed by
an undertow of guilt. Was this really it?

Oh, yes. He could feel pain and anger still lodged in
the damn trees.

He jumped out of the car. The ground squelched
beneath his feet. Wetter than it used to be, sinking into the
swamp around them. The road continued on through the
trees, but not for much further, he'd bet.

All gone. Except the memories, and he'd sure tried to
get rid of those. As shadows of the past crowded toward
him, he stiffened his back, like a gladiator ready to fight
for his life in the ring. He was angry as hell and done
keeping quiet. If Lizzie didn't like it she had no one but
herself to blame.

She climbed out the Jeep and picked her way toward
him. Her sandals sank into the dark mud.

"Home sweet home," he said coolly.

She hugged herself. Smacked at a mosquito on her arm. Her trendy outfit left her exposed and her forehead creased into a pained expression that softened him. Almost.

What had she expected? Lizzie figured it would be a shack in a swamp and here they were, the remains of a shack in a swamp. She was relieved there were no actual people here, but she'd never really thought there would be.

So where was her thrill of victory?

Con walked toward what was left of the stilt foundation and she followed, stick-littered mud squishing under her feet.

"This was the house," he said, scratching his head. He seemed to have regained his cool. "Up on stilts, 'cause as you can see, it gets wet around here. Two rooms." He gave a grim little smile that felt like a stab in her gut. "This what you expected?"

She nodded. Bit her lip.

"The bayou's right back there. You can see it if you're up a bit higher. We used to get around by boat. Didn't have a car except for one time when my dad won a few dollars in the lottery. Gone soon enough though."

He rested his hand on the blackened wood stump of the one remaining stilt. Stared right at her, his eyes black and focused.

Cool? He'd turned cold as ice.

She shuddered.

*Are you happy now?* His angry stare demanded the question.

Shame heated her face and scattered her thoughts. Had she thought it would be funny that he came from what was—at least to her—grim poverty?

"I'm sorry," she whispered.

"What for? It's not your fault I grew up dirt-poor. That some days I didn't eat. That my parents were alcoholics." He didn't move. Didn't blink.

After a long pause he looked down at the dark earth, then back up at her. "It's not your fault that my dad killed my mom, beat her to death."

Her blood froze.

Con stared, black eyes seeing right through her, into some horrible other world. "He said it was an accident, that she fell out of the boat. Drowned. But I saw him do it. I was right there the whole time. Watching. Just like you're watching me now."

Lizzie shuddered. Groped for words. For breath.

"And I lied. Lied for two goddam years. Kept his filthy secret and betrayed my mother's memory. Scared of his fists. Scared of being alone. Scared to death and wishing I was dead."

He hadn't moved a muscle.

Her hands shook and her breath came in gulps.

"He may be out there right now, walking around with blood on his hands. But I'm done keeping his secret." He stared at her, eyes fierce, voice low. "I'm done keeping his secret."

She tried to speak, but no words came out.

Finally Con broke the stare, shook his head and blew out a blast of air.

"I told you it was a long story, but it's not so long after all, is it? Just a few words."

She struggled for air. "Let's go. We'll leave right now. Go back to New York." Her voice was shaking.

"No. No, we won't." The resolve in his dark eyes stole her breath. "We're here now. I've been running from this place half my life, and I'm not running anymore."

At that moment the van carrying the rest of the crew rattled into view. Lizzie wasn't sure whether to be relieved or annoyed.

She wanted to reach out to Con, but his rigid bearing dared her to try it, like she'd get an electric shock if she touched him. She held up a hand to shield her eyes from the sun. She realized Dino was still rolling, recording everything.

Maisie leaped out of the white van, clipboard in hands. "This the place?" She looked disapprovingly at the black stump next to Con. "Not much left, is there?"

"Um, Maisie." Dino took the camera off his shoulder. "You need to see this."

"See what? There isn't anything to see."

"The footage. Con just… um." He looked at Con, then at Maisie. "You need to see it, that's all."

Maisie and Dino climbed into the van. Lizzie walked toward Con, slow, rigid and awkward. "Why didn't you tell me?"

"Did you really want to know?" His voice was quiet, his face expressionless.

*No.* "Yes. Of course. How can you carry a secret like that?"

"By burying it down real deep and pretending it isn't there." He looked down at the black mud, his voice toneless.

"By pretending you're someone else?" she whispered.

He met her gaze. "Yes."

The back doors of the van exploded open. "What do you mean by turning off the camera?" screeched Maisie at Dino. "Keep filming and don't stop until I tell you."

Lizzie cringed as Maisie stalked up to them, pale eyes flashing.

"Conroy—" Maisie turned to make sure Dino was filming. "Conroy, you've just shared some very painful revelations." She positioned herself so as not to block the camera's view of either Con or Lizzie. "Is it a relief to get this dark secret off your chest?"

He just stared at her.

Maisie sucked in a breath. "Your father killed your mother, right here on this spot."

"Yes."

"How does that make you feel?"

Again he just looked at her, as if he didn't understand the question.

"Do you feel angry?"

"Yes."

"Do you feel sad?"

"Yes."

*Leave him alone.* Lizzie fought the urge to take his hand, which hung by his side only inches from hers. She still didn't dare touch him. The whole situation seemed hotwired, explosive.

"Did your father ask you to lie for him?"

"There was no asking," said Con, face composed. "He told us what to say, and we knew better than to cross him."

"He used to beat you?"

"All the time."

Maisie's overdone expression of compassion made Lizzie's hands clench into fists.

"You said *us* just now. Who else was there? Did you have brothers and sisters?"

A long pause drew out into a painful silence. Mosquitoes buzzed in the thick hot air, and Lizzie felt one sting her right ankle. She didn't move.

"Yes. I have a brother." Con's voice was hoarse.

"Where is he now?"

"I don't know."

"When did you last see him?"

"Ten years ago." His voice cracked. His bearing was still rigid, regal, hostile even. But Lizzie could feel something breaking inside him. Her hand itched to take hold of his.

She'd brought him here, thrown him into this hell of past nightmares, and now she wanted to comfort him?

*She didn't have the right.*

"What was his name?"

"Danny."

Lizzie could see Maisie's growing irritation at Con's terse answers. Maisie tucked a stray piece of fine hair behind her ear and took a deep breath.

"Tell us, Conroy. When did you leave this place and how?"

Con shifted. Lizzie shifted too, a semiconscious mirroring of his movement. The spongy mud had crept up into her sandals.

"I left here when I was fourteen. My dad had beaten me, like he always did, for doing something, or not doing something, or for just being—I don't even remember what it was about—but I knew at that moment that the next time he hit me, I was going to hit back." Con raised a hand and wiped it over his mouth. "I knew I was going to hit back and try to kill him." He stared off into the dark swamp. "So one of us would be dead, either him or me. I'd be dead, or a murderer. So I had to go. I just took off. Didn't take nothing with me. Just left and didn't come back."

"And you left your brother behind." Maisie spoke very quietly, which gave the words the force of a secret, an accusation.

Con's sweat stung Lizzie's nostrils. Her own perspiration trickled down her back like a scratching nail.

"I left him behind. I told him I was leaving and that I couldn't take him with me. I didn't know how to survive on my own, let alone with a kid, and I figured things might be easier for him with me gone. More to eat with one less person around." He hesitated, looked at the ground, then lifted his eyes and looked right at Maisie. "I rationalized it." Lizzie could see his chest heaving beneath his shirt. "I'll never forgive myself for that. Never."

"Did you ever try to get in contact again, with either of them?"

"No."

Lizzie shuddered.

"Do you want to find out what happened to them?"

Con's Adam's apple moved as he swallowed. "Yes."

They all stood like statues for a moment. Lizzie could almost hear the blood humming in her head like the mosquitoes outside it. Maisie shoved her hair back. "Cut. Thanks, Conroy, I'm sure that was hard for you. So shall we go talk to the neighbors, see what they know about your family?"

Con looked at her for a moment, then nodded. His expression serious and dignified. Very controlled.

"Alright, let me just talk to the crew, and we'll roll to the next house down the road." She strode back to the van, all business.

Lizzie pressed her hand over her mouth. Spoke through her fingers. "I had no idea."

"Of course you didn't. Why would you?" He wasn't looking at her. "It's weird how clean the place looks.

There used to be a rusty boat hull I slept in sometimes, right over there." He turned and nodded at a patch of woods. "I'll bet you were hoping for some junk to give the place a colorful redneck flavor. Sorry to disappoint."

Lizzie bit her lip. His tone was cruel. Worse yet, he was right. How could he talk so normally after that revelation? But of course it wasn't a revelation to him. It was something he'd carried with him, every day, for the last ten years.

"Maybe the house got washed away in a hurricane," she rasped.

"Yeah. Most people would have come down here to check on the place after a big storm. See if their family was okay, if they needed help, don't you think?"

His look challenged her to respond.

"I... I..." She didn't know what to say. There were no right answers.

"I didn't." He let out a harsh sound somewhere between a laugh and a growl. "Deep down, I was hoping the place—and everyone in it—was gone. Washed from the face of the earth. Then maybe my guilt would be gone too."

He wiped a hand over his mouth. "But nothing's ever really gone, is it? It lives on in here." He tapped his forehead. "You can't get rid of that." He shook his head. "I've damn sure tried."

He stared around him, and Lizzie bit her tongue. Sure that anything she said would be a mistake.

"Come see the bayou." He reached out his hand. She looked at it like a snake that might bite, then gingerly took it. He gripped her hand hard, crushing her fingers together. She caught her breath and stumbled after him as he pulled her past the footprint of the house, into some scraggly undergrowth. He pushed through some damp, scratchy branches. "None of this brush was here. Place must have been uninhabited for years." A branch scratched her arm and a twig poked at her exposed toes. Her hair snagged, and she wrenched it loose.

"There it is."

Just through the thicket, they emerged on the bank of a river. The mud oozed thicker, closing over her toes, but

Con didn't seem to notice as he pulled her right to the edge. Murky blackish water gleamed in the midday sun. Lizzie shivered, despite the heat. Con gripped her hand with force, no hint of tenderness.

"It's beautiful, isn't it?"

Beautiful? No. Strange and terrifying. All that glittering dark water looked like a bottomless chasm. An abyss that held at least one skeleton.

"Look, a heron."

He pointed with his free hand as a huge, Wedgewood-blue bird took flight from a branch high above their heads. Lizzie flinched as it dove like a movie-screen pterodactyl, menacing in its great size and eerie color. Its beak cleaved the shining water, then with a massive flapping and splashing, it soared up again to the treetops.

"I haven't seen one of those in years. I spent hours studying their fishing technique, trying to figure out how to do that. Great way to get wet and come up empty-handed." He stared up at the now empty sky. "I always wished I could fly like a bird."

How could he be so calm? Carry on a normal conversation as if he hadn't just declared himself—on camera—to be witness to a murder? It was a burden he'd lived with and carefully hidden. Had spared her—until now.

She bit back tears that threatened.

Angry speech and rustling in the undergrowth heralded the arrival of Dino and Maisie.

"We didn't know where you went," hissed Maisie. "Why didn't you wait for the camera?"

"Didn't think of it. Sorry," said Con. Cool as the rippling water. "I was showing Lizzie my home. This is where I really lived, out here on the bayou."

"Are there alligators in it?" asked Maisie, wriggling her way into the shot.

"Sure." Con flashed an alligator smile.

Lizzie searched the undergrowth anxiously, her skin prickling. He softened his grip on her hand, gave it a gentle squeeze. "You can never be quite sure what to expect around here."

Lizzie swallowed, took in a deep breath.

"Want to see how Mudbug Flats got its name?"

"Yes," said Maisie. "I can see it's flat. And mudbug is a colloquialism for crayfish, isn't it?"

Con flashed another gator grin. "That's right. A *colloquialism*." His heavy emphasis on the word made it sound ridiculous.

He dropped Lizzie's hand and moved a couple of feet along the bank. He crouched down and reached right into the mud. Pulled his hand back with a wriggling thing in it.

"Here."

Lizzie cringed as he held it out to her, all flailing claws and spikes. He looked at her, waiting for her to take it.

"You got to watch out for the claws. They'll give you quite a pinch."

It was a challenge, and she knew it, but she couldn't bring herself to touch the nasty greenish-brown lobster-y thing.

"May I?" Maisie held out her slim hand.

Con placed the creature gently in it, and Maisie closed her hand around its tail. Beady black eyes surveyed the humans and claws waved.

"The tail meat is *delicieux*. You can boil 'em in salt water, or just eat 'em raw if you're really hungry."

"Raw?" Maisie sounded curious. Lizzie's stomach curdled. Was Maisie going to snap its head off and eat sushi right there? "I'll ask the chef to procure some. Perhaps we can eat them for dinner tonight." She handed it back to Con, casual as if it was a handkerchief she'd borrowed.

"I can procure some right now, if you like." He said, expressionless, holding the squirming creature. "They're all around us. Easy to spot if you know what to look for."

"I think we have bigger fish to fry," said Maisie softly.

Con swallowed. "Yeah, I guess we do." He put the crayfish back in its burrow and wiped his hand on his pants. "I guess we do."

# 16

Con pulled the Jeep up in front of the nice-looking place with the yellow flowers outside and jumped out, palms sweating. He waited for Dino to get his camera going, then climbed the steps to the front door. Lizzie hung back until prompting from Maisie pushed her into the shot too. He had no idea who lived here, but there was one good way to find out.

He knocked.

"Coming." A woman's voice. The door opened to reveal a pretty girl with a baby on her hip and a perplexed expression on her face. She glanced behind Con and Lizzie to the camera, and her hand flew to her mouth.

"Oh my gosh, did we win the Powerball?"

"No, no, nothing like that, I'm afraid," said Con. "Sorry to get your hopes up." He held his hand out, and she shook it gently as he spoke. "I'm Conroy Beale. I used to live just up the road." He indicated the direction with a nod. "This is Lizzie, my... fiancée." Fists clenched, Lizzie looked ready to explode with tension. "We're visiting the place where I grew up, part of a TV show they're doing on our wedding." He pointed to Dino and Maisie.

The baby started fussing.

"I'm Charlene. Pleased to meet you. Um, won't you come in?" Her expression was turning to one of alarm.

"Oh, that's okay, we don't want to impose, but would you mind if I ask you a couple of questions?"

"Um, sure." She shifted the baby on her hip and pushed her fingertip in its mouth. She had long dark hair and skinny shoulders. The baby was a curly blonde cutie with fat thighs.

"How long have you lived here?" Damn, he sounded like Maisie.

"About five years now. My husband works a shrimp boat down the bayou "

An irrational flare of hope soared through Con. "What's your husband's name?" *Danny?*

"Luke LeBlanc." His heart sank. "He won't be home for a couple of days. He's lived around here longer than me. I'm from Thibodaux originally."

Con racked his brain. Luke LeBlanc didn't ring any bells.

"Do you know what happened to the people who used to live down there?" He cocked his thumb back up the road.

She shook her head and pursed her lips. "Nobody's lived down there long as I've been here. Too wet now, I guess. The whole area's sinking. Luke says we'll have to move sooner or later." The baby let out a cry of distress, and she moved it to her other hip. "You should talk to Mr. Gaudry up the road. He's been here for ever."

Con nodded. "Thanks. I remember him. He still shoot squirrels if they get up on his roof?"

She chuckled and bit her lip. "Yup. Shoots pretty much anything. He's a mean old cuss. Hates kids." She lifted the baby higher.

"Hasn't changed then." Con smiled at her. "Your baby's very cute."

"Thanks."

He managed to get out an awkward goodbye and their entourage backed away to the cars.

Lizzie was white as a sheet. What was she all worked up about? This cozy little homecoming was all her idea. "You look like you're about to pass out. Are you running a fever or something?"

"No." she shook her head. Her gelled curls bounced around her shoulders.

"Your lipstick's smudged. Let me fix it." He reached into his pocket for a tissue, and wiped a smear off her upper lip. "Joe Gaudry shot our pig." He glanced at Dino, who still had the camera trained on them. "I told you we had a pig, right?"

"Yes, I think you did." Her lips tightened.

"Didn't have it for long." He pushed the tissue back into his pocket. "My dad won it in a poker game. It was just a baby. Danny and I caught food for it, fenced it in with sticks. It was a smart creature, I tell you." He tilted his head. "Affectionate too. Kind of a like a pet. Anyway, we had it a couple of months, and it was getting big. It got too strong for our fence, broke out and ran off up the road when no one was around. It got into Joe Gaudry's garden—he was proud of his peppers—and he shot it." Lizzie's moue of distaste gave him grim satisfaction. "My mom cooked it, but I couldn't eat it."

Lizzie looked away.

*Aw, but sweetheart, I'm just giving you what you want.* Did he feel sorry for her right now? Not really. He was working hard to hold himself together and being mean helped. Now he could see why Lizzie was so mean to him all the time.

"What a colorful story," said Maisie, after a short pause.

"Yeah, that's why I told it." He didn't smile. "I figured you'd want some color."

Joe Gaudry must be about a million years old, he tried to reassure himself as they pulled up in front of his house. Of course, that wouldn't necessarily affect his trigger finger. Funny how those old fears came crowding back, even though there was pretty much no way old Joe was going to point a shotgun at him with a camera present.

He half hoped Joe would be out, but the sound of a radio blasting Cajun music put paid to that idea as he stepped out of the Jeep. The old cuss had to have spotted them by now. The dog chained out back was barking up a riot.

Con waited for the cameras—he was getting pretty good at this—and climbed the wooden steps. There were at least ten of them. Old Joe's house was always the highest for miles around.

Lizzie waited at the bottom.

He rapped on the door, right where "Private Property: Don't Get Shot!" was painted in neat white letters.

He hauled in a breath as he heard someone fumbling with a chain on the other side.

"What?" snarled a throaty voice. The door swung open. Jesus, he hadn't changed at all. Hair still speckled gray and slicked right back with pomade.

"Hello, Sir. I don't know if you remember me. My name's Conroy Beale, I used to live just up the road."

"Conroy Beale." The rheumy hazel eyes narrowed. "The same Conroy Beale that let my dog loose and stole oranges from my tree?"

Con ran a hand through his hair. "Um, yes. And I'd like to formally apologize for that unlawful act."

The dog barked on.

The old man didn't say anything. His eyes narrowed further. Con almost wished Maisie would come on up and take charge. He had a feeling Maisie and old Joe were cut from the same cloth.

"I'm back in the area for the first time in years, and I wonder if you know what became of the people who used to live…in my old house."

"You don't know what became of your own family?" One gray eyebrow lifted. Con felt his disapproval like a smack.

He straightened his back. "No. I'm not proud of it, but I'm afraid I don't."

Joe Gaudry studied him for a moment. Looked down at his respectable shirt and pants. "Well, I admit I felt pretty sorry for you and your brother, even if you were both a pair of…" He licked his lips. "But never mind that. You do know your daddy died?"

"Did he?" Relief snuck through him, guilt hot on its heels.

"Yes. More than ten years back."

"Can't be. I left ten years back and he was still alive then."

"Must have died right around the time you left. Hit by a car. Drunk as a lord at the time, of course." He fixed Con with a hard stare. Con flinched. "The other boy, your brother, got sent off somewhere. The boys' home I expect. Don't think there were any other relatives. No one's lived there since. Place fell down, then what was left of it got swept away in one storm or another. Improvement if you ask me. Not that I ever had nothin' bad to say about your mother." Con stiffened. "She was a good woman, minded her own business."

*Yeah, that's what killed her.*

Con took a deep breath. "Did Danny ever come back? My brother? I need to find him."

"Why, you win the lotto?" Joe glanced down at the camera.

"No, nothing like that. Do you know of anyone who might know where he is?"

"Nope."

The dog kept up its barrage of noisy barking, and Con's nerves crackled to get going. "Can I give you my cell phone number in case you hear anything?"

"Don't have a phone. Got no need of one."

The radio launched into a lively dance number.

"Thank you for your time, sir."

The old man gave a single nod, stared at him for a withering second, then closed the door.

Con's blood pounded in his ears as he descended the stairs.

"Didn't get much of that. Damn dog," said Dino, as Con reached the ground. The dog still hadn't let up.

"He didn't say much. My dad's dead, my brother got sent away."

"Where to?" asked Maisie.

"Orphanage, he thinks." His rib cage felt tight, squeezing on his lungs and making it hard to breathe.

Maisie nodded, her pale eyes fixed on his face and her thoughts obviously whirring behind them. "Let's go back to the house and make some phone calls."

"Then you suck the head."

Lizzie grimaced as Con tipped the crawdad's head into his mouth and slurped. "That's the butter."

"You mean the brains."

Con shrugged. "Go on, try it."

With the camera on her and the entire crew gathered around the big wrought-iron table on the moonlit patio, Lizzie didn't feel like she had a choice.

She picked up a boiled red crawdad from the heaped plate, suppressing a shudder of revulsion. It was so...big. Why couldn't they be like tiny shrimp or something? Or big like a lobster so you didn't have to lift it? She snapped it, put the head down on her plate and cracked the shell off the tail.

The meat was tender and tasty. A lot like lobster tail. Con's anxious face broke into a grin as he saw she enjoyed it.

"Good, right?"

"Yes." She couldn't help smiling too. "It's great. But I'm still not sucking the head."

Con, back to the camera, winked at her. "Alright. Maybe later, huh?"

Her face flushed. Raoul let out a raucous laugh that echoed around the crew.

*This was all your idea.*

Con chuckled. "Don't let 'em get cold. That would be a tragedy. Come on everyone, dig in."

The entire crew fell on the steaming mound of bright red crustaceans that the chef had boiled in two giant vats of water. A variety of dipping sauces left everyone with garlic butter running down their chins and hot peppers stinging their taste buds. The conversation meandered from food to the eerie beauty of the moon-drenched garden, to the house.

"Who owns this old place anyway?" said one of the lighting guys.

Gia sucked her fingers. "A lawyer in town. He rents it out though an agency. They do weddings and parties here, and a TV movie was shot here last year."

"It's beautifully maintained," said Lizzie.

Con wiped his mouth with his napkin. "It's just plain beautiful"

"The rooms are very well proportioned." Maisie sucked the "butter" out of a crawdad head without batting an eye. "And the furnishings are really quite extraordinary. Worth an absolute fortune at auction. Genuine American treasures."

"Maisie interned at Christie's auction house in high school," said Lizzie. "The one thing that's still missing is air conditioning. I don't know how the rest of you stand it." Her armpits were soaked, as usual. She'd taken to wearing black so it didn't show so much.

"Doesn't bother me," said Maisie, who apparently didn't have any sweat glands. "But the A/C units are arriving tomorrow. They were booked up today with a convention, but tomorrow Con will think he's back in Canada with his Acadian ancestors." She picked up another crawdad, and looked around the group. Her eyes rested on the running camera. "The Cajuns migrated here from Acadia in Nova Scotia. A proud and fiercely independent people who maintain the cultural traditions of their native France, including an intriguing variant of the language. Did you speak French at home, Con?"

"Nope."

Lizzie, who'd been inwardly rolling her eyes during Maisie's pedantry, wondered if Con even was Cajun. Beale didn't sound particularly French, now she came to think about it.

"It's such a marvelously simple life, here in the swamps," continued Maisie, cracking open her crawdad. "Spiritual almost, in the lack of materialism."

"I think it's called poverty," muttered Lizzie. "Con's childhood doesn't sound all that spiritual to me."

"Well, obviously Conroy's family had its…Its challenges. But just imagine spending the day on the bayou, eating from the hand of Mother Nature, surrounded by the glory of creation…"

Lizzie couldn't suppress a snort.

"Hold on a minute." Con held up his hand. Finished his mouthful. "People down here live just like people in New York—we have TVs and cars and telephones."

"You had electricity in that shack?" Lizzie raised an eyebrow.

"Sure." Con sounded indignant. Then his mouth turned up at the corner. "Okay, so it wasn't turned on all the time, but it was there. Like Maisie said, we've got spiritual light from within, we don't need wattage." He winked.

Lizzie couldn't help chuckling. How did he always manage to make her smile? He was smiling too. In fact, he looked a bit too cheerful for someone who'd just learned his father was dead and his brother had disappeared off the face of the earth. Lizzie didn't know whether to be annoyed or relieved or worried.

As if he heard her thoughts, Con turned to Maisie. "Did you find anything out about my brother?"

Maisie wiped her fingers on a paper napkin. "Gia was on the phone all afternoon. We couldn't find a single trace of him. Social services never heard of him. Is there another name he could have used?"

"I don't think so." Con stiffened.

Lizzie swallowed. "Maybe he went to stay with a friend and they left social services out of it?"

"The woman at social services suggested we check records, you know, births, marriages..."

"Deaths." Con's mouth flattened into a line.

"There's no reason to believe he's dead." Maisie said it softly. Tilted her head to the side. *How sweet and caring of her*. Her blue eyes sparkled with moisture, and a simpering smile flickered across her pale pink lips. Lizzie's skin prickled with irritation.

So Maisie was starting her campaign to seduce Con. They were perfect for each other, both had the emotional depth of an alligator.

Lizzie grabbed Con's hand. "We should go into town and check the records tomorrow." It wasn't so much an act of reassurance as one of self-defense. This was turning into *The Con Becle Show,* and she was getting sidelined. If she didn't watch out, he'd end up marrying Maisie in the final moments of the show and no one would notice she was missing.

Taking her cue, Con shifted closer and wrapped his arm around her shoulder. He kissed her cheek. *Damn.* Why did his lips still spark a tingling reaction that sneaked right into her? His infuriating spicy smell crept up on her too.

"I'd like that." His lips were almost on her ear. "I'm glad you're with me, Lizzie. I couldn't go through this alone."

Her heart squeezed.

Yeah, yeah, cue the violins. "I'm exhausted. I think I'll hit the sack."

Would he follow her? Or would he stay down here chitchatting with Maisie?

"Me too." Con helped her to her feet.

She heaved a sigh of relief.

Of course, being Con, he took his time thanking the chef for the meal and working the room until everyone was smiling.

He really was her exact opposite, wasn't he?

As he finally took her hand and led her up the stairs, the horrible drama of the day's events started to pound in her head.

*This was all her idea.*

What on earth would she say to him now?

# 17

Up in the room, Lizzie stripped down to her black underwear, grateful to have fewer layers between her and the muggy night air. She didn't bother to suck anything in. He'd hardly care what her body looked like after the day they'd had.

Con undressed while she sat on the bed, scratching at the mosquito bite on her ankle.

He washed his face and underarms at the basin. Filled a glass and drank it. Gargled and spat, rinsed it, then held it up. "Want some water?"

She shook her head and drew up her knees, wrapping her arms around them. "You scare me. How can you act so calm after today?"

"What do you want me to do? Break down sobbing?" He tossed his towel over a chair and strode toward the bed. "Move over."

She moved, making room on the bed for him. She couldn't make him sleep on the floor after what she'd dragged him into today. Didn't even want to.

"Would you like a hug?" she asked shyly.

"Why? You think that's going to make me feel better?" He stretched out on the bed, muscles cracking. His onyx stare made hair rise on the back of her neck.

"No, of course not. I don't know." She turned on her side and faced away from him. Her emotions had been pretty much stretched to the limit today, and there was a real danger she might cry. She bit the inside of her mouth hard and dug her fingernails into her palm.

"Hey." He rested his hand on her hip. Her skin tingled under his fingers. "I know you just wanted to have a little fun with me. You didn't know what you were getting into."

"That's for sure." Her words emerged on a sob. She gritted her teeth as a tear crept from behind her squeezed eyelids.

"Don't cry over me. I'm fine. In fact, I'm glad we're here. I've been shit scared of this place for years. Now I'm back, it's just another place. And the old man is dead. It sounds a terrible thing to say, but that's a weight off my mind."

Lizzie turned to face him. He let his hand slide over her hip, soft and reassuring.

"But it's all on camera," she said, her lip quivering. "Surely you don't want the whole world to know…?" She swiped at a tear on her cheek.

"I don't mind." Con looked calm. He smudged her tear away with his thumb. "In a way I'm glad the camera's here, so I can set the story straight. I have a feeling I'm going to be a different person after this whole experience."

"You are? How?"

"Because I'm not pretending any more. I've been pretending since the day I left that patch of ground you saw today. Pretended I was older to get a job, pretended I was someone else so I could get arrested in Mississippi and they wouldn't send me back here. Pretended—"

"You got arrested on purpose?" she cut in.

"Sure." He picked up a curly strand of her hair and toyed with it. "Free food, school classes, you know? I used another guy's name so they wouldn't send me home."

"Oh." Another tear fell. Con leaned in and kissed it away. His lips soft and warm on her skin.

"I lied about my experience to get work as a mechanic. I'd finally found something I was good at, that I had a real knack for, but I didn't have any qualifications. I got used to working the angles, being whoever I needed to be to get by."

His face was inches from hers and she could smell his skin, musky and soothing. He leaned in and kissed her again, this time on the nose.

A strange crumpled sensation pulled at her stomach. Why wasn't she mad?

"I've always lied about my age. I honestly think you are the only person I've ever told my real age to."

"The same as mine," she murmured.

"Exactly. I'm even born in March, like you."

"Pisces?"

A smile crossed his lips. "Yup." He kissed her other cheek "Just like you."

"But we're not alike at all," she whispered, fresh tears welling in her eyes.

"Why not?" He tipped his head back and looked at her, dark eyes narrowed. "Maybe we're more alike that you think."

"Because you've been through all this..." She waved her hand in the air to compensate for words that wouldn't come to her.

"Hard times? Lies? Bullshit? Don't be so sure we're not alike. You're going through all that right now."

"Not like you."

"Sure it is. The circumstances are different, but the hurt is the same. You're all alone, making up crazy stories to hustle up some cash. Do you think they really believe you want to marry me?"

"You don't think they do?"

"I don't know. I think Raoul does. He's a true romantic." His mouth tilted into that familiar crooked smile.

Lizzie squeezed her eyes against the tears but they trickled over her cheeks anyway. Her throat was tight. "I'm sorry, I don't know why I'm crying, I just can't seem to—"

"Hey, that's okay." He stroked her hair. Leaned in and kissed her cheek in a way that made her skin buzz. "It's good to let your emotions out. Don't want to keep them all bottled up inside where they can drive you crazy."

"How come you don't?" She swiped at her eyes with the back of her hand.

"Don't what?" He stroked her shoulder.

"Show emotion? Cry?"

"I don't know. I guess I just don't feel that much anymore. Kept everything battened down so long the bolts are rusted. Don't let that happen to you."

He cupped her cheek, wiped a tear away, then leaned in to kiss her. "I'm glad of our lie," he whispered. "Because I like being with you. I like you, Lizzie."

The next thing she knew, his lips were on hers, hot and forceful, his tongue in her mouth. She shuddered as he gripped her round the waist and pulled her right into him, her belly pressed against his flat stomach.

Hot relief flooded through her as she wrapped her arms around him and hugged him tight. She kissed him back even harder as her hands groped into his hair and her breath came in loud gasps. Too much emotion, too much feeling, all with nowhere to go, and it hurt.

Suddenly they were tugging at each others' underwear and he climbed over her, panting and rolling on a condom he'd rustled up from somewhere. She couldn't think, couldn't talk, didn't know how to do anything but try to press her body against his.

He gave her a rough kiss as he entered her. Something ragged inside her tore a little further, splitting her open and making her cling to him tighter. He pressed against her, grinding, sending shivers of dangerous arousal rippling through her and crashing against the swells of raw emotion. She gripped his neck, gasped and moaned as he increased the tempo, thrusting her deeper and deeper into a frenzy of tortured excitement.

She clawed at his back with her fingertips, wanting him even closer as her teeth grazed his cheekbone and her lips sought his. *Oh, Con. Why do things have to be so complicated?*

He moved inside her more slowly now, rocking her hot, wet and slow. Their hips rolled together, and she wrapped her arms around him and hugged him so tight, not wanting to ever let go.

*I love you.*

The words danced on her lips for a split second before she bit them back.

Those days were over.

But as Con showered her face with tender kisses she couldn't help thinking that they might be at the start of a new day.

A series of hard thrusts and deep tongue kisses pushed her over the edge into an explosive climax. She heard her startled cry followed by Con's groan as he followed her into a post orgasmic realm of breathless silence.

Afterward they lay there, her fingers in his hair as his head rested between her breasts. His hands, one on either side of her torso, held her as if she might try to wriggle away.

"I've missed you, Lizzie," he said, after a long, peaceful silence.

"Missed me? We've been together every minute."

He looked up, hair dipping to his shiny dark eyes. "I've missed being close, being intimate. Affectionate."

She tousled his hair. "Me too."

Something inside her pulled sharply. A tug of warning.

"Con, why did you come after me? I mean, if you really never loved me. Why didn't you write the whole thing off as a deal gone south?"

How could she have been so sure he loved her if all the time he was just acting? No one was that good an actor.

A funny fluttering in her stomach accompanied the thought.

Con hesitated. Licked his lips. He slid sideways off her chest and moved up the bed until his head was level with hers.

He ran his thumb lightly over her lips, then pulled his hand back and shifted up onto his elbow. She heard him inhale.

"My father got my mom started drinking. She didn't drink at all until she met him. He used to brag about it. How she used to be such a prim and perfect little lady until he…" His expression darkened and he looked away.

When he looked back at her, the fierce expression in his eyes made her flinch. "I've always prided myself on being *nothing* like my father. Anything he'd have done,

I'll do the exact opposite. You'll not see me gambling, drinking myself under a table, starting fights. Never. I've never laid a hand on a woman and never will."

He combed his fingertips through her hair, gentle. "But I did give you those first sips of champagne."

Lizzie bristled. She wasn't the naïve innocent he assumed. "You think I never tried alcohol before? I've been dragged along to cocktail parties since I was eight. I probably had my first spiked Shirley Temple before I turned ten. My mother started cocktail hour at four p.m. every day."

"But you didn't. You didn't want to be like her. You were quite happy with a tall cool glass of chocolate milk—" he hesitated, and the corner of his mouth lifted into a smile.

She stiffened, gritted her teeth.

"And I loved that about you. A woman who knows her own mind! You didn't try and impress me with pomegranate martinis and champagne with gold bits floating in it. I'd never met anyone like you, Lizzie. You far exceeded my wildest expectations."

Lizzie's mind raced, trying to process all this information, most specifically the exact usage of the word *loved* in this context. "Loved" as in "I loved her like no other woman" or as in "I loved her Mary-Jane shoes." Her graduate-level classes in English Literature had not provided her with adequate interpretive skills.

"But," he looked sheepish. "You were hard to get close to. Suspicious." He raised an eyebrow. "Wary as a tiger someone's just thrown a fresh, thick juicy steak at. Like, where's the catch?"

"Little did I know," she said coolly.

"Well, exactly." Con shrugged and smiled. "You're a smart cookie."

"Not smart enough, apparently."

"Hey, I had more tricks up my sleeve. Champagne being one of them. A glass here, a glass there, and soon you were bubbling over into my affectionate arms."

His smile threatened to break into a grin.

"You know, you really piss me off, Conroy Beale."

"I'm just being honest. I guess that's new for both of us, but I think it's the best way to go, don't you?"

His wary glance, suddenly shy and boyish, snuck under her skin.

"I guess I do. So you felt guilty about getting me started drinking when your father did exactly the same to your mother."

The whole concept gave her a chill. She was nothing like Con's mother! Some poor downtrodden woman getting beaten senseless by a brutish husband. Goose bumps pricked her arms at the comparison.

"I didn't want to see you going down the wrong road, making poor choices—"

"I hardly think I'd have ended up like her."

"I don't expect she did either. But there was nothing I could do to help her. I could help you."

"You know, you make yourself sound almost heroic," she said, trying to squelch the weird warm sensation growing inside her.

Con's eyes looked distant for a moment. "She always used to say she came from a nice house, a nice family. Said she was rich even. None of us ever believed it, of course, since she was usually pretty buzzed when she came out with that stuff. But looking back, who knows?"

"Where did she come from?"

"I don't know. She was from Louisiana, for sure, but she never talked about where exactly she came from. It was like her whole past just got left behind somewhere. Forgotten. Anyway, if she started talking about the past or anything like that when my dad was around..." he trailed off.

"He'd hit her." Lizzie was surprised by how calmly she said it.

"Yes." Con looked down. "It's sad, I hardly know anything about her at all. Just that she tried to be a good mother to us, and she prayed a lot. Didn't do her a damn bit of good to pray, that's for sure."

"What about your father, where was he from?"

"Right there. Rose up out of the swamp for all I know. His parents died when I was a kid. I don't really remember them. Heavy drinkers too, though. The whole family was pretty much notorious as a bunch of total assholes. Lived on the same patch of swamp by the bayou forever. No stores would lend us credit, and they didn't have any friends. If my parents had other relatives they were all long gone. I guess disappearing without a trace is kind of a family tradition. I don't know how my mom got mixed up with the Beales, but she said my dad was very handsome and charming when he was young."

"Like you."

Con's eyes met hers with a look that ate right into her. "Yeah." He paused, then seemed to see through her into another world. "Like me."

"Well, then I guess I can see how that would happen." She stretched, trying to look casual, as tension crept through her muscles.

He tucked a strand of hair behind her ear. "I'm beat. You should get some sleep. You look tired. I know you had a rough night last night, even if you deny it." He stroked the end of her nose with his thumb. "You'll sleep just fine with my arms around you, though."

She tried to brush off the sensation that rushed through her. "I'm not really sleepy. I think I'll read for a while."

"Alright. I'll be right here if you need me." He gave her a quick, soft kiss on the cheek, then settled his head on his folded arms. "Night night, Lizzie."

"Night, Con."

She eased off the bed and pulled on a satin wrap. Despite the heat, she still had goose bumps. Unease. Too much sensation, too much emotion, too much everything.

She unzipped her suitcase of personal items to rifle around in there for a good engrossing read. In its search for a thick paperback, her hand settled on the little pile of letters she'd found inside the bedpost.

Her heart started beating faster. Why did she feel like she shouldn't read them? She closed her hand around the small stack of envelopes. Her fingertips stung with anticipation, with anxiety. Why? For all she knew they were a bunch of unopened bills.

She glanced back at Con on the bed. He'd rolled over and now lay with his back to her and the light. For some reason she didn't want him to see her reading them. Maybe because it felt like prying?

It wasn't prying. It was…research?

Yes, research into the history of the house. The letters were addressed to a Mr. Thomas Milford at the address of the house. Still, she felt like a spy as she stuck the edge of her nail file into the corner of the envelope and ripped a neat slit along the top.

The thin, yellowed paper tore easily. It was one of those privacy envelopes with the printed interior, and Lizzie inhaled a shaky breath as she drew out the piece of paper inside.

A single sheet of pale blue paper. Just a few lines of careful script, written in blue ballpoint pen.

# 18

*Dear Father,*
*It makes me so sad that we parted on bad terms. I still*
*feel like your little girl, even though I'm all grown up*
*now.*

An uncomfortable lump formed in Lizzie's throat as a
chill crept down her spine.

*I know you don't approve of my choice of husband,*
*but I'm a woman now and old enough to make my own*
*choices. He's very kind to me. I'm sure you'd like him*
*once you got to know him. He's saving money and hopes*
*to buy his own shrimp boat soon. There's a lot of money*
*to be made in shrimp and crabs, not that money is*
*important to me. There's a lot more to life than having*
*money and holding on to it, and I do wish you understood*
*that.*
*But I didn't write to scold, just to say that I miss you*
*and I hope one day soon we'll be friends again.*
*K*

Yeesh. Maybe opening these letters wasn't such a
great idea after all. A black hole had opened up in
Lizzie's stomach.

She glanced up at Con. His shoulders moved slightly
with each long, slow breath. Asleep.

She spread the letters out on the floor. There were six
of them altogether, and it suddenly seemed important to

read them in order. By chance—or because it was on top—she'd started with the first one. She studied the postmarks and noticed with alarm that there was more than ten years between the first and the last.

Someone here had received letters for *ten years* and never opened them?

Her scalp prickled and goose bumps rose on her arms. Part of her wanted to gather the letters up, put them on top of the dresser and...what? Throw them away? Hand them over to Maisie?

Like someone who can't take her eyes off a car wreck—because the car looked so much like her own— she picked up the next envelope and slit it open.

*Dear Father,*

*I never received a reply to my last letter, so I thought I'd write again, just to let you know that things are fine with us. It's odd to be so nearby, yet it's as if there were a thousand miles between us. Things have been hard lately, due to a poor shrimp harvest caused by bad weather conditions and buyers refusing to pay full price for the shrimp that is caught. I don't really understand the business but it looks like my husband will have to wait to buy his own boat. Anyway, we're managing.*

*I have some wonderful news, I'm pregnant! I'm expecting my baby in spring, which is such a perfect time of year for a new life to enter the world. I just wanted to let you know that you're going to be a grandfather.*

*Always your daughter,*

*K*

Oh dear, it was going to be a sob story. Had she expected anything different? Didn't anyone ever run off with the man they loved and live happily ever after, for crying out loud? Was that too much to ask?

Lizzie glanced back at Con. His shoulders moved slightly with the easy breaths of deep sleep.

Did she really want to see the rest of this car wreck?

She looked at the envelopes. They were all the same kind, as if taken from the same box. Who kept the same box of envelopes for ten whole years? This whole thing made her flesh crawl.

Come on, Lizzie. Maybe he gets his shrimp boat after all! Maybe he became shrimp king of the bayou and she was his queen?

She picked up the next envelope in date order. It had dirt on it, possibly from the cataclysm involving the bedpost. She brushed it off, and ripped it open with her nail file.

*Dear Father,*

*I wonder if the magnolias bloomed well this year after all the cool weather? Did John ever paint the arbor green the way you planned? I always thought that would look so beautiful, like the honeysuckle was floating right in mid air.*

*Is your gout still bothering you? It's so odd not to have talked to you in so long, and I do wonder often about how you're doing. Two years is a long time.*

*My baby is so beautiful. We named him Conroy Anthony—*

Lizzie heard a screeching sound in her head and black spots danced in front of her eyes. *Conroy?* How many Conroys could there be in this part of the world? She whipped her head around, breath coming fast, and was relieved to see Con still asleep. *Now she really was prying.* She read on greedily, holding her breath.

*We named him Conroy Anthony after the sailor in that book I used to love when I was a girl. He has black hair just like mine and he's just the sweetest, smartest baby. He laughed yesterday for the first time, and I've never heard such a beautiful sound. My husband is having to deal with the pressure of being a family man. Diapers are so expensive, and the baby will only settle when he's cuddled up in bed next to me, which makes it hard for my husband to sleep so he has to take a drink to help him relax.*

*I'm sure things will settle down soon. I'd love to hear from you if you can find the time to write. You know where I am.*

*Your daughter,*
*K*

There was a long gap between that letter and the next. Almost two years. Lizzie ripped it open with shaking fingers.

*Dear Father,*
*It's been so long since I heard from you that I suspect my letters aren't welcome. Still, you are my father and you always will be. As a mother myself, I understand that.*

*Conroy has a brother who we named after his father. He looks so different from Conroy, his hair almost white blonde and blue eyes like sapphires. Unfortunately he's been sick. He has a cough that won't go away and the doctor charges so much that I could only take him the once.*

*The shrimp harvest was poor again, or so my husband tells me, I don't understand these things too well. I got a job myself at the local store, but with a sick baby to take care of I just couldn't keep regular hours. My husband didn't like me working either, he thinks a man should provide for his family. I'm sure you'd agree.*

*I left everything behind when I got married, and I wonder if you kept my few trinkets, like the pearl necklace from Grandmother Adele and the gold locket with Mama's picture in it? If you could forward those to me, I'd most appreciate it.*

*Your daughter,*
*K*

Lizzie's heart was sinking lower and lower. Was this how it always happened? One minute she's seizing freedom and true love, and the next she's wistfully remembering old garden arbors and wanting to fondle trinkets from her old life.

*Who am I kidding? She wants those things so she can sell them for cash.* Lizzie had a nasty taste in her mouth.

She'd sold most of her trinkets already. The only one she couldn't bring herself to part with was the Bulova watch she'd been given on her eighteenth birthday. Right now its reassuringly familiar face read three a.m.

She picked up the fifth envelope and slit it open. It was from almost a year later.

*Dear Father,*

*You know I wouldn't ask for help if I didn't truly need it. The baby is very sick. He needs a course of antibiotics that costs more than we can possibly afford. Money has been especially tight this last year and I have not been able to work with the baby sick. I've prayed and prayed to the blessed virgin to grant us some relief, but the troubles just seem to pile up, with my husband drinking away what little we have.*

*I know you said I was making a terrible mistake in my marriage, and if it wasn't for my two beautiful boys I'd have to say you were right. I was young and romantic, as you said, and didn't understand the harsh realities of life.*

*Please Father, if you could find it in your heart to send $275, either in cash, or as a postal order, in care of the Dee General Store, I'd be eternally in your debt and I promise I won't ask for more. Please don't send it to the house, and put my name on the envelope, not my husband's.*

*Your daughter,*

*K*

Lizzie pressed her hand to her mouth. How could anyone write such a letter? She's asking for money from her cold hearted bastard of a father who won't even open her letters? The thought turned her stomach. This woman sounded painfully young. She also didn't sound too bright. *Thank God I'm nothing like her at all.*

The ballpoint pen was a reminder that this happened only a couple of decades ago. It had a horribly timeless ring to it.

She'd never write a "Dear Father" letter. What would she call hers though? 'Dad'? She'd never called him Dad. And Daddy just sounded silly once you were over, say twenty-one, and your father had betrayed your trust and bankrupted you and called you a *fat little nobody.*

She had a sudden urge to throw up, but a few deep breaths took care of it.

One more letter. She glanced back at Con and noticed with alarm that he'd rolled over and was now facing her. His frighteningly handsome features were still relaxed in deep sleep, one arm crooked under his head and the other sprawled over the white sheet.

He wouldn't want to see these letters. Wouldn't want to know they existed. He'd looked at them like a nest of poisonous snakes when she first found them. Was it possible that he somehow *knew*?

Inhaling a jittery breath, she picked up the sixth and last letter. Same identical envelope as the others. Same neat writing in a plain, blue ballpoint pen, but everything else had changed.


*Dear Mr. Milford,*

*You've ignored every letter I've sent, and it's like I sent you a piece of my heart and never got it back and now it's bled out and hollow and I don't feel too much pain any more. I know you don't love me, maybe you never did, and now that I'm a woman and a wife I can see that you likely didn't love my mother either. You didn't treat her right and I could see that even as a child. You see I'm a lot less ignorant about the relationships between women and men. Men have more power and they can use their strength to dominate, but don't you believe that you are winning anything of value.*

*I've said a thousand rosaries for you and for my husband and for all mankind and I think they are falling on ears as deaf as yours. Thank Heaven for my two strong young sons, who are the only joy I have left in this world.*

*You were right that choosing my husband was a mistake, but maybe staying with a heartless, cruel man like you who can cut off his only daughter as if she never lived would have been a graver mistake.*

*I don't suppose you've even read any of my letters and*

*I don't expect you'll read this one either.*
   *In sorrow over what has been lost,*
   *K*


   And that was the last one. A chill roamed over Lizzie as she read the bitter, angry words of the last letter.

   Could she really show these letters to Con?

   She bit her lip and slipped the folded bit of paper back in the envelope. Maybe it was better not to know some things.

   The screeching racket of the tree frogs outside made her long to close the windows, but the nighttime air was mercifully cooler.

   There was no way she could lie down and sleep with a secret like this on her conscience.

   "Con."

   "Hmmmm." His mouth shifted but his eyes didn't open.

   She gathered the letters and went to sit on the bed. She put her hand on his warm arm and shook. "Con, wake up."

   "What?" he squeezed his eyes, then cracked one open. The light was in his eyes.

   "The letters, I read them."

   "So what? It's nighttime. Tell me in the morning." He lifted the sheet for her to get in with him.

   "Con, I think they're from your mom."

   His eyes snapped open, but not all the way, just until they were dark slits peering suspiciously at her. "Impossible."

   "I'm serious. They're from a woman who ran away with a man her father disapproved of. She writes about naming her first son Conroy Anthony."

   "'S not me."

   "Anthony isn't your middle name?"

   "I don't have a middle name. Conroy Beale, that's all she wrote."

   "What was your mother's name?"

   "Rina."

"Oh." Her fearful excitement deflated a little. She'd been so sure. "Your brother, did he have blond hair?"

"Nope, light brownish."

"Oh. It's just that.... otherwise the details seem to fit. She married a man who she thought was wonderful and he turned out to be a mean drunk with no money. Will you take a look at them?"

"No, I'm tired. Come to bed, Lizzie."

"Please?" She hated the whiny tone of her voice.

"No. I don't even want to touch those damn letters. They give me the creeps." He slanted a suspicious glance at them where they lay in her hand.

"Can I read one to you?"

Con let out a loud sigh and pulled the sheet up over his shoulder. "If you must."

By the time she'd finished reading them all—which didn't take long—he was propped up on his elbow staring at her, lips parted.

"See what I mean? The details match right up."

"Well," he frowned, "some of them do, but like I said, my mom's name was Rina. What's the postmark on the envelope?"

"Breaux."

"Shit." Con bit his lip. That's the nearest town to Mudbug Flats with a post office. "I don't like this one bit."

"You know what this means, don't you?"

"What?"

"Your mom grew up in *this* house."

Con blew out a snort. "Well, that is just impossible."

"How? She's writing to her father at this address. We found the letters in this bed. This was probably her father's bedroom. It is the biggest."

Con squirmed, like the bed suddenly grew spikes. "No, really. There's no way my mom grew up someplace like this. She wasn't, you know, sophisticated or smart or anything. She was just a nice woman. There's no way..."

"If she ran away when she was very, very young, say fifteen or sixteen, then she wouldn't necessarily seem polished and sophisticated."

Con shook his head emphatically. "I don't think so."

"And, think about it, couldn't Rina be short for say, Katherine? That would match up with the K she signs. What was her maiden name?"

Con gave her a funny look. "I don't know what her maiden name was. But, you know, I think she did have Katherine written inside her prayer book. I asked her about it once." He sat up, an expression of deepening alarm on his face. "And—" He stared at her, a distant look that chilled her. "She kept a lock of my brother's hair taped inside her prayer book—he was sick a lot when he was little..." He tapped his chest, searching for a word. "He had um...respiratory infections. That lock of hair was real pale, almost white." He stared at her, blinking.

"It's her, isn't it?" Lizzie bit her lip.

"She never did say where she was from. I can kind of see why if she'd made a big step down like that." Con rubbed his hand over his mouth. "That kind of thing freaks people out. Better to keep it a secret, you know?"

"No, I don't know. You're the expert on secrets." Lizzie was getting a nasty prickly sensation up and down her spine.

"She always said my father was a good man when she met him." Con looked past her, out into the darkness outside the uncurtained window. "That he worked hard and they had big dreams. The problem was, he couldn't make enough money so he never felt like he was worthy of her."

Lizzie let out a breath she'd been holding for some time. "Is that why you pushed me away once I had no money of my own?" she asked quietly.

"What?" Con looked startled.

"Because you were afraid that you'd end up like your father, unable to support your family?"

"No," Con said indignantly. "No way. I didn't think about it like that at all. I'm nothing like my father..." His voice trailed off.

Lizzie placed her hand on his arm as strange heat flooded her chest. She looked at his face, at the confusion on his striking features. "You know, Conroy Beale, suddenly I understand you a whole lot better."

# 19

Lizzie sat at the dining room table munching a croissant as long slivers of morning sun crept across the wood floor. Raoul had accosted her at breakfast, set up a mirror in front of her, and started work on her shower-wet hair while she was still eating.

"Sweetheart, you are looking goooood this morning." Raoul's smiling face leered behind her in the mirror. "Guess you took my advice about ice on the bags."

"I just got a decent night of sleep." Actually, she didn't get all that much real sleep, but somehow unpacking some more of Con's baggage and spending the night in his arms was more restful than a week at a spa. For the first time she could really see where Con was coming from.

Raoul chuckled "Well, I'm glad you managed to keep young Conroy chained up long enough to catch some shut-eye. You'll be married soon. That boy needs to learn to pace himself."

Lizzie couldn't help smiling.

Raoul spritzed her hair with some shiny stuff. "I don't think any of us will get any sleep after they turn on those things." He jerked his chin toward three enormous blue air-conditioning units that were being wheeled into the house.

"Thank God!" Lizzie closed her eyes for a second as the promise of being cool again almost unhinged her. "I had no idea how totally dependent I am on air conditioning."

"Terrible for the skin. Dries it right out. The humidity has done wonders for your epidermis. It's positively glowing."

Yeah. Right. That glow has nothing to do with making love to Con and spending the night in his arms.

*Hold up. No love was made. We had sex.*

"You alright? You look tense. Like I was saying, now we've found the right routine—lots of moisture and a spritz of glycerine—the humidity makes your curls spring right up like Slinkys. Beautiful."

"Thanks Raoul." She took another a bite of her croissant and studied her reflection in the mirror. Perhaps her hair did look okay? Kind of like the "after" in a perm commercial. Would both Con and Raoul lie if they didn't think it looked pretty?

Well, maybe Con would.

"Darling!" Lizzie jumped as Maisie's voice boomed in her ear. "They're steaming some wrinkles out of the dress and we're going to do a fitting on-camera right after breakfast. Isabel Matsuo has outdone herself." Maisie leaned down and whispered in her ear. "You know I'm almost ready to defect to her myself. What she's done with the pearl beads is magnificent, the way it drapes—oh!"

Lizzie raised her eyebrows. *Whatever! It's just a dress.* Maisie took this stuff so much more seriously than she did.

"Raoul, you are the most talented hairdresser in the Northern Hemisphere. How on earth did you manage to get Lizzie's poufy frizz to make ringlets?"

Lizzie gritted her teeth.

"Didn't do a thing, sugar," said Raoul, without looking at her. "Lizzie's curl is 100 percent natural. This is what it does when left to its own devices, just as your hair hangs like wet shawl fringe." He winked at Lizzie, who fought to suppress an explosive chuckle.

Maisie's icy smile barely covered her teeth. "Well, I must go supervise the placement of the air conditioners."

"Don't know why we need 'em with her around here," whispered Raoul, before she was out of earshot. "Puts a chill in the air wherever she goes. But I guess I shouldn't talk that way about your cousin."

"Please do. It's music to my ears."

"Here comes Prince Charming." He smiled. Lizzie's stomach tightened.

"Hey, guys." Con wandered over, carrying a plate of food and looking his usual polished self. Lizzie tried to ignore the rush of warmth she felt at the sight of him.

"Guys?" said Raoul with a flourish of his hand. "Guys? Is that how you talk to your future bride? This is Lizzie Hathaway. Do you want her to think you fell off a turnip truck?"

"'S better than the truth." Con took a hearty bite of croissant.

"Yeah." Raoul stopped dusting a layer of fine powder over Lizzie's face and looked up at Con, suddenly serious. "I heard about yesterday. But don't you sweat it, sweetheart," he said. Con chewed his croissant casually as if a man called him sweetheart every day. "What happened back then was none of your doing."

"Amen to that," said Con. "And no one's going to be sweating around here once those things get fired up." He gestured to the blue monsters being wheeled into position and took another big bite of croissant.

Did nothing bother him? Maybe he really did have no feelings? Lizzie took a deep breath to combat tightness in her chest.

She had far too many feelings for Con this morning and anger and resentment weren't even among them. She bit her lip.

"No biting. Save that for later." Raoul rolled his eyes toward Con. Lizzie forced a smile.

She wasn't falling for him again. Really, she wasn't! She just felt sorry for him. Simple compassion, that's all. And strong sexual attraction. Just normal girl stuff, nothing along the lines of eternal love and all that crap.

It was a little disturbing she could only sleep with him in her bed, like a toddler with a smelly stuffed animal it can't let go of, but that was hardly the stuff of great romance.

"Lizzie, darling, we need you!" Maisie's distant voice startled her out of her rather panicked ruminations. "The dress is ready."

"Coming."

"I haven't done your eyes yet," protested Raoul.

"I'll sport the natural look for now." She rose out of her chair, relieved not to worry about mascara and liner streaking her cheeks for once.

"Later," she said to Con, trying to sound cool and casual.

Con just nodded, but the look he gave her—dark, wary and brimming with unspoken words—made her breath stick right at the bottom of her lungs.

"It looks a little tight." Maisie—who else?—loudly voiced the words on everyone's mind.

Gia struggled to get the zipper up. It was stuck right above her waist. A seed pearl popped off the front and rolled to the floor.

Lizzie gritted her teeth and sucked in harder. Lights, set up around the elegant sitting room they'd commandeered as a dressing room, beat down on her like sun on the Sahara. Dino winced behind the tripod-mounted camera blocking the Adams fireplace. The dress weighed a ton, and was all she could do to keep her shoulders steady.

"Is there any room to let the seams out?" Maisie asked the seamstress who'd accompanied the dress to Louisiana. The tiny Japanese woman looked at her blankly. She didn't seem to understand a single word of English.

"The seams," shouted Maisie, with a forced smile, as if the woman was deaf. "Fix?" The seamstress's smooth forehead creased.

Up on the makeshift podium, Lizzie closed her eyes.

Gia forced the zipper to the top with a lightning movement that left Lizzie's nipples begging for mercy. "Got it!"

*Thank God.*

A vision of seed pearls exploding over all the open boxes of shoes and gloves and silk stockings made her afraid to breathe except in tiny sips through her mouth.

All of a sudden the giant blue box hunkered in the corner roared to life.

"Yes!" cried Maisie, like a cheerleader. "They said it couldn't be done, and I simply insisted they do it anyway. A little determination, that's all that's required to accomplish most things in life."

The machine shuddered and hiccupped and a blast of freezing air shot across the room, sprinkling goose bumps over Lizzie's arms.

It felt really good.

It wasn't even all that loud.

Euphoria accompanied the icy air. No more sweat drenching her armpits and pouring down her spine! No more droplets beading her upper lip and wetting the hair at her temples! No more—

The machine shuddered to a halt at the exact same moment all the lights went out and Dino issued a resounding, "Fuck."

"Power's dead," yelled Roger from the other room.

"Someone give that boy a Pulitzer," growled Maisie. "Get it going again!" she yelled through the doorway. She tapped her foot on the floor for a few seconds. It was encased in a rather frumpy beige pump to match her slim beige suit. "You leave Manhattan, and it's like you're in another century."

*Would someone please unzip me?* was the only thought on Lizzie's mind, which felt as squished as her torso. She didn't voice it until Maisie had stalked out of the room, tut-tutting about primitive conditions and the need for hardship pay.

Gia unzipped her and she sagged with relief.

"I'm going outside for a smoke," muttered Dino.

"I'm with you," said Gia, already striding for the door.

Lizzie was left standing on the podium in a too-tight fifteen-thousand dollar dress, towering over a tiny Japanese woman whose name she'd not managed to catch.

*This was all your idea.*

Con's blood crept like Arctic ice as he and Lizzie stood in the Parish records office with Dino's camera trained on him. You weren't allowed to look in anyone's file but your own, but the kind young clerk had agreed to check Danny's file to see if it contained a death certificate.

She pulled a folder from the file drawer and flipped through it. It took all Con's strength to keep his face calm. He held himself steady as blood pounded in his head and cold fingers squeezed his heart.

"No death certificate."

He sagged with relief. "Thank God." Of course it didn't mean Danny was alive, but there was hope.

Lizzie let out a breath too. She looked almost as nervous as him, twisting her fingers together, her face white. He wanted to hug her, but didn't.

"Could Con see his own file?" she asked, as the clerk put Danny's away.

"Yes." The clerk looked at him. "Would you like to?"

*Not really,* was the answer that sprang to mind as a queasy sensation sneaked into his stomach.

"Come on, Con. You need to see your mother's maiden name." Lizzie put her hand on his arm.

*No, I don't.* He didn't want to know if she was that sad woman in the letters. His memories were sad enough already.

"Okay." He couldn't help feeling nothing good could come from digging up the past. Who knew what other skeletons lay rotting in the muck down there? He shivered in the air-conditioned room as they waited for the clerk to come back. Lizzie rubbed his back, and he took a deep breath.

"Conroy Aaron Beale." The clerk drew out the file. Aaron? How could he not even know he had a middle name? He became acutely aware of the camera on him, like he was being stripped naked. *It's just a piece of paper.*

"Can I see it?" His voice sounded disembodied.

The clerk handed it to him, and he pulled Lizzie close so she could see it too

"Father, Daniel Patrick Beale." That name still gave him a chill. Made bile rise in his throat.

"Mother," his voice cracked. He cleared his throat. "Mother, Katherine Marie Milford Beale."

"It's her," breathed Lizzie. "I knew it."

A hurt deep inside him started to throb.

"Can we see her birth certificate?" Lizzie asked quietly.

"I'm afraid birth certificates are confidential for 100 years." The clerk's soft voice was apologetic. "You can only see your own file."

"Why do you want to see it?" Con asked Lizzie.

"Just to see if her father really was Thomas Milford. But I guess we have our answer in her name. The puzzle pieces fit together. Your mother wrote those letters."

Con didn't say anything. He looked at the typewritten name, unwelcome tears blurring his eyes and pain seeping through him. *I miss you, Mom.*

His breathing became erratic. He shoved the paper back at the clerk. "Thank you." He needed to escape from the camera, from the punishing fluorescent lights, from the past.

"You really are descended from Louisiana aristocrats." Lizzie touched his arm, making him flinch.

"Let's get out of here." He strode for the door.


Back at the house there was still no electricity, and Lizzie tried hard not to laugh at the exchange taking place in the unlit dining room after a hurried take-out lunch.

"Well, yeah, I probably could, but I don't have an electrician's license so it wouldn't be legal," said Con to a fierce-eyed Maisie.

"But they said they can't get anyone out here until the day after tomorrow! That's supposed to be the day of the wedding! We're on a deadline here, for crying out loud. I have to be back in New York by the weekend."

Con shrugged.

"Don't you understand? There's no electricity. None at all! The entire main circuit is blown. There are no lights. We can't cook. We have no water. All the hotels are full because of some zydeco festival. It's a disaster!"

"A propane range works without electricity, and the bayou's out back." Con adjusted his cuff. He looked up at her. "Maybe you could fly out an electrician from Manhattan."

Maisie stared at him for a second. "You know, that's not such a bad idea." She stormed off, punching numbers into her cell.

"So much for our all-expenses-paid vacation in the lap of luxury," said Con. "Everyone keeps trying to put me to work. They're going to have me rebuilding the transmission on that van any minute the way Maisie's running it into the ground."

"I don't think she knows how to drive stick either." Lizzie winked. "Where's your spirit of adventure?" She punched his arm, feeling strangely cheerful for reasons she couldn't quite figure out. Maybe because she hadn't had any time to sit and think.

Probably a good thing.

"I managed to get you an appointment with a local lawyer for this afternoon!" Gia burst into the room. She looked from Con to Lizzie, glowing with excitement.

"Why?" Lizzie wondered if Gia had been smoking something other than Dino's cigarettes.

"He's famous for tracking down missing people— heirs of estates in probate that kind of thing. If anyone can find Con's brother, he can. And guess what?"

"What?" Lizzie said on cue.

"He's the same lawyer who owns this house!"

"Oh. Okay. So can't he do something about the electricity? Like, bribe a local electrician or something?"

"Oh yes, that's all under control. He said he'll have someone out right away."

"Thank God. Tell Maisie before she blows a fuse."

"Will do. Anyway, I have the lawyer's address right here. He's expecting you at two. No cameras, though. Something about attorney-client privilege. He wouldn't budge on it."

A strange buzz of excitement tickled Lizzie's skin. "We'll be there."

"So you're a Beale?" Eric Stapleton, esq., leaned into his wingback office chair and surveyed Con over his reading glasses. He was fiftyish, with silvering dark hair and a slight paunch straining his pinstriped shirt. Stacks of files climbed the walls of his office. Pictures of his perfect-looking family faced visitors from the top of his vast mahogany desk.

"I am." Con sat straight as a cypress.

"Well, well, well. I thought we'd seen the last of the Beales in these parts." The lawyer let out a laugh and wiped his nose with a large white handkerchief as if overcome by amusement.

Lizzie bristled.

"Things have been quiet around here since your daddy died. He sure did know how to stir up some excitement on a Saturday night." The lawyer looked steadily at Con with a supercilious smirk on his face.

"Do you know where I can find my brother?" asked Con stiffly.

"Can't say I do. As you said, there's no record of him after your daddy died. My assistant did some preliminary poking around, and he's off the school records after that year. Never registered with social services and nobody's seen him since."

He took off his wire-rimmed glasses and polished them with his handkerchief. "Must have left town. Do you have any relatives he could have gone to stay with?" He replaced his glasses and peered at Con through them.

"Not that I know of."

"Well, we are up a tree without a ladder then, aren't we?" His self-satisfied smile made Lizzie's scalp tingle. "But if you care to retain me in this matter, I'll have my secretary start doing some digging. She'll call around to see if she can find his name on any school rolls or in the record books of any other— Come in!"

A knock on the door had interrupted him and his cheerful-looking middle-aged secretary appeared. "Mr. Hodgkins on the phone."

"Thank you, Vera." He turned to them. "I'm afraid I must take this call. It's of the utmost urgency. A criminal matter, I'm afraid," he said with a wink. "Would you mind waiting outside for a moment?"

Lizzie and Con rose and left the room.

"What an asshole," muttered Lizzie once they were outside in the cramped hallway. "I wouldn't trust him as far as I could throw him." Con looked rigid with tension. She moved behind him and pressed her thumbs under the collar of his white shirt and into the muscle at the base of his neck. "Don't worry, if he's out there, we'll find him."

The secretary peered out into the hallway. "Would you care for some coffee?"

"Sure." Lizzie led the way to the spacious waiting room. The coffee actually smelled pretty good.

"That nice production assistant—Mia, was it?—told me you're staying at Dumas House," Vera said, as she handed a white mug to Con.

"Yes." He took a sip. "We're there filming our wedding."

Lizzie got a funny feeling in her tummy. He didn't say it with any undertone of amusement or mockery. He said it as if they were…getting married.

"How lovely. It sure is a beautiful place to get married. My niece had her wedding there two years ago in May."

"Really?" Lizzie accepted a cup too. "So the house is often rented out for events?"

"Yes. Mr. Stapleton has been managing it for nearly six years now, since the owner died."

"And he owns it now?" Lizzie peered over the rim of her coffee cup, holding her breath.

"He doesn't own it. He manages it as executor of the former owner's estate. We've been unable to locate any heirs. The old man was in his late nineties when he died, no family left to speak of. Mr. Stapleton's been using the attached trust to maintain the place. If you ask me he's made a world of improvements. I don't think it had been renovated since the 1950s before he took over."

"It must cost a fortune to maintain," said Lizzie.

"I believe he's had to invest a good deal of the trust in the house. He replaced the roof, updated some of the plumbing and electrical, and he keeps the gardens immaculate as it's becoming quite the place for any outdoor social event."

"Sounds like he has a pretty good business going," Lizzie took a sip of coffee, grateful for the air-conditioning in the offices. "So who, exactly, are the heirs he's been unable to locate?"

She heard Con choke on his coffee and recover himself, but she kept her eyes fixed on the woman.

"Apparently the old man who owned it—Thomas Milford his name was—had an estranged daughter. This all happened before my time, so I don't know the details, but I believe it turned out she was dead."

Lizzie shot Con a pointed look.

"No other descendants were found so Mr. Stapleton's been managing it while he searches for any remaining heirs." She blew her nose on a tissue. "But between you and me and the doorpost, he's looking to buy it himself. Once the trust is exhausted there won't be any cash in the estate to pay the local property taxes. At that point it becomes property of the parish, gets auctioned off and voilà! He'll be the legal owner. He's managed it like his own anyway, these last six years. You've seen the place, so you can tell just how much love and care has gone into it. Mr. Stapleton is a true guardian of our heritage."

While she was speaking Lizzie's breathing got shallow. Con stood motionless.

"Mind if I step outside for a smoke?" Lizzie asked, with what she hoped was a casual smile. Con shot her an odd look.

"You can smoke in here if you like," the secretary replied.

"I don't want to stink the place up. Come on, Con." She grabbed him by his sleeve, almost spilling his coffee.

Outside, cars whizzed past as they stood on the immaculate postage stamp of lawn in front of the law office.

"Did you hear that?" she hissed.

"Sure, I heard it."

"He's supposed to be looking for heirs. Those would be the descendants of Katherine Marie Milford. Also known as you."

Con's knuckles were white around his coffee cup. "I just want to find my brother."

"But don't you get it? The house is yours. And from the sounds of it, Mr. Stapleton here is spending the trust money hand over fist while he builds up a tidy rentals business there. That explains why it's so well renovated. He's probably poured a million dollars into the place. New roof, new upholstery, soon it will have all central air. I've never seen such a thorough renovation of an old house, but it all makes perfect sense now. He's deliberately trying to spend the money that came with it, so he can bankrupt the estate so it can't pay the taxes, then when the taxes go unpaid, the town takes over the property and he buys it for peanuts. He's trying to steal your inheritance."

Con let out a growl of frustration. "Lizzie, the house isn't mine. It never was and it never will be. I don't really get why you're—"

"Con, listen," she leaned into him and hissed in his ear. "That slick bastard in there knows you are the heir. How could he not? He must know who your mother was, if they found out she was dead. So I bet he knows she has two sons, and what their names are. He may well know exactly where your brother is. But is it in his interest to tell you? To let you find out about any of this? Hell, no."

Con stared at her.

She nodded. "Up until now he's been sitting pretty on a goldmine that no living soul has a claim to—then you turn up like a bad penny. Right now he's probably sweating bullets looking for ways to throw us off the trail. The one thing he forgot to do was scotch tape his secretary's lips together. We've got to run with this information."

At that moment the front door opened and Vera peered out. "He's ready for you."

Lizzie squeezed Con's arm above the elbow, and followed him back in. Eric Stapleton summoned them back into his office with an avuncular wave of his meaty hand.

"So, we're looking for Danny, aka 'Tiny' Beale..." he said, rifling in a drawer and emerging with a packet of extra-strong mints. "I'll make a note for Vera to check the local prisons. Mint?"

"No, thanks," said Lizzie, digging her nails into her palms. "We're very much enjoying our stay in Dumas House. It is a fine old place. Must cost a fortune to maintain."

"Labor of love, my dear. Labor of love. The place loses money hand over fist. Would have fallen down years ago if I hadn't poured every penny I own into it. My wife wrings her hands over it every year, but to me it's just my duty as a citizen of the parish." He gave her a saccharine smile. "Now back to the matter at hand. As I said, it may be impossible to find Mr. Beale..."

"Your secretary said the renovations on the house are paid for by a trust,' cut in Lizzie. "A legacy that came with the house."

"Why, yes, that is true. It was important to perform necessary repairs in order to preserve the integrity of the estate." He linked his fingers together, looking relaxed as if they were discussing the weather prospects for his weekend golf game.

"Exactly how much is in that legacy?"

"Sadly, almost nothing at all, I'm afraid. It's shocking the amount of money a place like that will eat through. As I said, it's been a labor of love. I'm just glad of opportunities such as the one provided by the fine production company you're working with. How many more days of filming do you have? Two, wasn't it?"

"It could be a few more since the power outage has slowed things down."

"I don't know if that will be possible. I believe we have a long-standing rental next week that will require the property to be vacant. I've taken measures to make sure the electrical problems will be solved immediately so there should be no further delays in your filming."

"Look," Con leaned forward. "I'm not here to talk about the damn house. Can you help me find my brother or not?"

Lizzie's ears pricked up at his aggressive tone.

"Regretfully, I suspect your brother has gone the way of so many of the men of your family." The lawyer tipped his head to one side and lifted an eyebrow. "A fate most of us around here had sadly assumed to be yours."

"Yeah? Well, guess what, I'm alive and kicking and I bet my brother is too."

"I see you've inherited the Beale temper." Stapleton leaned back in his chair and chuckled. "I bet you like a drink too, don't you, son? Bourbon?" He reached into his desk and drew out a small bottle.

Con blew out a disgusted snort and placed a clenched fist on Eric Stapleton, esq.'s cluttered desk. "I didn't plan to come back here—ever—but Lizzie brought me down here and now I'm up to my neck in the mess I left behind and I'm not leaving until I get some answers."

Lizzie stared at him.

"I have reason to believe you know where my brother is, and if you'll give me that information you won't see me again."

"I have absolutely no idea where your brother is. Drunk in a ditch somewhere, I expect, so don't you come in here with that tone of voice. I remember you when you were just a snot-nosed punk brought into court for stealing a frozen turkey." He broke into a grating laugh. Con seemed to shrink back a little. "You probably don't even remember that, but I do. Another one of *those* Beale's. Like father like son."

"Don't you talk to him like that!" Lizzie was on her feet before she knew what was happening. "We happen to know that he and his brother are the heirs of Dumas House and that you are deliberately concealing that knowledge from everyone in the hope of taking possession of the property yourself!" Her shrill voice startled her.

Stapleton's lips parted for second, then he drew them back together in a crooked line. "You have no idea what you're talking about, and I want you out of this office, now!"

He pressed his finger on the intercom. "Vera! Escort our visitors out immediately."

"You haven't heard the end of this, Mr. Stapleton," Lizzie said calmly. "Conroy Beale is back and he plans to demand his rights."

As Vera escorted them down the cramped hallway, Lizzie couldn't resist asking, "So is Mr. Milford's will kept in this office?"

"Oh, yes, Mr. Stapleton is the executor of his estate, but of course there's a copy filed with the—"

"Loose lips sink ships, Vera!" boomed the lawyer's voice from behind them. "Get them out of here and come into my office immediately."

"Y...yes sir," she stammered, giving Lizzie a wary glance.

Out on the tiny lawn Con ran his hands through his hair. "Why'd you have to go off on a tangent like that? We should have played it cool. Now he knows we know and he's basically the enemy. We'll never get anything out of him."

"That house is your right, Con."

"Bullshit. It's my nothing. That mean old bastard left my mother to die. Didn't even open her letters. I don't want nothing of his. You expect me to think about a house when we don't even know if my brother is—" He shuddered and broke off.

"So you feel you don't deserve it because you abandoned your brother? Help me out here. You didn't have any problem with planning to live the good life on the proceeds of *my* Grandfather's corporate greed, and now you're too moral to inherit your own wealth?"

Con's head kicked back. His eyes shone, fierce. "Look, I already said I was wrong to have tried to marry you the way I did. That's why I agreed to go along with your crazy TV wedding scheme and how I ended up back down here in the first place. Now I'm here, the only, and I mean it, the *only* thing I want is to find my brother. Stapleton can go live in that house himself and party all day and night for all I care."

Lizzie growled with frustration. "This is why poor people don't get ahead. You're afraid to stir up trouble so you let people walk all over you. I liked you better when you were a big faker trying to marry money and claim your place on top of the pie!"

"Can we get the hell out of here before he has us arrested for something?" Con turned to where Dino had parked the Jeep and they both noticed Dino at the same time, backed up against the outside of the building, camera rolling.

"Uh, hi Dino." Lizzie racked her brain to figure out what they'd revealed. *That Con had tried to marry her for her money.* Her face turned beet red. "Can you, uh, turn it off?"

He lowered the camera. A smile crept across his face. "I'll rewind over this on two conditions."

"What?" snapped Con.

"One, you have to buy me a six pack of beer."

"Done."

"Two, you have to go after that sonofabitch. I was listening at the window. His type makes me want to spit nails. Con, wouldn't you like to see Maisie sharpen her journalistic claws on that bastard?"

Con raised an eyebrow very slightly. "When you put it that way, I think we can make a deal."

"Any fine local brew will be acceptable."

Lizzie let out a silent sigh of relief. "Dino, you are a man in a million."

"And for the record, I think you two are made for each other."

Lizzie frowned and tossed her hair. "Let's go find a grocery store."

# 20

The power was still out when the local news crew arrived to do the arranged interview with Con. They brought their own lighting, which was lucky as dusk was falling and candles didn't do more than punctuate the sweaty darkness descending on the house. The dining room was ablaze with spotlights and floodlights and people milled about, stepping over trailing wires and talking urgently into cell phones.

The perky local reporter with her spackled-on makeup and molded wire hair made Maisie look washed out and girlish by comparison, but Maisie didn't seem to notice. She was too busy glad handing and name dropping.

Lizzie shook her head. She had ample opportunity to shake her head since she wasn't wanted on camera. No, it was *The Con Becle Show* and his impending wedding rated only a brief mention in the interviewer's introduction.

"The camera does love him, doesn't it," whispered Raoul, as he and Lizzie stood side by side in the shadows, watching Con's elegant profile on a monitor. "Cool under pressure, that one. You picked a winner when you chose him. And you didn't even know he owned this place!" Raoul slid his arm around Lizzie's shoulders and squeezed her affectionately.

A spore of guilt exploded inside her. Did Raoul really think she loved Con? Despite overhearing them in the bedroom, he didn't seem to get that they were just doing this for the money. Amazing what people will believe when they want to badly enough.

*She knew how that went.*

"He doesn't own it yet," she muttered.

"But these reporters are hot on the trail. Miss Thing there just said it." He nodded his head at the female reporter. "He'll get his due. I know it. You'll be living the high life again, by his side. It's like a fairy tale."

She froze. The script she'd written for her and Con didn't extend past payday, and here was Raoul conjuring up a Spanish-moss-bedecked happily-ever-after. Somehow, after last night's unexpected intimacy, that scared the hell out of her.

She blew out a slow, silent breath. "Can you really see Con living here in swamp-ville again?"

"Yes." He didn't even look at her. "He loves this place. Can't you tell? The way he's always pointing out the birds and the trees and all that. He's right at home here."

Huh? Were they talking about the same person? Or was Con giving jovial swamp tours while she holed up in the bedroom?

What did it matter? "Even if the house does turn out to be his, he couldn't afford to keep it. The lawyer's already spent the money and a place like this costs a fortune to maintain."

"Con will think of something. He's a hustler," Raoul said cheerfully.

"I won't argue with that," she murmured.

The reporter turned to face the camera. "So, Daniel Beale, Danny, Tiny, if you are out there, or if anyone out there knows where he is, please contact Eyewitness News at the number on your screen and reunite this family torn apart by tragedy."

"I guess they dub the violins in later." Dino snuck up behind them.

"Shut your mouth," whispered Raoul. "I'm all choked up."

He wasn't kidding. Raoul still had his arm around her, and Lizzie could feel his chest heaving. She slid her arm around him and patted his back. "You're a very caring person, Raoul."

"It's my downfall, sweetheart."

"That's a wrap," called the female reporter. "We're going to head back and cut a segment for the late news. We'll pass any information we get right along to you. Thanks so much, Conroy, I think your story will touch a lot of hearts."

Con said something inaudible and shook her hand. He searched the darkness, and when he found Lizzie, the look he gave her made her catch her breath.

*This was all your idea.*

"Excuse me." She disentangled herself from Raoul and pushed past Diro toward Con. "You did great." She stepped over a lighting cable just as someone swished it from between her legs.

"It feels weird to have people know so much about me." He looked rather dazed.

"Weird but good, though, right?" She squeezed his upper arm.

"Let's go outside." He grabbed her hand and pulled her to the back door

With a burst of excitement she followed him out into the darkened garden. The screech of tree frogs filled her ears and grass pricked her toes through her sandals as he pulled her off the slate patio out onto the lawn.

"Where are we going? I can't see a thing!"

She swatted at mosquitoes she could hear but not see. A firefly glow in front of her face made her gasp.

Con's gripped her hand tightly and sped into a run as they plunged deeper into the muggy blackness. He untucked his shirt with his other hand, and she smelled the raw tang of his sweat.

"You stink!" She laughed.

"No kidding!"

Lizzie stumbled over her sandal and he steadied her, then drew her in for a quick, hard kiss on the mouth that made her belly quiver.

Breathless, not knowing whether to gasp or laugh, Lizzie did both. Con unbuttoned his shirt and stripped it off, then unbuckled his belt.

"What are you doing?"

"Going in for a swim. Get undressed."

"What?" She glanced to her right and saw the sinuous movement of reflected moonlight on the black surface of the bayou.

"In there?"

"Where else?" Con kicked off his shoes and shucked off his pants. Moonlight glazed his face and shoulders as he grabbed her around the waist and kissed her again. She felt his erection hard against her belly, through her thin shirt.

"Get undressed," he growled, tugging at the waistband of her shorts. Suddenly he pushed up her shirt and closed his mouth over her bra-covered nipple with force, lashing it with his tongue through the satin fabric as his hands settled on her waist.

She gripped his hair with her hands, explosive laughter and fierce arousal surging inside her. Con's tongue on her breasts was driving her half wild.

But not wild enough to get into a muddy black river slithering with all kinds of creepy creatures.

"There's no way I'm going in there!" she rasped, hardly able to catch her breath.

"Oh, yeah?" In one deft movement he swept her off her feet—which didn't feel nearly as romantic as it sounded—and slung her against his hard chest.

"There could be alligators, snakes, anything!"

Con chuckled. He swiped a bite at her neck, grazing it with his teeth. "Snap snap."

"Con, please, agggghhhhh!" she screamed as he charged right into the bayou with her held firm in his arms. Water splashed her face and closed over her legs as she clung to him, shrieking.

"Shhh, they'll think I'm drowning you." Con's hot dark voice and the warm dark water swirled around her. "Feels good, huh?"

"It is cooler than the air." She tried to sound calm. Her arms were around his neck in a noose hold. "Don't put me down. I don't want my feet on the bottom."

"No prob. I'll just hold you. I'm enjoying the view."

She glanced down at her chest where her shirt was bunched up to reveal breasts lifted and separated by her now totally transparent bra.

"My clothes are all wet."

"You're a keen observer." The low vibration of his voice shivered into her ear. "Now all we need to do is get 'em off."

"No way, what if someone—" She shrieked as her shorts and panties slid down her legs with one silky movement of his hand under the water. She reached out to grab them as they floated, separately, to the surface a couple of feet away.

"Con, they're drifting. They'll get lost!" She kicked against him, splashing.

"They'll give someone downriver a nice surprise." His gator grin gleamed in the moonlight. She gasped as her bra came unhooked. "You'll have to loosen your arms so I can get it off."

"No way!"

He focused on the little buttons of her blouse, undoing them in the darkness with skill. "Come on, wrap your legs around me, like this." He maneuvered her thighs into position around his hips, so his erection teased her bare crotch. Moonlight glazed his striking features and the smile playing across his sensual mouth. "You look like a river goddess with your hair trailing out behind you." He kissed her lips with gentle intensity that stole her breath and made her heart throb. Suddenly her top and bra were floating away on the quicksilver surface of the water and she didn't seem to care.

"Did your Depo shot wear off yet?" His totally unromantic question made a giggle explode out of her.

"Why? You don't want to get me pregnant now you might have an inheritance to share?"

Con laughed, his face right in hers. "Is that how rich people think?"

"You bet." Her chest bumped against him as she chuckled. "And lucky for you I've still got another month left."

"Thank God," he murmured huskily, as he set about devouring her throat. As her fingers roamed over his back and up into his thick, wet hair, his erection thickened and hardened at her crotch. The silky water lapped at her breasts and she wriggled her hips, reveling in the sensation of the river water flowing over her sex and the delicious hardness of Con wrapped all around her.

She tightened her arms around his neck as his strong hands cupped her buttocks and he slid inside her, filling her. He buried his face in her neck for a hard love bite that made her nipples sting.

"Con, that'll leave a bruise," she gasped.

"I know." He grazed her collarbone with his teeth. "I want everyone to know you're mine." His dark gaze roamed over her face.

"They already know. We're getting married, remember?"

Con didn't answer her question, instead he thrust hard, and she shuddered in response, gripping him. His eyes squeezed shut, and he kissed her lips so tenderly that it made her heart constrict.

*Do you take this man to be your wedded husband, to have and to hold from this day forth as long as you both shall live?*

Con held her so tight, his arms wrapped around her with such force she couldn't imagine he'd ever let go.

*I do.*

She pulled herself even closer, wrapping her arms and pressing her cheek to his as her eyes squeezed shut. A surge of emotion threatened to choke her.

*It's just lust*, she tried to tell herself, but as Con nuzzled her gently and rubbed her back, she got a sneaking feeling she was up to her neck in something a lot stickier and more complicated than lust. She wriggled as sensation built inside her. Rocked her hips against him, making waves in the water as waves of emotion rolled through her.

*I love you.*

She struggled not to let the words slip out. She didn't want him to have that kind of power over her. Or if he did, she didn't want him to know about it, unlike last time.

*Why couldn't she control her feelings for this man?*

"What's the matter?" Con's soft voice made her realize that her sob of emotion had been audible.

"Nothing," she lied.

She honestly didn't know if it was love or hate or pain or tenderness or whatever, but she felt more for Con than she could express in words or thoughts.

He'd changed her, and if she wasn't mistaken, she'd changed him too.

"Hold your breath," he whispered.

"What?" she started to say, then she gulped air as he ducked them both below the black surface of the water.

Panic that tightened her legs around him turned to relief as they exploded up above the surface of the water again. Con's cock danced inside her, and she gasped, water streaming over her face. Hands on her waist, he drove her to a fierce splashing climax and a scream that echoed down the bayou and out to the Gulf of Mexico.

Con's wet hair hung to his gleaming eyes. The reflected moon danced in their black surface, vying with an expression so intense, so unreadable, that Lizzie couldn't look away.

"Lizzie! Where are you?" Maisie's voice pierced the viscous darkness, and the beam of a flashlight danced off a nearby tree.

"Oh, no." Lizzie hid her face in Con's neck.

"Don't want cousin Maisie to catch you bare-assed in the bayou?"

"Not really." She scanned the dark water for her clothes. Nothing.

"We can duck beneath the surface again."

"No thanks!"

"Lizzieeeeeee! ' That grating voice was getting closer. The beam bounced off the grass, illuminating Con's white shirt. "Conroy? Where are you?"

"We'd better disengage," whispered Con. Lizzie wiggled free of him. The water felt sensational on her aroused flesh. What did she care if Maisie saw her naked in the bayou making love to Con? She'd be jealous. You'd never catch Mr. Stick-Up-His-Ass Dwight going at it out under the stars.

"We're here!" she called on impulse. "No cameras though, please, we're X-rated."

Con chuckled and Lizzie buried her face in his neck with a snort of laughter.

She hid her breasts against Con's chest as the flashlight beam hit them dead on. "Oh, there you are," said Maisie, casual as if she'd found them reading. "We're off to a restaurant for dinner, and I didn't want you to get left behind."

"You hungry?" whispered Lizzie.

"Only for you," Con breathed against her neck.

"We'll find some leftovers in the kitchen. We both need an early night."

"It's a very famous restaurant. Authentic Cajun, Con, you'll really enjoy it."

Con shook with silent laughter. "Bring back some boudin for me, okay?"

Maisie paused, perhaps writing something down. "Will do. Alright then, see you later."

They collapsed in giggles as Maisie strode away, flashlight beam bouncing with her purposeful stride.

"You know, you can knock your cousin but she's quite a woman. Just needs the right man to straighten her out."

Lizzie bristled at his arrogance. "She's got one. His name's Dwight and he's a very dignified bond broker. I don't think she wants a Neanderthal to carry her off over his shoulder."

"Don't be so sure." His teeth flashed in the moonlight.

"Neanderthal! Just because you—"

Her words were lost as she gasped for breath when Con pulled them both under the water again. As they burst up, gasping, she pummeled him with her fists. It was a very token gesture as she certainly didn't want him to let go of her.

"I like the way you look with water running all over you."

"I bet you do. It's that Neanderthal thing."

"Yeah." He looked at her steadily, eyes shining. "I've got it bad. I want to drag you back to my cave and make love to you some more by firelight."

"We'll I'm not go ng anywhere with no clothes on."

"Then I guess we re stuck here. I like it. No one here but us."

"And the alligators and snakes and crawdads and herons and mosquitoes and…"

"Yes. Isn't it beautiful," Con's voice was dark with wonder. "Look." He pointed down the bayou where it rolled away in a lazy curve, iridescent with moonlight. Overhanging trees on the far bank kissed the water with their branches. The air pulsed with the heady thrum of tree frogs calling for their mates. "I'd forgotten how perfect it is here."

Lizzie's chest tightened, and not just because of the creepy crawlies.

"You're shivering. We'll get out." He splashed toward the bank, holding her tight. "The vans have all driven away."

"My hair's wet. I's going to tangle."

"I'll comb it for you." He pushed a soggy lock behind her shoulder, supporting her with one arm like she weighed nothing. "You have the most beautiful hair I've ever seen, my river goddess."

*Sweet talker.* Still, with moonlight and the warm night air on her skin she felt beautiful, sexy and alive as Con let her feet down on the prickly grass.

"I don't think I've ever been outside naked before." She giggled as Con handed her his shirt.

"Yeah, I guess you kept your top on that time in the desert, didn't you? This time was better. I could feel you right there with me."

Lizzie blushed in the darkness. She hadn't held herself back this time. Probably couldn't have if she tried. Con had gotten right under her skin again, damn him.

They strolled back to the house holding hands, Con buck naked and totally unself-conscious, even when he kissed her and grew hard again.

He'd been irresistible as a fantasy man, in the role she'd conjured and he'd so easily assumed. But somehow as a real person, with problems and hang-ups and deep, deep flaws, he was even more dangerously captivating.

"Let's find our way up to bed and get the sheets sweaty," he whispered, as he pushed open the door into the dark house.

"Okay."

# 21

They never did get around to combing Lizzie's hair, and by the next morning it was a rat's nest of tangles. Raoul was actually breaking a sweat trying to get a comb through it at the dressing table in the bedroom.

"Girl, whatever did you put in it?"

"River water," murmured Lizzie.

"You washed it in the river? Your hair doesn't need washing every day. You could have waited. And why didn't you use conditioner?"

Lizzie chewed her lip to stop a sly smile sneaking across her face.

Raoul tut-tutted. "I'll have to talk to that boy. He's interfering with my professional responsibilities." He spritzed more detangler on it. "Can you believe all the fuss they're making over him?"

"What fuss?" Maisie had whisked Con away while Lizzie was barely awake.

"The local paper ran a last-minute story about him that's out this morning. Got a big picture of him on the front page looking like a movie star. Has a whole bit about his tragic past and how he might be the missing heir to this place. They're eating it up like shrimp étouffé. "

"I guess it's a slow news day." Lizzie chewed her brioche, wondering why she suddenly felt nervous.

"Phone's been ringing off the hook ever since. Some other news stations want in on the act. There are vans from Baton Rouge and New Orleans out in the driveway."

"Well, that's good, isn't it? All the more chance he'll find his brother." So why did her stomach feel so queasy?

What would this brother be like if he was still alive? Not many people would have Con's sunny disposition after a childhood like that. Maybe what that asshole lawyer said about calling the local prisons wasn't so far off the mark.

She took another bite of brioche.

"Nervous about meeting the in-laws?" Raoul read her thoughts.

"I'm nervous about everything," she confessed. "Con never told me any of that business about his family. It was a horrible surprise. What's next?"

Raoul stopped combing. "Hey, if that was your story, would you tell it to the beautiful girl you wanted to marry?"

Lizzie bit her lip. "I don't know."

"You probably would. You're the up-front, in-your-face type. I like that about you." He started combing again. "And that's why you're perfect for Conroy. Some girls would have just let sleeping dogs lie. Who cares where he's from, right? He's cute." He winked. "But not you. You're not that easy."

No? She'd been ready to tie the knot when he was a virtual stranger with a past she'd unwittingly invented. *Sucker.*

Raoul paused again, held her gaze in the mirror with those all-seeing almond-shaped eyes. "I know why you're here."

Lizzie's stomach tightened. *To make fifty thousand dollars fast.*

"You have all kinds of reasons you think you're here for." He leaned in and she could smell his expensive cologne. "But you're really here because you needed to know all about Conroy. The good, the bad and the ugly."

*Did I?* She had no idea anymore. Hadn't it been just a cruel joke? Maybe it always was more than that. About getting under Con's smooth, tanned skin and seeing what made him tick. And now that she had...

*She was crazier about him than ever.*

"Keep your head still. What are you doing?" The comb tangled in her hair as she sprung from the chair.

"I need air!"

"You need detangling, sweetheart. I wouldn't go downstairs with all those cameras looking like this if I were you."

She collapsed back into the chair, heart thumping. "I really do love him."

"I know." He sprayed more detangler on her hair.

"But," she hesitated, watching his sharp profile in the mirror. "He doesn't love me," she said softly.

"Oh, yes he does," Raoul replied without breaking his combing rhythm.

"No, really, you don't understand—" She groped for the right words to explain without giving too much away.

"Sweetheart, there are a lot of things I don't understand, but one thing I know for sure, that boy is head over heels in love with you. Now sit still or we'll be here all day."


Lizzie came downstairs to find everyone outside, in front of the house, filming Con and his supposed ancestral estate.

She stood in the hallway, wondering why no one had asked her to come on camera. Gia crashed in through the front door, running.

"Gia, am I having another dress fitting this morning?"

"Um, I don't know. I need to find something. Ask Maisie." And Gia darted past her.

Lizzie didn't want to come out the front door into the shot, so she went out the back door and crept around the side of the house. Four TV vans with satellite dishes on top cluttered the long oak-lined drive. Con stood in front of a camera, next to a reporter in a bright blue suit. Dino crouched off to one side, filming the interview, and Maisie hovered next to him with her clipboard in her hands and an expression of fierce excitement on her face.

She tapped Maisie on the arm and pulled her out of earshot. "Maisie, what's going on?"

"The Eyewitness News team has been putting pressure on all the right people. They found an old will attached to the property." Her pale eyes gleamed with manic intensity. "It leaves everything to the owner's firstborn child. Since it seems Con's mother was the only daughter of the owner, and she's dead, it all belongs to Con."

Lizzie snuck a glance at the gleaming white façade with its double tier of balconies. Holy crap. No real surprise, though.

"The trust is almost completely empty, and they're starting an investigation into what happened to the money, as apparently there was almost two million in there when the old man died seven years ago. But—" Maisie glanced at Con, "they've uncovered other assets in storage, valuable antiques apparently, though at this point no one knows exactly what they are."

Lizzie didn't know what to say. Her brioche churned in her gut. "Any word on his brother?"

"Eyewitness News say they've had a slew of calls, but what with the inheritance they expect most or all of them are cranks wanting to get their hands on some money. They're weeding through them."

"So, um, the wedding, is it still on track for tomorrow?"

"The wedding? Oh, Don wants us to run with this inheritance story and get to the wedding after it's died down a bit. He thinks this is fresher and will generate more buzz. Roger's inside rough-cutting some promos already. It's a perk that Con's so great looking. I think we're going to get a lot of attention with this show."

*Now if we could just recast the leading lady...* Lizzie heard a subtext that made her glance down at the outfit she'd carefully chosen. She'd put some weight back on, and both the sage green capris and the turquoise blouse were a little snug. She'd have to keep her face to the camera so they didn't see a panty line.

Not that it was a pressing problem right now.

Another thought occurred to her. "The lawyer said we probably couldn't stay into next week. He said it was booked." What if they decided to drop the wedding altogether?

"Bullshit. That good old boy is sweating bullets right now with the attorney general's office breathing down his neck. It's Con's house, darling! He can stay here the rest of his life if he wants." Maisie squeezed her wrist. "Isn't it wonderful!"

"Oh, yes," she said weakly. "Wonderful."

The lord of the manor looked very handsome and earnest, talking with the reporter. What on earth were they gabbing about for so long? She couldn't hear a word.

For someone who'd wanted nothing to do with the past, with the letters, with any claim to the house, Con had slipped into his new role with alarming ease, and she was getting left out in the cold. Or more accurately, in the sweltering, armpit-soaking heat. The blue cooling machines had been carted away, apparently given up as a lost cause. She probably wouldn't get to feel cool again until she got back to New York.

If she ever did get back to New York.

Of course she was going back to New York. *You're not going to be living here by his side as lady of the manor. You'll be lucky if he even goes through with the damn wedding now. He certainly doesn't need the money. He can sell this pile for a pot of cash and cruise off into the sunset in a brand new gold Mercedes with a brand-new golden-haired mama by his side, no sugar even required.*

She realized she was chewing her nail and pulled her hand sharply away. Damn, it was hard to breathe in this humidity.

Was it possible that Raoul was right and Con really did love her too?

Making love. What a funny expression. They'd done it three times last night. But amidst all the moaning and heavy breathing there had been no professions of undying love.

He was horny.

And she'd gone soft on him.

Sucker.

"Maisie, do you have a minute?" Con wiped his forehead with his sleeve. Where was Lizzie?

"Shoot."

"Any word on Danny?"

"They've had eighty-three calls and more than three hundred emails, though a lot of those are just people who are interested but don't know anything. I think eight different people have claimed to be Danny."

Con swallowed. Would he even know Danny after ten years' absence? He sure didn't look anything like his scrawny fourteen-year old-self. "Anyway, the PA is updating me every half-hour. They're going to run something again on the evening news. The story is a local sensation."

He took a deep breath. "Could I ask you something in total confidence."

"Of course," she whispered, moving closer. Her eyes shone. "What is it?"

"Well," he shoved his fingers through his hair. "I was wondering if, maybe," he hesitated, his stomach tight. Where had Lizzie gone? "If maybe this story about me trying to find my brother might be enough to earn Lizzie the fifty thousand."

Maisie's eyes narrowed and her head cocked to the side like a coyote that just heard a rabbit in the bushes. "You don't want to go through with the wedding?"

"It's not that I don't want to, it's just that maybe…the timing isn't right."

"I can see your point." Her eyes narrowed to slits. "Your life is about to change very dramatically, so maybe now is not the time to make any permanent commitments."

Maisie's ill-concealed glee at his request deepened the unease in his gut.

"I'll have to have another chat with Don. We did line up a lot of donations for the wedding, people who are expecting sponsor credit and that kind of thing, but he loves this new long-lost heir/missing brother story. Perhaps we can use the wedding stuff for a follow-up series? A takeoff of *The Bachelor*, where beautiful young women compete for your—"

"Oh no, no that's not...Um, no. I was just hoping that Lizzie could still get her money if we didn't do the wedding."

"I'll talk to Don. Obviously, the series will need a climax, but since we ve got two options—you inheriting this place and you finding your brother, I don't think it'll be too much of a problem." She leaned into him, conspiratorial. "Thanks for coming to me, Conroy. I appreciate your trust. I won't breathe a word to Lizzie." With a look of compassion, she capped her pen and walked off to talk to one of the news crews.

Con sagged with relief. He hated himself for letting it all come this far. Lizzie didn't deserve to have her wedding—a once-in-a-lifetime event that should be a person's most cherished memory—be a cheap fraud for cold cash. He cared for her far too much to marry her under false pretenses. He'd brought her to this low point, and he'd get her out of it without her throwing away her dignity and integrity. If he was going to marry her it would be the real deal, from the heart, and for ever.

"Did Michiko manage to alter the dress yet?" Lizzie couldn't understand why everyone seemed to have forgotten the reason they were all here.

"Um, I'm not sure." Maisie seemed preoccupied, scratching something off her clipboard.

"What?" Yes, the power was still off, but surely even if the wedding didn't take place tomorrow as planned, it would be the following day or the day after that.

"This story about Con's family is taking up everyone's time for now. I just got the go-ahead to visit the storage facility where part of Con's inheritance is being held. We're heading out there right now."

"Oh, I guess I'll get changed." Lizzie smoothed the front of her wrinkled shirt. She'd spent most of the morning lying on the bed reading a paperback.

"There's no need. You can stay right here if you want. I'm sure it won't be all that interesting. Probably just a dusty box of stock certificates or something." Maisie scratched away at her clipboard.

"I'll get dressed." Alarm sizzled along her nerves as Maisie scurried off outside. Suddenly, she'd become totally irrelevant. No one had mentioned a single word about the ceremony. The arbor hadn't been decorated as planned; there had been no discussion of the intimate wedding banquet happening after the ceremony. It was all Con this, Con that, Con's brother, Con's legacy. What about her? She was going to be Con's wife for crying out loud!

*Well, not really.* Her breathing quickened. As far as Con knew, they were still getting a divorce right after the wedding as she'd decreed when she came up with this crazy idea.

She hadn't breathed a word about her fresh hopes that maybe they could forget about the divorce and...

Live happily ever after?

The house phone rang.

Where the heck was everyone? Probably outside doing more interviews. It certainly was peaceful inside with no power until the phone started ringing. The polished black antique had a painfully loud bell-driven ring. Was no one going to answer it? Her nerves were fraying.

She picked it up. "Hello."

"May I speak to Maisie Dixon please?"

Ah, she'd know those clipped pompous tones anywhere. "Hi, Dwight, it's Lizzie."

"Lizzie, thank goodness. I can't get hold of Maisie. I've left several messages on her cell but she hasn't returned them."

"She's been insanely busy. I'm sure she just hasn't had time."

"May I speak to her?"

"Actually, I can see her through the window and she's talking on her cell right now. Do you want me to give her a message?"

"Um, yes. She left me a message saying she won't be able to meet me in the Berkshires this weekend as planned."

"Oh, right. We're kind of stuck here. A power outage has delayed everything." That and Con's past exploding in my face.

"It's imperative that I speak to her. I've been trying to schedule some time with her for weeks now. Months, in fact. She's been so busy I haven't been able to... Anyway, I'm coming down there. I'm flying into New Orleans early this evening, and I've chartered a car to bring me there. I'm on my way to the airport right now, in fact."

"Okaaay."

"According to my itinerary, I should be arriving between 7:00 and 7 15 p.m. central time."

"I'll let her know." Lizzie tried not to laugh. Maisie with her clipboard and Dwight with his "itinerary" really were a perfect match. So self-satisfied and snooty they deserved each other. "See ya later, Dwight."

He'd love the lack of electricity. And the heat and the bugs. She chuckled. And Maisie probably wouldn't be too excited about being distracted from her work either. How long had they been engaged? They couldn't schedule time to have sex, let alone get married. In fact the very idea of them having sex... She shuddered as a vision of reptiles mating crowded her brain.

She pushed up the lower sash of the window. It went up smoothly. The sash-cord must have been replaced in the money-hemorrhaging renovations.

"Maisie!" she called out. About forty feet away, Maisie squinted at her, her phone still pressed to her ear. "Dwight called. He's flying down today. Got something important to tell you."

Maisie muttered something into her phone. She strode toward the window. "Today? You mean he's arriving tonight?"

"Yup. On his way." She smiled cheerfully.

Maisie's perfectly smooth forehead wrinkled. "What on earth for? It's not like I won't be back next week."

"He said he's been trying to schedule time with you for ages, but you've been too busy."

"He knows my job is demanding." Standing right under the window, Maisie glanced at her clipboard. "It's my time to build my career. He understands that."

"He sounded very anxious to see you."

Maisie's face brightened and got a strangely distant look. "I have a funny feeling he's finally going to set the date."

"Of your wedding?"

"Yes. We're always waiting until the timing is just perfect, and then of course we're both so madly busy—" She paused and pressed her pen to her mouth. "I wanted to get married last June, but his company was in the midst of a merger and he had an important bond deal to close. Of course it's given me more time to research and plan and develop a truly impressive guest list…"

Lizzie glanced sideways into the drawing room, where opened boxes of linen napkins and fine stemware lay gathering dust.

"That's it, I'm sure of it. We're going to set the date." Her eyes gleamed like ice cubes.

"Speaking of which, um, what day are we planning to do my wedding?" Lizzie's voice came out kind of high and squeaky.

"Um," Maisie tucked some hair behind her ear. "Has, um Con said anything about…No?"

"Con? What are you talking about?" The knot in her intestines tightened a notch.

"He has been terribly busy. Well, I must go. I need to get directions to the storage facility as we're driving out there right away. As I said there's no need for you to come." Maisie was already turning away and fingering her phone.

"I'm coming." She slammed down the window for emphasis. Suddenly she didn't feel like letting Con out of her sight for a single instant.


Con had planned to tell Lizzie the wedding was off on the way over to wherever the hell they were going. Maisie had the okay from Don, and he wanted to get that one mess straightened out. Things were so out of control right now he didn't know which way was up. People were talking about the house like it was his, and the story about his father and what he'd done to his mom was out there in the news and complete strangers with cameras were asking him questions about things he'd never even dared to think about let alone talk about and...

"So you guys think it'll be a big chest of treasure or something?" Roger's jovial voice from the backseat drew him back to reality. As soon as Rog climbed into the car, Con knew his news for Lizzie would have to wait.

"What exactly is it supposed to be?" Lizzie looked distracted and nervous, playing with her watch.

"I don't know. Some stuff in a lockup. The documents they found didn't have a list of specifics, just a key." Con drew the key out of his pocket and dangled it from its soiled string. "Hope it's not a bunch of skeletons or something."

"Too right. I never know what's going to happen around here lately." Rog shifted his long body in the Jeep's tiny backseat "So the house is really yours?"

"So they tell me. There's an old will involved, dating back to when the house was first built. The house goes to the oldest male of the line, failing that to the oldest female. Primogeniture or something, it's called. They did a DNA test on me to make sure I'm who I say I am."

"Smart move,' murmured Lizzie, eyes on the windshield.

Con chuckled. "Yeah. Anyway, they have to match it up with something of the old man's. I think they have a lock of his hair from when he was a baby or something creepy like that. They get the results back tomorrow."

"How do you feel about being related to him? To the guy who abandoned your mother to her death?" Lizzie turned to him, eyes flashing. She knew he'd caved under pressure and shown the letters to the news media, who'd slavered all over them. He also suspected Lizzie thought there was something pornographic about him splashing his unsightly family history all over the press.

"I hate him," he said with conviction that tightened his voice. "He didn't want to leave his precious crap to Mom. Only reason it's coming to me is because of some old will he couldn't change. I hope the bastard rots in hell." It felt good to get that off his chest after playing nice for the cameras all morning.

"So I guess you'll be giving all his money and possessions to a charity for battered women?" said Lizzie archly. She wasn't looking at him, but he could see her raised eyebrow.

"Maybe." The prospect of inheriting the house still seemed weird. Wrong. Damn he loved the area, though. Now he'd gotten over all those ancient fears, the thought of living back down here on the bayou held a lot of appeal.

"Are you serious?" Lizzie's head snapped round.

"I don't know. I barely know my own name right now." He gripped the steering wheel a little tighter, the firm leather and metal something he could at least hold on to.

"Your name's Conroy Beale, unless the story's changing again." Her tone was cool.

What was eating her anyway? He'd hoped all that hot sex they'd enjoyed lately would mellow her out a bit. He also hoped that after he told her the good news that she'd get her money without having to marry him, they could pick right back up where they'd left off in the early hours of this morning. Either that or she'd be pissed as hell he'd gone to Maisie behind her back. He was hoping for the former.

A surge of warm anticipation tightened his pants and he smiled at her.

"What are you smiling at?"

"You."

"Don't miss the turnoff!" called Rog. "It's the next right."

The storage facility was an old one. Long corrugated metal buildings set deep off the road in a weed strewn lot.

"Shouldn't think there's anything still in there." Lizzie scratched an itchy bug bite on her arm. "It's hardly protected by armed guards is it?"

"There's a security guard in the office, though he's about a hundred years old. He's the one who told me

where number four was. Says it's this whole building."
Patches of red rust-preventative paint were crudely
daubed over the peeling pale blue powder-coat of a
building at least two hundred feet long.

The van door slammed and Maisie strode toward
them, Dino close behind with the camera on his shoulder.

"What have we here, I wonder?" She rubbed her
hands together.

Lizzie crossed her arms and hung back, as usual.

Rog sidled up behind her and whispered in her ear.
"Maisie told the news crews we weren't coming until
five, she wanted to scoop them." He chuckled.

"Conroy," Maisie intoned, adopting her "on air" glow.
"We're about to uncover yet another legacy of a forbear
you never knew existed. How do you *feel?*" She leaned
into him, eyes glittering.

"I don't know." He ran his hand through his hair.

The lord of the manor's shirt was coming untucked.
Amazing Con wasn't coming right apart at the seams
considering all this drama she'd dropped him into. Could
they just go get married? Was that too much to ask?

"You have the key?" Maisie asked in deep, sonorous
tones.

Lizzie rolled her eyes.

Con held it out. They strode toward the door, Dino
following. A nasty twist of anticipation toyed with the
contents of Lizzie's stomach.

Con reached down to the ground to insert the key and
grab the handle of the giant rolling door. Then he seized it
and pulled hard.

The door came up about a foot, then stopped. "It's
rusty." He tugged at it. It budged up a few more inches,
then stuck again.

Lizzie instinctively took a step forward to go help,
then held herself in check.

Con yanked on it again, pulled it up a few more
inches, then levered himself under it and threw it up all
the way with an audible grunt.

"Holy shit."

Con and Maisie disappeared in the dark doorway with
Dino. With the blazing afternoon sun bouncing off the

metal building, Lizzie couldn't make out what lay inside the unlit interior. She hurried forward.

As she peered into the vast gloomy chamber, she saw shadowy hulking shapes, spaced at regular intervals, covered with dark tarps.

Cars.

Con and Maisie pulled back a tarp on one of the larger ones to reveal an immense, very ancient car—headlamps the size of soccer balls, seats like plush leather sofas and no windshield. Con's jaw hung open.

"It's in perfect condition," said Maisie. "I wish I knew what model it is."

"It's prewar Peugeot Phaeton." Con's voice sounded strangely breathless. Maybe it was the echo of his voice bouncing off the metal walls and high metal ceiling.

Maisie gave him a surprised look. She strode over to another car with a silver molded cover on it and started to peel back the edge. Con stroked his fingertips lovingly over the buttery paint of the Peugeot. Lizzie had a feeling it wasn't going to be donated to a women's shelter anytime soon.

"Conroy, come here! Even I know what this one is."

He took another corner of the silver tarp and they peeled it back. "A Rolls Royce Silver Ghost," they said in unison.

Rog let out a low whistle, which summoned a frown from Dino, who was still filming, silent as a shadow.

Lizzie lifted her hair off her hot neck. So Grandad left a bunch of cars behind. Big deal. Of course, it was kind of a coincidence the old man was a car nut like Con. Then again it wasn't a coincidence at all if they shared the same DNA. A lust for molded steel was probably encoded in the Y chromosome.

Con had opened the sideways folding hood of the Silver Ghost and was staring at its gloomy innards with manic concentration. "It's the original engine," he breathed at last. "I've never seen anything like it."

*Whatever!* Lizzie crossed her arms and rolled her eyes to the ceiling.

As if he'd heard her thoughts, Con closed the hood and looked around the unlit interior. "Lizzie, where are you?"

*Still alive, not that you care.*

Was she being petty? Probably. But heck, they'd come down here to get married, not to explore his ancestral legacy for crying out loud.

"I'm here," she said quietly.

"Lizzie, will you come sit in it with me?" The mischievous expression on his face made her insides jump. Okay, so he did look like a cute puppy dog who's found a new bone.

She walked forward, no faster than usual. No expression on her face. "Nice car."

Con tilted his head to the side and let out a snort of laughter. "That's the understatement of the century."

He pulled on the gleaming chrome handle and opened the heavy door for her. She climbed in, dust tickling her nose. The leather looked a little dull but totally unmarred, almost new. She sat down as Con walked around and climbed in the other side, with a goofy grin on his face. "Holy shit. I never thought I'd get to own one of these."

"Watch your language, you're on TV. Besides, if I still had money, maybe I'd have bought you one." The steering wheel stuck right out on a long pole.

"You wouldn't believe how much this is worth." Con ran his fingers over the smooth wood dash.

"Before or after I respray it for you?"

Her little joke cracked Con's smile into a huge grin and he leaned forward and kissed her. Naturally, being Con, he nailed her right on the mouth, lips hot on hers before she even had a chance to close them.

Chemistry boomed through her and suddenly her hands were clutching at his shirt, her tongue was in his mouth, his fingers were winding into her hair—

"Ahem." Maisie's deliberate throat clearing made her blink.

She jumped back. "How do you do that?" she hissed.

"What?" Con's lips were moist and his dark eyes shone.

"Nothing." She hoped her dark blush wasn't visible in the dim light. The hickey on her neck had begun sizzling, and she tugged her hair down to cover it.

Maisie approached the window, and Con rolled it down. "These cars are worth a fortune. Conroy, you are a very lucky man."

As Maisie turned to say something to Dino, Lizzie narrowed her eyes. "So, Conroy," she said, in an impersonation of Maisie's interviewer voice. "Will you be giving these fine automobiles away to charity?"

Con rested his palm on the smooth round head of the stick shift and looked up at her, dark eyes wide. "Hell, no."

# 22

"So they think this guy is your brother?" Lizzie was almost more nervous than Con. Neither of them had touched the plate of chips and salsa set out to stave off starvation back at the house.

"Yes." Con stared out into the gloom. "Eyewitness News said they interviewed him at the station, and he's on his way over right now."

It was dusk, and despite a large electrical crew working most of the day, the lights still weren't back on. Everyone sat out on the darkening patio, rubbing bug repellant on sunburned flesh and mixing hard lemonade with a jug of vodka and two cartons of Paul Newman's pink lemonade.

Con hadn't touched a drop. He kept leaping up and pacing about. Lizzie put down the alcohol-free lemonade that was making her stomach feel even worse and fanned herself with a paper napkin.

"They're here!" Rog called around the side of the house.

"Dino, get into position," said Maisie, leaping up with her clipboard.

Con rubbed his mouth nervously with his hand. Lizzie instinctively went up to him and put her hand on his shoulder. He looked almost startled to see her. "It probably isn't even him," he said, blinking.

"Maybe not," she said softly. "But it can't hurt to meet the guy."

"What if I don't recognize him?"

"It's been a long time; I don't think anyone would expect you to. Come on." She linked her arm though his and led him around the side of the house. A blitzkrieg of lights had been set up near the Eyewitness News van camped there, and Lizzie saw the reporter having a microphone attached to her lapel and the back of her waist.

A pickup truck pulled in behind the news van.

"Do you suppose that's his truck?" whispered Lizzie, as they hung back in the shadows.

"Could be." Con's voice was barely audible. The door of the truck opened, and someone got out. A big guy. Bigger than Con. It was hard to see much in the mauve semidarkness.

"Come on, Con," hissed Maisie behind them. "We need you in the lights."

"I'll just wait here," whispered Lizzie.

"No way." Con tugged her hand. "I need you."

A funny warm feeling smothered her jangling nerves and tightened her hand around his as they stepped cautiously toward the lights.

The reporter fiddled with her mike and said something to the cameraman. She gestured to the large man who'd climbed out of the truck.

He didn't look anything like Con.

She squeezed Con's hand.

As he stepped into the light, she saw the man had sun-bleached hair and rough-looking features. Totally unlike Con's dark hair and aristocratic profile. Nut brown skin, a worn T-shirt, dirty jeans and pale rubber boots completed the contrast.

Lizzie bit the inside of her mouth. There was no way this could be the guy. Was Con feeling the same pinch of disappointment?

Con made a strange sound and let go of her hand. He said something she couldn't understand. The big man let out a long, colorful curse, stepped forward and embraced him in a bear hug.

Lizzie stepped back out of the light. Did Con really think this was his brother? Wasn't he supposedly called Tiny because he was so small?

Headlights raked over her as another car pulled into the driveway. Dwight? Timing was never his strong suit. Gia rushed forward to intercept him.

Con and the big man had pulled back slightly to stare each other in the face. Con said something, but again she couldn't make it out. Too much emotion in his voice.

"You did what you had to do," said the other.

Con was crying. Tears glittered on his cheeks, and she could see his shoulders heaving. She bit her knuckle, suddenly horribly embarrassed for him, with all the lights and technicians and cameras and total strangers standing around gawking.

Shouldn't they all get out of here and leave him in peace? She started to back away as the brothers embraced again, even tighter.

Tears stung her eyes and she bit down harder on her knuckle, drawing pain, anything to distract from the uncomfortable mix of sensations boiling inside her.

"Lizzie." A hissed voice from the darkness made her spin around. A long narrow face topped by a thick head of wheaten hair emerged from the gloom.

"Dwight?" She wiped her eyes with the back of her hand and walked away from the lights and cameras..

"Why are you shooting out here in the dark?"

"No power in the house. Con's meeting his brother."

"Who?" Dwight wrinkled his face impatiently.

Did Dwight not even know about Con? A chill trickled through Lizzie as she remembered how she'd kept Con a secret from everyone. Her own prize, her dream, that she didn't want anyone to trample on. Or was it because deep down she knew he wasn't one of them and they wouldn't really accept him?

He'd be one of them now, though, as heir to this place and a fortune in vintage sheet metal.

Shame seared through her at the superficial thought. She didn't deserve someone like Con, who'd been through so much and emerged a warmer, nicer person than she'd ever be

Dwight tapped his foot impatiently on the tarmac. "Where's Maisie?"

Lizzie shook her head and gulped. "I don't know. She's out here somewhere. They're in the middle of shooting, though, so you might want to go wait inside."

Dwight smacked at a mosquito above the collar of his striped oxford shirt. "Ugh, this is ridiculous! I fly all the way down here and now—"

"Shhhhh!" came a hiss from the darkness.

Dwight stalked off to the house.

"Lizzie!" Lizzie jumped as Con said her name. "Come here."

Anxiety spiked inside her as he beckoned her into the harsh glare of the television lights. What did he want with her?

"I want you to meet my brother, Danny."

Her heart thudded as she walked toward him in slow motion. How did he know for sure it was his brother?

Con seized her hand as she came close. "Danny, this is Lizzie, the woman who brought me back down here. I wouldn't have had the courage to come without her."

Lizzie's breath evaporated, and the television lights stung her eyes. "Hello," she managed, as a large, very rough hand grabbed hers and shook it. "Nice to meet you."

Her words sounded stupid, but she had no idea what to say. She noticed that Con's brother had tattoos on both forearms. His features, blunt and forbidding in the harsh light, melted into a smile when he spoke.

"I'm glad to meet you too, Lizzie. I've wished for this moment for ten long years." A gentle voice, with its almost European-sounding accent. "Thank you for bringing my brother back to me."

Lizzie colored, partly as a result of the strong emotion zinging between all three of them and partly out of embarrassment that her motives were so very different. She'd dragged Con here to punish him, and her plan had turned inside out.

She heard harsh whispering off to one side, and the Eyewitness News reporter stepped into the light.

Lizzie barely heard a word of the interview that followed. She backed away out of the light, slipping her hand from Con's as he answered a question. Out in the darkness, Maisie fumed and stamped about being scooped, while a producer from the news station reminded her they'd been the ones to find Danny and she'd get her turn in a minute.

It seemed like an hour before all the news vans packed up their equipment and rolled off into the steamy darkness. Lizzie was ashamed to find herself hoping Danny Beale would climb back into his truck and roll away too, but of course he didn't.

Con and his brother talked, animated and excited, touching each other a lot as if they couldn't quite believe the other person was really there and they needed to make sure. Both beaming. She could see the resemblance between them now, even in the darkness. Not just features but gestures and the cadence of their speech. She knew she should feel very happy for Con, and part of her did, but the rest of her was...

Jealous? She wanted Con all to herself again.

The portable generator the electricians were using had roared to life again once the cameras turned off, and the jackhammer fury of its engine rattled her nerves.

"Dinner!" Maisie's voice penetrated the darkness. "Let's get out of here and into some light and air-conditioning before we all go mad."

"Lizzie, come with us!" called Con. He stood by Danny's truck. She swallowed and walked forward, tucking her hair behind her ears. She had a feeling Danny Beale would see right through her.

"I'll sit in the middle." Con climbed in, then held out his hand to help her up. The big old truck had a funky smell to it. She buckled herself in, then Con slid his arm around her shoulders and relief crept through her tight muscles.

"Danny, did you see the news story?" She'd missed that part of the conversation due to Dwight's arrival.

"I didn't, but when I went to get some breakfast after work, turns out everybody else in town saw it and heard my name." His deep voice was rich with humor. "So I called the number, they asked me to come in and meet with a producer. I went straight there. Haven't even changed my clothes. I don't think they knew what to make of me." He looked past Con and grinned at her. Two rows of perfectly straight white teeth, just like Con's.

"Anyway, they sat me down and a girl asked me my age and all my particulars." His hand on the wheel looked huge, dirty nails. They were following the taillights of the van with the rest of the crew in it, piloted by Maisie, and Dwight's rental car was behind them. "Then they asked me the trick question Con came up with to weed out the fakers."

"What was it?"

"They asked me what the name of our pig was."

Con grinned and tightened his arm around her. "I told Lizzie about our pet pig. That's what gave me the idea. I figured no one but you would know the answer."

The weight of his arm drew tension from her shoulders, and the spicy, musky scent of him made her want to bury her face in his neck.

"And what was the name?"

Danny looked at her. "Delilah." His mouth fought a smile. "Con came up with it. He always did have an imagination."

They both laughed. It was nice to see Con so happy. He glowed with pleasure. She could feel the heat of his excitement rolling right off his skin.

"Man, do we have a lot of catching up to do! You still live around here?"

"Been living over on Bayou Lafourche the last couple of years. I've got my own shrimper. It's a sixty-footer."

"Alright! I knew you'd make it."

"Yeah?"

"Yeah. Well, I hoped so anyway. I figured anyone who could make crab traps out of nothing the way you did was going to amount to something." They laughed again.

Something was hanging from the rearview mirror. A string of pointy teeth?

"And what about you? You look like you're doing alright."

"Me? Oh, I'm getting by. Finding Lizzie's the best thing that ever happened to me." He gave her a squeeze.

Her eyes popped open and a surge of warmth flooded through her. *The best thing that ever happened to me?*

"If it wasn't for her, I wouldn't be back down here. I'm not ashamed to tell you, I was running scared. I had no idea the old man was dead. But Lizzie decided I had to face up to my past, and here I am."

"And what's all this about you comin' into that house? I couldn't see much in the dark but it looked like a big heap."

"Yeah. Well, if it's mine, and they say it is, it's yours too, bro."

Danny chuckled. 'I never did too well in houses. I like to have water under me, but I'll be happy to come spend time with you there."

Danny obviously had an upbeat, easygoing personality like Con. He explained that he'd gone to live with an elderly fisherman friend in a nearby parish, dodging social services until he was too old for them to bother with him. When Con confessed the shame he felt at leaving him, Danny teared up and cursed at him for feeling guilty. His driving became a little erratic as he put his arm around Con and said he never gave up hope that they'd see each other again. Lizzie sniffed back her own tears. This reunion was partly her doing. A warm glow filled the cab, and she let herself bask in it.

The van ahead of them pulled up in front of a colorful seafood joint with Papa Ron's on the sign out front. It reminded Lizzie of a Cape Cod clam shack.

"Good choice," said Danny, pulling in next to the van. "I'm ready for some celebrating!"

Dinner was a raucous affair involving steaming platters of seafood and rice and shocking quantities of beer in iced jugs. Lizzie was the only one not drinking, and the conversation got more and more surreal as the level of alcohol rose in everyone else's blood.

Party-girl Maisie held court like an empress, eyes shining with power and drink, while Dwight smoldered in a corner, nursing a dry martini. She'd just started regaling the bartender with tales of her recent trip to Bangalore, and the huge crocodiles she'd seen there, when he beamed a smile that shone brighter than his bald head.

"Y'all want to come see the gator I've got out back. Ten feet long and snarlin' angry!"

Not really, thought Lizzie, but everyone else was already on their feet, following Maisie out the door. She heaved herself up and traipsed out into the muggy darkness.

An outdoor light beamed down on the alligator where it lay, looking small and oppressed, in a muddy pen surrounded by a low chain-link fence.

Poor thing.

"My nephew brought it here last week. Caught it in the bayou." The man leaned over the edge of the fence and brandished a stick at the alligator, which swished back, snarled, and snapped at the stick, revealing its fearsome spiked teeth.

"I don't know if Tiny here has told you," he gestured to Danny. "But he's done some alligator wrestling in his time."

All eyes swiveled to Danny, who looked down at the alligator. "Nice looking creature. Young male, I'd guess. Wouldn't want to get between those jaws."

"Don't let him fool you!" said the bartender. "He's taken down fifteen-footers. Learned it from the Indians."

"There are Native Americans around here?" asked Maisie.

"Sure," said Danny. "But he's talking about a stint I did out in Florida. I was a paid professional alligator wrangler for the Seminole tribe. Did it for two years."

"You're a Seminole?"

"Nope, but they don't care. If you can wrestle a gator out of deep water in front of a crowd of tourists, you're good enough. The Seminole kids have casino money now, and they want to work in a nice office. Not me. That's where I saved up the money to buy my boat."

Lizzie glanced at Con. He was wide-eyed like her. "Did you ever do that when you were a kid?" she whispered in his ear.

"Nope." He didn't take his eyes off Danny.

"Your brother is something else."

"Yeah." Con shone with pride.

"Danny, would you wrestle it on camera, please!" Maisie was suddenly right in front of him.

"Wrestle it into doing what?" asked Danny, with a smile. "It's just laying there."

"I don't know. Can't you make it mad and sit on it or something?" Maisie looked like she was about to start jumping up and down with excitement.

"Tell you what," said the proprietor slowly. "If one of ya'll New Yorkers want to help Danny carry this gator to the pen over there—" he gestured out into the darkness. "Your drinks are on the house."

"I can carry it by myself, chief," said Danny.

"I know, but where's the entertainment in that? I've got a bar to run." The bartender slapped him on the back. "Come on, who's willing to help move this magnificent creature for me?"

The tree frogs sang.

"Oh come on!" protested Maisie. "Conroy! Here's a chance to get back in touch with your bayou heritage."

Con laughed.

"Don't be a spoilsport! I'm sure your brother would love to have you do it with him."

"Sure, it'd be fun." Danny looked as relaxed as if he'd been dared to go floss his teeth.

Con hesitated.

Adrenaline surged through Lizzie. "No, don't! You'll get hurt."

"No, he won't," said Maisie. "Look, it's not even moving. And it'll make such a great cliff-hanger at commercial break."

"Well, I guess I—"

"No!" said Lizzie. "Con, you can't!"

"Why not? As Maisie said it isn't doing much."

"I'll take the head, and you hold the tail still. I'll walk you through it." Danny settled his hands on the rim of the pen, ready to jump the fence and get started.

"Alright." Con took a step toward the fence.

A vision of those hideous teeth closing around Con's arm, or worse, his head, swam in front of Lizzie's eyes and sent adrenaline surging through her. She grabbed his arm. "Don't you dare get into that pen, Conroy Beale!" she screamed at the top of her lungs. "Don't you care about anyone but yourself?"

There was a lengthy pause. Lizzie flushed violently.

"Nice to have someone who cares about you," said Danny softly. He lifted his hands off the fence.

"I just don't think it's a good idea, that's all," she mumbled. "I just..."

*I just love you.*

"Alright." Con slid his arm around her. "I won't do it if you really don't want me to, Lizzie." He kissed her forehead gently. "I won't do anything you don't want me to."

Lizzie tried to act like she didn't care much either way. Which was hard when Con settled his lips on her cheek and squeezed her waist, sending a current of heat and relief charging up through her.

Maisie scanned the group. "Roger?"

"I think I've drunk a bit too much," he slurred, swaying like a redwood in the wind.

"Dino? I'll take over the camera." Dino just looked over the camera, which was running, and raised an eyebrow.

"Raoul." She sidled over and slapped him on the back. "Come on. Just think of the great stories you'll have to tell. You'll be dining out on this for years."

Raoul lifted his chin in the air. "Sweetheart, I don't do mud." He straightened his shirt lapel.

"Ugh!" Maisie put her hands on her hips. Her eyes flashed in the harsh light above the door. "You're all such wimps. I'll do it!"

Even the tree frogs shut the hell up.

Danny looked down at her from his impressive height, and a slow smile spread across his tanned face. He strode up to her and gently lifted her hand, as if they were about to step out in a minuet. "I'd be delighted." He kissed her knuckles gently.

Maisie shook her hair back and stuck her chest out. "Good. Let's get started."

Lizzie covered her eyes with her hand. "That poor alligator."

# 23

Lizzie was the only one sober enough to drive home. Except for Dwight who'd zoomed off in disgust after learning from an arxious Raoul that his fiancé was about to get down and dirty with an alligator. Raoul had gone with him to help navigate.

Con sat on the bench seat of the big van next to Lizzie while everyone else, including Danny, piled into the rear. They'd retrieve Danny's truck in the morning.

The alligator was sleeping it off in a larger pen down near the bayou, the drinks—which had flowed for a couple more hours—were on the house, and Maisie and Danny—both covered in mud from head to toe—had been giving each other glances that could scorch the skin of a lesser mortal.

"Your cousin is something else." Con had also managed to get very dirty, and he was nearly as drunk as the rest of them.

Lizzie put the car into gear and pulled out of the space without stalling even once. "Yup, that's Maisie, loves to be the center of attention." Typical. Everyone in the bar had been drooling and falling all over her. Apparently, a glaze of mud only enhanced her Amazon appeal. "I'll never hear the end of her alligator-wrestling adventure. I can't believe Dwight didn't try to stop her."

"Do you think anyone could stop Maisie doing what she wants?" Con stretched and cracked his knuckles.

"Buckle your seatbelt."

He smiled, eyes soft with affection or liquor or both. "I love it when you worry about me." He obeyed with fumbling hands.

"I bet Danny let the alligator get loose on purpose just so he could have the fun of catching it again."

"Yeah." He grinned. "He sure knows how to put on a good show. It'll be a blast on TV."

"That's not what you were saying at the time. My arm still has white marks from you gripping it."

"Hey, he's my brother and I haven't seen him for ten years. I didn't want him to get eaten right after I found him again."

"He's quite a character. I guess it runs in the family." She winked at Con, who winked back, causing a teeny sizzle in her belly.

"What is Maisie doing with that Dwight? He seems a real stick in the mud."

"Dwight is from an old oil family. He's well connected and very, very rich."

"That may be, but he's not man enough to handle Maisie."

"And you're suddenly an expert on the subject?" Driving strange unlit roads in the dark was rattling her nerves enough without Con having opinions about Maisie's love life.

"I just know what I see. Maisie needs a real man."

"You're lucky she can't hear you through that partition, she'd show you which one of you is the real man."

Con laughed. "Too right."


What a day! Con sprawled naked on the bed, too tipsy to try and keep his thoughts straight. Finding Danny again was the best thing to ever happen to him...right after meeting Lizzie, of course.

The lights were back on so he got to admire the vision of lovely Lizzie coming back in from the bathroom, her robe held closed with one hand.

"Get that off, cher."

"You're drunk."

"I know. C'mere."

He could see her fighting a smile as she slipped her robe off and slid under the covers with him. Her lush silky body felt like cloud nine up against his.

How would he propose to her? It would have to be something really special. A carriage ride? Nah, too ordinary. A hot-air balloon? Since the TV show could arrange it, the sky was truly the limit. But maybe something closer to home—a riverboat ride? Maybe even on Danny's boat?

He squeezed her and couldn't help a groan of pleasure as he grew hard against her soft belly.

He wouldn't tell her the wedding was off. He'd propose to her, she'd accept, and they'd do the wedding in fine style, for real.

She'd say yes, he was sure of it. He'd seen her looking at him on the sly—those big eyes all wide and cautious. And when she screamed and got crazy when he was about to help with the gator...

*She'd say yes.*

He buried his face in her glorious hair. It smelled of almonds, probably some stuff Raoul put in it, but perfectly beautiful, like the rest of her.

The house made it possible. It made him good enough for her. Here she could live in the style she was accustomed to, no stepping down in the world. They'd install new air-conditioning and update the kitchen. There were plenty of bedrooms for...

*Get a hold of yourself Con! You have to propose first.*

"What are you laughing about?" Lizzie's soft voice tickled his ear.

"Nothing."

"Then why are you grinning like the Cheshire Cat?"

"The who?"

"Never mind. We need to get some sleep. You're going to feel like hell in the morning."

"I sure feel like I'm in heaven right now." He tightened his arms around her and inhaled the womanly sweetness of her skin.

He was looking forward to doing this for the rest of his life.

Lizzie emerged from a long, cool morning shower to a gloriously silent house. Everyone was sleeping off last night's bender and a big box of pastries had been delivered to the kitchen. She opened it and helped herself to a beignet loaded with powdered sugar. Mmmm.

Roger slept on the sofa in the "dressing room," one long arm trailing on the floor near the boxes of linen napkins.

A creak from upstairs brought her to the foot of the curved staircase in time to see a rumpled Gia leaving Dino and Roger's bedroom. So that's why Roger was sleeping downstairs. She took another bite and smiled. Gia winked at her on her way into the bathroom.

Lizzie polished off her beignet and licked the sugar off her fingers. Time to find Raoul before the hair got out of control. Of course she could just pull it back in a ponytail like she'd have done back home, but since the electricity was back on, maybe they'd do the wedding today as originally planned?

A shot of mingled fear and excitement jolted her.

*Do you take this man...?*

*Yes!*

She didn't think they'd get divorced either. She looked around the wide foyer, where the polished wood floors gleamed in the morning light. Maybe it was the way the sun streamed through the bright glass, or the easy warmth of the morning air, or all the hot sauce rolling around in her bloodstream, but she could see a clear vision of Con and herself living here...

*Happily ever after.*

Deep breath.

She climbed the stairs, and pushed her rapidly tangling hair out of her eyes as she knocked on Raoul's door. No answer.

"Raoul," she whispered, not wanting to wake everyone else.

She turned the knob—unlocked—and pushed the door open.

And gasped.

There were two men in the bed. Not entangled in the throes of passion or anything, but just sleeping peacefully, dressed in PJ's, one on each side. Raoul, and Dwight. One of them was snoring.

*Dwight?*

Was this why he wouldn't set the date? Because Maisie wasn't exactly his... cup of tea?

She closed the door. Phew. Okay, time to find a ponytail band. Maisie was going to go ballistic.

Why did that give her a thrill?

Gia came out of the bathroom, toweling her short hair. She jumped when she saw Lizzie.

"Where's Maisie?" Lizzie asked, biting her lip to keep from blabbing about what she'd just seen.

"Don't know." Gia had pale gray semicircles under her eyes. "I heard her going outside with Danny late last night. Don't know if she came back in."

This day was getting stranger and stranger.

"I'm just wondering what the schedule is today." Lizzie pulled her hair back, trying to ignore the prickles of anticipation and anxiety.

*To love and to cherish, from this day forth...*

Gia rubbed her eyes. "I'm not sure. Since the wedding is off and it's a Saturday I expect I'll just be packing up the—"

"The wedding is *what*?" The words flew from her mouth.

"You know, cancelled." Gia squinted against the light. "Since Con's brother turned up and all that."

*"What?"*

Lizzie stood there blinking. Blood rushed around her brain. "The wedding is *off*? Said who?"

"Maisie. Well, she told me. I thought it was something you'd all decided. It was Con's idea to turn the focus of the show to his homecoming. More unusual and better for ratings and all that. You didn't know?" Gia hitched her towel higher.

Lizzie's chest heaved as she struggled for breath. Black spots danced in front of her eyes. She wheeled around and headed to her bedroom.

She threw the door open and it slammed against the wall. Con—sprawled on the bed stark naked—didn't stir.

"Conroy Beale, wake up this instant!"

He grunted and turned over until he was facing away from her.

She stormed into the room, clapped her hand on his arm and shook him.

"Con! Wake up!"

He groaned. Ugh, she could smell alcohol fumes rising off him. "Wake up!"

He rolled onto his back again and held out his arms as if he expected her to fall into them.

*As if.*

"You called off our wedding?" The screeching sound of her voice bounced off the windows.

That got his eyes open. But sunlight closed them again after a quick squint.

"What?" he croaked. He pulled his arm over his eyes.

"You cancelled our wedding, you bastard!"

He shifted up onto his elbows, squinting at her, one hand shielding his eyes. "Yeah, but... You don't understand..." he mumbled. Then shook his head as if something heavy was clinging to it. "Ow."

"I understand only too well, you scheming trickster. You get your big house and all your fancy cars, and now you're ready to cut me right out of the deal!" Pain shot through her. It was all she could do not to pummel him with her fists.

"No, Lizzie, listen." He winced, apparently in pain. *Good.* "You still get your money, all of it, I made a deal with Maisie—"

"You made a deal with Maisie!" The words tore from her throat, raw. "About the *money*? Everyone knows about this, absolutely everyone except me!"

"No, yes... I can explain—"

"I'll just bet you can explain! You've always got a tall tale to tell—or not tell—when the occasion suits you. Well, I've heard enough of your filthy lies! I hate you! I wish I'd never met you and I hope you rot in hell!"

"Lizzie—" He reached out an arm to grab her and missed.

Before she could get suckered into anything by those dangerous dark eyes, she grabbed her wallet off the night table and fled.

Doors opened and faces stared as she thundered down the stairs, tears of rage and pain streaming down her face.

That bastard!

She shoved out the front door and ran to the Jeep, praying the key was in the ignition as usual.

Yes. She started it up, agony searing through her as the engine turned over and the car shuddered to life.

She'd been dreaming about their wedding being the real thing, and he didn't even want to go through with the fake one! How could he do that to her? After all they'd been through? She let out a low animal sound of anger and despair that fought with the noisy Jeep engine as she burned rubber through that accursed avenue of live oaks.

A thin morning mist still hung around the road, filtering the sun as she pulled onto the main road.

He would never see her again. Of that he could be sure. If he tried, she'd kill him.

The car ate up the road as she tried to shove Con, and everyone she'd ever known, out of her thoughts.

He was just going with the flow to get his money. Stringing her along and sweetening her up. Planning all the while to cut her loose.

And like a complete idiot she'd fallen in love with him all over again.

Houma.

Grey.

Thibodaux.

She sped through strange towns. At first it was all she could do to focus her thoughts enough to stay in lane. But as the sun rose higher and the muggy heat kissed her skin, she started to breathe deeply.

Vacherie.

Sorrento.

Gonzales.

She worked hard to clear her mind. To figure out a strategy before the car ran out of gas and she had to try to get some with a maxed-out credit card.

Next exit Baton Rouge. She'd sell her Bulova watch and rent a motel room, lay low for a few days. Right now if she had to so much as look anyone in the eye she'd go right to pieces. But she'd had her heart crushed to a bloody pulp before and survived. She'd figure out where to go, find a design or PR job, get an apartment and start over again as if none of the past few months had ever happened. As if she was a completely different person than the downtrodden ex-heiress Lizzie Hathaway who'd be the butt of every joke when that damn television show came out.

*It was all your idea.*

We all make mistakes. She lifted her chin. She'd made more than her share, and she'd make more before she was done, but she certainly wouldn't be making any more that concerned a certain silver-tongued, sleek-muscled, dark-eyed con-man named—

Conroy Beale.

She blasted the horn, just for the hell of it. Damn him to hell! And his brother too and all the rest of them for lying to her and laughing at her and...

Tears blurred her eyes as she pulled off the main road into Baton Rouge.

This time she wasn't going anywhere near any bottles of champagne.

She was all grim practical reality from now on. Shame she hadn't made Con pay her for the spray-paint job on the Corvette. Probably worth a few hundred dollars that would come in handy right now.

And people thought she had no survival skills and no talents of her own? Ha! She'd show them. She didn't need any of them and she'd prove it. She'd pay off all her credit card bills by herself and start over. Maybe she'd even change her name—you could do that without making the horrible mistake of marrying a man, something she didn't intend to do—ever.

Maisie couldn't seem to open her eyes. There was a heavy weight on her chest and something scratchy underneath her.

And something was ringing.

Her cell phone.

Her eyes popped open, then snapped shut under siege by sun knifing through the curtain of Spanish moss overhead.

The heavy weight on her chest was a large human arm, brown skin dusted with little blonde hairs sprinkled over a large circular symbol inked in bluish lines.

Her head hurt.

"My cell, where is it?" she rasped.

"S'up sugar?" The heavy weight lifted a little, and a larger mass next to her shifted.

"It must be around here somewhere, I can hear it." She hissed a curse as the ringing stopped.

It was grass tickling her back. That nasty dry prickly stuff they had down here. She groped around in it as the ringing started up again. Almost as soon as her fingernails tapped on the hard casing she flipped it open.

"Hello?" She sat up, realizing she was totally naked, the skin on her belly creased by the heavy weight of Danny's arm.

"This is Leeza from Eyewitness news,"

"Oh, hi, Leeza." She pushed a strand of hair out of her eyes. Danny lifted a big hand and placed it on her thigh in a proprietary manner. She tried to ignore the surge of heat that caused. "Any news on the DNA test?"

It was purely a formality. They all knew Con was the heir, but they planned to show the test on screen, with a brief explanation of the cutting edge technology involved. Once that was done they could pretty much wrap up and get out of here They'd already shot a bunch of establishing shots of Con in the house and garden; they had their touching reunion. As soon as they got these last shots she could get back home and—

Danny's mouth closed over her wet pussy. His tongue flicked and made her hips buck.

Maybe she'd have to take him home in her suitcase too.

He was twenty-one and totally uneducated. He knew what to do with that tongue, though.

"What is it, Leeza?" she said impatiently into the phone. Her nipples were tingling. She had better things to do than listen to dead air.

"I'm sorry." She heard papers rustling at the other end of the line. "I've got the test results, and I'm trying to make head or tail of them. This doesn't seem to make any sense."

"Con, what are you doing? You don't have any clothes on!"

Gia's voice penetrated his consciousness as he reached the front door. Holy shit, he had the hangover to end all and Lizzie was roaring off down the drive in the Jeep. His muscles itched to go leap in the van and chase after her, but as Gia had observed he was buck naked.

Idiot. He couldn't have grabbed some pants before running downstairs?

"Shit." He banged his fist on the doorframe. "Where is she going?"

"It doesn't really matter," murmured Dino, who stood at the top of the stairs next to Gia wearing nothing but a pair of boxers. "We don't need her anymore. Only a few last shots to wrap up and we can get out of here."

"I need her." Con stared out the door. Raw terror gripped him at the thought of losing her. He turned to face them. "I love her."

"Conroy, could you do us all a favor and put some clothes on?" Raoul stood in his doorway, wearing a Japanese robe. "I don't doubt she'll be back in your arms before sundown, but my blood pressure medication isn't up to your bare ass running all over the place."

Roger, sitting on the couch holding his head, tossed Con a pair of jeans from a pile on the floor beside him. Con caught them and put them on. "Can I take the van?"

"Why?" Dino itched his crotch. "You have no idea where she's going. Just relax. She'll come back."

*No, she won't.* He'd never been so sure of anything. He couldn't breathe.

"Conroy!" Maisie's voice rang out as he heard the back door slam. She marched into the living room wearing only a dirty white towel. She had grass in her hair. "I've just got a call from Leeza over at Eyewitness." She paused and sucked in a breath. Looked down. "There's some bad news I'm afraid."

"What?" He stared down the driveway, burning to get the hell out of there.

"The results of the DNA test came back and I'm afraid it appears there's a zero percent chance you're related to Thomas Milford." Her pale eyes looked almost soft. "So you're not the heir."

*Lizzie couldn't get far. She didn't have any cash.*

Maisie's words sank in.

"I'm not a match? But I thought they were sure?"

Maisie bit her lower lip. "I'm sorry, Con," she said softly.

Con scraped a hand through his hair. "I don't understand."

"Don't worry about the show. The reunion with your brother was beautiful. That's quite enough for us to put together an hour package so you'll get the full fifty thousand just like we—"

"Where's Danny?"

"Um," she tucked some hair behind her ear. Danny wandered up behind her wearing only his jeans. He also had grass in his hair and a sheepish expression on his face. Con felt a hot surge of relief that at least his brother was still here.

"Lizzie's gone," he burst out. "Just took off. She didn't understand that I want to marry her for real. She thought I was blowing her off and she—"

"Hey." Danny strode up to him. "Don't worry. We'll get her back." He embraced Con, who realized he was shaking. "Let's get some water. I'm hung over something fierce and I bet you are too."

"Um," Maisie hoisted her towel higher. "Has anyone seen Dwight?"

# 24

"**I** guess our mom was illegitimate." Con was trying to make sense of how the DNA evidence didn't mesh with the evidence of the letters and the will. "That could explain why the old man cut her loose and didn't read her letters. He might have known."

"So how come he left the house to her?" Gia asked. She and Roger were sitting with Con and Danny in the untidy dressing room, while Gia half-heartedly packed up embroidered tablecloths and silver cutlery.

"He didn't. I never saw the will," Con said, "but it leaves the estate to the owner's firstborn. No mention of names. It long predates that generation, so if we're not his kin, we're out in the cold. Maybe in the old days no one would have known, but now with DNA evidence..." He shrugged. "I don't know who'll get it. Probably that lawyer that spent up the estate money and is getting ready to buy it from the parish."

Nothing about this new turn of events surprised him. Being a no-count outsider was pretty much par for the course. As if someone like him could ever own a place like this?

That was as crazy as his idea of marrying Lizzie.

He felt cold all over.

Danny clapped a hand on his back. "Houses are nothin' but trouble. Leakin' roofs, lawns that need mowin', bills to pay. You don't need that."

"Nice try, bro." Con punched him lightly on his huge bicep.

"So, where d'you think your woman has gone to?"

Con shook his head. "The airport maybe? I don't know where she'd go except back to New York."

"We'd better get going then. But we need to get my truck from the bar. Who's gonna drive us over?"

Con put his hand on Danny's forearm. "No use going anywhere. It's over."

"What's over?"

"Me and Lizzie."

Saying it out loud socked him in the gut. He jumped to his feet and out of the room, damned if he was going to let anyone see him cry. He slammed out the back door and sucked in some air.

Danny was right behind him. "It's not over. You love her, right?"

"Yes," Con managed to keep his voice steady. "But that doesn't mean a damn thing. When I thought this house was mine and that I was rich I knew I could ask her to marry me, to come live with me here. But without it—" He shook his head. He'd offered to marry her out in the desert. She'd turned him down flat.

"What?" Danny's face creased into amusement. "You have to be a royal prince for this chick? I don't get it."

"She's from a rich family. Filthy rich, old money."

"So you'll live on her dough." Danny slapped his back. "What's the problem?"

Con let out a hollow laugh. "Funny you should mention it, but that was my original plan." He pushed his fingers through his hair. "Now she's broke too."

"Nothing wrong with that. You're even, you can build your empire together."

"Empire? Doing what? I'm a mechanic. She does graphic design, or something like that."

"Sounds good. What's the problem?"

Con wrinkled his brow. Hmm. What was the problem? "We fixed up a car together. I rebuilt the engine and she sprayed it. She's an amazing talent, a real artist, I've never seen anything like it. We turned a profit of eleven thousand dollars in a couple of days."

"That's what I'm talking about!"

"It was kind of an emergency situation, I don't know if she'd do it again." Con looked at him. His brother's eyes were so blue, like the sky out over the gulf. A heavy weight on his heart made it hard to breathe. "Our old man married a pretty rich girl and ended up ruining her life. She'll be better off without me."

"Big brother." Danny grabbed him by the shoulders and shook him. "Does she know you love her?"

"Of course she...well, I don't know." Con rubbed a hand over his face. "I guess I never did say it to her. I was waiting for the right moment. I wanted it to be perfect. But that was before, you know, the DNA." A funk crept over him like the sticky heat. "She won't want me now."

"So you say, bro, but from what I saw last night, she's crazy about you. Love doesn't have anything to do with money—it comes from in here." Danny tapped Con's chest with a brawny finger. "I bet you that right now she's cryin' her eyes out, wishing you were there to put your arms around her."

Con stared at him. The image of Lizzie crying cut into him like a boning knife.

*She thought he'd screwed her over.* Dumped her now he didn't need her money anymore. He had to set that straight, at least.

Adrenaline roared through him. "Let's go get your truck. And don't you start lecturing me on love, little brother. What the hell do you know about it?"

Danny grinned. "That's the spirit!"


Lizzie wasn't at the airport. She wasn't at the bus station, or the train station. Danny rolled his eyes while Con made nervous phone calls to the police and local hospitals, who'd never heard of her either.

"Must be still on the road." Con snapped his phone shut and drummed his knuckles on the dash of Danny's truck.

"Maybe we can check her credit cards? See if she's used one. You know the numbers?"

"Um, yeah. I'm afraid I do. I filched them from her wallet and made some payments without telling her."

"You still got that amazing memory?"

"Old habits die hard." Con winked and flipped his phone open.


"Dwight!" Maisie plastered on her biggest smile. "Finally, I have a few moments. I was so excited when I heard you were coming." The chef had whipped together some oyster po'boys for lunch and the remaining members of the crew were gathered on the patio. She'd been delayed by a phone call with Don so she was the last to attack the buffet.

"Really." Dwight helped himself to some coleslaw.

"I would have spent more time with you last night, but this show just sucks up every living second. You know how it is when you have one of your big bond deals going through."

"Oh, yes." Dwight picked up a little bottle of Evian. He wouldn't meet her eye.

"Is something the matter?" She smeared a dollop of mayonnaise on her bread.

"Is something the matter?" repeated Dwight, in a flat voice. "I'd say so, wouldn't you?"

Maisie's brow furrowed. She swatted a wasp away from the mayonnaise. "What do you mean?"

Dwight chuckled. Instead of asking her where she'd like to sit, he went and sat on the edge of a low wall, near Raoul.

"Would you like to join me at the table?" she asked brightly.

"Not really." He took a big bite of his sandwich.

"Sorry, Dwight, am I missing something?" She cocked her head, getting a nasty feeling that a scene was coming on. But it couldn't be, not with Dwight. That was the most wonderful thing about him. You could count on him to be discreet, tasteful and highly appropriate at all times.

"I'd say so."

Of course he wasn't the most sparkling conversationalist, Maisie reflected as she seated herself next to him on the uncomfortable stone wall and took a bite of her sandwich. But that's why you had friends. Choosing a husband was like picking a tasteful wallpaper pattern that wouldn't get tiresome for being too overwhelming. "This oyster is marvelous, isn't it? What's in the batter, André?"

"Beer," said the chef, as he stirred the fresh mayonnaise.

"Ah. Very cunning." She took another neat bite.

Dwight dabbed his lips with his napkin. "I'm obviously never going to get a moment truly alone with you, and I suppose everyone would know sooner or later, so I'll be frank..." Maisie's throat tightened around her last mouthful of oyster. "I came here to break off our pathetic excuse for an engagement."

"What?" Crumbs flew from her mouth. "You can't!"

"No? Just watch me." He took another bite. Raoul murmured something inaudible in his ear.

Maisie's ears buzzed as hot disbelief made it hard to think straight. "But the napkins have already been monogrammed. The silver commemorative wedding goblets are being engraved by artisans in Sierra Leone. My one-of-a-kind lace veil is being hand-netted in Lausanne—"

"Then tell them to stop," Dwight said through a mouthful. "Because the wedding's off."

"Why?" Her voice came out as a plaintive wail. She cleared her throat and asked more calmly, "why?"

"Let's see. Where do I start? Oh, yes, you don't love me, I don't love you, and I'm gay." He took another bite of sandwich.

"What?" she squeaked. "You're not gay!"

Dwight looked at her. "Trust you to think you know better than I do. I would feel sorry if I thought I was really hurting you. At one point I was delusional enough to think that we were a good match in a practical, looks-good-in-print kind of way. And I would have rather died than admit that I wasn't, shall we say, 'into' women."

Maisie blinked. Frankly, it explained a few things.

"Anyway, I've fallen in love. His name is Matthew, and he's a real estate developer and we're going to build a house in Greenwich together."

"I'm so happy for you," she spat. "And where exactly does that leave me?"

"Exactly where you've been all this time. Pursuing your own goals without regard for anyone else, and—from what I heard last night—screwing any thick-necked brute who grunts in your direction."

Maisie felt her face coloring. Had they heard? She'd been discreet. And that nasty characterization was uncalled for. At least Danny wasn't around to hear it. Since he and Con had gone off to look for Lizzie, the intoxicating effect he'd had on her had worn off a bit, but she wasn't quite sure what would happen when she saw him again.

"Now, now," said Raoul. "There's no need to get bitchy." He patted Dwight's knee. "Maisie has her needs that have clearly been going unmet."

"I'll say!" Maisie narrowly resisted the urge to throw her plate of po'boy at him. "You've got some nerve acting angry with me when you're the one who's been living a lie this whole time."

Dwight looked at her. She'd never noticed what a cold, gray color his eyes were. As cold as his voice when he spoke. "We were both living a lie. You never cared about me, only what I could do for you. I think we can both agree to end this extended-run farce of an engagement. Feel free to bill me for the napkins."

The sight of the white Jeep in the parking lot of the Cozy Suites Motel on the outskirts of Baton Rouge made Con's heart thump.

She must have had a nice surprise when her credit card worked, he thought with satisfaction.

"Why don't you knock on the door and pretend to be the maid," said Danny, opening a shiny silver laptop. "I'll just stay here and catch up on some record keeping. Then we'll all go to dinner."

"Confident, aren't you?"

"You're my brother. And from what I saw last night, you can charm a snake right out of its skin."

"No more pretending and no more charm. I'm on the straight and narrow, little brother. Nothing but the pure, unvarnished truth from now on."

"Sounds like a plan." Danny bumped his fist against Con's. "Just don't forget to tell her you love her."

Room fourteen, he'd been told when he called saying he was her new employer and needed to verify her address. Fourteen was one of a row of drab blue doors in a gray stucco wall.

He knocked. No answer. The next step was A) to start banging and begging and making a scene until either she opened the door or the police showed up, or B) to just break in. Option B was more classy, he decided.

He whipped his driver's license out of his wallet and slid it down over the lock. Irritation rippled through him at how easily it opened.

As he pushed in the door Lizzie sat bolt upright in the double bed, the blue cover clutched around her and her glorious hair streaming out in all directions.

Joy roared through him.

"You!" she hissed. "Get out."

"You need to take your safety more seriously and stay in a place with decent locks." He couldn't stop the grin ripping across his face. Damn, it was a huge relief to see her after a whole day of worry.

"I said, get out." Her beautiful brown eyes narrowed.

"I've got some explaining to do. I know you think I was trying to cut you out of the show by making a deal with Maisie and I'm sorry about that, but the real reason I did it was—"

She sprang forward so fast she almost knocked him off his feet, hair flying and eyes flashing. "Go away! I hate you!"

Her fists bounced off his shoulders and he grabbed them with ease. No one ever taught this poor girl how to fight. Heat flared at the feel of her skin on his.

"Will you listen to me a second?"

"No, I've heard enough of your lies!" She wriggled and struggled, kicking at him with her bare feet. Her lithe, lush body bumped against him in a way that did embarrassing things to his libido.

"Lizzie, I love you." Her breasts smooshed deliciously against his chest as he drew her close.

Her gaze met his for one stunning second. "No, you don't."

"I do. I was telling the honest truth when I said you're the best thing that ever happened to me." He tightened his arms around her, holding her steady. The almond scent of her hair and the musky warmth of her skin threatened to steal his thoughts. "Just lying with my arms around you makes me the happiest man alive—"

She struggled a bit but he held her tight..

"You make me feel loved, cherished—safe—something I've never felt before in my whole life. I grew up lying to save my ass, figuring out which hustle would get me through another day, but you wouldn't let me sweet-talk my way through life and you dragged me back here to face something I couldn't face on my own. Whether you know it or not, I believe you did it for my own good."

He felt her sharp intake of breath. "I just wanted to make a fool of you." Her words were cold, but her breath, warm on his neck, made him tighten his arms around her.

"I've been a fool, but I'm not one any more." He'd never had such a powerful urge to spill his guts. "I do love you, Lizzie. I love your sharp mind and your sharp tongue. I love that you're a strong woman, passionate and demanding. I love that you're an artist." He squeezed her. "I want to share my life with you, for better or for worse, for richer or poorer—"

She'd looked startled during most of his declaration, barely breathing, in fact, something that made hope swell inside him. But as he started reciting the marriage vows he hoped they'd share her lips drew together and he could feel her hardening against him. She lifted her eyes to his with a hollow look that made his words catch in his throat.

"I'm not dumb enough to think you're really here because you love me. Not any more." She shook her head. "What happened? Did the inheritance fall through and now you need to marry me to get the cash? That it? Huh?"

"It's not like that—" His voice had dropped low. She didn't believe a word he said. Didn't trust him at all. And she was dead right about one thing...

"No? Oh, do tell, what exactly is it like? You need a few more establishing shots of me being knocked on my ass by your betrayal? They didn't happen to catch my tearful departure on camera and you'd like a redo? You need me to be the maid of honor at your wedding to Maisie? What? This script changes so fast that it's hard for me to keep up."

Con dragged a hand through his hair. *He had to tell her.* "You're right about one thing..." he paused, when he spoke again his voice was very quiet. "I'm not the heir."

"I knew it." She stared at him for a second, open mouthed, then wheeled around and strode across the room. Since it was so small, three strides took her right to the bathroom door. "I knew you weren't here because you love me." Her voice was so empty.

Con held himself steady.

He didn't say anything for a long time. Lizzie stood with her back to him.

His mind raced with thoughts. Why hadn't he told her about his plans to cancel the phony wedding? Why hadn't he planned it *with* her? Concealment was so second nature to him that he couldn't even be straight with the woman he loved? He'd figured he'd just pull a fast one, skip the drama and charm his way out of it later with a sparkly ring and the promise of a fancy estate?

He deserved every word she'd said. Now he didn't even have the estate to give her. No sparkly ring either.

Just his honesty. And his true self.

He cleared his throat and straightened his back. "I don't have anything to offer you, not in the way of money or a fine house, at least." He paused and drew in a shaky breath. "But I do love you. I love you with my whole heart."

Back still to him, Lizzie tossed her curls and shifted her weight. His eyes fell to the curve of her full hips. So beautiful. He wanted more than anything in the world to put his arms around her and hold her close. To hold her and never let her go.

"For a moment there," she said at last, her voice trembling, "I thought I was experiencing déjà vu. I believe 'I don't have anything to offer you' were the exact words you used to cut me loose when you found out I wasn't rich any more." She turned to face him, eyes wide, lip quivering. "Then you had nothing to offer me, but now it's different, because you love me." She bit her lip. "You, who we both know is incapable of love, by your own admission." She drew in a deep breath, shivered as if she were cold. "I just wish I could figure out what you're after this time."

Con's muscles tightened. He deserved this. His own words coming back to bite him on the ass. The fruit of his deception.

"I offered you happiness once. You bring the money, I make your life sweet: That was the deal. I admit I wasn't upfront about it, but I knew I could deliver. I can't offer you that anymore, not really, because we both know that without money, happiness can be hard to hold on to. But, Lizzie," his voice cracked. He cleared his throat and straightened his shoulders. "You've given me my life back, my real life. I was running so hard all those years, afraid to trust anyone, afraid to care for anyone in case they got taken away from me again. I didn't want anybody to know the real me, the one who went through all that ugliness, so I tried to hide it, to be someone else, and somewhere along the way I lost myself."

He paused and took in a deep shuddering breath. "But now I'm in love with you...all the way." His eyes shone. "You've given me back the ability to feel—to truly feel, the good and the bad." He drew in a breath, hesitated. "I want to spend the rest of my life with you. I want to end each day with you in my arms. No pretense or trickery or lies, just you and me, together."

She was still shivering. Her hand had flown to her mouth and tears glittered in her eyes. "You really mean it, don't you?" She breathed.

"I do. I never lied to you, not in words. I love you, Lizzie, and I want you to be my wife."

Lizzie stood there, hand pressed to her mouth. Finally she drew in a ragged breath. "You're not the heir?"

Pain flooded his chest. Did it matter so much to her? "No. The DNA proved it. My mom was illegitimate or something. I found out this morning. It's kind of confusing."

"I'm sorry."

"I'm not." Strength roared through him at the sight of her, almost within reach. "I thought inheriting that big house made me good enough for you. Today I lost both you and the house. Losing the house was a blow, I won't lie, but losing you?" He shook his head. "I couldn't let that happen."

Lizzie stood there, fingers still pressed to her lips, tears dripping down her cheeks.

He crossed the room and took her other hand. Her soft skin on his was sweet relief. "You know what? I still think I'm good enough for you, money, or no money." He held his chin high. "I may be an arrogant son of a bitch, cocky and quick to turn on the charm when it suits me, but I'm also smart, caring and hard working. I love you, and I'll take care of you for the rest of my life. I can promise you that."

Lizzie let out a choking sob. He grabbed her and held her close, her face to his chest, her tears warm on his shirt.

Emotion surged through him, painful in its intensity, as he stroked her lovely wild hair. "You will marry me, won't you? Because I couldn't stand it if you said no. No cameras, no fancy napkins, just you and me." He breathed the words. "Just you and me."

Lizzie looked up at him, eyes glittering with tears, her cheeks flushed bright pink. "Yes, I will. Of course I will. Did you really think I could say no?" She laughed, crying at the same time. "I've been a sucker for you since day one, I can't help myself. I love everything about you. Your devilish charm, your bad-boy cool, your aristocratic sense of entitlement—" She blinked away tears. "The way you tell me I'm pretty like you really mean it—" She bit her lip, suddenly shy. "The way you like to cuddle after sex like a contented puppy—" Her smile sent pleasure rippling through him. "I'm awed by the way you know how to do *everything*—from eating an artichoke to picking a lock, and most of all..." She paused, eyes sparkling, "I love the way you've proved you really care about me, even when it's inconvenient, expensive and embarrassing."

She threw her arms around his neck and hugged him tight, and they kissed until he couldn't breathe. His happiness was so intense he didn't know how to handle it. Stripping off Lizzie's clothes was a good start.

He unbuttoned her flimsy blouse and unhooked her bra, worshipping her warm, fragrant body with his lips and tongue and pressing his face and fingertips into her satiny softness. He eased down her white cotton bikinis, his breathing audible as his tongue yearned to taste the honey sweetness of her sex.

As he buried his face between her thighs, Lizzie moaned his name and made his joy even more incandescent and explosive.

She helped pull off his clothes, and they fell to the bed, half blind with desire. They made love with total abandon and a tremendous amount of noise until they both lay panting, sweating and holding each other with fierce affection.

"Do you think we can get married today?" he said. "Before any other crazy shit happens?"

"We can try," she whispered, grinning from ear to ear. "But I'll marry you just as happily tomorrow, or the next day, or the next day..." she punctuated her speech with kisses that made his skin tingle and his cock harden— again. Lizzie wriggled against him, ready to start in on round— Three? Four?

A harsh rap on the door startled them out of frenzied kissing. They froze, naked on the bed, the sheet long gone. Con tore himself away from Lizzie and groped around for the sheet. He found it hanging off the far end of the bed and drew it up over them.

The knock came again. "Hey, Con, it's Danny."

"Um, Danny, we're kind of indisposed."

"Yeah, I figured. But it's Maisie. She won't quit calling."

"Whose fault is that?" Con winked at Lizzie as they both shook with silent laughter.

"She's not calling for me, big brother. She has to talk to you about something. It's *urgent*." The last word was a credible imitation of Maisie's clipped tones that made Con chuckle. "Could you do me a big-ass personal favor and call her back before she drives me out of my mind?"

"Ask him in," whispered Lizzie. "He's practically my brother-in-law." Her eyes shone. He planted one last kiss on her nose before diving for a towel and opening the door.

Danny came in looking very large and very shy.

"Hi, Danny. Thanks for driving Con here," said Lizzie cheerily.

"You're welcome. I'm glad you two made up. I didn't want my brother to be miserable for the rest of his life." He grinned. He handed the phone to Con. "I swear, she's called, like fifteen times in the last two hours."

"Two hours? We've been here that long?" asked Con.

Danny just looked at him, eyes twinkling with amusement.

Con ran a hand through his very tousled hair. "Sorry to keep you waiting."

"No problem." Danny kept a straight face as he handed Con the phone. "I'll be out in the truck." He winked at Lizzie, and exited.

Con hit call back. Maisie answered on the first ring with a curt, "Yes?"

"It's Con." He stretched out on the bed next to Lizzie, letting his hand wander into her soft hair.

"Conroy, thank God. There's been a development."

"Yeah?" He feathered a kiss on the tip of her chin. Her parted lips were swollen and rouged from kissing, inviting him back for more.

The phone kind of drifted away from his ear as Maisie launched into some detailed story about something, and Lizzie's hand slid under the towel. Her fingers closed around his hardening cock.

"Conroy! Are you there?" The high-pitched sound of Maisie's voice made him bring the phone reluctantly back to his ear.

"What?" he rasped. Talking was uncomfortable in his current state of arousal.

"Did you hear a word I said?"

"Yeah," he lied, "Sure." His breathing became labored as Lizzie's hand teased him.

"So you'll come right back now to sign the papers?"

"What papers?" he croaked, arching his back at the intense sensation.

"The papers transferring the house and its contents to your name, of course!" Maisie screeched with impatience. "Are you drunk or something? Put Lizzie on."

Con obediently handed the phone to Lizzie. Some distant part of his brain wondered what the fuss was about, but since his entire blood supply was pooling below his waist, he didn't much care. He eased himself under the sheet and went down on Lizzie, licking her crimson softness and losing himself in her wet warmth—until she pushed him out by crossing her thighs.

He looked up, confused. Lizzie was listening to the garbled sound of Maisie's voice, her mouth hanging open.

"We have to go back," she said at last. "Right now."

# 25

"So let me get this straight." Lizzie was almost delirious with exhaustion and happiness. She, Con, Danny, Maisie, and scattered crew members were gathered in the big living room back at the house at two in the morning. Mercifully Dino and his camera were absent, probably up in Gia's room. "Thomas Milford was not his grandfather, but Marie Ancelet, his wife, *is* Con's real grandmother and she's the original heir to the property?"

"Yes." Maisie, flushed with excitement and chocolate martinis, had Danny's big tattooed arm wrapped around her shoulders. "She was a famous circus performer. Called herself La Zoringa. She traveled all over the U.S. and Europe with a bunch of wild animals she'd trained. Snakes, crocodiles, that kind of thing."

"It's in the blood, bro." Danny grinned.

"She appeared at Radio City Music Hall in the 1950's and went on *The Ed Sullivan Show* three times. She made a lot of money and she's the one who put together the collection of classic cars we saw yesterday. She was famous for driving them from one engagement to another, and she liked to work on them herself."

"See what I'm saying?" Danny raised an eyebrow at Con and Lizzie.

"She sounds like quite a lady," said Raoul, sitting on the sofa in his Japanese robe. "I'd like to have met her."

"From what I gather she was estranged from her family," Maisie continued. "Eyewitness News dug up some old newspaper articles in the New Orleans *Times-*

*Picayune*. They didn't approve of having a female snake charmer for a daughter in the thirties and forties, but her two brothers died in World War II, so she inherited the house when her mother died in 1956."

"Do they have any idea who our real grandfather is?" asked Con. "If it's not Thomas Milford."

Maisie shook her head. "Not that I've heard. She married Thomas Milford in 1958. He was a respectable local businessman. Apparently, she wanted to settle in and join local society and he was her ticket into that rather closed elite."

"I guess he wasn't enough of a ticket to ride in the bedroom." Raoul winked.

"Or maybe she just had a hard time getting pregnant by him." Maisie shoved a strand of sweaty blonde hair out of her face. "She was nearly forty by then, and he was even older."

"So she had to find a hot young stud to breed with." Raoul pursed his lips.

"Raoul, would you keep your licentious thoughts to yourself?" Maisie glared at him. "Anyway, she died of a stroke when her daughter, Katherine, was only seven. The girl was left all alone with Thomas Milford and tutored at home because the local schools weren't the right sort of place for a proper young lady—"

"No wonder she ran off with a handsome bad boy at the earliest possible opportunity." Raoul blew on his nails.

Maisie rolled her eyes. "Listen to this. It's kind of bizarre, but Louisiana succession law dictates that property descends to children—not to the spouse of the deceased. Even if there's no will."

Lizzie's jaw dropped. "So even if Milford was her father, it was Con's mother's property the minute her mother died?"

"Exactly. Which could explain why Thomas Milford never opened the letters. He pretended Katherine was dead. As long as she was "missing" he had a right to keep the property for her. But if anyone learned she was alive, or if she came back claiming her rights…"

"She never knew she had any rights." Con stared at Maisie. "And he wanted to make sure she never found out."

"And Eric Stapleton wanted to make sure you never found out," said Lizzie. "He wanted to cheat you out of your inheritance the way Thomas Milford cheated your mother. The house has been legally yours since the day your mother died."

Con shook his head and blew out some air.

Lizzie squeezed him around the waist with her arm. "It really is yours."

"I guess so." He shrugged. "Still doesn't feel right, but I think my mom would have been glad to see me get it. I guess fate works in mysterious ways."

"Fate? I'd like some credit here." Lizzie put her hands on her hips. "I had to fight you every step of the way. I guess I just knew you were born to be lord of the manor."

"I don't know about that, but I'm glad my grandma was a snake-charming car freak. That feels kind of natural somehow." He flashed her a gator grin.

Maisie leaned forward. "So now the papers are all signed, sealed and delivered, there's no further risk of Eric Stapleton getting his claws into the property, which he was dangerously close to owning. Eyewitness News is doing a thorough investigation into all his business dealings, and Leeza tells me they've already raked up a good deal of muck. He was trying to gain title to the cars by setting up some kind of dummy corporation."

Con perked up. "So the cars are mine?"

Maisie nodded. "All yours to do what you like with. You could probably sell them and live off the proceeds for years."

Lizzie felt Con stiffen, probably horrified at the blasphemous thought. She chuckled. "I won't make you sell them," she whispered in his ear.

"Danny should get half of them. I don't care what the will says, this stuff is every bit as much his as mine."

"I have everything I need, bro. Grandma Marie would have wanted you to have her cars." Danny leaned down and grazed Maisie's neck with his teeth, causing her face to turn bright pink. "Only one thing I want right now, and it tastes like chocolate." Maisie melted like chocolate as he settled his mouth on hers for a hot and heavy kiss. After a solid minute cf smooching with no regard for the gathered audience, Danny swept a limp and breathless Maisie up in his arms. "See y'all tomorrow morning for the wedding."

The wedding! A surge of fear and excitement made Lizzie wonder if you could just explode with joy. They were going to do it for the cameras after all. Why not? Right now she wanted to share her happiness with everyone on the planet.

"I'm going to carry you up too, babe." Con wrapped his arms around her.

"Maisie probably weighs about ninety-eight pounds soaking wet. I'm more of a challenge." She raised an eyebrow at him.

"I enjoy a challenge." Con flashed a dark glance at her. "As you know." She shrieked as he slid his arm under her thighs and hoisted her into the air.

The sun was high in the sky by the time everything was ready for the ceremony next to the glittering bayou. Lizzie's gown had been let out enough to allow deep breaths, which was lucky as she needed them to steady her nerves. Her feet had protested the pointy-toed shoes so vigorously that she'd decided to go barefoot, and the grass felt cool and crisp under her relieved feet. Her heavy, pearl-encrusted skirt trailed behind as she strolled down the lawn toward the bayou like a splendid faery queen.

Con, dressed in a trim black Valentino suit, looked excited, cheerful and breathtakingly handsome. He grabbed Maisie's arm as she whisked past with her clipboard.

"Are you sure it'll be legal? I want it to be really legal."

"Conroy." Maisie clucked her tongue and tossed her freshly blow-dried hair. "Do I ever do anything by halves? Of course it's legal. We had all the permits in place before we even flew down here. Now, if you want it to be recognized by the Catholic Church, we could use the priest I suggested, but Raoul's certificate from the Universal Life Church is every bit as good as far as the law is concerned and Lizzie keeps insisting—"

"We definitely want Raoul," cut in Lizzie.

"My ears are ringing!" called Raoul, striding down the lawn, looking only slightly more elegant than Con in a double-breasted white suit with a matching cravat. "Are you ready for the sacred event, my children?"

"Yes," said Con and Lizzie at once.

"You'll be my third wedding. My first between a man and a woman." He beamed proudly. "What are we waiting for?"

"Dino, are we ready?" yelled Maisie. Dino had a bank of equipment set up under a canopy. Tripod-mounted cameras ringed the white arbor set up for the ceremony. The arbor itself was festooned with a bright mix of flowers Gia had hastily bought from every florist within a twenty-mile radius. The resulting riot of color fit the occasion far better than Sven's minimalist roses. In the background the bayou sparkled lazily under a bright blue sky.

"Danny!" yelled Maisie, making Lizzie jump.

"Yes, sugar?"

She startled again as Danny materialized a few feet away, sprawled on the ground in a shady copse of trees.

"Oh, I didn't realize you were right there." Maisie flushed. Lizzie didn't think Maisie had ever blushed—or shown emotion of any sort—before Danny turned up. Life was full of strange surprises.

Danny winked. Even in his rented gray suit he looked dangerously disreputable. A fun relative to have around. "I've got the rings." He patted his pocket. "How's my best woman?"

Maisie turned even redder and Lizzie couldn't help smiling. Danny was Con's best man, and Maisie was giving Lizzie away. Danny had decided that made her best woman.

Maisie glanced back at the house then hissed. "Let's get this show on the road before those vultures from Eyewitness News swoop in and try to steal our thunder."

Con had a big dumbass smile on his face that wouldn't subside and he didn't care. Lizzie glowed like a princess, and the sight of her in her wedding gown, with pearls in her glorious hair and bright roses in her cheeks, made his heart jump. He was torn between wanting to enjoy every single second of the ceremony and wanting to get her alone and take her lovingly apart, pearl by pearl.

In his capacity as officiant, Raoul had immediately nixed Maisie's impressive but stodgy program of events. As the oldest member of the group and the one who'd attended the most weddings, he insisted he would put together the perfect wedding for Con and Lizzie, and at one a.m. that morning no one had the energy to argue with him. By breakfast he had a printed program of music, readings and vows compiled off the Internet that made Lizzie bawl.

Con wasn't too crazy about anything that made his sweetheart cry, but Lizzie had insisted they keep it exactly as is, and he wasn't going to argue. He took up his place at the bottom of the steps leading up to the arbor, under the watchful eye of a very serious Raoul.

The music started. Maisie's planned string quartet had been replaced with a local Dixieland jazz band, who struck up a slow rendition of Louis Armstrong's "Wonderful World." There was no arguing with the skies of blue in Con's mind as he turned and saw his lovely Lizzie walking up the flower-edged aisle on the arm of her cousin.

Their eyes met, hers sparkling. She bit her lip and he hoped she wasn't going to cry. But if she did, hey, no problem. They were happy tears, right?

When she reached him he took her hand. She squeezed his palm, and he squeezed back as they climbed the two steps to the arbor together and stood facing each other, holding hands as Raoul had instructed.

Raoul himself radiated pomp and ceremony, and quite possibly divine majesty as well. "My name is Raoul Johnston, and I have the privilege of performing this ceremony today for Lizzie Hathaway and Conroy Beale.

We're here to celebrate the love they have found in each other and to witness and proclaim the joining together of these two persons in marriage.

His voice resonated across the lawn, each word ringing with dignity and sincerity. "This is the union of two individuals in heart, body, mind and spirit and is not to be entered into lightly, but reverently, honestly and deliberately."

Con whispered "Amen!" He'd be eternally grateful they hadn't gotten married just for show. He couldn't have forgiven himself for that.

The first reading was from some children's book and it had made Lizzie go completely to pieces during the rehearsal, so he held her hand tight as Maisie started to read it in her clear, ringing voice.

"*The Velveteen Rabbit* by Margery Williams.

'What is REAL?' asked the Rabbit one day, when they were lying side by side near the nursery fender, before Nana came to tidy the room. 'Does it mean having things that buzz inside you and a stick-out handle?'

'Real isn't how you are made,' said the Skin Horse. 'It's a thing that happens to you. When a child loves you for a long, long time, not just to play with, but Really loves you, then you become Real.'

'Does it hurt?' asked the Rabbit.

'Sometimes,' said the Skin Horse, for he was always truthful. 'When you are Real you don't mind being hurt.'

'Does it happen all at once, like being wound up,' he asked, 'or bit by bit?'

'It doesn't happen all at once,' said the Skin Horse. 'You become. It takes a long time. That's why it doesn't happen often to people who break easily, or have sharp edges, or who have to be carefully kept. Generally, by the time you are Real, most of your hair has been loved off, and your eyes drop out and you get all loose in the joints and very shabby. But these things don't matter at all, because once you are Real you can't be ugly, except to people who don't understand.'"

Lizzie's breathing got a little erratic in the middle there, so he chafed her hand with his thumb, feeling kind of panicky and raw and very very real.

He wanted to kiss her right now, to lose himself in her softness, but Raoul had been strict about the importance of sticking to his planned order of events so he straightened his shoulders and drew in a long, slow breath.

The next reading was by Danny, who recited from memory, hands by his side. During the rehearsal, Con had recognized the familiar prayer from their mother's prayer book, but hearing it now, at his own real wedding, he suddenly felt as if his mother was right there, kissing him on the cheek again and giving him her blessing. He squeezed his eyes shut, overwhelmed by the powerful sensation and by the almost painful joy of hearing his little brother's voice after so many years not knowing if he was dead or alive. When he opened them, Danny was smiling at him and Lizzie.

"I missed you, bro," he said. "And I'm not letting you and your lovely wife out of my sight ever again."

"Deal," Con croaked. Lizzie squeezed his hand.

Gia sang a song in her sweet clear voice, and Dino unveiled a limerick he'd composed for the occasion. The jazz band played a rousing interlude, then a hush fell. Con's heart beat faster. It was time for the vows.

Raoul had written them. Very simple and basic. When the wedding was a charade they'd planned to just respond "I do" to the usual questions. No sense telling a whole bunch of heartbreaking lies on camera. Now he and Lizzie really meant it, they wanted to say the words aloud. And he was up first.

He took a deep breath. Lizzie's eyes shone. His palms were sweating.

"I, Conroy Beale, take you, Lizzie Hathaway, to be my wife." A fist of feeling knocked his breath away. Lizzie blinked, and he saw tears hovering behind her smile. She bit her pink lip with those pretty pearl teeth.

"I promise to stand by your side, for better or worse, for richer, for poorer..." He paused, and they both smiled. *Been there, done that.* "In sickness and in health. To be open and honest with you—" He looked her right in the eye, wanting her to know he meant it. "And to love and cherish you as long as we both shall live."

He heaved a sigh of relief that he'd managed to remember it all. Again, he fought a fierce urge to seize Lizzie in his arms. To pick her right up and run away with her.

As Lizzie repeated the same vows, he grew lighter and lighter. He clung to her hands, as if he might lift up like a hot-air balloon if he wasn't anchored to her. Her voice was clear and decisive, not a trace of nerves, just sheer conviction that melted the ground under his feet and made his heart swell.

"May I have the rings, please," said Raoul.

Danny stepped forward and handed them to him, and Raoul placed Lizzie's ring in Con's hand. He knew there were some fancy words he was supposed to say, but they'd gone right out of his head.

"I love you, Lizzie." He'd never meant anything more in his life and it made the words come out kind of choked, but he didn't care.

He slid the delicate platinum band onto her finger. It didn't go on right away, and he had to wiggle it and jiggle it to get it on. Appropriate considering their rocky path to the altar.

They smiled shyly to each other, then Lizzie, tears glittering in her eyes, said, "I love you too, Conroy Beale," and pushed his ring on. He'd picked it himself from the selection Maisie brought. It was big and fat and gold and shouted, "I'm married." The sight of it on his finger made him feel solid and steady on his feet again. Rooted in something permanent.

"You may now kiss the bride," pronounced Raoul.

*Thank God.*

Con stepped forward and took Lizzie in his arms. His eyes shut as he closed his lips over hers. She melted around him, enclosing him in loving softness that made him want to cry with joy. Their tongues tangled and her fingers roamed into his hair as he held her tight, his palms pressing into the hard little pearls of her gown, squeezing her lush body as livid emotion burned through him.

Throat clearing by Raoul finally tugged him back to the present. They parted, painful, air rushing in where warm lips should be. Lizzie's whole face glowed, her lips red and her cheeks pink.

"Lizzie and Conrcy," intoned Raoul, "we have heard your promise to share your lives in marriage. We recognize and respect the vows you have made here today before us, and it is my honor and joy to declare you married and partners in life...for life."

"'Partners in life'? Raoul, this isn't a gay wedding, you know. Aren't you supposed to say 'man and wife'?" asked Maisie. They sat around the arbor-shaded dining table. The cameras had taken all the shots they needed and been turned off.

"I like the gender neutral approach." Lizzie lifted a steaming crawdad from the platter in the center of the table. She'd gotten over her fear of the tasty critters. "Otherwise, why shouldn't it be 'woman and husband?'"

"Exactly." Raoul delicately sucked the "butter." "One has to change with the times. Some would say marriage has had its day, but I happen to think two people wanting to spend the rest of their lives together is about the most beautiful thing in the world." He sighed as he wiped his fingers on a napkin.

"I agree." Con raised his glass. "To forever." Clinking ensued. "Now we've just got to get your parents back into the family circle. They'll like this place." Con glanced up at the mansion with a look of satisfaction. "And they'll like me too once they get to know me. I'll talk 'em around."

"I bet you will. Charmer." A smile crept across her mouth. "It'll be a blast proving they were totally wrong about you."

"Well," Con winked. "Not totally wrong..." He leaned over and her cheek sizzled under another hot kiss. "So where shall we put your art studio? How about the old carriage house? Then you could do either canvases or cars, depending on what takes your fancy."

Lizzie blinked. "I really could paint, couldn't I?"

"Could? Are you nuts? You're going to paint. You'll be a big success too. How else do you plan to support me? We old-school aristos aren't cheap to keep, you know."

She cocked her head and narrowed her eyes at him, her mouth fighting a smile.

Maisie stabbed her fork in the air. "You could always sell one of the cars."

"Well," Con leaned back. "What I'd like to do is have fun fixing them up then rent them out for weddings and films and that kind of thing. If Lizzie's cool with that."

"I'm cool." She smiled. "Con was up half the night fixing the Silver Ghost so we could drive away in it for the final shot." When he'd finally got the engine to turn over and run, he looked as if he'd just had an orgasm. Well, almost. She rubbed the back of his hand. "I want you to do what makes you happy."

"You make me happy." His dark-eyed gaze tightened her chest.

"You make me happy too."

"Uh, oh, I'm getting choked up again." Raoul reached for a napkin.

"Oh, Raoul. You're so sentimental." Maisie snapped open a crawdad. "Marriage is a lot of hard work. At least from what I hear. I seem to have escaped that particular burden of responsibility for the time being. Lizzie obviously has more discerning taste in husbands than I do."

"You had a lucky escape, Maisie," said Danny with a chuckle. "You've got way too much Tabasco for a man like Dwight."

Raoul peered at Maisie over his champagne flute. "Hmm. Dwight and Danny have the same initial. You wouldn't even have to get the silver goblets re-etched."

Maisie turned the color of a boiled crawdad. "I'm not marrying anyone."

"Me either," said Danny. "I'm too young and innocent." He took a bite of french fry and gave Maisie a look that was anything but innocent.

Lizzie glanced sideways at Con. "You really should stop your brother toying with my cousin's affections."

"Yeah, I really should, shouldn't I." Con grinned. "But it's too much fun to watch."

Maisie squirmed, as if something untoward was going on under the table. "Stop that!" she hissed to Danny. She sat up in her chair and glared at Con. "Don't get too cocky. Lizzie told me these Fleur-de-lis plates coordinate with a part of your anatomy?"

Lizzie bit her lip to stop a grin sneaking across her mouth. "They, um, celebrate Con's French ancestry."

"We have French ancestry?" Danny said through a mouthful.

"Who knows? Lizzie's being polite about the flaming dagger tattooed on my ass." He winked at her. "Want to see if it matches the plates?" He made a move like he was ready to unbutton his pants.

"I think we've all seen it, darling." Raoul dabbed at his lips with a napkin. "That man of yours has no shame. He was ready to run after you in his birthday suit until we stopped him."

"Clothes can get in the way." The cocky assurance in his expression was undercut by a swell of emotion that echoed in Lizzie's heart. She reached for his hand under the table cloth and gave it a squeeze.

"These two can't wait until we all get lost," Raoul muttered, picking up his glass.

"Only one more shot to do." Maisie dusted bread crumbs off her hands. "The happy couple driving away in the Rolls."

"Where are you going on the honeymoon?" asked Rog, after gulping back half a glass of wine.

"Right here. The most beautiful place on earth." Con smiled. "But certain people need a closing shot for their big TV show so we're going to take a drive to New Orleans before we settle in. Lizzie has some important business to take care of."

"Really, what?" Maisie could never hide her curiosity.

"Oh, we're just getting some items emblazoned with Con's family crest. You know, letterhead, towels…" *My butt.* Lizzie chuckled at how scandalized Maisie would be if she knew her formerly prim cousin was getting a tattoo.

It was the perfect way to celebrate her new badass self. A sexy secret between her and Con.

"Con, why did you tie all those shoes to the car bumper?" asked Raoul. "The Manolos will get mauled. It's a travesty."

"It's an ancient wedding tradition," said Maisie. "There are a variety of interpretations of its origins, dating back to medieval—"

"I just put 'em there in case Lizzie needs something to throw at me." Con slid his arm around Lizzie's shoulders. "We have a tradition of our own to keep up."

Lizzie gasped. "Con! You're terrible."

"I know." He winked. "And you wouldn't have me any other way."

THE END

# About the Author

Jennifer Lewis is the bestselling author of more than twenty books. She has lived on both sides of the Atlantic and been addicted to books since she learned to read at age three. Her stories have been translated into—at last count—twenty-two languages and are read on every continent, except maybe Antarctica. She lives in South Florida with her family, and when she isn't writing she's usually kayaking.

www.jenlewis.com

"The Velveteen Rabbit" by Margery Williams originally published 1922 by Charles H. Doran Co.

www.ingramcontent.com/pcd-product-compliance
Lightning Source LLC
Chambersburg PA
CBHW031701170626
46808CB00005B/1534